THE PROTECTOR

THE ACES SERIES, BOOK #2

New York Times Bestselling Author

CRISTIN HARBER

DEDICATION

She's got a little sass and is totally badass.
This book is dedicated to Aunt Courtney.

A NOTE TO READERS

Thank you for joining me on Chance and Jane's high-stakes adventure and love story.

If you are familiar with my books, you may notice familiar names or locations as you read The Protector. The Aces series takes place *before* the Titan and Delta books. You do not need to have read my other books to thoroughly enjoy this series!

If you have read my other books, you may see passing events from a new perspective. A new team comes together. Titan builds the Abu Dhabi headquarter. The younger version of characters you know. I hope this is as much fun for you to read as it was for me to write.

Hugs and Happy Reading,
Cristin Harber

CHAPTER ONE

PEERING OUT OF the tiny oval window onto a field of dark clouds below her, Jane Singleton took a deep breath and let it out as slowly as her churning stomach would let her. She chewed the stick of gum she'd popped in her mouth an hour ago, trying to keep her insides from doing the same gymnastics routine their single-engine plane seemed to be performing in the sky somewhere over western Asia.

Next to her, over the roar of the engine, Teddy Thane's little voice rang out, "Your turn, Janie."

She smiled over at the tiny, well-groomed boy and peeled her fingers from the armrest. The last thing she wanted to do was give her young charge the impression she was nervous—even though she really, *really* was.

Never mind where they were headed. As soon as they'd boarded an hour ago, Jane had gotten the creeping feeling that the pilot was out to kill them, even before they touched down in no-man's-land. Shrugging off the thought, she took one of her pins and put it in the corner slot of the tic-tac-toe board, leaving the middle open for him, so he would win.

Twenty-three games in, the two of them were still the most alert people aboard. Jane never could sleep on planes, but the photojournalist, Joe something, obviously had no trouble, from the snores emanating from the seat behind her. He'd been hired by the Thanes to document their trip and make it look as fabulous and glamorous as possible—despite the despair that awaited them when their group landed.

Jane snorted, deciding it was fine for him to take a catnap now. Pictures of them crammed into a smelly prop plane while getting their internal organs tossed around like beanbags by a suicidal pilot probably wouldn't make a great Twitter post anyway.

Truthfully, Jane was shocked that Teddy's mom, Gigi Thane, would even step foot in this flying tin-can. Not only had Gigi boarded, she'd promptly zoned out, likely a result of the wine-spritzer-and-Xanax combo she'd gulped while they waited for their plane at the airport in Amman, Jordan.

Yeah, Gigi Thane—an odd mix of Marilyn Monroe and Martha Stewart, who'd built her home-furnishing empire from almost nothing—was totally blitzed. Teddy's dad, Dax Thane, a ball of energy, jiggled his knee impatiently as his wife rested on his shoulder while his nose was, as usual, buried in his phone. Could he even get a cell signal wherever they were?

Jane shifted in her seat as Teddy finally put the peg in the middle square. The thirteen-hour flight to Amman in the Thanes' Lear jet was enough to make her restless, but this was more than just restlessness.

Syria wasn't exactly a hotspot for family vacations. But no one could tell that to Dax Thane, the brilliant and unconventional CEO of Thane Insurance. The idea for this trip was his brainchild: deliver a bit of Western goodwill while proving to his client base just how far Thane would go to cover their insane exploits. Once Dax got a stunt in his head, especially a thrilling idea for drumming up viral online attention, sanity need not interfere.

Nothing about Dax and Gigi Thane screamed "Parents of the Year," that was for sure.

Jane studied the handsome man in the plaid button-down and cargo pants. His face was as recognizable as Jeff Bezos's or Mark Zuckerberg's. Little had Jane known when she'd signed up to be a "nanny" to his busy four-year-old that partaking in those wild flights of fancy would become a part of her job description.

Jane ruffled the little boy's hair and placed another pin as she watched the pilot out of the corner of her eye. He'd been speaking into his headset in another language—Arabic? Kurdish? Aramaic?—in a way that sounded indignant. She wished she'd spent more time learning about the Middle East and Asia in school. But while she'd dreamed of traveling when she was growing up, solidly middle-class in the Florida panhandle, never once had she imagined traveling to *Syria*.

The pilot rubbed his nose with the side of his hand and barked into his headset again in a way that made her skin crawl. Was he disagreeing with someone? Hashing out an evil plan to take over the world? An alarm bell went off in her head, and Jane reached for Teddy and tightened his seatbelt.

Jane couldn't place her mistrust with the pilot. At first, he had seemed annoyed—here was a stupid American family, exercising their privilege in a stunt designed to profit off of another culture's tragedy. But the more time they'd spent in the airplane, the more Jane was certain the pilot wasn't disgusted by their opportunistic sightseeing.

In her job as the Thanes' nanny, she'd learned to watch for signs of chaos within the family. To anticipate the dangers that she associated with Dax Thane. Her neck prickled. There were too many red flags. Too many risks. She didn't like it, but that could be said as much for everything she did with this family.

This was a dangerous trip, but she had to stop overthinking. Disaster didn't always lurk. *You've been awake for twenty hours, and now you're letting your mind run away with you.*

But, hello, overthinking was her job. That was how she could best protect Teddy, and if her uncle had taught her anything in her self-defense classes, it was to stay sharp, keep her eyes open, and never ignore the tingling feelings that crawled up and down her spine.

"We should be there soon," Dax said absently, not looking up as he thumbed furiously on his phone. Gigi's head lolled, and her long eyelashes fluttered. She had a pretty face, albeit a billionaire's-wife face, with too much make-up for the occasion and just the right amount of plastic surgery to shave a few years off her advancing age.

Without warning, the plane hit turbulence. They jumped and jerked, and Jane's stomach somersaulted. She gripped the armrest again, feigning calm as Teddy shrieked in excitement.

"Fun," she muttered, swallowing the acidic taste in her mouth.

The pilot growled as they went through a series of smaller bumps. Seriously, was he *trying* to put them through the worst turbulence possible?

Every time the plane lurched, Jane closed her eyes and said a little prayer.

Dax leaned over and smacked Teddy on the foot. "Cool, huh, buddy? Rockin' and rollin'!"

Teddy nodded gleefully, as he usually did when he received some slight acknowledgement from his dad.

Now that his face was out of his phone, Jane hoped her employer would say something to reassure them. Something smart like, "Let's go home." After all, she'd been there when his sister, Courtney, had said a big *hell no* to this family-vacation-slash-social-media stunt on the grounds that it wasn't safe. Her exact words: "I'd rather wear a meat necklace in a cage of rabid wolves."

That was Courtney. Blunt. Practical. If only Jane could've been so forward. But she was staff, not family. And during the nine months Jane had been on Dax Thane's payroll, she'd learned to never expect the expected. Most insurance companies were about mitigating risk, but not Thane. He pushed the limits, broke through boundaries. Thane Insurance made insurance Insta-cool. Thus their literally asinine slogan, with the donkey mascot in the football helmet: *Risk it all. We'll cover your ass.*

So, as the prop plane started to rattle around them, Jane went over the reasons why she'd agreed to this job. One: Teddy was adorable, with those big brown puppy-dog eyes. Something about him had told Jane that he needed saving. Now, he was dearer to her than her own limbs.

Two: Gigi was desperate. Despite being a shrewd businesswoman in her own right, she had initially come off as having a deer-in-headlights thing going for her when it came to raising the kid. Not that Jane was any better, since the most experience she'd had was babysitting her cousins. But Gigi had assured her that was fine, because their family marched to the beat of a different drummer. Not to mention how Gigi treated Teddy as though he were a fashion accessory.

Oh, and three: Jane needed the money. The Thanes paid well, but with high reward came high risk. Sure, she didn't shy away from risky situations. Jane had certainly taken a risk when she'd prevented Gigi and Teddy from being kidnapped from thugs on the streets of DC earlier that year. The altercation had been a chance encounter and her first introduction to the billionaire Thane family. But she wasn't sure if she needed the money enough to *risk her life*.

She swept her long blond hair up into a ponytail and peered out the window as the plane descended below the clouds. *Oh goodie.* They were landing.

Teddy placed the last pin and won the game again.

"Hooray, cutie!" She gave him a high five. "You won that one."

"I've won all of them," he sweetly corrected as the plane lurched again and sent the game board tumbling off Teddy's knee and onto his dad's foot.

Dax, once again consumed by his phone, didn't notice, so Jane reached across and picked it up, once again finding reason to watch the spastic pilot.

Is it me, or is he unusually nervous? It was stuffy inside the airplane cabin, but sweat glistened at his temples.

Her warning tingle became worse than before. She stuffed the game into the pocket of Teddy's Pokémon backpack and smiled at him as the plane sank lower.

"I think we're landing," she said in a low whisper, as if they were having some great adventure. *Or crashing.* But that wouldn't do well to share with Teddy, and she willed herself not to think about dying in a fiery crash.

His cherubic smile pulled at her heartstrings. She bit at her lip. *We shouldn't be here. I should have prevented this.* His safety was her job, after all. Then again, his aunt had threatened and yelled, firing everything she had at her brother Dax to keep Teddy safe at home with her. It didn't work. The Thanes didn't even take their security detail. Big surprise… They never did.

Jane looked at Gigi, somewhat awakened by turbulence. Her head lolled again, her eyes fluttering, heavy—then Gigi was out again. Jane gritted her teeth and lambasted herself for not saying something before they left. Anything along the lines of "Let's avoid war zones" would have worked.

Teddy tugged on her arm. "Look."

Jane glanced out the window. She could see the ground in the distance. The plane rattled in her ears as she watched the dark nothingness morph into brownish ground cover. Finally, she could make out where bushes dotted the landscape, and the outline of distant buildings became visible.

"Almost there," Dax announced like they were heading to an amusement park.

Jane searched for what could make him so excited but saw a whole lot of nothing. The only difference was that they were much closer to the ground.

The distant buildings became clearer, though they looked more like ruins than modern day structures. Jane squinted and watched for the refugee camps she hadn't read enough about.

The nose of the plane abruptly tilted toward the ground, and Jane held her breath and gripped her necklace. Finally, up ahead, she saw what could pass as a landing strip awaiting them. It was more like a cleared straight area cut through the dusty, brush-covered sand and rocks. Awesome—they were landing in the middle of nowhere.

Approaching a runway should've been a reason to rejoice, but no. Her sixth sense buzzed with worry, and her body, from tits to toes, screamed out a warning. Dax rubbed his hands together. Jane glared at him.

He grinned. "Isn't this great?"

Not really. They descended at a nauseating angle. Teddy put his chubby hand in hers. Panic sloshed in her stomach. Gigi groaned. Alarm choked in Jane's throat. The pilot jerked the nose upright before she cried out. They touched down and bounced. Joe-the-photojournalist choked on his final snore and woke, cursing loudly. His equipment clattered to the ground as the metal frame of the plane rattled, finally touching down.

The harsh landing smacked Jane's teeth together. They jostled from side to side. The airplane jumped and jerked on the rutted airstrip. Brown dust billowed up around them as the pilot fought to slow down.

"Like a roller coaster," Dax shouted.

Motion sickness rolled over Jane as she ducked Teddy under her arm. The aircraft bumped along the pocked strip and coasted to a stop.

"Thank God," she whispered.

Dax popped his phone into the front pocket of his linen shirt and rubbed his hands together. "Now the adventure begins."

What had that plane ride been? A walk through the freakin' park? Jane leaned close to the window. As the dust settled, she took in a total wasteland. Scrubby, patchy bushes, and sand upon more sand. This didn't look like an airport, but more like someone had flattened a landing strip amid a few stone buildings. Other than that, there was nothing nearby.

Her throat felt thick. *Why couldn't Dax Thane be more like other billionaires and take his family to Hawaii for the month?*

She glanced out the other side. Men in kaftans with their heads and faces covered with dark fabric stood astride old motorbikes. Massive assault rifles were strapped over their shoulders.

The click, click, click of Joe's camera broke through Jane's concern. He was acting like they were on safari and the armed men were a tourist attraction. She elbowed him, muttering, "Stop that."

"Taking in the scenery." Though, grumbling, he scooted back into his seat.

The faces of the armed men were testaments to a lifetime of humanitarian crisis and war. Their experiences were weathered into their skin and hardened into their gaze. They'd been victims and aggressors, exploited and persecuted. She could see that in a glance as much as she could tell their group was unwelcome.

One of them motioned to the others, and they started to march toward their plane. The pilot made quick work of abandoning his helm. He escaped out of the hatch door, mostly ignored by the approaching group.

"Don't be alarmed," Dax announced. "They're used to receiving our kind. This is where NATO and your Red Cross outfits come in and drop supplies to help with refugee camps."

"Huh," Gigi managed. She groggily rubbed her hands across her face. "Not exactly what I expected."

Dax grinned. "They'll be friendly."

Jane pulled Teddy close to her side and wrapped an arm around him. She didn't care what her employer said. The men approaching the plane were not a Syrian hospitality committee.

CHAPTER TWO

THE HOT SUN beat down on Jane's shoulders. Their group shuffled down an uneven, sand-baked path, surrounded by their arguing captors. At least she thought they were arguing. Maybe they were just hot and angry like she was.

She didn't know where they were going, but they had to get there soon. Dax had already spoken to the leader of the armed group, an impossibly tall man in a long, dark tunic, and agreed to pay a ransom. Rescue or arrangements home should come at any time.

The armed man behind Jane shoved her and shouted words that she couldn't understand but had deciphered as *move faster*.

"We're trying." She grabbed onto Teddy's hand. The little boy tried to look over his shoulder, but Jane pulled him close. "Hurry. It'll be okay. But hurry." She'd told him the same thing so often that she felt like a broken record.

The heat was baking them alive. Jane finally realized why their captors were covered from head to toe in long robes, fabric, headwraps, and veils— they had to block the sun. What she would have done for a sun hat or a robe from the locals. Sweat soaked her clothes. Her tank top and shorts clung to her body, and she readjusted the straps fruitlessly to give her more coverage. It didn't matter. The hot sun scalded her fair skin.

They stumbled across the dirt, tripping over bushes and stones, and approached a meager patch of shade from a long-ago-burned-out bus. Dax's upbeat suggestion that they stop was rebuffed. The photographer clicked a quick picture.

Gigi threw herself to the ground. "I can't go any farther."

The photographer clicked again. Maybe it was the rising heat or the hazy and out-of-reach way the only signs of possible civilization loomed in the distance, but Jane couldn't help but think of Gigi as though she were acting in a soap opera.

The men ordered their group to stop abruptly, shoving them toward the carcass of a burned-out bus. Maybe Jane shouldn't have knocked Gigi's theatrics. They now had a slip of shade and could rest.

Jane crouched to Teddy's level. "This will make an interesting story to share when school starts."

"I'm thirsty," Teddy croaked.

"I know. Me too, and we can get a drink soon." She pushed his sweaty hair from his forehead, wishing she didn't have to lie. She had no idea when their captors would offer drinks again. She'd learned the hard way not to ask first.

"When?" he asked.

"I don't know, baby." She tried to sound optimistic. "It should be soon."

Teddy pouted and held his arms out. "Will you cuddle me?"

"Of course." Lord knew his parents weren't going to offer. She sat on the ground and cradled Teddy in her lap. The sand and rocks under her legs were hotter than hell. Teddy's body heat made her feel worse, but they both needed someone to hold on to. "Everything will be fine. Don't worry."

She blinked in the bright sun and studied the men. Their heads and faces were completely wrapped, leaving only their eyes visible. They held huge guns, and two of the men wore bandoliers of bullets around their chests. Their conversation seemed tense. Then again, what did she know? They mostly communicated through angry shouts. Maybe that was just their way.

Slowly, Jane shifted to glance at her employer. Dax rubbed the tips of his fingers together and regarded the men curiously, as if this was a history lesson. He almost looked confused. But maybe he was unhappy they didn't know his company's commercials. She wasn't sure he even understood the severity of what they were up against.

Gigi breezed over as she fanned her face and smiled down at Teddy.

"Don't worry. Everything's fine. Don't worry."

Joe's camera clicked as he captured the moment. "Nice shot."

Jane wanted to pull Teddy away and hide, but they had nowhere to go. She whispered the same words as Gigi against his temple. They all seemed to be speaking words of encouragement again and again. Except Dax. The only thing he repeated was, "Well, this is what our ransom insurance is for!"

Jane wanted to punch him in the nose. Especially when he followed up each time with a huge laugh.

Teddy turned toward two men. Their lively conversation morphed from terse words into shouts. He grasped her hand tighter. "Why are they fighting?"

"Everything will be okay." Jane managed the non-answer, wondering if she actually believed it. Deep down, she had the sinking feeling they were well and truly fucked.

She glanced at Joe-the-photographer, wondering why he was so calm. Jane couldn't understand how he'd been allowed to keep his camera or why he risked the occasional photograph. They were all crazy!

Dax acted like the danger was all part of the fun. Even Gigi didn't seem *that* worried. Surprisingly enough, she seemed more bothered by the heat and lack of water than frightened. Maybe the heat made her irrational. Or, maybe she was still coasting on her Xanax-wine spritzers.

Jane would have preferred Gigi's antics to this oh-well attitude. Why didn't she yell at their captors? Where was her big escape? Though the barren landscape didn't offer anywhere to go.

Ahead of them, the remnants of what looked like an abandoned city grew larger as they walked. She mopped sweat off of her forehead. It was nearly midday, and the sun felt like fire. Her throat was so dry. She would've killed for a bottle of water and sunscreen. Her skin burned, and poor Teddy's cheeks were as red as strawberries. They'd been forced to leave almost everything on the plane.

The three men with guns marched off, still arguing, sandals spitting up puffs of dust as they walked.

Dax carefully slid over to the photographer. "Joe," he murmured, "you getting all this?"

Joe nodded, patting his beaten brown rucksack that he'd been allowed to take. It hadn't had anything useful like sun protection, food, or water. Just his stupid camera equipment.

Jane eyed the bag and the awkward way Joe positioned it, then noticed the bag had a small hole. Joe was pointing the opening in the direction of the men. Was that a hidden video camera? *Is he fucking televising this? Live-streaming it on Twitter? For what?* She gnashed her teeth.

Gigi sighed loudly as though she needed everyone's attention. "Dax, I don't like this anymore."

Yeah, me neither, lady. Maybe the wine spritzer was wearing off and Gigi had just opened her eyes. Because this was a pretty easy trip to hate. Jane and Teddy hadn't been keen on it since before they landed.

"It'll be fine!" Dax's eyes were wide and wild.

Jane slumped. Whenever Dax rode an adrenaline wave, she knew to buckle her seatbelt and hang on. But how much longer could the man remain excited and oblivious?

"I mean it, Dax." Gigi fanned herself. "I don't think you're quite gripping this. Those men are carrying *guns*. Real guns."

Versus what? Fake guns? Jane managed not to roll her eyes. At least someone else besides her now seemed to know that they were in deep shit and rapidly sinking deeper.

"I didn't realize it would be so—rustic." Gigi looked over at Jane. "I think Teddy's frightened."

Dax brushed dirt from his white linen shirt. "Relax. Guns or not, nothing'll happen to us."

Gigi pursed her lips and sighed heavily again before turning to her husband. "What if something goes wrong?"

Hello? *Something has gone* very *wrong*, Jane wanted to scream. Instead, she kissed Teddy's temple.

"In case you forgot," Dax pointed out, "we're worth a hell of a lot of money to them. They won't hurt us."

"But Teddy," Gigi whined, clinging to her new interest in her son.

Dax kneeled in front of Teddy and faked a punch to his shoulder.

"You're okay, right, buddy? My big man?"

Teddy straightened in Jane's arm and smiled hopefully at his father. He rarely got Dax's attention and was over the moon when it happened.

"Great." Mollified, Dax winked at his wife. "He's fine."

Gigi's lips thinned. "Filtered ice water would be nice."

Jane almost snorted. Filtered and cold would be a little more than nice... Jane wondered what the symptoms of heatstroke were as she watched Gigi pout.

"We can't always get what we want." Dax rubbed a finger over his teeth, then wiped the shine from his tanned forehead as though he wanted to look nice for his public.

Obviously, they both were having heatstroke problems. Or! The joke was on her and Teddy. Gigi and Dax had forced them unknowingly to take part in a reality television show. An odd spring of hope quickened Jane's pulse.

It wouldn't be totally unheard of for either Gigi or Dax to act absolutely insane. Maybe their whole thing, from capture to caravan to the ransom, was just an act. Maybe the men with guns were just actors that Dax had hired. This could all be for a publicity stunt!

Optimism surged. Insanity ruled the roost at the Thane residences. They might be a few minutes away from ice-cold water and a luxury suite in a hotel. At least, Jane hoped.

She peered around, hoping to see a poorly hidden camera crew, complementing the closeups Joe had managed. The crew would pop out after all of this was over, hand them ice-cold drinks and snacks, and tell them, "You should've seen your faces!"

She held her breath, waiting. No such luck.

Teddy stirred from her lap and found a stick.

"Good idea," Jane encouraged.

He drew pictures in the sand. A circle, a house, then a *T* for Teddy.

Jane leaned over and kissed the top of Teddy's head. Despite the hours trudging through hell, she could still smell the faint lemon shampoo from the bath she'd given him right before they left.

He wrote the *E* backward and asked, "Everything's okay, right, Janie?"

"Oh, yes. I'm sure," she lied. Her hopefulness plummeted as the secret camera crew failed to appear.

A quick, loud rat-a-tat-tat rang out, somewhere near the city in the distance. It echoed across the desert plain and pinched at her heart. *Gunfire.*

"Is everything still okay?" Teddy asked again.

"Yes, baby." Again, she lied. "I'm sure."

But now she was nearly certain this wasn't one of their games. A camera crew wouldn't pop out from behind the burned-out bus. Gigi and Dax wouldn't joke about their ransom insurance. Things were most definitely *not* all right.

CHAPTER THREE

Two Days Later
Abu Dhabi, United Arab Emirates

CHANCE EVANS LEANED back and swept his eyes over the lavish hotel in downtown Abu Dhabi. Even "closed for construction," as the sign outside proclaimed, it was way more opulent than anything he was used to in the States. He was more of a cheeseburger-and-beer kind of guy, but this place was definitely steak and scotch.

All this wealth? It made him antsy. For the thousandth time since the Titan Group's jet had touched down in the Emirates, Chance wondered how the hell Jared Westin, the man, the myth, the legend—also known as his employer—had ever thought Chance was made for this kind of lifestyle.

Abu Dhabi was a far cry from the shit he had to slog through while in the Army and an even bigger step away from his humble country upbringing in southwestern Virginia, in a house that was about as middle-of-nowhere as one could get east of the Appalachians.

Honestly, he couldn't see how anyone on the Aces team fit in with the swank and sizzle of a city so glitzy that the call to prayer bellowed from a mosque that could have doubled as a palace. Then again, some of his teammates had worked in espionage, while others had been on assignments in exotic locations. He'd, more or less, been a grunt like his friend Liam, who'd also joined Titan's newest covert team.

Whatever it was that had prompted Jared to offer Chance the opportunity, he was grateful, and even if he was a fish out of water, he would make it work. Once he got used to this place, he would be fine. It had been almost a year, so… any day now.

He walked through the magnificent lobby, with its arched doorways and colorful frescos, to what had once been the hotel's reception area. It would be so again, but unknown to the public, the walls would be armored and the glass bulletproof. Somewhere in the middle of the skyscraping towers that would again one day house tourists and business travelers was a central command center shaping up to be Titan's Abu Dhabi Headquarters.

It'd be state of the art, with at least one floor dedicated as a central nerve center. Several floors would include suites that were actually impenetrable safe-house locations—everything the elite team of agents needed to provide security for their clients on this side of the world.

A film of dust lightly coated the marble floor as the most technical construction crew that Chance had ever come across ran wires into the walls and ceiling. He eyed them and then saw Parker Black, the Titan Group's Director of Intelligence, scowling at blueprints. The large papers were laid across a makeshift table, and Parker's brow knit as he spoke with one of his many construction-security consultant minions.

With nothing much to do, Chance ambled over. "Working on the death rays today?"

The security minion wasn't amused, stepping from Parker and scurrying away to wait by the far wall.

"I didn't even get a smile." Chance grimaced dramatically. "I don't think they like me."

He snickered as he glanced from the schematic. "They don't like to socialize."

"They seem like a bunch of spooks."

Parker shrugged. "What are you up to?"

Now it was Chance's turn to shrug. If he had to be honest, he was up to a shit-ton of nothing. "If not death rays, then what?"

Parker laughed. "Right now, we're in a holding pattern. Everything's hurry up and wait."

"Sounds familiar." Army life had been the same, though new orders always seemed somewhere on the horizon. Even post-Army, as a contractor, downtime hadn't existed unless he wanted it to. Right now, no one needed anything from Chance. Their team was still forming and the jobs weren't lined up. They spent more time training and working out than jumping into battle zones. That was probably why he was antsy.

"You look bored." Parker rolled the large paper and tucked it into a long, black container.

"Yup, you nailed it."

"Something's in the pipeline. But until then, Hagan's running the stairs in the west tower if you're that bored."

"Ha. Not bored enough to sprint up staircases." Though the day was looking bright if the possibility of a job loomed. "If a gig is coming, I'll stick close. Maybe grab some grub and people watch."

"If you returned with muhammara or moutabel from the restaurant across the street, I wouldn't turn it away."

"Sounds fancy," he joked.

"Better than that shit you keep upstairs in your kitchen."

"Don't knock my canned food stash." Though, he would have killed for a burger and fries.

Boots thundered down the hall, and Chance turned as Jared stormed into the lobby. He paused, glowering like he'd woken up on the wrong side of the bed every day of the last decade. Then he nodded to Parker.

"Boss Man," Parker said as way of greeting.

"Both of you." Jared glared at Chance and threw a thumb over his shoulder. "Get into the office." Then he pulled out his phone, barking similar orders as he stormed away.

"Glad to see he's all piss and vinegar today," Chance muttered with a half-cocked grin.

Parker signaled to the security consultant that he'd be back and then slapped Chance on the back. "That, my friend, is what you get for being bored."

A little work? Chance snorted. "I'll take it."

They filed behind the reception desk and through the door to their makeshift office. It was nothing more than a few chairs and a bare desk holding a laptop.

Parker moved to the computer, and Chance pulled up a chair as a sweat-soaked Hagan walked in, guzzling a bottle of water. The other men filtered in as Jared reappeared. He took his position at the head of the improvised table and leaned back in his chair. His dark, laser-focused gaze landed on Parker. "It looks like we'll have to put our little redecorating job on hold."

"Looks like," Parker said.

Chance sat on the edge of his seat. Welcome anticipation surged in his chest. They were finally getting away from the wealth and privilege.

Boss Man cracked his knuckles. "There's a civilian rescue in order."

CHAPTER FOUR

C HANCE DIDN'T WANT civilians in danger, and he hadn't signed up to sit back and twiddle his thumbs. Still, seconds ticked by, and Jared didn't share anything. Instead, he and Parker managed to have an intense, nonverbal conversation, leaving Chance to guess at what was happening.

He came up short. Both men were impossible to read. Jared didn't let anything slip from his close control beyond what the big guy wanted Chance to know. Parker, less guarded but more analytical in nature, played his cards close to the vest as well.

Both men seemed like good people to work with. Chance even liked Boss Man all right. So far, he'd been fair. Even when he was an asshole.

"Something funny, Midas?" Jared barked.

He hadn't realized he'd been smirking. "No, sir."

Across the table, Camden coughed to cover a laugh.

Sawyer didn't bother hiding his amusement. "That's Chance's happy grin. The man's ready to get to work."

"Not a lie." Chance leaned back in his chair.

"Anyone else? Hagan?" Jared groused and muttered, "Anyone got anything to add to this chit chat before we get down to work?"

"Well." Hagan placed his elbows on the table. "I—"

"For fuck's sake, Hagan. *No.* Your answer is no." Jared rubbed the back of his neck. "*Son of a bitch.* Now, as I was saying…"

If Chance were a betting man, he'd guess that their team bullshitting around the table pleased Jared to no end. Even if he constantly reminded them that he wasn't ready for their team and they weren't ready, period. The more Boss Man said that, the more Chance thought he approved of their work. They meshed well. Chance had fallen in with a handful of the guys—Liam, Hagan, Camden, and Sawyer—and got along with others. Though, he got along with just about everyone.

Noticing the quiet that had fallen over the room, Chance refocused on Jared. He glared at Parker until he stopped typing. "If you're finished sending dirty messages to your special lady friend."

Parker smirked but didn't deny it.

Boss Man shook his head then slammed a fist on the table like a judge ordering a court to order. "*Thane Insurance*. Everyone knows them?"

Hagan snorted and leaned back in his chair, crossing his arms. "Who doesn't?"

Sawyer hummed their familiar jingle.

Camden chucked a pen at Sawyer. "Thanks, asshole. Now I've got that stupid jingle in my head."

"'Risk it all. We'll cover your ass,'" Sawyer belted for Camden's benefit.

"Right. Those people," Jared confirmed. "And you all know Dax Thane."

Chance nodded. Some of the guys rolled their eyes. It wasn't possible to exist in this world and not know Dax Thane. A world-class pretentious prick. Dax Thane might be the exception to Chance's belief he could get along with anyone. The guy was a social media showman, the P.T. Barnum of the insurance world. His recognizable face was plastered on every Thane Insurance ad, along with that smiling donkey in the football helmet.

Sawyer took the pen that landed in front of him and tucked it behind his ear. "What's that walking ego gotten himself into now?"

"Something that needs a rescue." Hagan elbowed Sawyer.

Jared rolled his eyes. "You guys need to get out more."

"That's the truth," Parker chuckled.

"Our newest client is Thane Insurance." Jared's lips thinned before he added, "And their esteemed leader has found himself in something of a hostage situation."

The room settled down. Chance leaned forward. Hostage situations were interesting, even if they involved Dax Thane.

"Everyone's favorite billionaire stepped in it big this time," Jared explained. "In one of the most dangerous places on the damn planet."

Of course Dax did. But, where? Each man in this room would have a short though debatable list of the worst places.

Jared pursed his lips. "We're going in for the rescue, but be prepared to hear online about how far Thane Insurance will go to protect its client base."

They were going to risk their lives so Dax Thane could score a few publicity points? Chance wanted to work but maybe not as much as he'd thought.

Hagan hunched forward, dragging his hands down his face as he shook his head. "You've got to be shittin' me."

Jared's face darkened. "We can bitch and debate all we want about that guy. But this is the game changer. He brought along his loving family."

"His wife and four-year-old son," Parker clarified.

At that, a low grumble erupted from around the table. Jared and Parker remained stoically expressionless, but neither told the team to shut up.

After the 'what the hells' and 'asshats' were done, Jared called for quiet again. "Our job isn't to provide a running commentary. It's to save lives and keep our own."

"So where we are talking about, boss?" Sawyer asked. "Syria?"

Syria was the leading contender on Chance's list of shitty places to avoid.

"Bingo." Jared's jaw twitched. "Parker, fill 'em in."

"From what we can tell." Parker shut his laptop. "The Thane family is in or near a Syrian refugee camp outside of Aleppo."

"Sounds like a high-stakes mission for a high-stakes—" Hagan caught a short look from Jared, obviously censoring himself as he finished, "*client.*"

"They're high-value targets." Jared's glare eased. "No one is in better position to rescue the HVTs than this team."

A totally preventable hostage situation. Chance chewed the inside of his mouth. The HVTs should never have been in Syria. That was the problem with people with too much money. Were they so bored that they had to invent life-or-death problems?

Parker removed a folder from a shelf behind him and passed out the mission details. "We have five HVTs."

Chance flipped to the page profiling the family.

Parker continued, "Dax Thane; his wife, Gigi Thane; their son, Teddy Thane. Then there's the nanny and a photographer." He retook his seat and ran through pertinent information on the family. "No security."

Chance skimmed ahead, disgusted that the parents had brought their kid, and of course, that they couldn't leave the nanny and photographer behind on their suicide mission.

"Forty-eight hours have passed since they landed," Parker explained. "A ransom request of fifty million dollars came into Thane HQ last night. The abductors swear that once that money is deposited into their account, they'll let the prisoners go."

"Right," one of the other guys said. "We all know how honest rebels who abduct billionaire families tend to be."

"In your mission packets, we've designed a plan for every contingency," Parker said. "Ranked by threat analysis and a risk assessment to human collateral."

That was a cold, scientific way to categorize the situation, including the possibility of death. Chance grumbled, "We've got intel on the *exact* location of this refugee camp?"

"Nothing's exact, and there's more than one camp." Parker flipped through their briefing papers. "Best we can do is piece together a series of delayed satellite shots and layer it with a thermal map from friendly drones."

"Sounds far from exact," Sawyer added.

Parker's jaw tightened. "Statistically, we have a pretty good idea of the location."

"And that's saying a hell of a lot," Jared grumbled, continuing to explain the best option that came with the smallest amount of risk. Their course of action depended on how the ransom exchange and ensuing negotiation would fall out. The quick and short explanation was for a secondary team to fly in and haul ass out, preferably with the HVTs in tow, when the ransom exchange went bad.

Parker directed the room to turn the page of their briefings to the possibilities of schematic. Various entry and exit points were mapped among what was an always-changing landscape. They didn't have hard data on the site, because blocks of what was once a city were now obliterated, abandoned buildings.

Some called it a fucking wasteland. Others, a humanitarian crisis. The only thing Chance knew for certain about Aleppo was that the urban area had been decimated by war over the years, making it completely uninhabitable. Anyone still living there was in danger, while anyone who fled for their life had been labeled a refugee.

"We'll divide into two teams. One will arrive by vehicle." Jared thumped a fist on the schematic. "The area's marked on your map."

"Who chose the location?" Hagan asked.

"Thane Insurance agreed to the ransom and terms prior to contacting Titan Group."

"That was smart," Sawyer muttered, rolling his eyes.

"*When* the deal goes south," Jared said by way of agreement, "the secondary team will already be airborne. Collect the family and go." Jared met the eyes of all the guys, one by one. "Got it?"

They all nodded.

"We've got to do this right the first time," Jared added. "We fuck up, and there'll be hell to pay."

Chance shifted to the edge of his chair.

Jared cracked his knuckles again. "One final thing that's not in your briefing. You know what kind of trouble to expect in Syria, but you need to know what kind of people we're going in for." He paused as though searching for the right words. Tension ticked on his face. Diplomatically, he continued, "The contract was for the family. No specifics for the staff." Jared's jaw set. "Once you've thought that over, forget about it. We don't leave without everyone."

Whoa. That kind of disloyalty hit Chance like a concrete-cast sucker punch.

"Any other questions?" Boss Man met every person's gaze, one by one.

When he reached Chance, his personal turmoil brewed. He had several questions, starting with what kind of idiot would work for Dax Thane? And, what kind of parent would travel to Syria despite the government travel warnings? Chance didn't want to be around any of those people, whether they were family or staff.

"Midas?" Jared asked.

"None," Chance managed.

The meeting wrapped, and they filed out, marching orders in hand.

Syria occupied Chance's mind. He'd been there years ago. Right outside of Aleppo, too. His first tour. When he'd left, he clearly remembered thinking the same thing. *You couldn't pay me enough to go back there.* Guess he was wrong.

If there wasn't a kid involved, Chance might wonder if it would be better to let natural selection do its job. But the kid didn't deserve to die just because he was surrounded by fools.

CHAPTER FIVE

"READY TO GET this shit-show on the road?" Hagan asked Chance as they flew over Syria in the back of the stealth copter.

"As I'll ever be." Chance peered out the open door of the copter. Night had fallen, but the orange glow of little bonfires occasionally lit up the ground below.

The night breeze whipped against his face, cooler than the oven of daytime. It felt good to be back in the saddle again, back in tactical gear, but he couldn't say the last memories he had of Syria were pleasant ones.

Just as they'd expected, the exchange was starting to fall apart. The kidnappers wanted more money, and now they were only willing to give up half the family. The plan had been all of them or nothing.

Hagan growled. "Could've called that one from half a world away."

Chance tightened his gloves on his wrists and got ready for the drop. "Then let's get to it."

JANE JUMPED AT the sound of more gunfire outside, just when things had been settling down.

They'd spent what felt like hours walking toward the compound. As the sun set, the men had led them into a crumbling building and left them in a room with a dirt floor and no furniture. That had to have been over an hour ago.

They sat, shivering, in total darkness, except for a slim shaft of moonlight that shone against the far wall. In quiet whispers, Gigi and Dax kept repeating more of the same: "This is fine. We're okay. Everything will be all right."

Jane had started to think they really were losing it. No job was worth this. How dare they risk her life like this? And their own son's? She'd considered telling them both to go to hell, and she would have, if not for Teddy.

She'd just curled her body around Teddy, trying to make him comfortable, when a sound much closer than the gunfire cracked the air.

"What was that?" Gigi hissed.

Dax rose to his feet and pulled his wife next to him. Jane lifted Teddy's sleepy body to hers. Joe didn't move as fast. Jane assumed the poor lighting and anticipated picture quality made him slower.

"I can't see a damn thing," Joe complained.

"Figure it out. It's your job," Dax snapped.

Yeah, because who wouldn't want to recall these happy memories of a family vacation… Jane held Teddy close and pushed herself from the floor.

"Janie," Teddy mumbled against her neck.

Her ears hurt to make sense of the sound of footsteps shuffling in the corridor outside their locked door. "Everything's okay."

"They're coming closer," Gigi warned.

Dax put his arm over her shoulder. "Everything will be fine."

Metallic clicks turned on their door, and it flew open. Jane jumped back. Gigi screamed. Dax and Joe shouted in surprised as several men poured into their cell.

"Dax! Dax! What's happening?" Gigi screamed.

Their captors reached for Gigi. She clung to Dax's arm as they pulled her away. Jane didn't know what to do. Help Gigi? Protect Teddy? Joe and Dax stood like shocked statues as Gigi kicked and yelled, acting for the first time like she might be in danger. "Dax!"

Other men held Joe back as he lurched into action. Dax still didn't move.

"This isn't supposed to happen! Dax!"

As much as she hated Gigi and Dax, she couldn't handle this. Jane covered Teddy's ears and held him against the wall, promising that everything would be okay in a whisper-prayer against the back of his head.

"Gigi." Dax jerked from his stupor. "It's okay. All right? Everything's good. Just listen and do as they—"

The door slammed shut. Gigi and the armed men were gone. Their cell was eerily quiet.

CHAPTER SIX

"T HEY'RE SPLITTING US up," Dax announced as though he were well-versed in terroristic abduction tactics and strategy. "No one will hurt her. Or us." The door flew open again. Two men entered. Dax held out his hands. "Ease up. Okay? You've made your point."

Additional armed men flanked the two Dax faced off with. Joe and Dax stood shoulder-to-shoulder. Jane curled around Teddy, trying to become one with the wall.

A flourish of words flew around the cell. As fast as the armed men had entered, they easily subdued Joe and Dax then dragged them away.

Jane trembled. Her knees threatened to buckle. She wanted to shield Teddy's eyes, but he already knew what was happening, and there wasn't anything left to see.

"The door didn't shut," Teddy whispered.

"What?" She wanted to cry, and rubbed Teddy's back. Holding him nearly took all her energy, but she couldn't let go—for both their sakes.

"It didn't shut. Like when Mom and Dad fight. They shut it so hard it stays open."

Jane turned toward the door. Teddy was right. The door had been slammed shut so hard the latch hadn't caught. Carefully, she inched over, waiting for the guards to burst in again. Minutes passed. They felt like hours. Finally, Jane reached for the door and tried the knob. It didn't turn—but the door moved. "You're right, Teddy." She kissed his cheek, pulling the door farther ajar. Jane peeked into the semi-dark hallway and didn't see anyone.

"Are we going to go home?" Teddy asked.

"Absolutely." She squeezed him close but realized her arms were shaking with weakness. If they were to leave, she couldn't carry him. "But I need you to walk. Can you do that for me?"

"Yes." Teddy wriggled from her arms.

Oh, God. She hoped this was the right thing to do. Jane inched it open. A dim, flickering light danced on the wall far from their cell. That had been the direction she'd heard the noise and gunfire come from. The other way seemed much darker, but quieter. She opted to head away from the gunshots. "Let's go."

Hand in hand, they rushed down the hall. The uneven floor and winding walls didn't make sense. Her free hand helplessly felt around in front of them.

Teddy tripped. "Ow! Janie! My knee!"

"Shhh!" She pulled him back to his feet and lifted him to her chest. Her muscles ached under his light weight. "We'll check on it later."

Walls pocked with gaping holes allowed moonlight to guide their way. They stumbled over uneven ground. "There has to be a way out."

Gunshots fired again. But this time, they were so close that Jane was surprised her heart continued to beat. Teddy clung to her, shaking and whimpering, and she let him bury his face in her shoulder. At least then, he couldn't see what a clusterfuck his father had created.

They raced from the sounds until she had to stop and catch her breath. They leaned against what had at one time been a wall. Now it gaped and allowed the frigid night air to blow over them.

Her eyes swept a half-circle around them, scanning outside their building, trying to make sense of the dark landscape. Far away, bonfires glowed. Maybe they were from refugee camps. Maybe someone from the UN or NATO would be there and could help. But, the longer she stared, the more impossible it seemed to reach the lights.

Suddenly, hands came down on her and Teddy. She fought against the powerful hands wrenching the boy from her grasp. "No!" Relinquishing Teddy was one thing she was prepared to fight to the death over, and not just because it was part of her job description. She slammed the heel of her palm under the man's chin. His jaw snapped back under her force, and she kneed him in the groin.

The man toppled forward, and Jane released her grip on Teddy. She dropped a leg back into her fighting stance. She could barely see her target and didn't want to hit the boy between them, but sighted him as best she could, pulled her knee up, and attacked with a kick that landed only because of years of repetition.

The man grunted. Teddy fell between them, and Jane scooped the crying boy to her chest.

"What are you doing?" Teddy cried.

"Baby—" She rounded a sharp corner. "We have to run."

CHAPTER SEVEN

ON THE GROUND, the men stole toward the orange light. The compound was nothing but a shithole of burned-out walls fortified by rubble and whatever the refugees could get their hands on. They had scattered about, huddled around bonfires under the starless sky.

Hagan motioned with his hand, indicating that the team should spread out. After volunteering to do the clean-up sweep of the compound, Chance hung against the wall, waiting for the signal to engage.

In his earpiece, Headquarters calmly stated directives to the first team. But other than that, he might as well have been alone. The only sign something was wrong was the faraway rattle of gunfire.

His radio crackled with a teammate checking in. "We've located Subject Five."

"Subjects One and Two have also been located," another voice said. "We're bringing them out. Rendezvous point Alpha."

On the other side of the compound, Chance barely saw anything of interest. He continued his scan. The broken transmissions crackled in his earpiece, and Headquarters responded, "Stand by for incoming helo extraction."

"Good," Hagan grumbled. "The dad is giving us shit. Says he wants everything fucking documented, and I'm doing everything I can to keep the mom from screaming her head off."

Chance kept his aggravation quiet. If he was in Hagan's place, there was no telling what he'd say to the mother. They'd purposefully flown into a wasp's nest. What did they except?

"Who we got left?" someone asked.

"The kid and his nanny," Headquarters responded. "Midas, stand by for backup. Do not continue without coverage."

"Holding," Chance confirmed, not feeling very Midas-like as he wait-ed. He'd earned the nickname during his first few weeks on the ground in Abu Dhabi with Aces. Boss Man had joked that every job he'd worked on metaphorically turned to gold.

For a brief and yet hellishly long week, his new teammates had pushed his buttons, giving their boneheaded explanation that Midas had some-thing to do with how Chance looked; his golden-boy good looks. The angrier it made him, the funnier the guys thought it was, until he nearly came to blows with Camden. After that, they stuck with Boss Man's golden-touch version.

Hell, he wasn't one for nicknames. There was a short-lived time in college that his roommate called him Gomer because of the backwoods shithole where he grew up. Good thing that one hadn't stuck. Though he'd take a backwoods dig over mention of how he looked, as though that type of attention ever came with any depth worth trusting.

The stealth chopper arrived. The comms system relayed the chaos of loading the rescue targets into the helicopter. Gunfire erupted. New commands scrambled the team as their defensive position came under attack. Chance balanced on the balls of his boots, waiting for new orders to provide backup.

"Go," Headquarters demanded. "Get that bird back in the air."

Not a second later, their plans were thrown into a tailspin. The pilot pulled up and hauled ass out, and from the turbulent conversation, Chance wondered who else had stayed behind.

"Son of a bitch," Jared growled.

The realization struck. No one had stayed behind, and no one was happy about it. Chance tensed and waited for Parker's emotionless voice to issue next order.

"Midas, you're on your own for the time being."

His eyes closed. Parker's even tone from HQ hadn't belied the predic-ament Chance was in without backup, but anyone who'd heard the transmission now knew why Boss Man had cursed.

"Wouldn't have it any other way." He brushed off their strategic problem and trusted his training. It certainly wasn't the first time he'd been without backup. Though, it was one of the firsts for putting his dick on the line for a family with more money than brains.

He rolled his lips together and focused. Even if the rescue targets were a bunch of rich asshats, he loved saving the day when all odds were against him. Hell, he *thrived* on it. Risking certain death was usually the only time he truly felt alive.

Parker relayed a new game plan. Chance envisioned each step and every risk, picturing his end goal: Teddy Thane, four, and his nanny, Jane Singleton, twenty-five.

"You got this," Jared said. "Now bring their asses home."

Chance let out a breath, counted to three, and moved.

CHAPTER EIGHT

J ANE SMASHED HEAD-FIRST into another wall. Her arms tightened around Teddy as they stumbled back. The air had been knocked out of them. They gasped and wheezed. Her tired mind struggled to define the problem as she finally gulped in air.

No, that had not been a wall. Jane tore Teddy from her chest, wrapping the boy behind her. She lifted her hands and dropped into her fighting stance, unable to make sense of the darkness ahead of them.

Her eyes adjusted in the faint moonlight that poured through rips and craters in the building. The man in front of her wore black tactical gear. His face was mostly obscured by a night-vision goggles and a helmet. Even his hands were gloved, with his finger resting on the trigger of the biggest rifle Jane had ever seen. He was quiet possibly the scariest, most wonderful thing she'd ever set eyes on.

He held up a hand in a way that said hello and be quiet. "I'm one of the good guys."

English. He was an American. "Thank you."

"Grab the kid and listen to what I say. Let's go," the man said gruffly and turned.

Jane straightened. This was the wrong time to take issue with the guy's manners but, hell, his tone worked down her nerves like nails on a chalkboard. "Okay, but you don't have to be an ass about it."

He paused then turned slowly, head cocked. "Are you kidding me, lady?"

She realized that his proclamation as a good guy didn't mean much. Why would she blindly trust another person simply because they spoke English and said they weren't the enemy? Were his clothes even issued by the US government? "I don't know who you are—"

"You people," he muttered. "And this fucking job."

She balked. "Excuse me?"

He leaned closer like a bull pushing an invisible fence. "If you want to stick around and die, be my guest. But I'm taking the kid with me."

Jane threw her arm out like a barrier between the grouchy-warrior dude and her sweet little boy. "I don't think so, Rambo."

He cackled. It wasn't like a laugh, because the sound was too full of disdain and reproach.

A thunderclap of a nearby explosion shook the walls, and she jumped.

"You ready now, Mary Poppins?" He reached over her and lifted Teddy. "Or were you going to stay put?"

For as coarse and gravelly as he was to her, he had an immediate magic touch with Teddy, somehow making him laugh.

Teddy's laugh was nearly the only reason she lamented and agreed to follow. That, and the fact that she'd worked too hard to stay alive since they'd landed in Syria to let a little spite toward the big guy with a gun be the reason she didn't make it out of this hellhole.

They took off and plunged into complete darkness, which was great for him, with those night-vision goggles. But she ran with hands outstretched and groping to keep her balance.

"Hang on," he ordered.

But Jane was a millisecond too slow to comprehend. Her outstretched hands landed flat on his back before her face smashed against him also.

"Try to keep yours hands to yourself, Mary Poppins," he muttered.

Teddy giggled.

Whose side was the kid on? "A little more warning would be nice."

"Our pathway ended," he explained.

Jane peeked around them and could barely tell they had reached another T-intersection. The man listened intently to their surroundings. At least, that's what she thought he might be doing. She tried to as well… and heard absolutely nothing.

"Do you know where we are?" she whispered.

He ignored her.

Jane's lips flattened. "Do you know where we're going?"

Again, he ignored her.

"Great." She scrubbed her hands over her exhausted eyes. They were lost in a dungeon-like tomb of a half-collapsed building, and their saving grace didn't know which way would lead them to safety. She decided they should go left.

"Let's go." He turned right.

She hesitated. "Are you sure?"

"*This way.* Now." He motioned to her forcefully with his gloved hand. "Keep up."

After a few more turns, they came to a place where one of the walls had partially collapsed. The man set Teddy down and crouched. "We might need to crawl through there."

"Um…" She wasn't sure if his armored body could slip through the broken wall. "I don't know if we can fit."

Teddy scampered forward. "I can!"

"Teddy!" Jane dropped to her knees. "Wait!"

"Hold on, kid." The man produced a flashlight.

"It's easy," Teddy called from on the other side of the stone wall.

"*Teddy!* Hang on." Jane wriggled through the opening to follow after the little boy. Debris shifted under her hands and knees, and she maneuvered around concrete chunks connected to thick metal rods. Behind her, she heard the man close on her heels. "Are you okay?"

"Yeah. Why?"

She shrugged, crawling forward. "I didn't think you'd fit."

He laughed. "Heard that before."

Had he just made a sex joke? Jane's jaw dropped. "Crass."

"What?" he deadpanned. "I—"

Another explosion ripped through the building, knocking her off balance. Dust fell. Rocks tumbled. "Teddy!"

"Damn it." The man pushed ahead of her.

Jane tried not to choke on the flurry of floating dust. The man cursed again, and she blinked in the darkness to clear her view. Wait, no. Dust hadn't clouded her eyesight. A new section of the wall had shifted, creating a barrier between her and Teddy.

Jane rushed forward. The worst possibilities came to mind as fear burned her eyes and throat. Was he trapped? Crushed? "Oh my God!"

"Don't move" the man ordered.

"Oh, screw off." She strained to see through the rubble. "Teddy! Can you hear me?"

A faraway and faint voice hit her ears. "Janie! Help me!"

Breathing a sigh of relief, she grabbed a handful of small rocks. "I will, honey! I'm coming."

Then, the little boy let out an anguished sob that tore Jane in half. Aching to wrap her arms around him, she started to dig harder, oblivious to skinned knuckles and the grit burrowing under her fingernails.

"Stop." The man tugged her shoulder back.

Jane slapped his hands away. "Why would I stop?"

"You need—"

"I need to get to him," Jane cried. "He's trapped, and I'm Mary freakin' Poppins! So why don't you help instead of slowing me down." She whirled back to the downed wall.

He yanked her away. "You keep digging, the whole wall'll fall on you."

Jane stopped and understood he might be right. But she couldn't do nothing. Desperation made her dizzy. "Then what do we do?"

His answer didn't come. She tried to stare him down, which was impossible. The darkness, his height, and the impenetrable dark goggles were a combination that even her best glare couldn't fight past.

"This way." He motioned her to turn around. "We back out and go around."

"What? Leave him?" She shook her head. "No way. I…" She didn't want to leave Teddy all alone. "I can't."

"Look at me," he said quietly.

Her chin snapped up. "I can't even see you."

The man laid his hands on her shoulders. "Then you'll just have to trust me."

CHAPTER NINE

"Janie!" Teddy cried. "Don't leave me!"

Jane had no choice. She stared up at the faceless man. How could she trust him when she couldn't see him? Jane had no better options, but she was still frozen with fear.

"Listen to me." His low voice rumbled, pouring over her in the dark. "If something feels off, it is. Do you read me?"

Her lips parted.

"So you either follow me, or you don't. That's your decision to make. Trust your gut, Mary Poppins."

Jane jerked from the man, wanting to push him and his ridiculous nickname away. But he was right, and her gut instinct told her to get out of her own way. Jane placed her hand on the rubble. "Teddy, I'm coming back." His sniffles and tears shattered her soul. "I promise."

The man took her hand in his, and Jane gripped it with every ounce of strength she had. He pulled her from the pile of rocks and rubble. She couldn't stop her tears. What if that was the last time she ever saw him? What could she have done differently to prevent this? They never should have gone on this trip!

Teddy was her charge. It was all her fault.

But beating herself up wouldn't save Teddy's life. She steeled herself and pressed on. At another intersection, her leader went right. She would've gone left. "Wait. What about—"

He held up a hand, silencing her.

She hesitated. "Are you sure we can get to him this way?"

He gave her a gruff nod. "It's better than the other way."

Something in his voice gave her pause. It wasn't that same confident voice that told her to listen to her gut. Jane's feet turned to stone. "I think we should go the other way."

He silently studied her.

Jane stepped toward the left. "I'll go this way. You go that way, and we'll meet up."

"If we split up, you're gonna get the three of us killed, and that's not in my plans today." He regarded her through the black lenses of the goggles. She couldn't see his eyes, but she figured they were full of *Fuck you, lady.*

"Teddy's my responsibility," she continued. "We're out here because I didn't say something when I should have. *Now I am.*"

He let out a muffled curse under his breath and conceded. "We'll go your way." He wheeled around and took the passage she'd wanted.

"Thank you." He didn't seem to hear her, and she guessed it didn't matter, anyway. Their odds were the same, either path they took. Pretty fucking dismal.

He spoke as though in a quiet conversation with someone else. Jane realized he was in communication with others. A team? The military? Someone with the know-how and weapons-power to bring them home safely?

"Who are you talking to?" Jane asked.

Once again, he ignored her, and the seconds ticked by as though they were centuries passing. Then, out of nowhere, he laughed and then grumbled, "If you call me Midas before I get on that chopper again, bro, you're never gonna hear the end of it."

Midas. Wasn't Midas the king with the golden touch? She wondered if that meant he did everything right… and she'd gone and forced him to do something different.

"Hey." She elbowed him. "Would you mind saving the small talk with your buddies for when you get us out of hell?"

He ignored her. Big surprise.

She tried to step in front of him. "Who are you talking to?"

Midas sidestepped her to the lead again.

Enough with this bullshit. Jane grabbed his arm, trying but failing spectacularly to make him stop. The guy kept trucking.

"Hey, *Midas.*"

That did the trick, and he turned abruptly. "What?"

Exasperated, she tried to keep her attitude on an even keel. "Who are you talking to?"

"My team."

That wasn't so hard. "And what did they say?"

For the billionth time, he didn't answer. This time, though, she didn't grow more irate. A heavy sense of dread swirled in her stomach, and suddenly, Jane didn't want to know any more.

"They said to get a move on, or we're all dead."

CHAPTER TEN

NOW THAT CHANCE had the nanny's complete silence and attention, he hustled them through the winding turns until he found another crater where a wall had once been. "This will take us to Teddy."

She didn't second guess, following obediently. For one absurd moment, he wished she'd run her mouth and question him. It made him double-check his thoughts instead of fly by instinct. Then again, he didn't need to double-check a damn thing. His intuition was the best barometer he had.

Chance eased through a space that became more confined by the inch until he needed to crawl on his knees.

Behind him, the nanny kept up and stayed quiet. He thought about baiting a conversation by sharing his thoughts on Dax Thane. Then again, he needed to concentrate, not fight about the travel habits of the billionaire's family and staff.

For the fifth time in as many minutes, his comm piece crackled in his ear. "Move it, Midas."

"Haven't found the kid yet," he huffed out, on his elbows.

They ignored that, and Boss Man barked, "Hurry the fuck up."

Great. Nothing better for his concentration than a pissed off Jared Westin. Chance blocked HQ from his mind and got to his feet when the height of the space allowed him to do so. Chance turned to check on the nanny and found her on his six. "You holding up okay?"

She dusted herself off. "I'll be fine when we get Teddy."

His night-vision goggles showed a trickle of blood smeared across her forehead. "You're bleeding."

"I don't care." She shoved him out of the way. "Let's go, Hercules.

Lead the way."

He took a quick few steps and glared at her. *Hercules?* "Stay behind me."

"Or what?" She forged ahead.

"Someone might shoot that pretty face of yours off if you're not looking."

Irritation colored her features, and her lips pursed, but she stopped and let him go by—not before giving him a two-handed shove. "Then keep going."

He smiled at the move but grabbed her wrists and squeezed for a long moment before he released them by her sides. He lingered closer than he needed to, for longer than he needed to, making sure his message rang through loud and clear. He was in charge. He'd given her some slack, appeased the attitude—he even enjoyed their back and forth—but if she tested him again, the consequences would be a fuck-ton stronger.

Mary Poppins didn't shy away. Of course not.

Chance was about to say something when HQ announced a count-down in his earpiece. Three minutes until their evac air crew would arrive. Shit, he hadn't secured the kid. "Let's go."

This time, she stayed on his six. They moved fast, until finally Chance peered around the corner. They'd found the kid. He hadn't realized he was holding his breath.

Teddy's high-pitched sob pierced the air, and Chance stepped aside for the nanny to rush by.

She scooped him into her arms. "Teddy, are you okay?"

The little boy's head bobbed.

Another wave of relief rolled through Chance. He took a deep breath and updated HQ. "Got the kid. Heading to extraction point now."

"You've got a minute, fifty-eight, fifty-seven..." HQ urged. "Hustle."

No shit. He motioned to the nanny and child to follow him, which for the first time since he'd met her, she did without uttering a complaint, suggestion, or question. *Small favors.*

They retraced their steps, and he paused for a half-second to let them catch their breath. She kissed the boy's forehead as she repositioned his body against hers.

Chance studied their interaction for longer than he meant to. Maybe she wasn't only duty-bound or asininely stubborn after all. Maybe she really cared about this kid. He had to give her that. "Let's roll."

They climbed through a labyrinth of decaying stone and twisted metal until they finally exited onto a dark street. "The extraction point is on the other side of that." He motioned a few hundred yards away to the skeletal remains of a two-story building. It was an unsteady, mostly demolished structure, much like every other one on the surrounding dark streets. "We've got less than two minutes to get around it."

She stopped and slid the boy to the ground. Doubled over, hands on knees, she drew in breath after breath. "How? You're not Superman."

"Maybe not." His eyes scanned upward. "But you did mention something about Hercules."

She gave him a doubtful look. "Ha, ha."

He didn't hear the helicopter's blades beating through the air, but that didn't mean it wasn't waiting for them. "Either way, we gotta roll."

She snorted. "I wish this whole thing was a joke."

"Yeah, well, tough cookies, Mary Poppins. It's not." Chance took off and kept them close to his side.

"But, knowing my boss, it just might be."

HQ barked the countdown in his ear, along with a harsh reminder they needed to get a move on. Chance lifted Teddy into his arms and positioned him over his shoulder like a sack of potatoes.

The kid squealed. "Hi, Janie."

Chance clapped a hand onto his back to keep the wriggling four-year-old in place and out of the way of his weapon. He jogged toward the extraction zone, occasionally eyeing Mary Poppins. She kept pace, but he slowed. Chance wanted to take a corner carefully and make sure she didn't run herself into the ground before the helo arrived.

He waved her against the wall, sliding a small mirror from his pocket and checking around the bend. "All clear."

"Just like in the movies," she said.

"What?"

She motioned to the mirror.

Chance shoved it into his pocket and eased them around the corner. "That's a Boy Scout trick."

"I wish this was fake. All of it."

He choked on his laugh. "Wishful thinking."

She barely shook her head. "I wouldn't put it past him to pull this shit in the name of going viral."

He glanced over his shoulder. "Who?"

"Dax."

His lips curled in disgust. "Are you kidding me?"

"No. This trip's like a sex tape for an adrenaline junkie." She rubbed her hands over her face. "Never mind. I shouldn't have said anything."

Chance didn't understand her point, but it didn't matter. He had no time to think. The countdown from HQ and the hint of movement in the far-off darkness forced Chance to forget about anyone's family drama.

They needed to get to the evacuation zone pronto. The only way to meet the chopper in time was to go through the building instead of around. "In here."

They rushed toward a stairwell that had seen better days. The busted concrete and rusted rebar were like an altar to tetanus.

"Watch yourself." He picked a path and gestured for them to follow. "We have to go up there."

She looked up, then her face fell. "You're kidding, right?"

"Not today. You can do it." Chance lifted Teddy to the top of a broken wall and turned for the nanny.

"I'm okay." She shooed his hand away. "I've got it. Just stick with Teddy."

He studied her for a split second, deciding she could manage to hoist herself up, then he turned for the boy. The nanny came up behind Chance and said exactly what he was thinking: "This is impossible."

She was right. Half the floor didn't exist anymore. The walls were rubble piles mixed with tangled, rusted rebar. Chance pinged HQ. "We don't have a path to the top of Alpha location. Expect us directly below, on the outside ledge."

"Roger that," HQ acknowledged. "They're coming in hot. Be ready."

A bullet buried itself in the wall above Chance, raining stone on him. "Hell, we are too." He reached for the woman and flung her ahead of him, and reported to HQ, "Taking fire again."

"Son of a bitch," Jared snapped. "I've never seen assholes so intent to fight a losing goddamn battle."

"Go, go!" Chance waved them ahead and then returned fire. He couldn't see where the shots had come from, but by God, he hoped he got lucky with a bull's eye.

"Fifteen seconds," buzzed in his earpiece.

Bullets whizzed again. They seemed to come from every direction. Chance didn't have time to take cover. He struggled to maintain a foothold on the uneven pile of broken concrete underneath him. "Fuck you."

The gunfire paused, and he ran like hell toward the boy and the woman, not giving them a moment's notice as he scooped their cowering bodies into his arms and hauled ass across the buckling concrete.

"*Ten.*"

Chance hurdled them toward a gaping hole in the exterior wall. The ledge, broken and damaged from years of war, came into view. Relief flooded his heart. "We're here!"

"Roger that, Midas."

Chance placed the boy down first. Mary Poppins wriggled from his other arm as an explosion shook the skeletal building. He covered their bodies until the repercussion faded, then urged them forward. "Go. Get onto the ledge."

She didn't move, wrapped around the little boy like the reverb-shaken building had been the final straw before her shock set in.

"Come on, Mary Poppins. You've got this."

"Why couldn't this be fake?" she whispered.

"I have news for you. None of this is fake." Time wasn't on their side. He held on to the remaining shred of his patience. "We need to move."

"Incoming," HQ announced in his earpiece.

"It doesn't look safe."

"It's not." Nothing in this place was safe. "But it's better than staying here." Chance stepped onto the ledge. "We've gotta go."

"Promise me it will be okay?" she asked.

Hell, he couldn't do that, and he couldn't lie to her either. For that moment, time suspended as he struggled to find a response. He looked at her. *Really* looked at her. She was a civilian. Scared... and beautiful. Vulnerability shone in her eyes, and while he always did his best, he wanted to do better than that. So long as he could ease her nightmare. "I promise I'll do whatever it takes to keep you both safe."

Chance stepped through the broken wall onto the shoddy ledge. He reached for the boy. After a closed-eye squeeze, she urged Teddy to Chance. He hoisted the boy outside and onto the ledge.

Once Teddy pressed against the wall, Chance noticed how much smaller the space was then he'd envisioned. "Stay there, kid. Don't move a muscle."

"Teddy, be careful," she shouted.

"He's not the one I'm worried about." Chance held out his hand. "Come here."

Mary Poppins stepped closer. Her fingers rested on broken concrete, and she ducked under the metal rebar, onto the ledge. "Oh, God! There's not enough room out here for all of us!"

"There is. Hold on to the boy's hand and follow me." Chance led the way across the rickety ledge. Every step seemed to shake the concrete strip that led them to the far side of the building. "We have to reach the corner. Then it's a piece of cake."

"What if we can't?" she called.

Chance wasn't about to explain that the chopper couldn't get as low and close as they needed. "Positive thoughts, MP."

"Don't be cute!" she yelled, then followed behind.

The ledge tilted as they shuffled forward. Chance cursed and backed them against the building. "I promise, I won't let anything happen to you. But we have to keep going. Okay?"

She didn't answer.

"Or,"—he shook her shoulder, hoping to break her trance—"we can stay and test out the theory this is all pretend?"

CHAPTER ELEVEN

J ANE'S CHIN JUTTED up. Of course this wasn't fake! If she hadn't been scared that drawing a deep enough breath to yell at the man might catapult them over the edge, she would have torn him to pieces. But, she didn't think the ledge could handle that much movement. "I know it's not!" The fairytale part of Jane's brain wanted to assure her that nothing bad could happen. The rest of her brain screamed with common sense. "Teddy, take the man's hand. Let's go."

Teddy obeyed, and she watched the juxtaposition between the armored man and her sweet little boy. The man looked back, catching her eye, and she dropped her chin, flushing—and then stumbled. Her gaze slipped down the long drop. "I thought you said this was the second floor."

"Don't look down," he ordered.

That wasn't an answer, and she looked again anyway. Her stomach tumbled. They were very high. The ground looked very rocky. Falling to her death in this spot would be particularly painful. "We're definitely not on the second floor," she muttered again, inching forward.

"It's called a slope." The man crept forward with Teddy in hand. "Stop looking down. We have to move faster."

Teddy ran ahead.

"Not that fast, kid." The man bolted after him, gripping his shoulder in half a stride.

Chunks of concrete crumbled in front of her. Jane watched the chunks fall and crash down the rocky slope below. She couldn't move.

"Grab my hand, Janie," Teddy called.

Her heart ached. He was so young, so brave. She couldn't show him her fear. "Okay." Gingerly, she stepped closer to him and took his little hand in hers. "Thanks."

Unencumbered by Teddy, the man continued on. Teddy followed, and she tried to take careful steps. Too bad the sound of falling gravel seemed louder than the gunfire ever had.

A huge chunk of the pathway fell off the ledge. She faltered. "I should go back and find another way to the ledge."

The helicopter arrived with a pulsating *womp, womp, womp* and hovered a dozen yards away, near the corner. Ropes hung down. Men dressed like the military seemed almost close enough to touch but still miles away.

"Don't," he barked. "Do *not* go back in there."

"The ledge isn't safe!" she shouted, then looked ahead and pointed to a large gash in the stonework ahead of them. The entire ledge might fall at any moment. There were cracks and missing chunks along the short path. The ledge was covered by evidence of war and explosions, with black spots scarred on the light stone and pocked concrete.

A portion of the edge gave way and crumbled, proving her point.

He beckoned them to keep up. "You won't fall. Keep moving."

Jane gulped and searched for the safest path on the narrow space. "Teddy, keep close to the wall."

"Okay." He put his back against the building and sidestepped toward their rescuer.

Her heart hammered as she followed. The deteriorating pathway lost another chunk. Teddy jumped over it before she could cry out.

A sickening crack sounded ahead of Teddy. She rushed forward and grabbed him as a large piece of the path fell away.

"Damn it." The man carefully eased back toward them. "Give me the boy's hand."

She looked down.

"Don't do that," he ordered. "You have to trust me."

Jane had no choice, even as Teddy cried and clung to her. "Give him your hand."

The transfer seemed effortless. Before she knew it, Teddy was safely tucked behind the man.

"Now you." He held his hand out. "Give me your hand."

She inched closer. Rocks fell away under her feet. She stumbled back as the man turned Teddy away. For a terrifyingly grateful moment, she appreciated that the little boy wouldn't watch her plummet to her death.

More stone cracked between them. Paralysis froze her muscles. He reached for her again, offering her a lifeline across the chasm. "Grab my hand."

"I can't reach you." Her fingers dug into the concrete wall. "I can't—"

"Yes, you can." Rocks crumbed underneath his boot. "Shit." He backed Teddy farther away and then pulled his face mask off. "*Jane.* Look at me."

He knew her name? She met his gaze. His fiery eyes were unlike anything she'd ever seen. She could see determination and loyalty mixed with dark blue and flecks of gold. He wasn't a man who failed. She could see him in a way that she didn't understand, as though she could see his soul, and understood he simply refused to back down from death.

"You have to trust me," he whispered.

Her bottom lip quaked. In that moment, she couldn't imagine trusting anyone more than this man. His life was in danger to save hers and Teddy's.

"Remember, my team calls me Midas," he said. Rocks fell from under the toe of his boot, and he reluctantly shifted his weight back. "Everything I touch turns to gold. I won't let anything happen to you."

Midas. Didn't he know that the story of King Midas was a tragedy? The gold blessing was nothing more than a vain curse. Disaster loomed, she was sure of it. "You won't let anything happen to Teddy."

He jaw tightened. "I won't let anything happen to *either* of you."

The ground weakened beneath her shoes as well. Jane inched back and studied the rapidly expanding gap that separated her from Midas. Even if the ground didn't soon give out under her weight, she couldn't reach him. "Come back and get me."

"No, ma'am." He pulled his earpiece out and reached for here again, dangerously toeing the edge. "Eyes on me. Listen to me."

Jane's heart had never beaten so fast. She committed his brave face to her memory, then took a step back. A chunk of concrete fell from where she'd just stood. "You can't save both of us." He'd kill them all trying and die in vain just like Midas, the king with the golden touch.

His hard jaw set as though he refused to accept their fate. "*Jane.* Give me your goddamn hand."

A sense of peace wrapped over her shoulders. A warrior like that man would keep Teddy safe.

Gunfire rang out again, but this time, it wasn't aimed at her. She jerked toward the helicopter. Midas's team was returning fire. The rapid-fire cracks mixed with the splintering sound of their ledge loosening. She jumped back and reached for the broken wall. Her fingers couldn't find a hold. Jane scrambled back, knowing they'd run out of time, and looked at Midas one last time.

His lips were pinched. A hard fury flexed in his jaw, and he didn't look away. His boring gaze drilled Jane with exasperation. "I'm coming back for you."

Then he spun to Teddy, wrapped the boy protectively between him and the wall, and sprinted across the disintegrating ledge. A rope waited, and he secured them as Teddy wailed her name.

A second later, the helicopter disappeared. Jane rushed onto safer ground, pressed her hands to her heart, and fought for a deep breath. If nothing else, at least Teddy would be safe.

CHAPTER TWELVE

CROUCHING INSIDE THE burned-out building, Jane listened to silence. The surrounding quiet overwhelmed her. She couldn't hear the helicopter or gunfire. All was eerily still.

Jane pinched her eyes closed and ducked her chin to her knees. She couldn't shake the incensed expression on Midas's face. But there was something else profoundly reassuring about his overbearing presence. He would see the job was done correctly. That meant someone, somehow, would come back for her. But, more importantly, Teddy was safe. And that was all that mattered.

Distant gunfire tore peppered the silence. She backed into a corner and said a quick prayer. For what, she didn't know. Another helicopter? Guidance on what to do next? No miracles fell from the sky, and she decided she needed to form a plan. Her concentration came in fits. Adrenaline made her hands shake. Her legs cramped, and she desperately needed to sleep.

"Think," she whispered.

The only thing that came to mind was retelling this story at one of the Thanes' excessive events. She always needed fodder for cocktail parties. The idea made her laugh. A trickle of humor mixed with sheer, utter exhaustion.

Jane stretched her legs and sat down, deciding to stay put and watch for another helicopter. That seemed as good of a plan as any. After a few minutes of waiting, she wondered if it would return for her in the morning. Daylight always made problems seem more manageable.

Could she sleep here? She didn't know if it was safe—all things considered. Jane peeled herself from her hiding spot and tip-toed to a gaping hole that could've once been a window.

The dark velvet night sky enveloped the world in a coldness that went beyond the temperature. She scanned the remains of a war-torn city. The moonlight created ghostly shadows. Was this what Dax had wanted to catch on film? Absolute devastation? Some buildings barely remained, while others seemed impossibly untouched.

Voices echoed from below her. She pushed away from the wall and raced to find a better hiding spot. Jane crouched and searched for the voices. She saw no one. But now, the voices sounded like they were coming from above. "What the hell." That was one of the many problems with partially destroyed buildings. Noises bounced and echoed in ways that she couldn't wrap her mind around.

Another voice and footsteps broke the quiet. This time, Jane was certain the proximity was much, *much* closer. She rushed down the semi-demolished hall. The scenery blurred together. She tried to reorient herself and turned in time to see three men hurrying in the direction she'd just come from.

The hell with thoughtfully planning her escape. Jane needed to haul ass from here if she wanted to survive.

CHANCE DID HIS best to stymie a torrent of curses in front of Teddy Thane. *But fucking hell. How did I not see that coming?* The woman was a nanny with a superhero complex. He should've expected a stunt like that from someone who worked for the Thanes.

Except it hadn't been a stunt. If she hadn't jumped back, she'd be dead. If she hadn't demanded they leave, the helo wouldn't have been able to stay. The kid would be dead. Hell, they would all be dead.

Begrudgingly, Chance acknowledged she might've made the right move. But he sure as shit wasn't accepting it. *He* was the one who was supposed to risk his life for civilians. Mary Poppins wasn't going to die on his watch. Protecting her was his job, and he'd failed.

Chance took out his garbling earpiece and pulled on a headset. "HQ? You read me?"

"Loud and clear, Midas," Parker returned.

He rubbed a hand over his face. "Drop me back."

Next to Chance, Hagan's chin snapped up. "Are you suicidal tonight, man?"

"No." He gnashed his molars, waiting for HQ to give him the go-ahead. He didn't hear a word, and unlike his earpiece, the transmissions were clear. Chance readjusted his mouthpiece. "Drop. Me. Back."

"Negative, Midas," Parker replied. "The current circumstances aren't working for—"

"Give me a break. She's a civilian, and we're not leaving an unarmed woman to fend for herself."

"No, we aren't," Parker said. "She'll hang tight and we'll send in another team."

"No." Chance's hands balled into fists. "I know the area."

Hagan put a hand on his shoulder. "They know what they're doing."

Chance shrugged Hagan off. "There's not a single reason to wait. Drop me back in."

"Negative," Parker repeated. "We can't let you risk—"

"Damn it, Parker. If you don't, she's as good as—" Chance choked off *dead* when he caught sight of Teddy's tear-swollen eyes locked on him. He cleared his throat and dropped his voice. "I need to do this."

No one spoke. Teddy didn't look away. Chance felt like he might explode.

"Midas." Boss Man broke the silence. "If you go after her now, I don't know when we can get back to you."

"That's fine." Chance could keep them safe until the team returned. "I told her to trust me. I said I'd be back." He glanced out a window. Miles and time were speeding by. "I have to keep my word."

Eternity passed.

"It's your call, Midas." Boss Man let out a long breath. "The odds aren't good now or later."

"So we go now," Chance requested.

The transmission went silent.

Chance waited, adrenaline flowing, hoping that headquarters was communicating directly with the pilot.

Suddenly, their helicopter angled and circled round. Determination flooded his chest as he braced for the chopper's hard turnabout. "Thank you."

"Roger that," Boss Man said. "We'll stay in contact, best we can. Until then, do what it takes to come back alive."

CHAPTER THIRTEEN

J ANE RAN FROM the building, threading in and out of alleys until she saw a burned-out truck that looked familiar. *Think, think.* Where had she seen that before? Was that one different from any of the other burned-out and stripped trucks? Her brain was too tired to connect the dots.

Maybe... maybe she'd seen it on the way from the airstrip. If so, hurray! She'd been going in the right direction. Dax had pointed toward the distance at a number of white tents. They were scattered as far as they could see. He'd said the tents were part of a refugee camp.

And, hadn't Dax said something about peacekeepers? She'd tuned out his attention-seeking conversations for so long, she hadn't realized this time it would be important. *Think...* He'd said that they'd arrived at the same airport that UN and NATO peacekeepers had used. Hope squeezed her heart. Maybe there were friendly people at the refugee camp. She could find the peacekeepers and explain that she was American. They would help her. Or, if they didn't, she could drop Dax Thane's name, and maybe that would help her.

Or, not. The Thane name could cause the whole disaster to start over again. She could be captured and put up for ransom again. There had to be good people there. Weren't there always good people everywhere? Folks who didn't want to barter, trade, or kill her? Was that too much to ask? The refugee camp was the safest bet... probably. *Do you have any better options?*

Jane turned toward the building she'd been in, waiting one last minute for Midas to swoop in again.

Then she waited another, more anxious minutes as a small-and-scary, but oddly contained fire blazed on one of the upper floors. No Midas with his night-vision goggles. No stealth helicopter with dangling save-the-day ropes. The refugee camp still seemed like the better option.

Something small and furry skittered over her feet, and she jumped. *Yes, a much better option.*

Jane trekked from the building, and the image of her hometown popped to mind. In all of her days growing up in Pensacola, she'd never once thought life would lead her to the opposite side of the world. What happened if she died here? Had she made any important contributions to society? Would she leave behind anyone heartbroken and missing her? Not really. Suddenly, the piles of money the Thanes had thrown at her in paychecks sounded like a pittance. The only good thing about that job still was Teddy.

Jane headed in the direction of the refugee camp. Her travels took far longer than she'd estimated. Her feet hurt. Blisters rubbed her heels, and her tongue felt thick and dry in her mouth. Even with her slow pace, her muscles strained. But, finally, Jane reached the outskirts of this makeshift, ruined city.

The open space between her and the camp seemed like no man's land. Animals made unrecognizable noises. The darkness became impossibly darker, and the ground far harder to navigate. In some sections, she crawled on her hands and knees.

Jane couldn't guestimate how long it took to close in on the camp. The only sense of time she had was how the cover of night remained overhead. But she'd made it, and Jane collapsed in the shadows to catch her breath and work on a plan.

Purple light warmed the dark sky, promising dawn would soon come. But even with the slowly brightening sky, she realized that the refugee camp wasn't what she'd expected. It looked far less inviting with its seemingly unending chain-link fence topped by barbed wire. The barricade separated her from rows of pale tents.

The tents were stacked on top of each other. They sprawled for as far as she could see.

Cautiously, Jane approached the towering fence. For as large as the camp seemed, it was painfully silent. She didn't see any signs of life.

"Hello?"

No one answered. Was it possible that every occupant was asleep?

Or, maybe the entire facility wasn't in use. After all, her information had come from Dax Thane. Not the most reliable source.

She called again, "Hello?"

Nothing.

Jane slowly walked along the fence, but, despite her watchful gaze and careful pace, her breaths tightened. A mixture of wild anxiety and sleep deprivation pummeled her with doubt. How safe was a refugee camp? Why didn't she listen to the news or prepare for this trip more than she had?

Her fingertips ran along the rough, rusted fence, hoping to see a gate or friendly face.

Finally, she found an opening in the fence that was large enough for her to crawl through. Would the camp be safe? Would Midas and his helicopter look for her there?

She glanced over her shoulder and searched the sky for a helicopter. Nothing caught her attention, and Jane dropped to the hole in the fence. If another plan was to come to mind, now would be a good time…

No other plans surfaced. She had to find someone in camp who would help her. How hard would helpers be to find? Jane pushed herself through the rusted fence and rolled to the other side. Her uncertainty grew as she sat up, somewhat surprised that she didn't miraculously feel safer inside the camp.

What next? She searched both directions, finding nothing new, and pushed herself off the ground. It was time to explore.

The tents were as long as tanker trucks, but not nearly as high. She found that they were made of a canvas material and lined up in rows many tents deep. After she passed the front of several tents, deciding that the overlapped fabric served as doors, she picked one and carefully inched apart the heavier-than-expected fabric.

Her nose twitched at the stale air. Rows of people slept, huddled on the floor or packed onto cots. She couldn't imagine this many people living in this tight of a space.

A baby cried deep within the tent, and Jane scrambled backward, suddenly terrified to be caught. Her plan hinged on *helpers*. How could she ask anyone for help when they didn't have enough space to simply sleep?

She hurried away and wound through the unending rows of tents, now knowing of families piled on top of one another, sleeping in inhumane conditions.

Suddenly, Jane stopped. Which direction had she come from? She turned then spun on her heel again. *I'm lost.*

You've been lost for a while, she reminded herself. But now, she didn't know which direction to go in.

The faint sound of footsteps crunching on rocky sand broke through her momentary paralysis, and as they came closer, her fear escalated. She bolted the opposite way. So much for her grand plan to find the helpers. She should've waited on the outside of the fence until she found a gate. Why had she snuck inside?

She stopped again. Not because she wanted to. But her head was swimming. Jane ducked behind the far side of a tent and bowled over. Her hands rested on her knees, and she panted to catch her breath.

An uncertain voice startled Jane. She jerked toward the voice. The quick move made black spots skew her vision, and she stumbled to the ground. Jane lurched back and saw a man towering over her. He barked angrily. She didn't understand and couldn't find the words to explain who she was and the help she needed.

She choked over the dirt in her mouth, but finally managed, "I need help."

He motioned for her to stand, beckoning and calling over his shoulder. Time barely moved. She swayed on her feet, blinking sand from her eye as another man approached. This guy carried an assault rifle—he pointed it at her.

"Help." Her voice cracked, and she raised her hands. "I'm an American, and I need help."

Understanding crossed their faces. Grins tugged at their weathered faces, and in an instant, Jane knew that had been the wrong thing to say.

CHAPTER FOURTEEN

HER PLEAS FOR help remained unanswered, and their faces turned predatory. If they understood Jane, they didn't seem to care. Another man joined them. He was also armed. Were they guards? Where were the peacekeepers she'd heard about? Hell, what *were* peacekeepers?

With short commands and gestures, they made their orders clear. She needed to turn and walk down the aisle between the tents. Jane staggered forward.

After another minute of walking down an endless lane of identical tents, they stopped. She sensed they were toward the center of the camp. After a moment of heated discussion, the man without a weapon pulled the flap of a tent open. The other man nudged her inside with the barrel of his gun. Bile tickled the back of her throat. She tried one more time—"I need help"—before stumbling inside.

Her eyes had to adjust to the darkness—and then the bright flame when the first man struck a match. It flickered in front of his face. Jane realized that peace was the farthest thing from his mind.

The flame settled on the end of the match, and he lit a lantern. An eerie orange glow danced on the canvas walls. This tent was far smaller than the others she'd peeked at. It was more like a portioned room that held a handful of cots, a makeshift desk, and trunks. She guessed it was some kind of officers' quarters.

What would they do with her? Both men studied her, doing nothing to ease her panic. They exchanged a clipped conversation, then, unexpectedly, left.

She sank onto the packed dirt floor. Sand and grime coated the room. Jane waited. Time ticked. An eternity passed. Her eyes fought to close.

Every part of her begged for sleep...

The tent opened, and she jerked awake. The same men returned, and as they entered the tent, she saw the sky had changed to a morning light with teases of grays and oranges. Dawn! Sunrise! The new day arrived.

Beyond this tent, Jane heard the camp coming to life. That had to be good news!

The tent flaps parted, and a new man walked inside and greeted the others.

The first man who found Jane yanked her onto her feet.

Dizzy, she wobbled and groaned. When her head stopped spinning, she realized that the new man was speaking to the others. Unhappiness coated his words.

As fast as she was jerked to her feet, she was dropped unceremoniously. The man who'd held her rushed from the camp.

No one said another word until the man returned, seemingly apologetic to their newcomer. He held up a canteen and torn flat bread.

Jane didn't recall him offering them to her. She almost felt as though she stood next to her body, watching as she shoved the bread into her dry mouth and choked over the gritty water.

Before she could appreciate the quench of her thirst, the newcomer reached for her. He gripped her jaw with one large hand and pinched until her jaw hinged.

She cried out, gagging as his other hand hooked inside her mouth and yanked her head back, stretching her lips apart. Jane fought the hold but was too weak. The man peered inside her mouth and then pushed his fingers under her lips, as though he wanted to see her teeth and probe her gums.

As if he was pleased to find she had teeth and a tongue, the man released her face and ran his fingers through her hair, tracing a pattern over her skull.

"Stop." She leaned from his inspection, but he easily shifted her to the side. "What are you doing? Stop."

He ran his across her shoulders and arms as an EMT might do while searching for an injury. He did the same to her legs. At her blistered feet, a long conversation ensued. She tried to jerk from their hold, but they held her ankles, still deeply engrossed over her raw, wounded feet.

Then they let go. Jane sprawled on her back, staring at the top of the tent. They'd avoided her breasts, between her legs, and her backside, but they'd still managed to make her feel like an animal, rather than a person.

They conversed as though she weren't there. Did they think she was a spy? Transporting contraband?

The conversation paused, and the men turned toward her. One shook his head. Another pursed his lips, and the others remained still.

The newcomer offered a single word. Again, the first man shook his head.

The newcomer pursed his lips and spoke quickly. Like before, the first man shook his head. But this time, he reached for Jane and grabbed her arm. She felt like Gumby, putty in his hands, and didn't pull away when he positioned her fist above her elbow and then, with his other hand, squeezed her bicep.

Each man studied her bicep. Her mouth soured. Dread rolled through Jane like a runaway locomotive. They were negotiating over *her* as though she were livestock.

Her knees shook, and her stomach threatened to regurgitate the dry bread and water. But the faintest surge of adrenaline reminded her she wasn't dead. Her pulse jumped erratically, and even though she was weary enough to faint, she closed her eyes until her mind cleared. Midas was coming for her. Somehow, someway, he'd harness that crazy determination that had been on his face and hunt her down.

Goosebumps spiked at the back of her neck. She opened her eyes. Nothing had changed. The heated negotiations over her sale had their complete attention, but they were blocking the exit to the tent.

Jane gripped the necklace around her neck. No one had thought to remove it, but the little knife wouldn't be of any help now. It did, however, help her focus. She could picture her uncle training her in martial arts. She could see his face and hear her complaints when she was a child. He'd drilled her with repetition over and over again, promising her that her limbs would know what to do when her mind did not.

She rotated her torso, spotted a target, then tornadoed her body with a roundhouse kick. The oil lantern flew across the tent. The fuel spattered over the cot and tent walls. When the glass shattered against the trunk, the flames were instantaneous. Jane sprinted out the tent door as the men flanked the fire with furious shouts.

She'd never been a runner, but her blistered feet covered as much ground as her legs could manage.

It only took a moment before angry cries called out behind her. She cut a corner. The voices followed. Where was she going? Every row looked identical.

Jane turned another corner and ducked into a tent. A group of women gasped and jumping away. She held up her hand, wanting help, needing them to hide her, but she could only gasp for breath.

Outside the tent, a rush of footsteps pounded by. Every woman looking at her knew what the men were after. But they didn't call for help.

"Thank you," Jane managed, and waited for the longest three seconds of her life. She ducked out the tent and ran the opposite direction.

The morning sun allowed her to see small differences in the tents, to better catch the expressions on faces and assess enemies and potential allies. Despite that, she never stopped, still having no idea how to escape.

Her heart slammed against her sternum, and its rapid beat drummed in her ears. She had to stop again or she'd drop dead. Jane slipped into another tent. Miracle of miracles, it was empty.

Jane sagged onto her knees, too tired to continue and too scared to cry. She wiped away the sweat and dirt that coated her face. It wasn't until a figure in a black kaftan robe stood directly in front of her that Jane realized she wasn't alone.

Enemy or ally? Jane slowly tilted her head back and met the dark eyes of a woman. A black veil framed her face, flowing into the layers of black fabric wrapped around her body.

Jane weakly lifted her hands. "Help."

The woman roared and peppered Jane with questions that she couldn't understand. She had no idea how to communicate but put her finger to her lips, begging for silence.

Silence didn't come. The woman's voice grew louder with more authority. Clearly, she wasn't an ally. It was only a matter of time before the men heard her warning cries. At any moment, Jane expected her pursuers to enter the tent. Then the woman stopped. Her dark eyes bulged as though she were waiting for an answer.

Jane's head dropped. "I'm so sorry. I don't understand."

Did she have enough energy to keep running? Jane struggled to tap her reserves that had been depleted again and again.

The woman turned, and Jane tried to stand. Her leg swayed, and she wobbled, but she wouldn't give up. Finally, she managed to stand upright. The woman clamped a callused hand over Jane's shoulder.

Her eyes closed. She was too weak to fight—soft fabric pressed into Jane's hands. Her chin dropped, and she stared at the folded black linens before snapping her gaze to the woman's. Their eyes met. A powerful conversation unrolled between them without a spoken worry. Then, the woman spoke urgently but slowly. Quietly. Jane didn't understand, yet she did.

The woman took the fabric from Jane, unfolding the bundle, and with breathtaking carefulness, wrapped Jane from head to toe in her disguise as she remained immobile—simply, gratefully stunned.

A commotion outside the tent broke her trance. "Thank you."

The woman assessed her with a sharp eye, then walked toward the tent entrance, pulled open the flap, and pointed down the long aisle of tents.

Each step toward the morning sunlight was harder than the one before. She hesitated, not knowing if she could blend in. Her adrenaline had dissipated, and Jane didn't know how she could find the energy to move.

She paused next to the woman and stared into the now-bustling camp.

The woman touched her back and leaned close to Jane's ear. "Go."

A shiver of appreciation rolled through Jane. That single word was enough to power her again. "Thank you." She squeezed the woman's forearm, then stepped into broad daylight.

CHAPTER FIFTEEN

THE FIRST FEW minutes after Chance dropped in, the radio communications that crackled in his ear weren't of the friendliest nature. His team didn't outright call him an idiot, but he knew they weren't certain of his decision. Everyone had heard Parker's grim statistical likelihood of his success versus his death. Chance was pretty sure that wherever Jared was, he was giving him a big double-finger salute and popping antacids.

Hours had passed. The longer Chance went without finding Jane, the heavier his thoughts became. He'd searched several burned-out building without success. Pressure ticked in his chest. The adrenaline-high buzz from his teammates dropped off, and a grim reality set in. She wasn't where he'd expected her to be.

The team's guesses as to where Jane might be weren't alleviating Chance's concern. Their list had been short: She'd been captured, gone into hiding, or taken off. But the variations and unknown factors were sickening.

Finally, as morning light cast a depressing glow over the ruins of what was once a beautiful city, he crouched and checked in with headquarters again, fully expecting HQ to demand his extraction until a better plan was determined.

"Actually," Parker said in a noncommittal tone, "I might have found something worthwhile."

A small flame of hope ignited. "What does that mean?"

Parker hummed. "Truthfully, it's a crapshoot. I can't tell you for certain, but since you're out there, might as well check on it."

The edge of hesitant deliberation in the IT-maven's tone gave Chance warning. "All right. I'm here. I'll check it out."

"I ran a walkable radius of satellite footage against thermal disturbances that mimicked how a person moves."

Definitely a crapshoot. His heart sank. "There could be a hundred people walking the city's perimeter."

"Actually, no."

Chance looked up like the voice in his comm piece was coming from the sky. "Really?"

"There weren't any people traveling alone and on foot. Except for one. That person headed toward the closest refugee camp."

Chance rubbed his temples and groaned.

"Yeah," Parker agree. "Those can be hit and miss and, at best, aren't great situations for a woman traveling alone."

"What do you know about this camp?" Chance asked.

"The basics that have been reported by humanitarian groups. The most recent report shows minor paramilitary group involvement.

Chance pinched the bridge of his nose. "That's good, right?"

"Depends on what we're comparing to." Parker paused as though he was re-reading the report. "Your biggest concern will be the locals' loyalty to a growing criminal regime."

"Awesome," he deadpanned. "Got anything on those guys?"

"You've already been acquainted," Parker said. "That'd be the nutjobs who took the Thanes and sprayed bullets for fun."

"Maybe she was right to get moving." The nutjobs had been fanatical about hunting the Thanes down. "But an unknown camp…"

"Yeah," Parker agreed. "If Jane Singleton was hoping to find a friendly face, she would have done better by jumping into a pit of vipers."

"Jeez, man." Chance grumbled. "Did you run a statistical analysis on that too? Or just trying to lift my spirits?"

Parker snorted.

Chance shook his head. "So, I head west, huh?"

"West. Right dead center of the encampment." Parker continued with details on the last thermal marking picked up, a rundown of threats and possible entry points as Chance worked his way west. Once he was clear of the battered buildings, he could see the faint outline of the refugee camp in the distance. How did Mary Poppins cover that much ground?

He checked his compass, memorized the coordinates where the thermal imaging had lost sight of her, and set off.

The sun beat on the back of his neck as he crossed the deadlands. Heat radiated from the ground. Sparse clumps of grass and brush provided little shade or area to rest. Chance covered the distance as quickly as he could. He couldn't shake the image of Jane's face the very moment they both realized he couldn't save her.

At least, couldn't at that moment—because now, he'd be damned if he didn't bring her home safe and sound this time. But he couldn't fault her anymore for staying behind. The more time he spent reviewing what had happened, the more he saw her bravery for what it was. She didn't know what she was doing, but the nanny had erred on the side of caution to save the boy.

Stupid. But impressive.

That was a combination he didn't like that he liked.

The longer he trekked across the desert, the more badass he thought her actions had been. Not that he condoned the stunts that the Thanes were famous for.

Finally, Chance was close enough to the camp to review his next move. He paused approximately a hundred yards out and assessed the situation. The main gates were nearly two miles from this spot. Would Jane walk the fence perimeter, not knowing where a gate might be? It'd be the most practical option given the circumstances. But this was Mary Poppins, the superhero nanny. Would she jump the fence?

He examined the fence and couldn't think of a way she could manage the barbed wire. Without training, it'd be nearly impossible. He crossed scaling the fence off of his list and walked parallel to the camp, keeping his distance and searching for any factors that would influence her choices.

Engines roared behind Chance. He crouched and watched a pack of motorbikes race across a dirt-packed road that led to the camp gates. Dirt plumed in their wake, casting a dusty cloud as they disappeared from sight.

While he didn't have a good look at group, his senses tingled. The motor bikers could be part of the local crime regime, or worse, related to the group who'd abducted the Thanes. He checked in with HQ again, but got nothing. Their last transmissions had been spotty, and like they had planned, he was on his own.

He edged closer to the fence line and picked up his pace. Despite the sun and limited water and supplies, he jogged until an irregularity in the chain-link fence caught his eye. He squatted and studied the rusted, broken links. The hole in the fence had been repaired more than once, but it was clearly in use again, large enough for a person to crawl through.

Would she have seen this at night? Chance squinted both ways in the distance and then searched for any signs of the refugees. The long, narrow tents on the other side of the fence didn't have openings. From the wind-blown patterns on the ground, it was clear that people didn't congregate behind the tents.

Again, he heard the motorbikes, though this time their engines roared from deep in the camp. A cold chill shivered down his spine. He had no proof that Jane had entered this way, but his intuition said time wasn't on his side. He needed to move in immediately, or this job would change from search-and-rescue to recovery.

Chance pushed through the tight breach in the fence and hustled to the narrow space between the tents. He stood out against the dirty white tents and decided to stick to the outskirts of the camp. The camp layout became apparent, and he threaded himself closer to the sound of activity.

A few women and children saw him. Every time, they ducked their chins and scurried away without so much as a questioning look or the sound of an alarm.

A commotion and revving motorbikes served as his beacon. He crept deeper into the belly of the beast, crossing pathways that reminded him of dirt-road intersections. Diagonal from his position, tent flaps separated. A man with an overstuffed basket pushed into the daylight. Chance froze, unable to hide. Eternity passed as he held his breath. The basket had blocked the man's view.

He ducked between canvas walls again and analyzed the light foot traffic. Several men with large bundles made their way down the path. They gave Chance hope of a nearby marketplace or meeting space. But the rising influx of motorbikes gave him heartburn. The bikes rattled and raced. Every rider wore an assault rifles over their chest. At least that kept things interesting.

He'd seen enough and moved out. He stayed off the pathways, skirting the spaces between tents, until he reached a cross-section that forced him from the shadows earlier than he'd anticipated.

A bellowing commotion rolled through the dry air. It sounded less like a marketplace and more like an angry pep rally. Motorbikes and irregular pops of skyward-bound gunfire punctuated the tension. He closed his eyes, praying for a sign that this was the right time to make his move.

Chance wiped sweat off his brow and moved out. He jogged several strides and stopped. Across a clearing, an old, beat-to-hell motorbike practically glistened in the sun. So long as he could hot-wire the rust bucket, he'd take this as his sign.

Adrenaline pumped through his veins. Without cover or disguise, he sprinted to the bike and marveled at its simplicity. There wasn't much to hot-wire. Only a simple switch.

"All right, all right." He straddled the narrow seat, positioning his weapons for better access, and wrapped his hand around the rickety handlebars. "Here goes nothing." He pressed the ignition button. An ear-grating whirr whined from the engine. "That's what I'm talking about!"

He scanned the area then pushed off, twisting the throttle. The bike cried as it picked up speed, defying his expectation of what it could handle. He turned from the commotion and sped back the way he'd come, searching for the area where women congregated and crossing his fingers that they'd have what he needed.

And they did. He sped toward a line of linens drying in the arid heat. He tore by and grabbed an armful of linens and clothes, then hightailed to the ignored area by the fence.

Chance had absolutely no idea how to cover himself with the fabric swaths he'd grabbed, but so long as he could configure a semi-decent disguise, he'd be fine. The likelihood of locating Jane had to have immediately increased. At least in his opinion. HQ, with Parker and his number-crunching formulas, might disagree. But for now, Chance couldn't shake his grin.

With newfound confidence, he roared toward the center of the camp, only stopping when he could see the gaggle of men and bikes a hundred feet dead ahead.

He gripped the throttle—but his stomach dropped. The commotion was different. Less like their battle cry and more like… wild excitement. The enemy was *celebrating*.

Was he too late?

CHAPTER SIXTEEN

I N THE SAFETY of her disguise, Jane could finally catch her breath and survey her surroundings. The encampment was abuzz. People moved about the maze of tents. The motorbikes raced by and random, rapid gunfire occasionally cracked through the air. The harsh smell of burning plastic and gunpowder hurt her raw nostrils as she tried to blend in with the crowd, but she felt like everything she did called attention in her direction.

Did her walk stand out? Were her eyes too light? Should she say hello or avoid eye contact? If anyone gave her a second glance, she didn't have the strength to keep up the rouse.

With her head down, Jane picked a path forward, lifting the hem of her skirt from under her feet. The layer of darker clothing provided a disguise, but it also added a hot layer atop her shaky frame.

A vicious round of air horns blasted, and she jerked from the path. A fleet of ancient motorbikes zipped by, spitting chalky dust in her face. She coughed as her eyed filled with tears.

Everywhere, men carrying guns argued. Just when she thought she'd moved away from them, she would see them again. Either she was traveling in circles, or the military element in the camp was everywhere.

Swallowing the grit in her throat, she headed away from the center tents, toward the back fence where she had started this mess. Where was the broken part of the fence where she'd first entered?

Jane scanned the fence line. It seemed to travel for miles. Warily, she took an unsure step closer, considering ways to escape. A wild animal cried out from the other side. She couldn't see it in the rocky, desolate land-scape, but it sounded hungry and large.

Maybe this time, she shouldn't cross the fence line without a plan. Though if she stayed here, nothing good would happen. Would Midas and the helicopter think to search for her at the camp?

Or, maybe they wouldn't come back at all. They'd saved the intended targets—the Thane family. Thane Insurance had likely paid dearly for the rescue. *Their* rescue, not hers. Jane could almost hear Dax and Gigi casually deciding to leave her alone and abandoned in Syria. They'd believe that Jane's death—or rather, losing the nanny—was simply a cost of doing business. The realization was a morbid and terrifying. They saw people as commodities. *Poor Teddy.*

Her vision blurred, a mix of tears and exhaustion, until she shook her head. When she looked up, her saw a man straddling a bike, watching her from several tent lengths away. Jane gulped and decided to move quickly. She gathered her flowing skirts and ran into the camp again.

This time, she had a better idea where to go, and Jane let herself be swept into the crowd. She collided with a man, then tripped on her kaftan. Her body shook from hunger and fatigue, and her stomach revolted against its emptiness.

She squeezed her eyes shut, and when she finally tried to open them again, her eyelids didn't want to obey. Her vision tilted, and her head felt as heavy as a cinderblock. She hadn't slept in so long, hadn't had enough water. Jane staggered forward and saw the man on the bike again. He didn't look angry, only curious. Would he help her like the woman had?

She made her way toward him. Every step took more energy than she had, but she closed the distance and stopped in front of the man. His expression shifted, his lips turning up into a hint of an encouraging smile.

Oh, thank god. She smiled at him and whispered a dry, throaty, "Help me."

He grabbed her arm and raised it in his hands, calling out for others.

"No." She didn't have the strength to fight, and her free hand clutched her heart, certain it would stop beating. It didn't.

The man jerked her like a prize. Jane lost her balance. Her feet went out from under her. They tripped. He took the brunt of her fall. She sprawled over him. He yelled and pushed her away like she was flea-invested and diseased. His angry cries shocked her back to life, and even when she knew she couldn't run any more, she did.

The maze of unending hell turned her every which way. She stopped when she couldn't take another step and found herself cowering between lines of clothes.

Jane crawled into a corner and caught her breath. She must not have gone far. She heard booming voices multiply. From her crouched position in the laundry area, she watched gaggles of men become an army. Were they all searching for her?

Catching a couple more breaths, she took off and nearly ran into a dead end. Shit. She doubled back and took another path. Another dead-end. What was this? A market? She stood in front of a stall that sold old metal pieces. She was thinking of hiding behind their boxes when an old, prune-faced man snapped at her.

The angry search party marched nearby. She was certain their jeers were for her. She ran down a lane that seemed suspiciously empty and wondered what would happen if they found her. Shoot her? Or, did they still want to sell her?

Maybe capture wouldn't be so bad. She could escape again, and they'd give her food and water.

"Stop," she wheezed, realizing that the voice of surrender had gained footing in her thoughts. She refused to be captured again. Jane didn't care if she ran herself to death. She wouldn't stop fighting.

Wavering on her feet, she choked on a sob. Damn it, she was just one woman. What did they think she could possibly be worth? Her feet were bleeding. Her sunburn had turned to blisters. Hell, her will to live had all but left her. She couldn't take this anymore.

The rattling whine of another motorbike forced her to turn. It raced down the long aisle, and she needed to run but her feet wouldn't move. Jane's eyes closed, and she thought of dropping to her knees in surrender— no! She spun, refusing to give up.

Her skirt tangled with her feet, and she tripped, and as she looked up, the aisle filled with the angry mob, flanking the motorbike that was almost upon her. Whatever these assholes wanted, she vowed to give them hell until she took her last breath.

The motorbike screeched sideways. Dirt spit into the air like a landmine had exploded. Sand and grit rained down. Jane wiped at her face and blinked until her vision cleared.

"Mary Poppins." An outstretched hand reached toward the ground. "It's time to move boots, babe. Get on."

CHAPTER SEVENTEEN

G IVEN HOW MUCH Jane had questioned him before, Chance was surprised by the nanny's willingness to jump on the back of his bike without a thousand inquiries.

Was he sure he could ride a motorcycle?

Could the bike hold two people?

Chance was also surprised at the skill and speed with which she lofted herself behind him, considering she looked like she'd outmaneuvered death more than once.

He didn't have to tell her to hold on. She wrapped her arms around his waist. But jumping on the bike was one thing; staying on it was another. "Are you injured?"

She shifted. "Um…"

Well hell.

"No," she finally decided.

Not like their plan would have changed much if she had been. He squinted at the approaching mob. The group stopped hesitantly, uncertain of who he was. If they were to capitalize on the confusion, they needed to leave now. "Are you going to pass out?"

"Not right now. But, definitely later."

He snorted. "Good plan. Hang on."

Jane tightened her arms around his waist and buried her head into his back. Another body on the bike might push the ancient thing to its limits. That'd be fine, so long as they broke through the crowd. He throttled the bike and sped straight ahead.

The group shouted and jeered, parting at the last second. Some hands grabbed for them as they burned dead center through the crowd. Someone fired warning shots, and Chance hoped the men on the other side of the mob would think twice before firing at them with others so close behind the bike. If not, their ride would be a short and painful one.

Jane's hold squeezed, and she cried, "Oh," as hands continued to tear at them.

"You've got it." They bumped and skittered through the throng of people. Then he spotted his exit. "Almost there."

He banged a quick left, and they were free of the horde. But the rest of the camp wasn't empty. Chance gunned the motorbike down a row of tents. He wanted to get closer to the fence line. After they passed another tent, he cut around a corner. "Shit." Women and children and baskets littered the narrow aisle. "Move. Coming through."

Jane shifted. Her chin rested on her shoulder, then she squeaked and ducked down again.

"Don't worry." He rocketed down a straightaway, angling his torso forward as though willing the bike to go faster. It was far from a smooth ride. Even if they'd been on flat asphalt, the piece-of-shit bike would've vibrated and jerked. Their ride was enough to give veteran thrill-ride seekers a run for their money.

They broke free of the sea of tents. Ahead of them, only the fence remained, reaching endlessly on either side. Chance eased off the throttle, and they stuttered to a stop. He glanced over his shoulder, and while he didn't see anyone, he could hear the sputter and whine of kickstarting motorbikes.

Her limbs loosened. She inched from his back. "What are we doing?"

"Planning our exit."

She shifted, glancing over her shoulder as he pulled out a pocket grenade launcher. It was locked and loaded with one charge. "Cover your ears."

Her hands tightened around his waist. "Are you insane?"

"Probably."

Her hands broke from his waist, and he felt her bury her face between his shoulder blades, covering her ears.

He pointed the handheld launcher at the fence. "Here goes Plan A."

The launcher fired, spitting smoke and kicking back in his hand. The grenade hit the base of the barrier fence. Even with the space he'd allowed, the reverb rolled over them. Jane screamed and cursed. He shielded his eyes from the brilliant fireball. If the locals had any question about where they'd gone, the large explosion would offer a pinpoint-location.

"Hang on." The flames licked across the dry ground cover. The smoke and dust cleared. He aimed them toward the hole in the fence, ballparking that it was large enough that they could fit through. But just in case... "Duck."

Then he barreled toward their only chance of escape.

THE MAN WAS an angel. A fucking insane angel. But an angel, none the less.

There was no other explanation for Midas. He'd saved her from certain death. Jane looked over her shoulder. One by one, motorbikes slammed to a halt inside the fence. A cloud of dirt mixed with smoke and darkened the air around them like an ominous cloud.

She swallowed hard over her dry throat. If Midas hadn't blasted through the fence, they would both have been dead by now. "Why did they stop?"

He glanced to his side. "That's their thief-dom, and out here, we're not worth the chase."

"Really?" Everywhere she went, she'd been chased.

"It's hotter than hell, and the sun's just getting stronger. Limited resources." They crested a small hill and he slowed as they rolled over the uneven path. "And me. I'm an unknown."

The Unknown. A damn angel. She believed it through and through. How, in that maddening maze of tents, had he known where to find her? There could be no other explanation. He had to be a divine miracle.

Her body swayed. Maybe she was hallucinating.

Because she'd already met Midas. He wasn't an angel. Actually, he'd been more of a pain in her ass.

"Whoa." His hand reached back to brace her. "You okay?"

"Sure..." Then the daylight turned black.

CHAPTER EIGHTEEN

J ANE TURNED HER head and groaned. Every muscle ached. Her tongue licked her chapped lips. Something was different. Her mind fought through the fog to wake.

Softness brushed her cheek. Her hair pulled from her forehead, and her eyelashes fluttered. A low, deep voice urged her awake, but she fought against it. A headache pounded suddenly, and she thought she might get sick.

Jane rolled to her side. Sore and dizzy, she opened her mouth. Nothing happened. Her stomach convulsed. She curled into the fetal position. The thrum of her heartbeat raced in her ears, and a reassuring hand rested on her shoulder, rubbing gently. Steadily, her racing heart slowed back to normal.

The nausea abated. She licked her lips again, realizing the skin was chapped, but also free of dirt and grit. She opened her eyes. A small, smoldering fire of red embers burned in the dark. Jane propped herself onto an elbow, realizing it was nighttime.

"You've been out for a while."

That voice. She jerked upright, but the quick move made her head spin in sickening circles.

"Careful."

Jane let the spinning stop, and then she twisted to face Midas. Her foggy stupor vanished with squeaky-clean clarity, and the previous days flooded her thoughts. She recalled the hell and fear, and then the escape. After eons of processing what had happened, she whispered, "You saved me."

He offered her a canteen. "Drink. It wasn't easy to hydrate you while you were going in and out."

Her fingers pressed to her lips, then skimmed over her cheeks. Her skin wasn't covered in grime. She reached for the water, and the small container weighed down her hand.

"You'll get your strength back." He rifled through a small pack. "A little more water, protein, and calories. You'll be back to new."

Her arm quivered. She rested the canteen against her thigh and tried to remove the cap. Her stiff grip wouldn't allow her fingers to close around it. Midas uncapped it with one hand, shifting to her side, and lifted the water to her lips.

Jane drank like he'd offered nectar from the gods. Water dribbled out the corners of her mouth. She didn't care, greedily gulping.

"Not too fast." He eased back, but her strength returned enough to grip his forearms and hold him in place. "Hang on. You'll get more in a minute or two."

Her eyes burned, and if she hadn't been dehydrated, Jane would've cried. "Please."

"Too much too fast will make you sick."

She slumped onto him, and Midas propped her up with his arm around her back. Her eyes closed. "Water. It's all I can think about."

Midas hummed. "Do you see the stars?"

"I can't open my eyes."

"There's a constellation over there. Something that translates to something like 'big fish.'"

She grinned against his hold. "You're making that up."

"Swear I'm not."

"Tell me more," she whispered hoarsely.

Midas hummed in thought again. "Don't bust my ass if I get the details wrong."

She managed a small laugh. "Promise."

"In mythology, a fish saved the life of a goddess. Its descendants became stars, and that's why some Syrians avoid eating fish."

Her eyes cracked open until she stared at the sky. Midas noticed and pointed. She couldn't see a fish, and though she believed him. Still, she added, "I'll Google that when I get home."

"I'd expect nothing less." Then he quietly continued, explaining where the planets would be able to be seen if it were a different time of year.

Jane listened, and his voice lulled her weariness away.

"All right." He eased the canteen to her mouth again. "Try not to drown yourself."

Her lips quirked. She'd almost forgotten her desperate need for water. This time, with newfound knowledge about the stars and some water already in her system, she drank more slowly.

"Good?" he asked.

She nodded.

"Hungry?"

She should have been. But her unsettled stomach rose at the mention of eating. "I'm not sure."

"Try to eat something anyway." He removed a small package from the side pocket of his pants and handed it to her. "Protein bar packed with calories."

"Oh, calories. How I've missed thee." Jane tore the dark green wrapper open and, after a few bites, wrinkled her nose and took a small sip of water. "It doesn't taste that good."

He laughed. "Sometimes that's not the point."

The little voice in the back of her head—or maybe, from in her stomach—told her to keep eating. Like Midas said, she needed protein and calories.

He took the wrapper when she finished and then picked up a stick, poking at the red, glowing embers. "Are you cold?"

Jane realized she was so out of sorts that her basic needs weren't coming to mind. If it weren't for this guy, urging her along, she might not have woken up, much less hydrated and fed herself. "A little."

He reached behind them and then added another layer of fabric over her legs.

It was a robe like the ones she'd been given. "Thanks."

He nodded and studied the small fire. Jane listened to it crackle and watched how it cast an orange glow over his face. He was handsome, in a rugged sense. She couldn't picture him in the posh world of the Thanes, wearing designer clothes and striking poses for Instagram, but he didn't need that kind of pomp to showcase his sharp features.

He had a strong jawline, a straight nose, and eyes that never stopped searching for danger. She recalled, from seeing him in the daylight, that they were blue. A deep, cobalt blue. Up close, she'd sworn there'd been flecks of gold. Tonight, his eyes were dark and serious. The corners of them had slight crinkles, as though he'd spent more time squaring off with threats than Jane could imagine.

She shivered. His hand reached over, pulling her to his side and shielding her from the elements. The protective move reminded her of their escape, and her chill lessened. Little by little, the shivers stopped.

"Do you want to go back to sleep?" he asked.

"I'm not sure." She leaned into him and realized she couldn't recall anyone helping or sacrificing for her like Midas had. Not her parents or her friends. Certainly not the Thanes. She'd been the one always sacrificing to help others make up for the lack of caring she'd received growing up; it came naturally to treat people the way she wanted to be treated. But others didn't always act the same way. No one would lay their life on the line for her. Except, this man had.

And he was a stranger. Or, not. He was Midas.

Overwhelmed by his selflessness, Jane wrapped her arms around him and hugged. He stiffened, obviously uncomfortable, but she didn't care. She was alive and safe and had no one else to thank but him.

He awkwardly patted her on the back. When she didn't let go, choking on a grateful sob, he begrudgingly returned the hug as though that might do the trick. But she didn't want to let go. The hug had gone on far too long. She didn't care and could have hugged him for the rest of her life and still not conveyed how grateful she was. "You came back for me."

He shifted. "I gave you my word."

He did. She didn't know why that struck her as a surprise. Finally, she released him with a self-conscious laugh. "No more torture. Sorry."

"Don't apologize." He pushed her hair behind her ear and then repeated his question again. "Are you still tired? Do you want to go back to sleep?"

Her head tilted. "What about you?"

"Me?"

She twisted to get a better look at his face. "Are you tired?"

"I'm exhausted." He chuckled.

Her hand pressed to her chest. "Did you get any sleep?"

"I will, but first wanted to make sure you didn't die on me."

"Oh, well… I didn't. Now you should sleep. I can…" She gestured to the dark blanket of night, having no idea what surrounded them. "I'll stay up and make sure everything is fine."

His lips quirked and amusement danced in his eyes. "Generous, but I think it'll be okay."

Her brow furrowed. "You can't stay awake indefinitely."

"I'll close my eyes and get a little rest."

Good. She nodded. Though who would keep an eye out for… everything and anything. "What if something or someone—"

He squeezed her shoulder. "Don't worry about it. I'll hear if anyone comes close."

"What?" Her furrow deepened. "You've got superhero hearing?"

He laughed. "Maybe."

Jane pursed her lips. "You're awfully confident."

"We're in a good place, and I set up a few hair-trigger traps *should* anything slip by my superhero faculties."

Her lips twitched, and relaxing somewhat, she couldn't shake the feeling they shouldn't sleep at the same time. "What about…" She recalled the howling animal from across the camp fence. "Coyotes or cougars. Whatever they have out here?"

"We'll be okay."

Sleep beckoned, and she wanted to believe. "Midas." She fought off a yawn. "I haven't come this far to become someone's dinner."

Midas tilted his head and urged her bed down. "I won't let that happen." His voice gentled. "Promise."

"There you go again. Who makes so many impossible-to-keep promises?"

"I do, MP."

Mary Poppins. She felt a stab of guilt for being so difficult with him now and when they were with Teddy. "I'll just rest a little." She pulled the robes up like a blanket, tucking them under her chin. "Make sure you sleep too."

He positioned close. They weren't touching, but she sensed his proximity. And, she sensed how much larger he was than she'd realized. Taller, broader, stronger. It reminded her of how she'd called him Hercules.

"Good night, Jane."

Her insides warmed, and she didn't know why, but his steadfast voice made her smile. "Good night, Midas."

The still night hung low, dark. There should've been a cacophony of sounds, but she only heard the faint crackle of the fire embers. For as tired as she was, the night wasn't ready to release her to sleep. Silence dangled between them like an unfinished conversation.

"My name is Chance."

She felt his whisper as much as she'd heard it.

"Chance Evans."

She wondered how sharing a name could seem so personal. "Good night, Chance Evans."

"Sleep tight, Jane Singleton."

She grinned then shivered, not 100 percent sure that she was that cold. Jane rolled onto her side and pressed her back against his side. Chance pulled in a slow, deep breath and then let it go. Her eyes closed, and she finally felt like she could almost fall asleep.

He repositioned and hooked his arm over her side, molding his body against hers. Her shivers faded. A small smile curled on her lips as she finally drifted to sleep.

CHAPTER NINETEEN

THE DESERT GREW so cold overnight that if Chance had any light, he would've seen his breath puff out in front of him. But as the first rays of daylight began to break over the horizon, he knew that would change. And quickly.

Until then, he stayed close to Jane. She'd slept more soundly this time. He'd caught a few Zzzs on and off as well. When he woke the last time, her head rested on his bicep like he was her pillow *and* his leg was thrown over her thigh.

Given the circumstances, staying close was always a good idea. But that wasn't the reason he didn't move. Holding her warmed him from the inside out. Then again, he wasn't within his right to touch her like that. There was no need to tangle their legs to keep her warm. Chance grit his molars and lifted his leg from her thigh.

Jane mumbled in her sleep and turned to face him. She cuddled and nuzzled herself into the crook of his arm, and son of a bitch, he liked that the testy blonde had a soft side. He liked a whole hell of a lot about her in addition to her attitude, and if he wasn't very careful, the way she curled her body to his would make him hard as a rock.

He closed his eyes and tried to find sleep again, knowing it wouldn't come. It wasn't that he'd had enough rest. The warm tickle of her breath against his skin would keep him wide awake.

Chance wasn't sure how long they stayed like that. The inky black sky showed wisps of purple in the east. Dawn would eventually arrive, and he hoped it took its time. There had never been a time when a woman rested in his arms for the basic need of safe sleeping. She didn't care about looks. She wasn't there because they'd gone to bed. She simply needed him to protect her while she rested. He liked that.

Which was a problem. They were in as safe a location as he could find, but now that day was breaking, he should've scanning the perimeter. Instead, he was staring at Sleeping Beauty.

He liked that better than Mary Poppins.

Actually, he liked Jane.

No matter the name, he couldn't allow attraction to distract him from his duty. Jane shivered and burrowed against him and showed signs of waking. A pang of jealousy lumped in his chest. Those sleepy sighs and quiet, almost awake murmurs weren't for him. Who did she normally wake up with?

Maybe, no one.

He wondered what would happen if they'd found each other at another place, in another time—And that thought was all it took to realize he was losing his touch with reality.

Regretfully, he moved her head from his arm, separating their bodies. Jane sleepily grumbled, fighting for her heat source, leaving Chance now surer than ever that she would wake up, notice how they had clung together and think he was a perverted asshat.

At that moment, her eyes flickered open. Big, blue, and bottomless, they landed on his. *Held his.* The moment stretched on for an eternity. "Good morning, Chance."

As if he needed any confirmation on how dangerous Jane was, he now had it. They were on their own in war-torn Syria. Enemies could arrive from any direction. But here he was, immobilized by the woman at his side.

JANE HAD BEEN having a nightmare. Teddy was ripped from her hands over and over again. Everywhere she ran, chasing after him, she ran into roadblocks and had to watch his anguished expression as he was pulled farther and farther away. And then, at the very end, right before she had awoken to face Chance, was a man with dark, sea-blue eyes who promised everything would be okay.

Now that she was awake, staring into those same blue eyes she'd dream about, she felt safe. Even as the terror of her time in Syria flooded back, she didn't worry. Not when this guy was by her side.

"Morning." His voice was thick with sleep, but he pulled abruptly away.

Her chest twanged, and self-conscious, she sat up, finger-combing her unruly hair. "Not a morning person?"

Big surprise. He didn't answer.

Then again, she'd been *very* close to him. When was the last time she'd taken a shower? How awful did she smell? Jane ran her tongue along her teeth, grossing herself out. No wonder Chance jumped from next to her. There was a strong chance she resembled Medusa.

Heat crawled up the back of her neck. Somehow, she hadn't noticed that Chance Evans was hotter than the Saharan sun. And, oh boy, did she know it now.

Attractive people were fairly constant in her life. The Thanes tried to associate with only *beautiful* people. Most of the beautiful people had egos to match the depths of their amazing looks.

But this guy? He was worlds apart, and if left to her own devices, she could've laid next to him and stared all day. How was it possible that he seemed better looking today—with his stubble-covered face and his piercing blue eyes, dark and troubled, like an icy sea during a winter storm. Apparently, there was nothing better looking in the entire world than a smoking-hot mercenary.

Actually, there was nothing better than staring at the man who rescued her from the shittiest armpit one could find in Syria. She owed him her life. That would make anyone weak in the knees.

She pushed up and looked away from Chance. There wasn't much to see. The sun blazed low in the morning sky, harshly changing the air from frigid to burning. There was nothing but desert, dead brush, and rocks and a million variations of the color beige. "Where is everything? The refugee camp? The burning fence?"

"Long gone. I hauled ass for a while," he offered.

Jane snapped and pretended to pout. "I was asleep and missed everything."

He laughed. "You passed out and missed a lot." He handed her the canteen of water. It felt woefully close to empty. "Take a sip," he said.

"You don't have more, do you?"

He shook his head. "Don't take too much right now, and we'll be okay."

She pursed her chapped lips. "That's not the *'yup, more water right here'* that I was hoping for."

He chuckled then turned to his bag. "Soon as I get my comm device linked up, we'll get airborne and you can have all the water you could possibly desire."

He fiddled with his earpiece, and she stood up, stretching. The muscle aches had lessened, and after a couple of stretches, she focused on her real pain. The blisters and sunburn. There wasn't much she could do for them out here, so she eased back onto the sleeping mat that he'd arranged for her. Chance continued to fuss with his equipment. She guessed things weren't going well. "No one's picking up on the other side?"

"It's not like a phone call," he muttered, distracted.

Well, no kidding. She thought about picking up a stone and pelting him. Maybe he'd realize his tone was a touch too condescending, but she decided against it since he *had* let her sleep on him.

She opened her mouth to ask him whether he was okay, but he must have anticipated it, because he cut her off with a "shhh."

Okay. Jane reconsidered a quick stone pelting, again deciding it wouldn't do any good.

Chance repeated the same action several times and then paced, stony look on his face.

Ruh-roh. Something wasn't going well for fearless Hercules. "What's the problem?" She readied to retaliate if he shushed her again. But how? Give him a little kick? She wasn't sure. But the shushing and clipped talk could ease up.

She didn't have to kick him, because he stopped by their motorbike and kicked it. "We have a broken-down bike." He shook the comm device. "And a broken-down mic."

"Wait. What?" The motorbike worked before she'd passed out.

"We ran out of gas."

Her lips rounded. "That seems like an important thing you failed to mention."

Chance shrugged. "It happens."

She blinked. "No one knows where we are?"

"For the time being." His lips thinned.

Her heart sank. "That throws a kink in the works, huh?"

"It's a complication," he agreed.

"A complication is more like when you miss a connecting flight at the airport."

His lips quirked. "That could be one too."

How the man could lump a missed flight with sitting alone in the desert, she didn't know. "Chance, do you ever panic?"

He raised an eyebrow. "What do you mean?"

"I mean." She rubbed her temples and tried to think of wording a Herculean-Midas-person might understand. "Do you ever freak out?" She put her hands in the air and pretended to scream, then added, "Ya know, *panic*?"

His chest trembled as though he were holding back a belly laugh. "Why?"

"Because!" She threw her hands into the air—not panicking yet but definitely feeling the possibility loomed. "If you're not the kind of guy who can give me a heads up when the end is near—"

Chance tipped his head back and released a belly laughed he'd been wrestling with. He laughed so hard the man gasped.

"Chance, I'm serious!"

He buckled over. "When *the end is near*."

She clamped her hands on her hips. "Pardon me, but this is my first abduction-escape-desert-debacle."

He didn't stop laughing, and for good measure, threw in an "oh, shit" and slapped his thigh.

Jane crossed her arms. "I'm so thrilled I can make you laugh."

"Oh, Mary Poppins." He staggered over as though he could barely walk and draped his arm over her shoulders. "I needed to laugh."

She rolled her eyes. "Then, jeez, you're welcome."

Just when she thought everything would work out, her hero rescuer was cracking up before her very eyes. She tried to stop her despair from getting too low. After all, how many times in recent days had she thought she was at the end of the line? More than she could remember. If she'd given up, it would've been the end. But she didn't. Something always worked out. Even in the midst of an insane good-looking hero who was losing his mind.

Eventually, he stopped laughing and released her from under his arm.

"Did that slip from reality help you come up with a plan?" she asked.

He chuckled again. "We walk."

"Walk?" Jane flinched when said the words that her blistered feet were hoping to avoid. "Are you sure?"

Instead of answering, shielding his eyes, he studied the uninhabitable terrain before them as if he might be able to pinpoint the promised land.

"Where to?" she asked and mimicked his stance. Jane shielded her gaze from the sun, turning to face the same direction and scanned the desert. There didn't seem like much to see, though she supposed he had some kind of superhero training that left him well-prepared for life's little hiccups. What military mission guy didn't prepare for a communication failure in the devil's backyard? Right…?

"Um…" She cut her fruitless search short and glanced at him. "What are we looking for?"

His lips pursed, and he didn't offer an immediate answer.

"Can you hear me? Or—"

He grinned. "Sometimes no answer is an answer."

"Not really."

Chance sobered and pulled a handheld device from his pack. "Sometimes I'm just thinking."

Her nerves skittered, because while she was not a superhero-rescuer, she considered herself a master of reading faces. At least when it came to little kids. But, it wouldn't be the first time Jane had lumped grown men and little kids into the same category. Chance's expression didn't bode well.

That look mixed with her limited knowledge of the Syrian landscape—yes, she had only glanced over that section in the brochure when Dax announced their final location. Who would fault her? There was a level-four travel ban in effect. She hadn't planned to go merrily skipping along what was called one of the most unforgiving places *on Earth*—Jane didn't blame her nerves for somersaulting like delirious, dehydrated little anxiety explosions. "Do you know where we are?"

"We're right here, Mary Poppins." He checked his device.

Her eyebrows snapped together, and a growl that surprised both of them rumbled from her throat.

The corner of his mouth quirked and then he extended the device. "Our GPS coordinates."

The screen meant a whole bunch of nothing to her, and she lifted her shoulders. "That's good? Right?"

"Yeah." He pocketed the GPS tracker. "But it'd be better for headquarters to have them also."

"Ah, yes."

"We'll continue toward the last evac zone." Chance checked his compass. "But there may be a small problem we deal with on the way."

Jane chewed on the inside of her mouth, wondering what he considered a small problem. She could name a half dozen concerns without having to think. "The suspense is intense. You know that?"

He rolled back on the heels of his boots and smirked. "We broke from the camp on the far side and judging by the typography map—"

"What? Typography?" Jane extended her arms. "Everything is flat, slightly flat, sandy, dead, or dying."

"With the occasional promontory."

She groaned. "I don't suppose a promontory is a fancy word for a dance hall or something that serves ice water."

He grinned. "Not quite."

"More like a club? A disco?"

"It's good that you've kept your sense of humor, MP."

Jane sighed dramatically. "If it's not a place to grab a drink and shake my booty, then what?"

His eyebrows arched.

"Oh, it's something horrible."

He quietly snorted. "Not horrible."

"A canyon? Cliffs? A mountain?"

"I think a large land mass would be a good description."

Her shoulders slumped. "All joking aside, every part of me hurts. Especially my feet."

"We'll be out of here soon."

She sighed and tried to cling to his optimism.

Chance scanned the horizon for the millionth time. "Have you ever been hiking?"

"Not in the desert while taunting death with dehydration."

"That's the spirit." He smiled like Jane announced hiking was her favorite weekend activity. Perhaps the man was certifiable.

She marched up to him and grabbed his biceps. "It worries me *a lot* that you only hear what you want to hear."

He winked and adjusted his pack onto his shoulder. "Ready?"

She gave a longing glance to the motorbike, bade it farewell, and gave him a thumbs up.

With that, he strutted off with a cool, easy gait.

CHAPTER TWENTY

JANE REGATHERED THE loose hairs that stuck to the back of her neck, tied her hair into a ponytail once more, and then caught up to him again. She wasn't sure how far they'd gone before the ache in her feet numbed or why he never needed to stop. "Are you worried that we're going to die?"

He paused, waiting for her to fall in-line with his side, then urged her to keep his pace. "Nah."

"Why not?"

"Because this is what I do," he explained.

"And you never fail?"

"Of course, but it doesn't stop me." He gave her a sideways glance. "I don't think it stops you either."

"Ha," she muttered.

"How many times could you have died?"

Sweat trickled down her back. "In the last twenty-four hours? Or, since, I don't know, I got into a rickety puddle jumper to come here?"

His laughter rang clear and crisp despite the shimmering heat and dusty sand. "Think you proved my point."

She licked her dry lips. "Normally, I think of myself in a protective role. Like you, but without the desert and grenade launchers."

He glanced over. "How so?"

"Taking care of Teddy." Her heart tugged. "I'm not sure how many people out there have his well-being in mind. Everything's royally screwed up."

Sand crunched under his boots for several steps before he grumbled. "Huh."

Emotion panged in her already parched throat. "I worry about him."

"I bet. That kid…"

She waited but he didn't continue, trudging ahead. "What?"

Chance tilted his head to look at her. "You don't want to know what I think."

"About Teddy?" Her stomach clenched. "He's great."

"No. About everything that surrounds the kid."

The idea that Chance disliked her work with Teddy bothered Jane. "Tell me anyway."

He wiped a hand over his forehead. "I think the 'royally screwed up' part was just coming out here in the first place."

"Tell me something I don't already know."

They didn't talk as the sandy ground rose into a small dune. Climbing wasn't easy. The gentle angle still made her muscles burn as much as her sunburn, but she didn't want to complain.

"Do the Thanes mess with everyone's life like this?" he asked.

They crested the top of the dune, and panting, Jane stopped. She struggled to take a deep breath. Chance handed her the canteen. The top of the canteen bottle burned her lips. The hot sip of water didn't quench her thirst.

Jane capped the canteen, still catching her breath, and nodded. "That depends on what you mean. But, they—Dax especially—have a knack for drama and chaos."

Chance snorted, gesturing his hand toward the expansive landscape. "I hope he pays good overtime. You deserve one hell of a Christmas bonus for this shit show."

"Dax is… a very eccentric man." Jane struggled to defend Dax and explain herself. "Working for him, more importantly the family, has its good and bad points."

"I think Dax Thane sounds like a grade-A asshole."

Jane didn't bother hiding her laughter. "Tell me what you really think."

"That none of you should have been over here. Whether he's an asshole or not."

She sighed, glad she wasn't the only one to see the absolute folly in her employer's antics. "I know. His sister warned him from the get-go that we shouldn't go. *That Teddy shouldn't.* I should've tried harder to stop the trip, and before I fully grasped what was happening—" She cut herself off, dangerously coming close to saying too much.

"What?" he asked.

She shrugged. "I shouldn't say."

"Why?"

"Everyone who works for the Thanes signs a nondisclosure agreement. It's pretty far reaching." She bit her lip. "Actually, I'm not sure if I'm allowed to say that I've signed one."

"Once again, what an asshole," Chance quipped.

"They have an image to protect," she explained, somewhat defensive. At least of Teddy and maybe even Gigi. "Reporters and paparazzi try to bribe me for insider stuff. Some photographers offer huge amounts of money for exclusive knowledge of their schedules."

"Have you ever taken them up on an offer?"

Her jaw dropped. "Absolutely not!"

Chance's mega-watt grin defied their circumstances. "I didn't think you would."

Jane dialed back her reaction. She wanted his respect, and for that pinprick of a second, she worried that he'd lumped her with the Thanes as though they were a tidy, attention-seeking group. "Can we change the subject?"

"Sure, tell me something that has nothing to do with the Thanes."

Her mind blanked. Suddenly, she was struck with the awkwardness of a twelve-year-old who had a crush. Was *she* developing a crush on Chance? Jane had been too tired to think straight, much less flirt and fall for a guy. And yet… she was drawn to him.

Jane listened to their steps and watched him walk a stride ahead of her. He was so strong, large, and masculine. And to think, she'd slept in his arms like a baby last night. She'd probably drooled. Her cheeks heated. That would be just her luck.

He stopped and waited for her to catch up. "Is that so, Jane? Riveting."

Jane smacked his arm.

"Tell me something."

"My brain is fried," she admitted. "I can't think."

"What's the first thing you think of—" he snapped "right now?"

"I've never been camping and slept with a guy I didn't know." The second she said the words, she cringed. Definitely something a twelve-year-old would say. "I mean, like that. Camping and sleeping, *resting*, with a stranger."

He chuckled a little. "Technically, I didn't sleep much, so I don't think it counts against you either way."

She laughed for exactly one heartbeat then realized that he'd been awake all night. Holding her. Watching her. Watching her drool and probably snore. Her cheeks blazed. "I offered to trade shifts!"

He shrugged his shoulders. "You needed sleep."

"Everyone needs to sleep."

Chance shrugged again as if to say no big deal.

"Are you tired now?" she asked.

"More hungry than tired," he admitted.

At the mention of hunger, her stomach growled so loud that she was surprised it didn't cause an avalanche of sandy dunes. She gripped her stomach. "Tell me about it."

If he noticed her crazy stomach, he didn't say anything. He reached into one of his pockets and pulled out a granola bar and handed it to her. Usually, Jane wasn't a big fan of granola, but recently, she considered herself a huge fan of anything that semi-resembled food.

"Oh, you're my hero." She started to tear it open. "Wait. Do you have any more?"

He shook his head but waved her off. "I'm good."

"No, we'll share." She opened it, ripped the bar in two pieces, and held out half to him. "I'm not letting you starve on my account, Midas."

He chuckled but shook his head. "Really, I'm good."

Jane lifted her chin and tilted her head in a way that never failed to get her point across with little kids. "I've perfected my we-always-share speech. Would you like to waste our time and hear me recite it?"

"All right, Mary Poppins." He grinned.

Every time his smile appeared, she floated for the second it took to absorb.

He held out his hand. "Since you insist."

"I do." She set half of the granola bar in his palm. He inspected the half of the bar, which was little more than a mouthful. "I don't think this is going to make much of a difference."

"I don't care. It's yours and we share."

"Yes, ma'am." He popped the piece into his mouth whole.

They chewed in silence and then sipped from the canteen. Chance checked their location and his compass, nodding that he was pleased with their progress. Then, off they went as the sun rose higher and her feet felt heavier.

With no shade or cloud cover, Jane stayed close behind Chance, using his body as a shield from the sun. But as large as he loomed, it didn't help much.

She wondered how people around here wore so much clothing. How could *Chance* manage, wearing a uniform and body armor? Jane was sure she would melt into the dusty ground at any moment. "How long can the human body last without water?"

"There's a depressing question."

"Not an answer," she panted. "Though I appreciate you said something."

He snickered, then added, "I didn't expect you to be like this."

"Like what?" He'd thrown around a saccharine Mary Poppins enough to give her a toothache. Had he expected her to be more like a princess? Weak and pathetic?

"To be this entertaining." He shrugged and looked the opposite direction. "I thought someone on a billionaire's staff would be a hoity-toity snot."

"What?" She balked. "Why?"

"You were a little hard to read at first," he said. "But you've mellowed."

"I'm trying not to die."

He laughed. "And doing a bang-up job. Keep it up."

"On that note, I need a break."

Chance stopped. "Sure."

She leaned over and rested her hands on her knees. "Tell me something right," she flipped her wrist, not bothering to snap, "now."

Chance crossed his arms and waited until she looked up before he said, "I projected the Thanes' worst qualities onto you before I knew you. Sorry for that."

She smiled. "That's okay. I might've made assumptions about you, too."

"Oh, yeah? Something to do with Hercules?"

"Ha." Once again, Jane's cheeks flushed. She prayed that her toasty sunburn would cover the way she continued to blush. "Nothing, really."

He adjusted the length of fabric she'd laid over her shoulders to protect her skin. "Now I want to know."

Her skin prickled under his touch. His calloused palms were painstakingly gentle over her skin. Whatever she might've said floated from her mind as his hands drifted over her biceps, inspecting the sunburn he tried to cover.

"What'd you assume?" he pressed.

"I would've guesses you were a rigid warmonger."

He smirked. "I'm not?"

"You know what I mean."

"A warmonger?" Chance crossed his arms, amused. "Nope. You'll have to clue me in."

Way to go, foot-in-mouth syndrome. "It just seems like only a specific personality type would want to work in these conditions."

"What are you talking about?" He winked. "This place? It's like working at the beach."

Jane laughed, then added, "I didn't spend a ton of time thinking about you, anyway."

"Of course not."

"I didn't." She elbowed him. "Cocky."

"Better than a rigid warmonger." Chance reached for his pack and handed her the canteen.

She tilted it to her mouth, taking only enough to wet her lips and alleviate her dry throat. She handed him the canteen, and Chance capped the top and stowed it in his pack. She worried he wasn't drinking enough.

With a tilt of his head, he signaled it was time again. They walked with their arms brushing, occasionally reassuring her they were still alive. She couldn't have done any of this without him. "I know it's your job…"

He watched her for a beat, waiting, as they walked toward the never ending see of sand.

"But I couldn't have done this without you."

Chance chuckled, dropping his chin with a small shake of his head. "Don't be too hard on yourself. I've had years of training."

"I mentioned that I'd made an assumption about you."

"Yeah."

"Truth is…" She mopped her forehead with a swath of fabric. "My assumptions were more about me."

"Oh, yeah." He shook his head. "Who doesn't think they can handle a marathon walk in a triple-digit sandbox after escaping captivity?"

"Ha, ha."

"What? That's what happened."

Jane marveled at how well Chance put the ordeal into a few tiny words. Maybe she was too tired to do anything more than live in the moment. "I assumed I was strong enough to take care of myself and Teddy." She wiped sand off of her lips. "In any situation."

"Like a weekend in Syria," he muttered.

"You're missing my point."

"I don't think I am, Mary Poppins."

"I'm not the kind of person who needs a white knight to come in and save me. But I was wrong."

Chance stepped in front of her. His brow knitted. "So, in this scenario, I'm the white knight?"

Her eyes rolled. "Out of everything I just said, that's what you heard?"

His lips curled impishly. "Yup. Chance Evans, White Knight. At your service."

"Nothing about my philosophical struggle with my mortality," she deadpanned.

"Oh, yeah. I heard that too." He took a half-step closer until his boots were toe-to-toe with her worn out sneakers. Chance slipped his hands under the fabric shawl she'd draped over herself and rested his palms on her sun-tender shoulders.

Jane waited for him to speak. Sand blew over their feet, and her chin dropped. She watched the light grains slide over his dark boots. She hadn't meant to sound pitiful, and she hadn't been hoping for a pep talk. Shame nipped in her chest. They'd stalled because of her pitiful ramblings. She tilted her head back, and damn, the way he looked at her.

A subtle red hue colored his deep tan skin. His stubble had thickened, and his blue eyes, intensely powerful, were like watching the cold, churning ocean. No one had ever looked at her the way he did now, full of belief and certainty. "What?"

His fingers curled into her skin. Tension ticked in his jaw. The corners of his eyes crinkled, and he pulled a long breath—then Chance stepped away. He cupped a hand over his forehead, shielding his gaze, then just as abruptly turned back.

"Are you mad at me?"

With a sardonic laugh he shook his head. "Let's forget for the moment that *you* were the one who sacrificed yourself on the ledge for Teddy with the helicopter." Chance pressed his lips together, then added, "And, I'm not going to mention how hard you're being on yourself."

"So, you're not mad at me?" she asked again.

With a quick head tilt, he started them on their never-ending journey. "I never wanted to be someone's white knight before. But coming from you, Jane, it's a goddamn honor."

She faltered.

He stopped. "Do you get what I'm saying?"

"No." Her whisper barely made it beyond her lips.

His nostrils flared, quietly snorting. "Of course not."

Chance turned away. She grabbed his arm. "What does that mean?"

"You're nothing like I ever imagined—" His laughter broke the tension, and he patted her hand like someone who needed to placate a toddler. "I'm just glad you're not some clueless lady living the high-life, courtesy of some asshole who likes to see himself go viral."

Whatever she'd felt between them a dozen yards ago was gone. Or maybe it wasn't really there. She took an unsteady breath—and caught the way she smelled; it was *miles* from pleasant.

Chance led the way, unfazed. For a moment, she thought there had been a buzz of attraction, some wayward blip of chemistry. But what was she thinking? Jane watched him truck over the sand. Her fingers swept over her cheeks and temples, wiping the sand and sweat into her dirty hair. Whatever she'd thought she'd felt between them, one thing was clear: This man was not attracted to her.

He turned to look over his shoulder. "You coming, MP?"

Yeah, there wasn't a single storm darkening in his eyes. No churning oceans. No cool, cobalt breezes. Her ability to differentiate fact from fiction had now been called into question. She held a thumb up, not trusting herself to talk, and then hurried to fall in line.

CHAPTER TWENTY-ONE

CHANCE STOPPED AND turned. He acted as though he'd heard someone call his name. Jane didn't hear anything new. "What?"

He didn't answer. Of course. She peered across the bleak landscape. Maybe he'd spotted a new challenge to defeat. Something to keep his spirits up, like a rattlesnake or landmine.

Chance shielded his eyes and searched the sky. Jane's stomach knotted as his intense focus tightened. Then she heard it, too—a faint beat. Her spine stiffened. The sound grew louder, lower. Helicopter blades? Her heart jumped. *Rescue.*

"Piece of cake." He opened his pack.

Jane shrieked, then pointed. "There! I see it!"

"Good eyes." He extracted a small canister and ripped a pull-tab off. Bright red smoke hissed free. "I told you we'd be fine."

Chance waved the smoke signal, and Jane waved her arms.

He laughed. "Thanks for the help."

"Oh, be quiet!" She wanted to drop to her knees and thank God—and she wanted to kiss her white knight. Instead, she wrapped her arms around him, squeezing with everything she had as they watched the helicopter in the distance change course and move their way.

A sudden, painful realization hit her like an avalanche. This was it. Their journey was over. Would she see Chance again?

After an eternity spent searching for their rescue helicopter, it suddenly seemed to arrive too fast. The blades displaced the air, and it had grown from near pinprick in size to a massive black beast.

Sand swirled as it descended from above them. Chance pulled her makeshift veil farther over her face and then covered his eyes. "Your chariot awaits."

She stole a look at the helicopter hovering above them. Ropes dropped. Chance gestured to a man that hung out the side. She couldn't understand their hand signals. Looking up and then down again, her balance faltered. Dizzy, she didn't feel as strong as the last time the chopper had come. Jane gripped his arm. "I can't."

"What?" He ripped the black fabric from her head and shoulders.

He couldn't hear her—and he wasn't paying attention. Did he expect her to hang on a rope? She'd drop off. With rescue in sight, pure exhaustion whipped through her mind and muscles. "I can't."

Black spots scored her vision. She swayed. Her knees threatening to buckle. Jane closed her eyes, barely feeling Chance pull her close, tightening his grip around her like a belt.

"Jane?"

She didn't want to open her eyes.

His hands cupped her cheeks. "Come on. The hard part's over."

Her eyes met his, then dropped to his mouth.

"I've got you."

She noticed the ropes between them, the harness and the carabiners clipped between them. The slack tightened.

"Good to go?" he asked.

"Good to go." She stepped into his embrace, wrapping a hand onto the rope. The harness pulled, and the helicopter rose. Her dirty sneakers dangled, and they lifted higher and higher.

Jane closed her eyes and clung so tightly to Chance that she probably cut off circulation to some of his important body parts. Days-old stubble grazed her forehead, and the arm around her remained steady and strong as a steel bar on a rollercoaster.

They swung, turning and jerking as they were pulled to safety while traveling across the desert. She took one last look at where they'd come from, then buried her face into his protective hold. Even as the ropes jerked, his arms never once wavered, and she never felt unsafe.

She turned from his chest and saw the opening of the helicopter. A uniformed man reached out and pulled her aboard. He did most of the work. Her legs were jelly.

Jane turned for Chance. He easily hopped in, released the carabiner clip, and met her gaze.

"You did great, Mary Poppins."

Her weak smile barely showed. An overwhelming urge to bawl like a baby clogged her throat.

"*Jane?*" the man in front of her said as though it weren't the first time he'd tried to get her attention.

She noticed he had his fingers on her wrist as though he were checking her pulse. But her attention followed Chance. He moved to a bench and pulled on a headset. He seemed to be holding more than one conversation between the guy next to him and whoever was talking in his ears.

A pinprick jabbed her arm. She watched the man, maybe a medic, start an IV bag of fluids.

He ran through a battery of questions, ranging from who the president was to where she was now. Her bleary vision clouded, and she curled into a ball. The helicopter's vibrations and white noise lulling her toward sleep— She shot up. "The little boy." She gasped, and her heart raced. "Teddy. Is he okay?"

The man shined a light in her eyes.

"Stop." She batted his hand away. "You already did that."

"Ma'am—"

"Is Teddy Thane okay?"

"We'll update you shortly." He flashed the pen light again. When he finished, he produced a bottle of water. "Thirsty?"

She clutched the cold bottle, taking a greedy gulp.

"Slowly." He eased it from her lips. "The IV fluids will hydrate without cramping you up. Slow, small sips."

She obeyed, taking small drinks as instructed until his scrutiny waned, and gave him the okay to check her over.

Chance slid onto the bench next to her, bottle of water in hand. "Doing better?" He offered her another one of the protein bars that she didn't like.

Appreciatively, though, she took it. "I haven't heard how Teddy's doing."

He nodded then motioned to the man hung out the helicopter, pulling them in.

"Teddy Thane doing okay?" Chance asked.

The man nodded but she couldn't hear what he said. Chance fitted a set of headphones over her ears.

"The kid's doing well," the man said. "Cleaned up and playing on his iPad, last I heard."

"Thank you—" She realized she didn't know his name. "Thanks."

Chance hopped on the opportunity to make introductions. "Jane, this is one of my favorite assholes. Hagan Carter."

Without missing a beat, Hagan smiled, adding, "We're glad your back, but sorry you had to meet Midas. By now you know he's the *whole* ass."

"Hardy, har," Chance snickered.

She laughed at their banter. Despite where they'd come from, the men surrounding her seemed relaxed, doing their job like this day could be interchanged with any other one.

Suddenly, she shivered and then couldn't fight her jittery chill. Days of adrenaline spikes had run their course. She was more depleted than she knew possible, and the warring emotions of fear, gratitude, and fragility overwhelmed her.

Chance slipped his arm around her shoulder and held her close, whispering that all would be okay. Hagan and the medic faded away, and Jane reveled in his attention. She wasn't used to relying on someone, but right then, she needed his support. As he continued the low, rhythmic croon that everything would be all right, she believed him for the time being.

Jane dropped her head onto his shoulder, and he rested his chin on the top of her head. Tears pricked. Soon, she'd have to let him go, and that pained her. A realization hit her as though symbols had crashed in her ears. He wasn't just the good-looking white knight with a backside she liked to ogle. He was the man who saved her life, who lived on the other side of the world, and who she'd fallen for somewhere on their journey through the depths of hell.

CHAPTER TWENTY-TWO

TRANSITIONS HAPPENED QUICKLY. From the helicopter, Jane was bustled in and out of a military hospital for a speedy medical check—her sunburns and blisters were far worse than she'd thought—and then into a heavily guarded, private waiting room at a military airport.

Now alone, and with nothing to do but resist the urge to pick at her blistered skin, Jane let herself recount her conversation—likely the last conversation—with Chance at the hospital.

He'd told her that the Thane family had been evacuated, and Teddy was blissfully binging on cartoon videos. Chance explained that arrangements had been made for her to meet the Thanes in Abu Dhabi. She had been drowsy during their conversation, having slept fitfully whenever she could. But, she also recalled Chance mentioning that his team was stationed in the same city.

Her foot tapped on the tile floor. Why had he mentioned he lived in Abu Dhabi? Why hadn't she paid more attention to his tone? *Hello, Jane.* Catching up on sleep and water took precedent over reading between the lines with a man who was far, *far* out of her league.

She crossed her arms, and a wave of pain burned over her shoulders. She clenched her fingers and took a slow breath, reminding herself that she'd refused pain killers. Imagine how foggy her memory would have been if she let the doctors numb her pain. She wouldn't have remembered Chance mentioning how he lived in Abu Dhabi.

"That doesn't matter now," Jane told the empty waiting room. She could endlessly analyze the reasons he'd mentioned Abu Dhabi, but his motivations simply didn't matter. They made no plans to see each other again, and she'd been far too chicken to suggest it herself.

Why hadn't she, though? An invitation to recount the horrors of their last few days didn't exactly yell romance. He could show her around a city she'd likely never visit again. Jane had only needed to open her mouth and ask.

Or not. Alone in a waiting room, as clearheaded as she'd been in days, Jane couldn't fathom an invitation beyond the musings of a horny cavewoman.

Me Jane. You hot.

Yeah, that wouldn't work with Chance. She imagined that he regularly declined invitations from other damsels in distress—ugh! Did Jane just lump herself into a distressed damsel category? Not a chance—

"Hey, Mary Poppins." Chance strode into the waiting room, clean-shaven and more handsome than he'd ever been. "I caught you."

"Chance." Jane jumped from her chair then faltered, clinging to the last thread of her dignity. She ignored the impulse to throw herself into his arms like she was the leader of the Distressed Damsels Society. "I didn't think I'd see you again."

"Turns out, we're headed out now, too." He hooked a thumb over his shoulder. "Some of the team is back there, but I knew where you were and had a minute."

Why had he known where she was? Her heart skipped a beat, and she swallowed around the awkward knot in her chest. "I'm glad."

He crossed the waiting room. "If I'd known we'd be airborne at the same time, you could've ridden back with us—" He grinned. "Turns out our jet's nicer than what the billionaire could muster for you."

"Next time." She laughed as though the working-vacation from hell would ever happen again.

Jane expected him to leave, but he stepped closer. Only two feet remained between them. She could extend her arm and touch his chest, and that thought made her nerves dance. If her chair hadn't been directly behind her, she would've backed away. The air crackled and sizzled when he stood this close and taking a normal breath seemed impossible.

"You should know." He shoved his hands into his pockets. "You were a total badass out there."

Jane choked and rolled her eyes. "Yeah, I'm sure."

His head cocked to the side, and the corner of his deep blue eyes tightened. Chance met her gaze. "Don't believe me?"

"No," she whispered.

"Well, Jane." He inched into her personal space, not letting her gaze drop. "You should."

The pounding beat of her pulse thumped in her ears. If he couldn't hear her heartbeat, he was deaf. And, he wasn't. The man heard the step of faraway enemies and the rotors on helicopters beyond where the eye could see. Heat rose up Jane's neck. Her cheeks flushed. Damn him; he didn't back away and knew his effect on her.

"Next time," she managed.

The corners of his lips quirked. "Next time."

This was her opportunity. She could ask him on a date. Fate had thrown them together one more time just in case she found the nerve.

After I shave my legs and triple wash my hair, would you be interested in another night alone with me?

Or, not. Because, they'd been there, done the private overnight, and she had the blisters to prove it.

He was just as capable of asking her out. More so, probably. But he didn't. Meaning... he wasn't interested. The man before her wasn't the type to ignore what he wanted.

That was what she should ask him. What did he want? Standing that close, smelling that good, what the hell did he want—

"Midas," a voice bellowed from outside the door.

Chance licked his bottom lip and pivoted toward the door.

Jane recognized Hagan's voice when he called again, "Where you at, brother?"

She crossed her arms over her chest and hugged. "I guess it's time for you to go."

His jaw ticked. "Sounds like it."

The waiting room door flew open. "Chance?" Hagan bound into the small space. "What the—*hey, Jane.*" His gaze quickly cut between them then he turned for the door, pausing long enough to add, "Waiting on you, bud. Whenever you're ready."

Hagan disappeared, and Jane couldn't fill her lungs.

"Jane," Chance said in a careful way that made her throat burn with unshed tears.

Embarrassed, she shook her head and pinched the bridge of her nose. "I hate goodbyes." At least she did with him.

Chance extended his hand to her. She wasn't sure if she could take his hand because this was their goodbye. She tried to reason with herself. The meaning she'd assigned to her rescuer was irrational. This wild rollercoaster of emotions was a byproduct of her trauma.

With that, she met his grip then forced her chin up.

His stormy eyes met her watery ones, and his tough, warm hand surrounded hers trembling one. Her heartbeat raced like a lawless locomotive, and she couldn't help it. Hot tears fell down her cheeks.

Chance swore and pulled her to his chest. His arms wrapped around her, hiding her distress until she could pull herself together.

"I'm sorry," she whispered against his chest.

He rubbed her back and dropped his chin onto her head. "Don't be. It happens."

This is what his Damsels do. This was what always happened. Jane squeezed her eyes shut and hated how foolish she felt.

From outside the waiting room, someone other than Hagan called for Midas. Chance hugged Jane tight enough to make her sunburn scream. She'd take that pain again and again if he didn't have to leave.

Chance kissed the top of her head and pulled away. "I have to go." Then he left without looking over his shoulder.

CHAPTER TWENTY-THREE

EVERY STEP THAT Chance took away from Jane made him sick with guilt. He should have stayed away, but hell if he couldn't stop himself.

That was only the first thing he shouldn't have done in the last ten minutes. He shouldn't have held her, and he sure as fuck shouldn't have kissed the top of her head.

What had he been thinking? He hadn't.

Even if he had, he couldn't have guessed that those few minutes would amount to the closest he ever felt to another person. Fully clothed and at an airport, that had been the most intimate embrace of his life.

He returned to where his teammates had been. The area was empty, and he was thankful for a few more seconds to get his ass in gear.

Chance rubbed the back of his neck then grabbed his go bag and strode out to the tarmac where Titan Group's sleek jet waited.

A few dozen yards away, a far crappier propeller plane readied for Jane. His molars grounded. The Thanes were assholes. If they wanted, they could've transported her home on a chariot padded with gold-threaded pillows. But nope, the billionaires didn't go out of their way for their employees.

Chance shifted his bag onto the other shoulder and charged up the stairs. Cool air conditioning from their jet hit him before he ducked in. He made his way to an open seat and ignored Hagan's expectant expression. "Not now."

Hagan let out a long, slow whistle.

That was all the conversation they would have about Jane. Chance settled into a seat as the lights dimmed. He unwrapped a set of noise-canceling earbuds from a console panel and dropped his head back, closing his eyes. The earbuds dulled the jet's engines but didn't do a damn thing to quiet his mind.

What if Jane hadn't been a client?

What if he didn't live in another country?

What if he never experienced that zap of chemistry with another woman again?

Their electricity burned deeper than he knew possible. Jane Singleton had a smart-mouth and a strong body. He could easily explain his attraction, but he didn't understand their magnetic pull. How could he fix what he couldn't comprehend?

OF ALL THE cliché things that Jane could've done, she opted for the most pathetic. She had cried—and he'd pitied her.

She swallowed several times like she might get sick. *You cried on him.* Her head dropped into her hands. He didn't even look back.

Of course, he wouldn't. Jane had let the desert bake her brain cells away. Why would Chance have fallen for her when she was at her weakest—and smelliest? This wasn't a fa-la-la, rainbows-everywhere movie where the macho hero runs off with the woman who had stolen his heart. What on God's green earth had she been thinking?

Jane dropped onto an uncomfortable plastic chair and focused on what would come after her flight. *Comfort. A warm bed. A hot shower.* Those should make her swoon. She couldn't wait to pamper herself. Room service was definitely in order. Most of all, Jane couldn't wait to see Teddy.

"Ma'am?"

Jane turned toward a man wearing desert camouflage. "It's time?"

He nodded and held the door open. Jane stood and her arms felt empty. No purse. No phone. No one to lean on.

She followed the man outside and was introduced to the pilot of her airplane. They traded a brief conversation as she studied his face, searching for any hints that he might be like her last pilot. Nothing seemed out of place as the pilot took painstaking care to make sure she was nicely settled into the cramped, somewhat antiquated plane.

"Thanks." Jane shifted uncomfortably as he continued to fuss over her comfort. "But you don't have to do all this. I'm not a Thane. Just one of their staffers."

The pilot paused, crooking his head. "I'm sorry?"

"You don't have to waste your time on me. I'm just Jane. Not a billionaire."

He straightened. "Just Jane," he repeated and then reached for her hand and squeezed. He spoke Arabic, and then with a grandfatherly expression, translated, "There will always be people who do not see your worth. Don't let one of them be you."

Her lips parted as the pilot let go of her hand. She wanted to explain that he'd misunderstood her intent. Jane knew her worth!

The pilot situated himself in the cockpit and spoke into his headset. The propellers revolved and drowned the conversation away, leaving her with the weight of his words and the question: *did* she know her worth?

Jane was a realist. She didn't have low self-esteem.

Perhaps she had a few insecurities. But who didn't? Especially when her surroundings were glittery photoshopped perfection.

"One hour," the pilot announced. "To Abu Dhabi."

"Thanks." She closed her eyes and a strange sadness clogged her throat. Soon as the regular routine of her life came back, she would forget about her dashing white knight and carry on like she'd always done. The last thing she needed was to pine on over a man who lived half a world away, who would jump into danger on his next job, maybe saving another woman who'd fall in love with him. She'd be a distant thought…

The trip went by quicker than she expected. They began their descent almost immediately, and Jane watched as the barren landscape changed to an extravagant city of ocean-side skyscrapers.

The plane lined up for a runway and smoothly touched down. She stared out the window as the pilot taxied and then the small private plane stopped.

The outer door of the airplane was unlocked by the ground crew as Jane thanked her pilot. The plane door unfolded. Jane unfastened her seatbelt and stretched as the captain disembarked.

"I left before saying everything I needed to."

Jane jerked the opened hatch. "*Chance?*" She blinked twice as if that might clear her vision. "What are you doing here?"

"Like I said. I didn't leave our conversation the way I wanted to." He held out his hand. "You got it?"

"Um—" She broke from staring at Chance but didn't take his hand. "Yeah."

He led the way down the clamshell staircase like they weren't skinny, narrow, and tedious. This time when Chance offered his hand, she took it. "This thing's easier to get into."

Her feet touched the tarmac. Their fingers lingered for half a heart-beat—or not. She didn't know, hating how she immediately reverted to her quest for secret meanings in benign gestures. Then again, he was standing in front of her. "Thanks."

"The guys would never let me live it down if we survived Syria, but I let you break your neck falling out of the airplane." He tilted his head toward the exit. "You ready for the big city?"

They crossed the smooth, clean tarmac. The exterior of the airport gleamed. Even the vibrant sky seemed well-appointed with the cotton ball clouds.

Chance escorted her into an unmarked door and into the cool, lightly perfumed airport. Wealth poured from the rafters. Designer-clad travelers walked through the grandiose terminal. Jane lived and worked in the Thanes' extravagant world, but this airport was still a sight to be seen.

Then she noticed how others stared at her. Her cheeks flushed. She could only imagine what they thought of the sun-blistered woman who wore hospital scrubs and her dirty shoes. She tugged on his elbow and whispered his name.

When Jane had his attention, she pointed out, "People are looking at us."

He didn't bother to check. "You should wave."

"What? Why?" She crossed her arms over her chest as though she could curl into herself and hide.

"A pretty lady looking like she escaped hell?" He looked her up and down. "They probably think you're from one of those reality shows. Amazing Race. Survivor. Something like that."

She chuckled, relaxing the slightest bit. "Right."

Chance stepped in front of Jane and held his arm out. "Stay back."

What in the world—

"No pictures." He blocked the invisible paparazzi.

A blush rocketed from her forehead to her toes. "Oh my God. Chance, would you stop?"

"No autographs." Chance placed a protective hand around her back, shielding her from absolutely no one, and then ducked her through a door. His laughter bubbled as the door clicked shut.

Jane couldn't help but laugh. "You're insane. Do you know that?"

He shrugged without disagreeing and led her through a maze of private halls.

"Do you know where we are?" Jane asked.

"More or less."

She groaned. "If I end up in Abu Dhabi police lock-up because—"

He turned, stopping Jane short. "Thought you trusted me?"

Well, hell. Here they were, too close for her brain to function properly. "I do."

He swept an arm behind her back and led her to another door and out into the sunshine again. Jane blinked and shielded her gaze. A black Mercedes sedan waited curbside. A chauffeur greeted them by name.

She slid into the backseat and muttered, "Guess you do know what you're doing."

Chance laughed as the driver shut the door. "Sometimes I just have to see what happens next."

CHAPTER TWENTY-FOUR

TWENTY MINUTES LATER, they arrived at a hotel. Its gleaming windows reached into the cloudless sky. Jane didn't want to leave the close confines of the Mercedes' backseat, but for both of their sake, she needed to shower. Her only shower since Syria had been at the hospital where she'd had just enough time to scrape off the first layer of dirt, sand, and sweat.

Bright light spilled into the sedan as Chance opened the door before the hotel bellboy or chauffeur had the opportunity.

She grabbed his forearm. He was half out of the car with one foot planted on the driveway. This was one of her most awkward moves yet. Hurray for consistency.

He raised his eyebrows then ducked back into the car. "What's up?"

Well, hell. She should've thought this through. Variations of 'Me Jane. You hot.' filled her thoughts as a flock of twitchy butterflies flipped in her stomach. She had no idea what she wanted to say and still held an iron grip on his forearm. Her fingers held his arm so tightly that Jane had to will herself to let him go.

Concern darted across his face, and she couldn't blame him. This was one those situations they likely warned white knight heroes to look out for in potential stalkers.

Jane yanked her hands in her lap. "You said something about finishing our conversation."

"Yeah."

Well, wasn't that vague. "So... did we?"

"Finish our conversation?" he asked.

She lifted a shoulder. "Yeah."

Chance turned to face her and settled against the door. "No."

"Are we going to?"

"Sure."

She laughed and rolled her eyes. "When?"

"Later. You good with that?"

Ha, ha, ha, no. "Sure." Jane wanted to shake him. If he ever said something about women being hard to read, she would recall this two-part conversation verbatim. Then she remembered that it might be a good idea to take a breath.

"We can wait until you're ready," he said, unaware of her urge to shake the words from his mouth. "I figured you wanted to crash when you got to the hotel."

"Shower," Jane agreed. "Then crash."

"Good." He squeezed her knee.

Even as more oxygen made its way to her brain, Jane was left feeling like a groupie unable to function near their rock star. "Good," she repeated.

He opened the door. A professional-looking woman in a long black skirt and long-sleeved white blouse waited a few steps away with a friendly but curious smile. Chance got out and exchanged greetings with the woman.

Jane stepped out and cupped her hand over her forehead to block the bright sun.

"This is Angela," Chance said. "She'll take care of you while you're here. If you need anything, she can make it happen."

Angela extended her hand. "At least, I'll try."

Jane detected a faint southern accent as they shook hands. "Nice to meet you."

"Likewise." Then Angela pointed at Chance. "And, you, my friend, are late."

He held up his hands. "I had a good reason."

"Uh-huh." Angela clucked then turned to her. "He was a perfect gentleman?"

Jane blushed and hoped her sunburn hid her reaction. "Of course."

Chance gave Jane a wink. "I'll check on you later, okay, Mary Poppins?"

"Okay." She laughed awkwardly, explaining to Angela, "Inside joke."

"Uh-huh."

With a quick salute, Chance strode away.

Thankfully, Angela gave Jane a few seconds to take in the view before she cleared her throat. "Ready?"

"Yes." Jane straightened and followed Angela toward the hotel entrance. "Chance was late?"

"He was," Angela offered, all business.

Did they go out on jobs again so quickly? "Where's he going now?"

"To get his ass chewed out by Boss Man."

"Oh." Jane hadn't expected anything about an ass-chewing to come out of the woman's well-lined lips. But since when had Jane's expectations squared with reality?

Angela guided Jane through the hotel lobby. The marble floor was a mosaic of whites and gold. The walls held bright and gilded tapestries. But as beautiful as the surroundings, Jane couldn't stop asking questions about Chance. "Why would he get chewed out?"

Angela stopped. Her lips quirked as her eyebrows delicately arched. "I haven't quite figured that out yet."

Jane was somehow the answer to the question. At least according to Angela's curious expression.

Angela turned briskly. "We'll head to your room. After you clean up and rest, we can review your itinerary."

Jane rushed to keep up. "Thanks."

They stopped again at a bay of elevators. A hotel staffer pressed the call button for the elevators, creating a small line queue. "Before we go to my room, can I swing by and say hi to Teddy first?"

"Oh." A line creased across Angela's brow. "Did no one tell you?"

Her stomach churned. "Tell me what?"

"The Thanes and their photographer were evacuated home earlier this morning."

Jane's head swam. "They're not here?"

"No," Angela said more softly.

Jane didn't know why this was a surprise, but yet, she couldn't grasp that they hadn't waited a few hours to check on her. "They left without me…" Had that been what Chance had wanted to share?

Jane closed her eyes, mortified *again* that she let her romantic thoughts lead her so far astray. Talk about insult to injury.

Angela grimaced. "I'm sorry."

"Never mind." Jane opened her eyes and waved Angela's unnecessary apology. "It's fine."

"Mr. Thane said he had important business matters to attend to—" Angela faltered, clearly unaccustomed to the derailment of her smooth plans. "This is my fault. I thought, well—"

Jane forced away her disappointment. "It's no one's fault, and honestly, it makes sense. The family is so busy." And she didn't mean anything to them. A decent boss would've checked in on an employee who nearly died, wouldn't they?

Maybe Jane had a pie-in-the-sky idea of how connected she was to the Thanes. They played house and family, and because of her upbringing, Jane had little to compare how real, normal families worked. After all, Jane had left home when she turned eighteen, and she wasn't certain if her parents had noticed she was gone.

But she'd assumed that being part of the Thanes' household, being invited on this trip, meant that she was part of their family. Or, at least, part of Teddy's family.

Emotions shuffled through Jane's head as Angela led her into the elevator and then to her room. Jane always played by their rules. She signed gag orders, put up with Dax and Gigi's ridiculous behavior, and had given Teddy the best care she knew how to give. She dropped everything to accompany them on this trip that Aunt Courtney had correctly assessed as a disaster. And… Dax and Gigi had just left her.

No. They weren't her family. She hadn't known them more than a year. Even Teddy, who she instantly and immediately had loved as her own, wasn't hers. They could take him away whenever they felt like it, and she could say nothing about it. Teddy's aunt hadn't even been able to stop their trip. What was Jane thinking? She'd had no family before, and she had none now.

Angela stopped, startling Jane, and opened the hotel room door. "This will be your room."

Jane stared through the threshold but didn't cross it. The hotel room was more like a grand suite. Her stomach turned. Did the Thanes throw money at her the way they did any other problem, certain all would be fine?

"Jane?"

"This room… I can't."

Angela came to her side. "I can't imagine what the last few days have been like, but I think you'll feel better if you come in and relax."

Jane let herself be coaxed inside. The sight of the bathroom and the bed gave her enough of a reason to stay.

Angela ran through Jane's remaining travel as she stared out the window and soaked in the city of Abu Dhabi. The massive buildings gleamed in the desert sun, above throngs of people, some dressed in Arab kaftans, wraps, and veils, while others dressed in Western fashion. She never thought she would be anywhere as exotic as the city.

"Which would you prefer?" Angela asked.

Jane blankly turned from the window. "I'm sorry. What?"

"We can make arrangements for you to leave in a few hours after you've rested. Or…" Angela tilted her head as though she preferred the next option. "You don't push yourself and leave in a day or two."

As much as Jane wanted to hug Teddy, she reminded herself that they'd left her behind. Not Teddy's fault. But when would she ever get an opportunity to be in this city again? She deserved a small vacation. "I suppose I don't need to rush back."

"Perfect." Angela smiled and walked toward the door, only pausing to leave a business card on a side table. "If you need anything, let me know."

With that, Angela left.

Jane stripped her scrubs as she walked into the luxurious bathroom. As steam filled the air, Jane wondered if Chance had meant to tell her about Teddy. Or had there been something else?

Then she stepped under the hot water. This shower and hours of sleep were her only priorities.

CHAPTER TWENTY-FIVE

CHANCE STEPPED FROM the harsh sunlight into the hotel that housed their headquarters, however makeshift as it was. He ducked under a clear plastic tarp that lined the lobby out, threaded his way behind the front desk, and into the hotel offices that continued to serve as their temporary nerve center for team operations.

The seemingly slow progress on the hotel wasn't likely to make Jared Westin's mood any better, and what Chance wouldn't give to be freshly showered and shaved with a good night's sleep in his own bed under his belt before meeting up with Boss Man.

The job had gone well. But Chance wasn't oblivious. The way he went about his second re-entry was low on Ace's list of ways to get a job done.

"Well, look who it is. The renegade." Jared bounded down the hall, wearing workout shorts and an old shirt that read 'When life closes a door, breach the wall and show up like a boss'.

Chance kept his amusement to himself. Boss Man had never seemed the type for small talk—and he'd never been one to stare at a door without blowing through it. "What are you looking at?"

"Nothing," he growled and nearly ripped the door from its hinges before he stormed in.

Yeah, that'd be a big fat no on small talk with Boss Man. This was going to be a great meeting.

"Get your ass in here," Jared boomed.

Chance stopped at the door and read a paper sign duct-taped slightly off center.

WARNING
Aces Team Be Like…
Ninjas and Pirates
Lasers and Slingshots
Proceed at your own risk.

"It's not that interesting." Jared sounded like a fire-breathing dragon with a bad case of heartburn as he snatched the WARNING notice from the door and threw it onto the floor. "Fuckin' imbecile children." He threw the door shut, muttering, "What the hell have I got myself into?"

Yup. This was going to go about as well as surprising Jane at the airport, skipping over the key part of his plan—asking her to dinner—so that his surprise appearance closer resembled a creepy stalker who wanted to capitalize on her naïveté. Chance waited until he was certain Jared wouldn't toss the table before he sat down at it and looked at his boss.

"*What?*" Jared barked from across the makeshift war room.

Sorry for forcing the team's hand in Syria. Wish I could've got the nanny out the first time. Chance had nothing that sounded like a conversation opener. "I like your shirt."

"Shut up."

Gladly… "About my request to drop back in—"

"That's what you're calling it?" Jared crossed his arms. "A request?"

Chance eyed his boss and saw cold eyes paired with a soul so ancient it surpassed Stonehenge. "You have a different phrase?"

Jared's eyes narrowed. He strode to the table and planted his fists on it like two thunderbolts. "I'd call *your request* a piss poor position that you put me in."

True enough, but it was the only one they had. "I—"

"You could've waited." Jared's nostrils flared in challenge.

This would be their sticking point. Chance ground his molars. "Waited for what? Her to die?"

"Don't be a smartass." He pounded a fist. "You shoulda waited for more intel. For a better route. For goddamn anything where you wouldn't find yourself skipping rocks through the desert for a girl you want to impress."

Chance's jaw dropped. "Wait a minute."

"You heard me."

Tension scraped up his neck, and Chance shifted in his chair, positioning so that his boots were underneath him as though he might leap into action.

Jared glared. "You were lucky it worked out in your favor. But get this through your thick skull, I won't have my orders disobeyed."

A righteous strain of pissed-off coursed through Chance. "With all due respect, Boss Man. You signed off."

"You pushed my hand."

"You're damn right I did." Chance rose from his chair and leaned into the table like Jared. They were two muscled-up pit bulls ready to scrap. "I either went back for her then or it wouldn't matter. The job wouldn't be a rescue. We'd have a body to recover, and you know it."

Jared's jaw flexed. He didn't disagree, and that was something. If he did, Chance wasn't sure how well their conversation would continue to go. Not that this one constituted a great chat.

"You know we call you Midas for a reason—"

"You know what?" Chance snapped. "I never asked for that."

"For fuck's sake. Stop talking and listen, because one of these days, if you pull shit like that again, it's gonna catch up with you."

Chance pressed his knuckles into the table until pain burned into his forearms. "I wouldn't change a thing."

"No one's invincible." They silently faced off until Jared pushed from the table. "I didn't put you on my payroll because you're stupid. Don't do stupid shit again." He cracked his knuckles. "Do you read me?"

Chance paused and recalled Jane's retelling of King Midas. *Well… hell.* He chewed the inside of his mouth and rolled back on his heels. Boss Man wasn't wrong. Chance took a deep breath and then admitted, "Yeah. I read you loud and clear."

"Finally." Jared rounded the table and clapped Chance on the back. "Glad you're still alive. Don't cause me any more headaches."

And that was that. Jared was gone.

Chance arched his eyebrows and turned for the door that'd Jared had slammed shut on his way out.

Holy mother of adrenaline rushes. He dropped back into his chair and ran a hand over his face. That'd been more intense that he'd expected.

From what he'd heard from others on the team, a slap on the back and a commendation for still breathing was as close to a "good job" as Jared Westin ever gave.

Chance laughed. A huge smile cracked across his face, and with that, he decided today was one hell of a great day. Tomorrow would be even better, because he wouldn't screw up while trying to impress a girl who'd done nothing but impress him.

CHAPTER TWENTY-SIX

THE MORNING SUN blanketed Chance's bed with a bright, white light. It always worked better than setting an alarm clock. Too bad he woke up hungry and horny.

Neither were a great way to start the day. Mixed together? They propelled him toward Jane Singleton in a much different disposition than he'd initially planned.

His bedroom was in an old hotel room. It had once been a suite before Titan closed the hotel for repairs. For the time being, the Aces team considered the thirteenth floor their home sweet home. He wondered more than once why that floor had been chosen but hadn't found a good time to ask Boss Man.

After a quick shower and shave, Chance flipped through the mostly empty cupboards in the kitchenette. *Popcorn. Beef stew. Jerky.* Even as his stomach rumbled, nothing caught his eye. Finally, he opted for a breakfast of beef stew, cold and out of the can as someone banged on the door.

"Midas," Camden called. "You up?"

"Yeah, yeah," Chance mumbled around the spoon in his mouth. "Hold your horses." He let his teammate in. "What?"

"Morning to you too, dick." Camden noted the can of beef stew and beelined for the kitchenette. "Got any more of that?" He didn't wait for an answer, grabbed a can from the cupboard, and popped the lid with an old P-38 can opener from his keychain.

Chance shook his head. "By all means, help yourself."

Camden rifled through the utensils. "The spoons clean?"

"If they weren't, they wouldn't be in the drawer." Chance leaned against the wall. "Ever thought about that?"

"Maybe." Camden inspected a spoon and then dug into the stew.

Chance snickered. "What's going on?"

"Dunno." Camden shrugged.

"You came to forage for food?"

"Actually," Camden said around a mouthful. "I want to know about the nanny."

Chance clamped his teeth around the metal spoon. He forced himself to swallow the last bite, noting that his breakfast had lost its taste. He dropped the spoon into the half-eaten stew can and set it on the counter. "Mary Poppins?"

"Who the hell's that? You mean Jane Singleton?"

Chance scrubbed a hand over his jaw, working it side to side, as he picked the best way to handle what should've been an easy question. "Yeah. They're the same person." He crossed his arms. "Why?"

Camden cocked his dark eyebrows and half-laughed. "Why'd you think?"

For an ugly second, Chance assessed himself against his teammate as though Camden was just some young guy from Jersey. Chance decided his superiority, from looks to—he stopped short and could've kicked his own ass. How often had Chance futilely tried to ignore his own appearance? He wasn't blind. He knew he was a good-looking guy. Good looks caused more grief than they were worth.

But yet, at the mention of Jane, he wanted to call upon physical traits to one-up a teammate? Nope. That was a dick move. If Chance wanted Jane's attention, he'd get it another way. "She's nice."

"Nice?"

His back molars ground, but he managed, "If you think you have a shot—"

"*Me?*" Camden hooted. "What the hell? No, man. What's up with *you* and Mary Poppins?"

He shoved his hands into his pockets. What the hell? Boss Man tore into him for *impressing* Jane. Now Camden had questions? "Nothing."

"Right." Camden smirked. "Because that wasn't you who held her on the flight back in."

The back of his neck heated. "On the helicopter? She'd been through hell." He rolled his eyes. "Tell me you didn't come over this morning to bust my balls over the nanny."

"Her name's Jane."

Tension vibrated up his spine. "I *know* her name."

Again, Camden laughed. "Easy, buddy. I'm here for the food."

"Which you have." Chance gestured. "You gonna leave now?"

Slowly, Camden set the stew can on the counter. "It's interesting, ya know. I ask you about Jane. Then you tell me to take a hike."

"You need to get out more if you find *that* interesting."

"You like her, huh?"

"Jesus, dude. Are you trying to get under my skin?"

Camden flipped his hands up defensively. "No, jackass. I was trying to make fucking conversation, but I guess that isn't going to fly."

Chance walked out of the kitchenette and settled onto the couch. He hunched over. His forearms rested on his legs, and his fingers steepled together under his chin. "She surprised me. That's all."

Camden picked his can of stew off the counter and ambled over to the chair across the room. Chance used more as a coat rack than for company, and it was piled high with hoodies. Camden knocked the clothes to the ground, sat down and kicked back. "What are you going to do about it?"

Chance looked up. "Her?"

"Yeah. It. Her. *Mary Poppins.*" Camden's forehead creased as though he'd been asked if an alien Santa lived on the sun. "What the hell else are we talking about?"

"It's not that easy."

Camden snorted. "Never would've taken you for a pussy."

Chance squinted and shook his head. "Are you only capable of conversing in streams of insults?"

"Yeah. Got a problem with that?"

Chance snorted and tried to remember that Camden was younger than all of them. He could hold his own and knew what to do—but he was still green and inexperienced. Chance had never seen himself as the older and wiser type. Mentoring a teammate never crossed his mind. But Mary

Poppins had shown him that the unexpected had a way of making itself known. Even if Chance wasn't a good mentor, he could push Camden in the right direction. "How old are you?"

Camden straightened his shoulders, and the corners of his eyes tightened. "Fucking old enough."

From out of nowhere, one of his grandmother's saying thundered to mind. *Rudeness is a sign of insecurity.* His amusement faded, and Chance met Camden's hard, dark stare. They both had uncertainties, and Chance wouldn't let those issues caused problems on their team. "Want another can of stew?"

Uncertainty ticked in Camden's jaw.

"I could use another." Even though Chance hadn't finished the first can. He stood up without waiting for an answer and walked to the kitchenette, pulling out two new cans. "Yeah?"

"Yeah. All right."

Chance gave another can to Camden and decided that he would mentor the guy along in his time on Aces. Whether Camden knew it or not, he had a long way to go.

CHAPTER TWENTY-SEVEN

THEIR BULLSHIT AND bluster changed. Chance and Camden ate their beef stew breakfast and joked over the WARNING sign that had been taped to the war room door. Camden swore up and down that he hadn't been the one to hang it up. Chance wasn't sure he believed him, but it didn't matter.

After their breakfast of champs, Camden left. Chance felt as though he'd done a good deed for the day. Not only would a better partnership pay off in the field, but now he had another buddy to shoot the shit with.

More importantly, chilling out with Camden forced his mind to focus on his current mission: finding Jane.

Angela had been surprisingly less than helpful when he'd asked her for Jane's room number. No matter. He was a determined man. If he'd have to sweet talk the hotel receptionist or canvas the building, he'd find her.

Chance grabbed his phone and hustled down thirteen flights of stairs. He ducked through newly hung plastic tarp and exited their hotel. The overpowering sun hit him like a steamroller. The day would be nearly as hot as their jaunt through the desert, and he arranged for a car service as he walked to Jane's hotel.

The quick walk took far too long. Finally, he pushed through the opulent hotel entrance. A shower of cold air rolled over him as he ambled into the marbled lobby. The tiles beneath his feet probably cost more than his childhood home. He tried to ignore the excess. Gold on the walls. Gold inlaid on the floors. With every step, he saw excessive wealth, and Chance wondered how the world had strayed from the idea that simple could be exceptional.

Like the woman he spotted across the lobby. Chance couldn't see much beyond her long, red dress. But, as she faced the opposite direction, he couldn't help but appreciate her elegant simplicity while sitting on an ornate bench.

The woman on the backless bench kept his attention, even as she ducked from his gaze as she bent to the side to adjust her sandal. Chance stopped abruptly. The hairs on the back of his neck stood like a porcupine's quills. The familiar sensation served him well on the job. But he wasn't in danger. He was breathless and only beginning to understand why.

The woman sat up, and her long blond hair draped over her covered shoulders. Though he couldn't see her face, there wasn't a question about who she was. Jane was the only person who'd ever made him react like he might not survive if he walked the other way.

Chance savored the realization and took his time as he approached. Nerves tingled along his forearm. The corners of his lips curled in a way he couldn't shake. She smoothed the flowing skirt over her legs and picked up a travel brochure from a pile by her side. He was close enough to see a photograph of Sheikh Zayed Grand Mosque Center and then quietly, he sat down on his side of the bench, facing the opposite direction.

Only her pile of tourist brochures separated them. Chance picked up the top flyer up and leaned toward Jane. "You can't go to that mosque until later."

She twisted. Surprise lit her features in a way that did something painfully amazing to his chest. "*Chance?*"

He grinned and flicked the brochure in his hand. "But this place is great, and it's open now."

She wrapped her arms around him. "Hi."

"Hey, MP." He savored the way she fit against him, and he drew out the seconds it took to return her hug. Holding her was somehow exactly the same as he'd done in the desert. His protective, possessive instincts hummed in his chest. He inhaled, and his mouth watered. The scent of jasmine, rich and fragrant, reminded him of early fall, when the days were warm as summer but the nights crept in, early and cool. Now, it would remind him of her, too.

They pulled apart and set down their tourist brochures.

"Look at you," she said with a nervous laugh. "You're so... *clean.*"

"Ha." He'd been hoping for something like "handsome beyond reason," but clean was fine—of course it was fine. Since when did he want to lean on a crutch of looks? "So are you."

"Clean is exactly what I was going for. But..." She looked down at the modest red dress and picked up the flowing skirt with a small shrug. "This isn't exactly my usual style and color. But what can you do? My luggage is long gone."

"Sorry. We're not big on rescuing luggage. Just people."

"I know." She folded her hands and repositioned her legs, crossing them at the ankle. "I wasn't complaining, and Angela had several options available in my closet. But they were so... bright."

"Why don't you like bright?"

"It's so..." She raised her hands and threw her fingers out like they were fireworks. "*Bright.*" Jane laughed. "I much rather blend in."

He could appreciate that. "They taking good care of you?"

"Yeah, of course. Angela's amazing."

"Did you sleep all right?"

"Eh." She seesawed her hand. "I never sleep well in strange beds."

"Oh, yeah? But you slept pretty well in the desert." He laughed.

Her cheeks pinked. "That wasn't *really* sleeping."

"It was. I remember." Chance leaned close and dropped his voice. "There's the possibility you might've snored."

She swatted his arm playfully. "Never."

He bumped his shoulder to hers. Jane hadn't snored but damn he liked making her eyes go wide and her smile light. "Maybe even a little bit of drool."

"Absolutely not." She rolled her eyes, blushing furiously.

He leaned back, pretending to think back to their night together. It wasn't a hard memory to search for. "All right. Maybe you didn't snore or drool, but I saw you sleep."

Jane met his eye for a moment.

I saw you sleep. They were both replaying what he had said. What a simple statement. Except it had been anything but simple.

"No." She glanced away with a self-deprecating laugh. "Not sleep. That's what you'd call a full-body shutdown brought on by complete exhaustion and near-death experiences." She brushed her hair off her shoulder, not meeting his gaze. "What about you? Sleep well?"

He snapped. "Out like a light."

Jane tilted her head, and then she grinned as though she'd learned a secret.

"What?"

"I heard you were called to the principal's office."

Chance chuckled and imagined Jared Westin as a high school principal, ruler in hand and glowering from behind a desk. "Something like that."

"What happened?"

He waved her concern away. "Nothing. Don't worry about it."

"If you say so." She swept a lock of blond hair off her face and twirled it around her finger. "Hey—did you know that the Thanes left?"

"Not initially."

Her forehead furrowed as though he'd answered incorrectly. "Really?"

Chance lifted a shoulder. "Angela mentioned it today when I gave her a quick call. Why?"

Jane studied him and then ducked her chin. "I don't know. I'm just surprised they left me here, high and dry. Sort of sucks."

Well, hell. Here he was, ready to make plans without considering that she didn't want to be in Abu Dhabi. "Sorry about that."

"No, it's a good reminder. I work for them. I'm not family." Her bitter tone matched the way she thinned her lips. It was as though she didn't want to care but couldn't help it.

Perhaps a date wasn't in the cards. He'd still help her out. "I can help you get back home if Angela wasn't able—"

"Oh, no. She could, and I appreciate that." Jane took a quick breath. "But I decided it might be good to let Gigi fend for herself while I take a mini vacation at their expense."

"Yeah. They owe you that much." He tapped the pile of travel brochures. "What's on your agenda?"

"No idea. I'm an Abu Dhabi virgin. I haven't been anywhere outside of the United States, really."

Lord help him. His body jerked to life at the word virgin like he was a kid in the midst of puberty. Chance shifted and cleared his throat. "You should see the sights." And, he should ask her to go with him. What the fuck was wrong with him? "With me," he tacked on.

Mission somewhat accomplished. Not an articulate invitation. But, apparently, the best he could manage.

Jane curled her fingers into her skirt, fidgeting. "You don't have to be my tour guide."

There was literally nothing he would rather do. "Jane." Chance laid his hand over hers, again feeling his body react explosively. "Spend the day with me."

She blinked as though she didn't understand his offer. "Are you sure?"

Why was this so hard? Had anyone ever turned him down? No. Chance stood on her side of the bench and pulled her to her feet. He kept his hand over hers. There wasn't any space between. In his mind, there wasn't any question as to where he wanted to be or with who he wanted to be with. "Do you need to get anything before we head out?"

Jane shook her head.

Green light. Their day together was a go. "Let's go see what we can get into."

CHAPTER TWENTY-EIGHT

J ANE TRIED TO accept that her day couldn't get much better if she'd planned it. True, her thoughts had meandered with wistful dreams about drinks with Chance. But this was absolutely surreal. He had his hand at the small of her back, guiding her out the hotel. They didn't seem to have a plan, yet she had a feeling he was never without one.

They stopped to let an elderly couple walk ahead of them. It gave Jane a minute to take in all that was Chance Evans. It was as though the sun cast a spotlight on him. His stormy blue eyes sparkled. The desert had left his skin golden and tan, and his trim, sun-lightened hair gave him clean-cut glint to his military-hardened edge.

Hands down, he was the most attractive man she'd ever met. Maybe she'd known that before, and her survival-mode brain had merely categorized him as hot. But, oh no. He was leaps and bounds beyond hot.

Now that Chance was well-rested and wearing a nice shirt and jeans, there wasn't a question. Jane wouldn't have been surprised if he'd been a model in a previous life. Not the kind of model that walked runways, but the models who reigned king of the perfume commercials. The kind where he would lay on a beach and let waves crash over his sculpted stomach and thighs—and, now she was a first-class pervert.

In a way, the perverted title fit, given her blistered and burned ogre-like appearance. Couldn't he see how she looked? Or, had the bright dress done the impossible and allowed Jane's damaged skin to blend into the fiery red fabric?

"Here we go." Chance led her to a waiting sedan.

"You ordered a car?"

"It's hotter than hell and I don't want to worry about parking."

Pragmatic. But when had he done that? She let him help her into the car and realized that he'd planned the car service before they talked. What did that mean?

The sedan whisked them into the fast-paced stream of traffic. Jane gawked out the window. Exotic cars and pristine landscaping. She lived with one of the richest families in the world, but they didn't live like this. The streets gleamed. Locals and tourists alike seemed as gorgeous as their possessions on display. Jewelry and designer brands met the eye as far as she could see. Everything—and everyone—shined. No wonder Chance lived in Abu Dhabi. Here, he was amongst his fellow beautiful people.

The sedan pulled over. Chance opened the door before the driver had the opportunity.

"Where are we?"

"The carpet souk." He spoke briefly to their driver then led her into the market.

They were swept into the crowd. Vibrant colors dazzled them from every direction. Displays of rugs, prayer mats, and cushions mapped any and every color. They were chaotically stacked, shelved, and sold. Jane watched in rapt fascination as storekeepers and customers haggled. She eavesdropped on conversations in languages she didn't know but could still understand through tone and gestures. "This is amazing."

Chance's hand rested on her lower back. Occasionally, his fingers gave a quick squeeze as they threaded through the crowd. They pointed to interesting patterns that caught their attention. Chance liked ones that were simple. As for what she liked? After canvassing rows in the market-place, Jane still didn't have a clue what she liked best. But she'd never had more fun figuring that out. It was almost as though she were learning her own taste as they went.

The sedan waited for them as they stepped out of the far side of the carpet souk.

"Want to do that again?" he asked.

Jane laughed. "I'm not sure how many more carpets I can look at."

His grin danced. "How about something almost the same but different?"

"Why not!"

Their driver took them to the next spot—a *gold* souk—and then to a souk that sold bolts of fabric. Both were identical and completely different than the carpet souk. Jane tried on gold bangles and rings and couldn't stop laughing when Chance swathed himself in gold necklaces. They wrapped brilliant fabrics around themselves and then each other.

By the time they left the fabric souk, incense clung to their clothes and scented their hair. Jane had let loose and forgot how she looked—and maybe more importantly, how beautiful he looked. They played. She couldn't remember the last time that had happened with an adult. And, maybe, they'd flirted? They'd certainly touched a lot. Though every touch had a reason; he adjusted a pashmina on her shoulders, or she wrapped dark, exquisite silks over his shoulders, around his torso.

Their sedan awaited them again. Chance opened the door and then settled into the back seat after her. She stayed close to him and dropped her head against his shoulder. "I am *exhausted*." She expected him to laugh or agree and cast her eyes to his. "You're not?"

"Maybe we should've done something more low-key."

She sat up. "What? No! I loved that. Why—"

"I forgot everything you've been through."

"Ha." She choked on her laugh. "Liar."

His brow furrowed. "Meaning what?"

All day long, Jane hadn't a clue where they were headed next, but she was certain he couldn't forget where they'd been. One look at her, and he could see the evidence of their time in the desert. She was pocked, peeling, bandages, and just plain ugly. Jane shook her head and then watched the landscape pass by.

"Hey."

She didn't look away from the window. "Hm?"

"Jane?"

He wasn't going to let this drop. Next time, she should control her thoughts better. Jane pulled a deep breath then looked at him.

His eyes were tight and assessing. "Why would I lie about forgetting?"

Her stomach turned. "Please don't pretend. Okay? It doesn't make me feel any better."

"Jane—what are you talking about?"

Incredulous, she tilted her chin up to give him a good look at her neck. She tugged a dress strap to the side of her shoulder and then let go, opting to just hold out her arms.

The man had the gall to feign cluelessness. Was this supposed to make her feel better? Did she need to pull up the long skirt and remind him how her legs looked? No, she didn't have to do that. Even though the dress offered a great deal of coverage, it showed enough bare skin that she shouldn't have to parade wounds to make her point. "Don't act like I'm not a walking, talking billboard for the dangers of the desert."

His forehead creased. "What are you talking about?"

Tears burned the back of her throat. Her sunburned face had to be greasy with the amount of lotions and ointments she'd applied. Chance couldn't have missed that. But, just in case, she framed her face with her dry, cracked hands, disgusted and embarrassed. "I did everything I could to hide what I look like. But I'm not blind." Tears spilled down her cheeks. "I look like a leper."

"Jane…"

She shook her head. "I get it. It's cool. You're being nice. But you can't pretend you forgot. And you certainly can't pretend that people haven't stared at us like we're a backward Beauty and the Beast."

His mouth hinged but nothing came out.

CHAPTER TWENTY-NINE

I F CHANCE HAD had an assault rifle pointed at his nuts, he wouldn't have been able to come up with Jane's explanation. "Wait—*what?*"

Even as that fell out of his mouth, stuttering through what felt like a mouthful of cotton, he knew there were better things he should've said. But his brain wasn't connecting the dots in a meaningful way. The nerve endings that should've conveyed a response did nothing.

Jane had sunburn. The most painful he'd come across. Burns and blisters sucked. He didn't deny that. But so the fuck what? They went away and had *nothing* on the woman. Inside *and* out. Because, again, gun to his nuts, he'd swear the truth. Jane made his dick jump to attention.

"You're..." Hot. Sexy. Lush. Sexy. Sexy. Fucking sexy *again*. More than that, Chance wanted to tell her that she was wrong, and even if she weren't, he didn't care.

She wiped a rogue tear. "Don't."

His heart twisted. She was *beautiful*. But so fucking what? That wasn't what made his cock jump in his goddamn jeans. She was smart and strong with a lot of sass behind deceptively innocent eyes. Jane was sweet and caring. And, brave. He swallowed hard. "I can come up with a hundred thousand reasons why you're incredible."

"I look like a freak."

"Yeah, okay. So you say. I disagree."

Her gaze flitted away. "Even if I wasn't—" She lurched back. "Oh, God. Come on. I mean, I'm shedding on you."

He laughed.

"Do *not* laugh at me."

"Jane—"

"You don't get it." She shook her head. "If I wasn't burnt to a crisp, smelling like a medicinal coconut, aloe—"

"For the fucking record, you smell like a flower."

Her brow furrowed as if he'd started singing in Greek. "Compared to you, I'm plain—" Her eyes widened, then she nodded as if she'd finally uncovered a secret. "Plain Jane. I normally blend in, except when I finally stand out, I'm like a flaky…" She gestured. "A flaky something red. Apple. Or, lobster."

"Kind of a cute lobster."

She slugged him in the chest.

Chance caught her hand between his palms and held her fists to his sternum. "Careful there, Mary Poppins. I'm not sure I trust myself around you if want to get physical."

She gasped, half-heartedly yanking her arm, but he held firm. He could feel her pulse thunder under his palm, and Chance didn't know what he was doing, but he didn't plan to let her go just yet.

His day had been a rollercoaster. At the first souk, Chance decided he'd never been more drawn to a woman. But, by the last souk, he knew they couldn't have a future. Their jobs kept them on opposite sides of the globe. No matter what her opinion of the Thanes, she cared about that boy. It was crazy and unfair that he wondered whether or not she might leave Teddy while she wrapped silk fabric around his stomach.

The driver slowed in front of a restaurant Chance had planned for dinner. It didn't cater to tourists but still had the splash that the city was known for. The sedan came to a stop. His thumb caressed her wrist before he released her hand. "Hungry?"

"I'm not sure."

He chuckled. "That's a better answer than no." The driver opened his door. Chance stepped into the heat and waited for Jane to join him.

Tentatively, she stepped out. He offered her his arm, and when she took it, he led her through an opulent arched doorway, and he held the door open for her. "Want to get a drink first?"

"I could use one."

She excused herself to the bathroom while Chance spoke with the hostess. When Jane returned, he led her to an elevator which them took to a rooftop bar.

The bar was more crowded than he expected, but he found a small table next to the glass rail that overlooked a bustling market below as the orange sun melted against the horizon.

A server greeted them, offering the drink list, and introducing himself as Sagar.

Jane looked it over after Sagar departed. "What are you having?"

He skipped the cocktails and perused the extensive beer list. "I don't know."

Sagar returned, and Jane handed him her drink list. "I'd like to try a great beer that's not readily available in the US."

Sagar interest had been piqued. "Would you consider a flight that would meet your request?"

Chance grinned, raising his eyebrows. "I'm good with that if you are."

"That's perfect."

"Sweet." He flipped the menu over. "What about something to eat before dinner?"

Jane nodded. "I'm good with whatever."

"Yeah, but what do you want?" He nudged her drink list closer to her. "Other than the moutabal sitti, because I'm not leaving this place without trying it."

She rolled her lips together, smiling as she reviewed the menu. "And, the labneh with mint."

"Nice choice." Chance nodded and thanked Sagar. Once they were alone, he admitted, "I pegged you as a fruity cocktail girl."

Her eyebrows arched as she playfully shook her head. "You'd be wrong."

"So I keep learning."

Jane rolled her lips tightly and then laughed. "When I first met you, there was a small chance." She pinched her fingers together. "That I thought you were wrong *a lot*."

"Shocking."

"I thought you couldn't tell," Jane laughed and brushed her hair back.

"What else have you been wrong about?"

He snorted. "When you're around, I'm starting to think *everything*."

Their flight of beer arrived and cut off her response. Chance let his attention linger on her before appraising the small glasses that rested on a skinny wooden plate. The beer samples were arranged in color from lightest to darkest.

"You choose first." He waited as she picked the lightest beer. He selected its opposite; the darkest sample. "Cheers to those who have seen us at our worst and our best but can't tell the difference."

The corners of her eyes tightened, and she waited a beat. "Cheers."

His lips quirked and then they sipped the beers. After trying the other samples, they agreed that Sagar had done right by them.

The cold mezzes plates arrived, and their conversation died as they devoured the dishes.

"Guess I was hungrier than I realized," Jane admitted with a laugh. "And it was delicious. All of this is so... amazing."

"A little trendier than my style." He shrugged. "But I couldn't do this all the time like you."

"*Me?*"

"You know. Living life with the Thanes. Everything perfect and just, I don't know—" he snapped, "arrives when you want it."

"That's how you picture my life?"

He chuckled. "The Thanes are as close to royalty as Americans can get."

"Oh, no." Her nose wrinkled. "Their lifestyle is way out-there, but it's not for me. I'm more of a homebody."

A homebody he met in Syria...

Jane tilted her head. "What's that look?"

"I'm a bit of one too."

She leaned forward and dropped her voice. "Want to know a secret?"

"Always."

"During the summer, Teddy and I sit in the backyard when the sun goes down, and we watch the fireflies."

"Nice." Chance wondered how hard Liam's global commute was.

"Why's that a secret?"

"If he's up late, Dax and Gigi would prefer he attend events with paparazzi and photo lines."

Teddy's parents were first-class douche canoes. "I'd watch fireflies with you guys."

A sweet grin curled on her lips. "Wouldn't that be crazy."

He finished the last swig of a beer, thinking it wouldn't be *that* crazy.

Wistfully, she glanced over the glass rail. The sun had sank behind the horizon, painting the sky a deep orangish-red that wouldn't last. It deepened the red of her dress and warmed the lightness of her hair. He wouldn't have noticed the light at any other time. But now, her sunset-cloaked image burn into his memory. "What should we do tomorrow?"

She met his gaze. "I'm leaving tomorrow."

Oh, right. Here today, gone tomorrow. Likely never to cross paths again. "So…" He didn't know what should happen next. Asking her to go home with him seemed like the obvious and cliché thing to do. Plus, Chance was certain she'd demure. He didn't blame her. There was something odd about a one-night stand with a woman he wanted to see again. "Do you need to head back?"

"Not necessarily."

What the hell did that mean? Was that a vague way of asking to go back to his place? Chance leaned closer and whispered, "I don't know what the hell that means, Mary Poppins."

Her eyes brightened, and she mimicked his behavior. "You don't have to babysit me all day and night. I'm sure you have things to do."

Wait. What? He jerked back. "Do you always put others before yourself? Or, only when I'm around. Because I can't tell if you're—"

Her shoulders stiffened. "I'm a nanny."

"That's a job. Not who you are."

"Sometimes that's not true. Look at you—"

"Me?"

She bit her bottom lip. "Why do you have your job?"

"Easy. Because I feel a sense of duty."

Jane smiled as though Chance had walked into her trap. "A lot of jobs could fulfill a sense of duty. But you live where the job says. I bet you only socialize with your teammates. Unless, there's a woman you meet on the job—"

"I *never* meet women on the job—present company excluded." He held her gaze until she pulled away.

"You are your job, too."

He pursed his lips, knowing that his fuckin' job was keeping him from whisking her off this rooftop bar and into his bedroom. She wouldn't be a one-night stand if not for Aces. Chance pulled his bottom lip into his mouth, frustrated and not wanting to admit defeat. But she'd made her point.

Abruptly, he stood and tossed his napkin on the table. "Let's go."

Carefully, Jane folded her napkin and placed it on the table, then pushed out of her chair. He moved close enough to rest his hands on her hips and yank her close. Instead, he shoved his fists into his pockets, refusing to step back. His heart thudded, knowing that only a few inches of space remained between her warm, soft body and his.

Jane angled her head back to meet his gaze. "Where are we going?"

A server brushed by. They stepped out of the way, and Chance seized the excuse to rest his hand on the small of her back. "Hell if I know."

Then without another word, he guided her across the rooftop bar. A hot wind blew over them. Flowering vines lined their path to the elevators. Their thick green leaves rustled.

She stopped and turned. "What are we doing?"

That was one hell of a loaded question, and far harder to answer than where were they going. Except, Chance knew the answer. He'd been falling for her. That was the truth, whether it was a good idea or not. "No idea." Which was an absolute lie, but he followed it up with the God's honest truth. "But I'm not ready to stop."

CHAPTER THIRTY

JANE COULDN'T MOVE. She couldn't breathe. Chance had locked her in place with quiet words and his all-consuming presence. Her back touched a wall covered with plants. He towered over her and arousal hummed around them.

She had no idea what to do. The most beautiful man she'd ever met was acting as though he might kiss her. The possibility terrified her. She didn't want the moment to end, and she'd never survive the certain disappointment that would course over his face if he, for some insane reason, actually kissed her.

The elevator chimed. A talkative group exited, and Jane threw herself out of Chance's reach, practically running to the safety of the open elevator.

He followed behind her and reached over Jane's shoulder to catch the elevator door as it tried to close on her.

Jane scurried through the doors, mumbling, "Thanks."

"Sure."

When the doors finally shut, Chance pressed the button for the first floor and stayed on the opposites side of the small space. Between them, Jane stared at the ornately patterned floor that looked as though it were drawn with gold.

Thankfully, Chance had more manners than she did. He was a perfect gentleman, not asking why she sprinted away. She couldn't imagine what he must've thought, and her cheeks flamed.

The elevator made its slow descent, and Chance pulled out his phone, typing until they arrived on the first floor.

Finally, she glanced at him as they stepped out. His casual demeanor was a lesson in cool. Nothing could faze him. He slowly ambled out, and she self-consciously walked by his side. They passed through a small hallway then he held open the door as they exited, acting as though nothing had just happened.

Well, *nothing* had happened.

Maybe nothing had even been about to happen. Jane could have projected her fantasy into a perfectly benign conversation.

Their driver waited for them at the curb, and they slid into the back seat. Chance was still cool as cucumber. Her embarrassment grew, and she recalled his words. *No idea* what they were doing. Of course not, because they didn't make sense! She could've slapped herself on the forehead.

The car sped off. She didn't trust her voice enough to ask where they were going. It would kill her when they arrived at her hotel. She didn't want to end the night like this, didn't understand what Chance saw in her—or didn't—and Jane wanted to scream.

"We're here."

This wasn't her hotel. How long had she zoned out? They couldn't have been in the car for that long. Their driver opened the door, but she didn't see the bright lights that lined Abu Dhabi's now-dark streets.

Chance helped her out. The sounds of the city became clearer. Jane chewed on her bottom lip and scanned the dark parking lot. There wasn't much to see beyond a large partition. Perhaps it was a retaining wall. Then she realized scent of water hung in the air. "What are we doing?"

"We're going kayaking."

Jane turned toward Chance and could faintly see his face. "Did you notice that night fell?"

His lips quirked. "I did." With a tilt of his head and a grin that was more than enough to make her heart trip, he led them toward a dock.

She'd grown up in Pensacola and had seen her fair share of docks. By those standards, this dock was *nice*. Just like everything else in Abu Dhabi. Chance took her hand and pulled her stiffly around the gate. He didn't let go. Her gait only became more awkward as they walked by a deckhouse.

And that's when she saw the kayaks that stole her breath. "*Chance?*" The kayaks glowed. "Those are..." She didn't have words. Kayaks weren't beautiful things. Yet, the two that floated side by side *were*. They left her breathless. She turned to him, met his eye, and know *he* had made her breathless.

"Greetings, Mr. Evans!"

She turned toward the voice as a stout man emerged from the shadows. His belly was as large as his smile. "Welcome!"

The men spoke as though this activity had been quickly planned. She couldn't look away from the kayaks. Underwater lights were attached at the front of each, and the result was magical.

"Cool, huh?" Chance stepped to her side. "I always wanted to do this."

Cool wasn't in the same universe. She peered over the side of the dock as they were fitted with life jackets, given woefully few instructions on how to kayak and where they could go, and before Jane knew it, the stout man situated her in one kayak. Chance floated beside to her side.

Their movement disturbed the shallow water. Clouds of sand whirled to their sides.

"Are you ready?"

"Sure," she said.

His kayak glided away, and she tried to follow her instructions. Apparently kayaking was easier said than done.

Chance called over his shoulder, "Come on, Mary Poppins."

The Disney nickname was yet another reason Jane was sure this wasn't a date. But, at the moment, she didn't care and had bigger problems: *moving*.

She fumbled with her paddles, splashing when she meant to stroke. The impossible little boat moved sideways instead of following Chance.

He glided back as easily as he'd left. "Stuck?"

"No, thank you very much." She paddled again just as fruitlessly as before. At least this was an activity she didn't mind embarrassing herself over. "I'm enjoying the view. That's all."

Chance snatched the end of her paddle.

"Hey!"

With his other hand, he effortlessly padded from his kayak, towing her along. Maybe if she hadn't run from him at the rooftop bar, this would be embarrassing. But she just laughed. "Show off."

He chuckled, easily sliding his paddle from one side to the other, not letting go of her.

"Pretty impressive, Hercules."

"Obviously, my goal."

She smiled and relaxed. Chance did all the work. It felt as though they were sliding across glass until he stopped paddling. They drifted, and he used her paddle to pull her by his side. A beautifully lit circle surrounded their boats. Beyond them, the night sky and dark water blended together into a black abyss. "I feel like we're the only people on earth." Fish darted by. Underwater plants moved with the underwater currents. "I didn't know anything like this existed."

Chance made up names for the fish, providing fantastical details about the Great Abu-Dha-bowskis and Purple People Eaters. He regaled her with impossible stories of goldfish that were strong enough to sink pirate ships and seaweed that could be used as dental floss. Jane laughed and laughed and laughed, already missing him before they said good night and goodbye.

"I've never met a guy like you before." And, she was certain that she'd never meet someone like him again.

He gave her a strange look but then joked. "Guess I'm one of a kind."

Sadly... She had to go halfway around the world to find the most interesting person she'd ever met. Forget how freakin' hot the man was. Who else would come up with this day? No one, except for Chance.

Chance paddled them closer to the dock, and they returned from where they'd set off from. The stout man reappeared out of thin air. Jane didn't know how Chance had known where and when to go, but she realized, he always had an innate sense of what came next. At least one of them did.

She was plucked from the kayak as easily as she'd been put on the water. The man took their life jackets and disappeared again. "My legs feel like wet noodles."

He slung his arm around her shoulder, and she didn't pull away. They ambled up the dock, and she breathed in the faint scent of their day together. She'd never smell incense again without thinking of souks—and him. Jane wished she hadn't run from Chance on the rooftop.

Embarrassment had changed into regret, and she wished he'd forget what had happened and would kiss her now. She wouldn't run. *Chance, kiss me.* Jane slowed. The dock ended soon. The sedan would be in the parking lot. This was their last moment alone.

He paused then stepped in front of her. Her pleading heart clenched, and she dared to lift her chin, to meet his stare.

Chance towered over her. With the city lights and sounds held at bay, with the moonlight streaming down upon his chiseled face, she couldn't look away. He gazed at her as if hungry and tormented, as though she caused him pain that he simply *craved*.

A warm breeze rolled off the water, loosening her hair. He tucked the wayward strands behind her ear.

"You did that in the desert."

He touched her hair again and then his knuckles swept over her cheek. Jane's eyes fluttered shut. Her lips parted, and Chance trailed his fingers across them. Her breath weighed heavy in her chest. His fingertips skimmed over her chin, her jaw with a touch fainter than air. Jane quietly moaned as his touch slid down the strumming pulse in her neck.

Cold electricity bled over her when he pulled away. Jane almost protested—until his hands threaded into her hair. Chance tilted her head, and Jane trembled. Their bodies touched. The anticipation of his lips on hers made her weak—a brash chirp of a cellphone blared.

She jumped then lurched back. Her hands covered her face. Jane didn't know if she would scream, cry, or curse. Chance cursed, long and low before he opened his eyes again. His jaw ticked, and his hand went to his side. "Sorry. That's an emergency call from headquarters."

Jane blinked hard. "Sure. Of course."

Chance stepped back as he answered the phone. "Yeah?" He listened and rubbed a hand over his face, into his hair. "*Yeah.*" He dropped his head back. "No. She's here." He paused, shaking his head. "*Yeah. With me.*" He hung up, pocketed the phone, and when he finally turned to her, she thought he might smash his phone. "Or, as it turns out, *not* an emergency call."

"They called about me?"

"Angela was worried and jumped up HQ's ass to make sure you were okay."

"I'm okay," Jane whispered.

Their moment was gone. Judging by the blissful seconds before his phone rang, she was sure that she'd missed out on the world's best kiss *ever*.

CHAPTER THIRTY-ONE

A PHONE CALL shouldn't have changed a thing, but Chance would be lying if he didn't sense the mood sober. Perhaps, there was a reason for the interruption—like he had no business kissing their client. Too bad Jane Singleton clouded his mind from the moment they clashed in Syria. Soon, she'd be gone. Abu Dhabi would be a distant memory, and he couldn't afford that kind of distraction.

"So." He shifted his weight onto his heels. "We should go before Angela requests a search squadron to confirm proof of life."

"Sure. It's late anyway."

Chance didn't miss the forced edge to Jane's nonchalant response. "Right."

They returned to the waiting sedan. With barely a word, their driver whisked them toward her hotel. Jane sat close to his side, but their tension wasn't the same. He wished the night wouldn't end. Or, maybe, he should have wished that it had never started. Everything would be easier if they'd part ways yesterday.

The driver pulled into the driveway of the hotel.

She turned sideways in her seat as though ready to sprint from him again. "I guess this is it."

Or, not. He wasn't above dragging their time out until the very end. "I'll walk you in."

Jane's skeptical look didn't confirm he'd said the right thing, but she didn't protest. Chance told the driver he'd walk home from there, releasing the man from duty, then stepped out of the car and held out his hand for Jane. She took it, joined him on the curb, but let go and stepped away. The push-pull of their tension remained. Without giving her an opportunity to shy away, Chance placed his hand on the small of her back and led her inside.

Somewhere between the front entrance and her elevator, he started to silently remind himself that walking Jane to her room didn't mean inviting himself into her bed.

The elevator arrived. His jaw tightened, and he steeled himself not to go upstairs. Chance gave her side a squeeze and urged her into the empty car. "Have a good night, Jane."

"Oh." She spun to face him instead. "I didn't realize this was—" The doors eased together. She twisted and stuck her arm out to catch them. They re-opened, and she turned to him again. "That this was goodbye. I thought you were coming upstairs." She blushed. "I mean. Not *coming upstairs*. I didn't assume you were coming up for, ya know—" The elevator door tried to close again. "Damn it, hold on. I'm not ready—" The doors tried to close again. She slapped at them, flustered and tongue-tied.

He couldn't help himself. Chance captured Jane between his arms and strode into the elevator. Her mouth parted. He towered over her, caging her against the wall. The elevator doors closed, deadening the murmur of the hotel lobby. Only theirs racing breaths punctuated the thick silence. Her chin tilted up. Chance savored the slip of time before he took what he'd been dying to taste. Then he claimed her mouth.

Electricity scored his nerves. Jane came alive. His palms clasped her cheeks and he held her face until their tongues clashed. She knotted her fingers into the front of his shirt, twisting and pulling him closer until her knuckles sandwiched between their stomachs.

This was more than he expected. Hell, it was everything that he had needed and then some—and that was the problem. Kissing Jane wouldn't temper his desire for more, and more couldn't happen.

Reluctantly, he slowed their mouths and smoothed his hands down her neck and over her arms until he cupped her ass. She quietly moaned, and the throaty vibrations purred against his lips, making him feel as though her velvet tongue had stroked his cock.

Unable to let go, Chance flexed his fingers into her soft curves. Jane arched, and he couldn't pull himself away, instead skimming his lips to her neck. When he found a sweet spot, she blessed him with a husky moan.

His swollen erection pressed against his jeans. Uncomfortable, but he didn't care. His arousal thundered. He'd no idea it was possible to find growing, addictive satisfaction simply from worshipping this woman's neck.

The elevator doors chimed then opened. Surprised, scandalized voices disrupted their privacy. But the interruption hadn't been enough to tear them apart. Their breaths raced. Their eyes locked.

Chance swallowed hard, forcing himself to inch back. "I wasn't ready to say good night."

"That wasn't a good night kiss," she whispered.

No kidding. It was also far beyond an invitation to bed. His blood rushed, realizing that he didn't know shit about the best things in life; a list starting with Jane's insatiable kiss.

The elevator remained empty. The doors closed, and the quick trip to her floor wasn't a particularly comfortable one.

They exited and walked down her hallway. Every passing step weakened his will to say good night and leave, and then a crowded field of questions overtook his thoughts. The most basic being, why would he leave? He was selective, but Chance wasn't a goddamn monk. Judging by their kiss, the sex would be cataclysmic. Why did he hang on to the asinine idea that sleeping with Jane would screw everything up?

Jane slowed by a door and slipped her motel key from behind the top of her sundress. "This is me."

He stopped by her side, hesitating. It should've been easy to pluck the key from her hand and let them in. He wouldn't have to say a word. As soon as the door shut, they could pick up where they'd left off. But he didn't move.

Neither did she.

Shit. "Let's go in."

That wasn't strong enough to dictate what would happen next. Hell, he didn't know what he wanted to unfold in the next few minutes.

Wordlessly, Jane unlocked her door. That simple, silent agreement made his cock throb. His pulse beat in his neck. Both sensations did a bang-up job in clouding the cautionary questions of his conscience.

They stepped through the threshold. The door clicked shut, and they stood close in the darkened hallway of her suite. The only light came from the windows. The curtains had been drawn open, allowing the city's nighttime cityscape to take center stage.

"The view's amazing," Jane whispered.

God, he didn't give two shits about the view in this room unless it was her, naked, in the middle of a bed. "Uh-huh."

He pretended to marvel out the large windows as she walked them farther into her suite. Truly, the view was unforgettable. But Chance didn't want to stop looking at Jane. It might be the last night he'd see her—no—there was no *might* about it. He *wouldn't* see Jane again.

She continued to the window and placed her palms on the glass. "Beautiful but..." She tilted her head, glancing at him over her shoulder. "But nothing like everything we did today." She turned and stayed against the window. "Thanks again for that."

Chance had left a few feet between them, and he couldn't decide if that space felt like miles or millimeters. "My pleasure."

The desire to feel her skin on his overpowered most of his sane thoughts. Still... He wasn't blind. She'd pressed herself as far away from him as the woman could get. The silence hung heavy like a warning shot: Jane couldn't be a one-night stand.

He licked his bottom lip and forced a small grin. "I should go." He couldn't think of anything else to say or do, and awkwardly extended his hand.

Jane ignored his offer of a handshake and wrapped her arms around his neck. Their hug could've been very PG rated, if not for the massive hard-on her touch instantaneously inspired. He didn't want to forget the way they fit or the scent of her jasmine shampoo. His eyes sank, and he didn't pull away for a long moment.

Her arms drifted down. "Thanks for everything."

For a scary second, he thought she might cry.

Then Jane shook her head with a deprecating laugh. "It's been an adventurous few days. Saving my life, taking me kayaking."

Kissing her senseless didn't make her short list. Chance lifted his chin. *Walk away. Go. Leave. Walk out the door.* Moving his feet was like tearing concrete anchors from the ground. "Get some sleep."

"You too." Her lips pressed together. "Maybe, one day, I'll see you again."

That was what he needed to hear. The hope for the impossible. If she thought there was the slightest possibility they might meet again, he couldn't stay another minute. He kissed the top of her head then turned, not willing to face Jane when he lied. "Maybe one day."

He left in a hurry, granting himself only one look back at Jane's door, already knowing he would regret the way they'd left things—even if it was the best decision. The only decision. There wasn't another choice. Tomorrow, she would be gone, and he'd be shipped off to God only knew where.

Chance headed past the row of elevators and opted for the stairs. He flew down the steps, hoping to feel lighter as he put more distance between them. Instead, a weight bore down on his shoulders. He wanted to run back up the stairs with every passing floor. Finally, Chance arrived at the lobby and jogged out of her hotel.

The night air didn't do him good as Chance walked back to his hotel. One of the towers came into view, and Chance glued his gaze to the partially lit skyscraper. Under construction or not, that hotel was the home base for everything that mattered: Titan Group, his Aces's teammates, and his home. His job and home life were entangled, yet Chance clearly saw the difference and couldn't mix business with pleasure. Distractions would cause failure. Failing his teammates meant injury and death. Tonight, he'd made the right choice, but it sucked.

Chance trudged through the security parameters that protected the building overnight and stopped in the center of the dark, empty lobby. His boots echoed hollowly, and he tried to imagine this place as a fully operational luxury hotel. He couldn't.

Worse, Chance tried to picture the future of this young team. He wondered what other teams existed. Would his perpetually be off-the-books? He'd never worked for an organization like Titan before, and

Chance wasn't sure if teammates came and left as life dictated changes or the other way around.

He pinched the bridge of his nose, frustrated that answers didn't surface. Chance walked up several flights of stairs and let himself into an area that would one day become their war room. For now, it was an empty space, sparsely decorated with wires that dangled from the exposed ceiling and piles of metal framing, yet to be soldered together.

He meandered to a metal fold-up chair and eased into it. The cold frame squeaked under his weight. Chance leaned back onto two legs and stared at an empty wall. One day, it would hold the best equipment the intel community had at their disposal. Everything would be different...

Chance let the front legs of the chair drop. The harsh sound reverberated in the empty room. He rubbed a hand over his face and wondered how Jared knew how to envision the future. It seemed to come effortlessly. Boss Man met with architects and security experts, redesigning a hotel from the inside out, just as easily as he had created Titan Group's teams of military operators. Chance respected Jared for many reasons. But he didn't envy Boss Man's ability to foresee impossible ideas and force them into fruition.

What would it feel like to be aware of such potential? He dropped his chin and cursed, realizing that it had to be similar to falling in love.

CHAPTER THIRTY-TWO

JANE'S FITFUL SLEEP had done nothing to ease her heartache. The sun had come up too early, shining through the windows. She had pulled herself from bed, wondering what parts—if any—of this city would remind Chance of their time together. Maybe none, but she'd be hard-pressed to forget anything.

How had she let this happen? She'd had fallen for him in a way that made air hard to breathe. Now, sitting in the backseat of a chauffeured Mercedes with Angela on the way to the airport, Jane still couldn't catch her breath—or ignore the sad, dull ache in her chest.

Angela momentarily looking up from her constantly buzzing phone and gave Jane a long look. "Are you okay?"

Jane leaned against the window. "Not really."

She'd said that in such a way that Angela could understand. There was nothing to discuss. No words that could help.

Silence hung over the remainder of the drive, only broken when the Mercedes pulled into a private entrance and the chauffeur spoke with the security officer. Their short conversation led to the entry barricade lifting. The sedan glided onto the tarmac, and they stopped planeside. The driver opened Angela's door, assisted them as they stepped into the bright light, and then he removed a small carry-on bag from the trunk.

For a pathetic second, Jane hoped that carry-on bag was for Chance, that he would surprise her at the airport like he did when she'd arrived.

"This bag is for you." Angela added an unnatural chipper tilt into her voice. "There's a pair of shorts and a tank top for you to change into if you want more Western clothes. I also brought a pair of pants and a sweater." She handed the bag to Jane. "You never know how cold flights can be."

Jane glanced at the luxury private jet. "You didn't have to—"

"Nonsense." She shooed away the wayward compliment. "It's my job, and it was far more fun to pick clothes for you than to make sure the guys have their jock itch powder or whatever."

Jane laughed. Out of the corner of her eye, she saw another vehicle approach. Her stomach flipped as the SUV stopped next to the Mercedes.

Hope layered upon hope, and she almost prayed that Chance would open the door. Hagan did instead. Disappointment tightened her throat.

Angela touched her arm. All signs of her chipper attitude had disappeared. The corners of her lips tightened, offering a worried smile. "Are you okay?"

"I'm tired." They both knew that was a truth and a lie. Angela possessed a sharp ability to assess a situation, and given too long together, Jane would admit she'd committed the ultimate party foul and fallen in love with her white knight.

Fallen *in love*?

Oh no. No, no, no. She'd *fallen* for Chance. That was leap years away from fallen *in love*.

"My contact information is in there, too." Angela angled closer. "If you ever need to talk."

Jane didn't want to talk. She was panicking! Falling for Chance. Falling in love with Chance. How had her mind confused the two? They weren't the same thing. Like vanilla yogurt and vanilla ice cream. Both were great. But there was a time and place for yogurt. The breakfast table. After a workout. Snack time after a playdate. Ice cream, however, wasn't an everyday occurrence.

Was Chance ice cream or yogurt? Jane pressed her fingers to her temples. She was losing her mind. "I need to go home." Jane muttered a quick thanks to Angela, grabbed the bag, and hurried onto the jet.

The jet's cool, dry air and quiet white noise surrounded Jane as she disappeared into the aircraft. The pilot and an attendant greeted her, but she didn't make sense of their words. It wasn't until a hand squeezed her shoulder and Jane whirled that she snapped out of her fog.

Hagan watched her carefully from behind mirrored sunglasses. He took them off, gave a nod to the pilot and attendant—as if to say, *don't worry, I'll handle this one.* Then he gestured. "Is that your only bag?"

Her gaze dropped to the carry-on dangling in her hand. "Yes."

"I'll stow it."

She let him take it from her hand and let the attendant guide her to a seat. Jane stared out the window, feeling pathetic and foolish. The distinction of how she felt for Chance didn't matter. Especially not when her subconscious had concocted an insane idea that he might surprise her again at the airport. She could almost picture him in place of Hagan, holding a dozen red roses like her life was a Hallmark Channel Christmas movie.

But no, her life was far closer to a *True Hollywood Story.* She dropped her forehead into her hands.

Hagan settled close by and quietly conversed with the attendant, ordering a bottled water, then met Jane's eye. "You okay?"

Wow, that question came up a lot. She shrugged. "Do we have the plane to ourselves?"

He nodded.

"I didn't think I'd have company."

The attendant came by and offered luxurious blankets. She accepted. Hagan declined and flicked his sunglasses over his eyes again. "I have a training session and someone I need to see. Figured I'd hitch a ride."

Someone special? It didn't matter. She tugged the blanket to her chest. "Does that happen a lot?"

Hagan paused, then admitted, "No."

She couldn't tell if he hadn't wanted to disappoint her or if she were projecting her misery with such force that he didn't know what to say.

"I planned on sleeping." He reclined his chair and crossed his arms over his chest. "You okay with that?"

Jane translated his meaning as "I promise, I won't talk to you" and then laughed to herself. "So long as you don't snore too loudly."

"If you go to sleep also, you'll never know."

She should've laughed but couldn't.

Hagan's amusement faltered. "Look, Jane. Sorry you were stuck with me."

Versus Chance? She clutched the blanket with a BS-nonchalant shrug.

He quietly assessed her, then added, "I have a sister who worries. I like to visit. It keeps the family happy."

"Sounds like you're a good brother." And, it sounded as though his team wasn't always in the Middle East. Chance made it sound like they were.

"Do you have family?" he asked.

She pursed her lips. "Not so much. Why does your sister worry?"

Hagan snort-laughed. "She thinks I spend my days igniting dynamite while hanging with the devil."

Jane arched her brows. "That's a lot."

His laughter died. "She has her reasons, but that imagination of hers doesn't help."

Jane sighed and peered out the window. "It's easy to let wild ideas run away."

The jet taxied down the runway. The engines roared, ending their conversation. She settled into her seat and watched out the window as land and water became farther away. They reached a cruising altitude and clouds obscured the view. She glanced at Hagan as he uncapped his water.

"Thought you were going to fall asleep."

"Maybe. Unless you need anything."

Without thinking it through, she blurted, "Is Chance dating anyone?"

Hagan choked on his water. When he finished coughing, he wiped his chin with the back of his hand and capped the water bottle. "Midas?"

She didn't know what had prompted the question, but now that she'd asked Hagan already about Chance, it didn't seem to matter if she pressed. "Is there another Evans on your team?"

"No. Not that I know." Hagan twisted the bottle cap many times over though it was clearly secured in place.

"Does he usually hang out with you and your teammates?"

"Yeah."

"What about people you pick up along the way?" Jane's fingers knotted under the blanket.

"You mean like..." Hagan stared at the ceiling.

When she figured he'd never finish his example, she clarified. "Women."

"Women," he repeated.

"That you rescue."

"Rescues don't make up a majority of our jobs."

She snickered and closed her eyes. Her uncle had taught something just as important as martial arts; how to call a bluff in poker. Evasion. It was at the root of all defensive tricks. Right now, Hagan was the poster child of dodging and avoidance. "You're not very good at covering for your friends."

He scowled. "I'm not covering for anyone."

"You're not being up front."

He flipped his water bottle and caught it. "You're asking open-ended questions."

She sort of liked how he wouldn't lie to her but continued to protect his friend, not knowing why she was asking. "Has Chance..." Oh, she didn't want to dig into specifics. "Dated..." Date seemed like an all-encompassing generalization. "The *few* women that your team has rescued?"

He glared. "Jeez, you're an undercover ballbuster."

"I'm curious." *And pathetically obvious to the point that everyone asks if I'm okay.*

Hagan flipped his water bottle. They hit turbulence, and his water jerked out of reach. It landed on the aisle between them. Jane grabbed the bottle before it could roll away.

He extended his hand as though she might do the polite thing and hand it over.

Instead, Jane put it in her cup holder. "You'll never get this back if you don't tell me what I want to know."

He smirked. "I can get another bottle of water."

"But you won't."

Hagan cocked his head, not hiding his amusement. "Yeah, and why not?"

"Because I asked nicely." Jane fluttered her eyelashes, gave her most syrupy grin, and preened.

"Yeah." Hagan snorted. "And held my water *hostage*."

"And because I want to know." Her pitiful tone was impossible to ignore. Jane wanted to cringe. Instead, she straightened her shoulders and tried for a laugh. "High stakes, I know."

He rubbed his face. "Don't put me in the middle of this."

"Of what?"

"I can tell something happened between you two."

Her cheeks flamed. It was one thing for him to know and pity but another to make assumptions out loud. "Nothing—"

"I don't know what." He shook his head. "But obviously, you got under each other's skin."

She got under Chance's skin? "We camped in a desert and outran people wanting to sell me to the highest bidder," she offered flatly. "I guess you could say he made an impression."

Hagan snickered and side-eyed her. "Is that what the kids are calling it these days?"

Jane chucked his water bottle at him.

He caught it. "Thanks."

"Ass."

"Look." He tossed the water bottle twice more. "Midas is one of the good guys. I promise you that."

His admission was great news. Except, it didn't matter if Chance was a good guy or not. He wasn't on the jet. They'd purposefully not made future plans. No matter what happened in Syria or Abu Dhabi, no matter how she felt then, or now, nothing would change. They'd be thousands of miles apart. Nothing would change that. She couldn't act like Chance had done her wrong.

"Good to know," she eventually, albeit quietly, added.

"Jane, he'd never intentionally hurt a woman."

She nodded. "I believe you. Thanks."

"No more questions?" He laughed to lighten the mood. "I can sleep now?"

Jane recalled what Chance had said about her—that she was worth remembering. The same was true of him. She grinned to herself. It was buttery warm and nostalgic. A sad kind of happy.

CHAPTER THIRTY-THREE

UPON JANE'S RETURN, Gigi denied her time off, mentioning that Jane wasn't due any more vacation days. She'd been too dumbfounded to ask her boss to reconsider. It wasn't as though the Thane-family-trip-turned-abduction-nightmare had been a weekend away at Four Seasons.

But instead of griping, Jane decided it was best for her and Teddy to barricade themselves in the poolside cottage that served as her apartment. After all, the Thanes's sprawling estate looked like a vacation getaway.

For a few days, the staycation plan had worked. Jane worried she pressed her luck as they secretly devoured good books and streamed movies—activities that his parents considered pedestrian. But what Dax and Gigi didn't know wouldn't kill them.

That morning after breakfast in the main house, they once again slipped to her cottage. No one seemed to notice. Teddy sprawled on the soft carpet as he listened to a Minecraft audiobook and colored on a pad of sketch paper. After the chapter ended, he turned the drawing and held it up. "What'd you think, Janie?"

Jane studied the little boxes stacked into columns and tried to decipher what he made. "Is that a castle?"

He laughed like she'd intentionally guessed wrong. "No."

"Hmm." She pursed her lips. "A bridge?"

Teddy's giggles didn't stop. "No!"

She paused the audiobook. "Give me a hint?"

"It's what just happened in the book."

Well, awesome. About ten minutes ago, the Minecraft tale of apple hunting and bridge building had turned into background noise. "It's a house?"

"Yes!" He squealed in delight and returned to his sketchbook. "This is my house. And that's my front door. The waterslide to keep zombies away. This is my cow and chicken."

How did she miss a herd of animals? She leaned over and squinted. The waterslide must've been the black squares. The yellow and gray squares could've been the chicken, though she couldn't find the cow. Unless he was part of the black waterslide. "Is the cow taking a bath?"

Teddy rolled to his back in a fit of giggles. "No, Janie. Cows can't take baths."

"Then what's he doing?" she asked.

"He's riding the waterslide."

She thumped her forehead. "Ah, of course!" Janie tickled his tummy. "The water-sliding cow."

"I'm gonna peeeeeee."

That was a great reason to stop tickling. "All right." She pulled him into her lap. "What should we do today?"

"Eat hot dogs."

Not likely if Gigi had anything to say about it. Maybe the chef could find some kind of macrobiotic organic hot dog lookalike that they could smother in ketchup. "We can ask."

Voices neared outside the cottage. Gigi's lyrical laughter floated in the mix of the conversation. Teddy froze and put his finger against his lips. "Shhh."

"We're not hiding from your mom." Though, they actually were…

He curled into her lap. "Is she coming in here?"

"Maybe." But she hoped not. Jane stroked his soft hair. They waited for the group outside the cottage to leave, but the conversation lingered. "Let me see what's going on." Jane set Teddy to her side and snuck over to the window. Gigi dressed in a fashionable black strapless jumpsuit. She'd begun wearing black all the time, as if the Syria trip had put her in mourning. For the loss of what, Jane could only guess. Clearly, their sanity had left them long ago. A camera crew surrounded her, and the group faced the enormous in-ground pool.

Teddy moved beside Jane. He wrapped an arm around her hip and skirted himself in front of her, pressing his face into her belly as though he couldn't watch. "Are they coming?"

She rubbed his shoulders and recalled a similar conversation when she was Teddy's age. The only difference was that she had asked her uncle what her parents were doing. He never had a good answer because there wasn't one. Instead, he let her hold onto him. She'd needed a comforting touch.

Her uncle hadn't known how to give affection. It was one of the reasons he focused much of their time together on martial arts. Jane wondered if Teddy received enough affection from her and his aunt. They could always spend more time with Courtney…

Jane watched the camera crew. They were different than the ones she'd seen over the last week. Since they'd arrived home, Dax and Gigi worked the national news networks. Their harrowing story had been recounted again and again. But this one was interested in the gardens and the pool. Perhaps it was something like HGTV. The cameras pointed toward Gigi. Microphones lifted and others fanned out. Gigi smiled and began her well-rehearsed bit. Her gestures pointed this way and that—then at the cottage.

The gaggle turned. Jane jerked them away from the window. The swaying curtain was the only evidence they'd been snooping.

"Are they coming in?" Teddy asked.

Her stomach turned. "I hope not." She wasn't exactly expecting a television crew to pop by her apartment, *and* Jane wasn't the neatest person on earth. Given their recent death-defying trip, Jane had given herself a break from laundry and dishes. They were corralled in a laundry basket and lined on the counter, but it wasn't pretty. *Please don't let her come here.*

Voices came closer. She dropped onto her knees and faced Teddy.

"We should run," he suggested.

In the back of Jane's head, she saw the value in his suggestion. But the front door was the only way out.

Outside on her porch, Gigi conversed with a television interviewer. Their bright and lively chat focused on the craftsman-style cottage that Jane called home. Gigi recalled the pains she'd taken to decorate the backyard oasis, then lightly knocked on her door. "And in here—"

Were they live on-air? Would a producer yell "cut"? Jane couldn't breathe.

Someone sneezed. An audible groan welled as someone profusely apologized, and a deep voice yelled, "Cut."

"She needs a touch-up anyway." Jane recognized Gigi's publicist Lark. "Where's the makeup girl?"

As quick as the group appeared, they departed. Jane sighed in relief.

"That was a close one," Teddy announced.

This poor kid. His life seemed so nice from the outside. But really, he needed parents that wanted to spend time with him, not showcase their gardens. "If they came in, it would've been fine." She tried to reassure him, wrapping him into a snuggle-hug. "We could've said hello and waved for the camera."

He shook his head and tilted his head back, revealing watery eyes. "Janie, I didn't tell you."

"What's the matter? It would've been fine."

"No." He shook his head. "I colored on my shorts when I was drawing."

"Oh, honey. That's fine. Crayon washes out." And even if it didn't, he was a little kid!

"Because, I sat crisscross applesauce and my hand drew off the paper. Onto my leg." He covered a spot on his khaki shorts. "My mom could have seen it."

Jane lifted him into her arms and placed him on the counter, blowing raspberries on his neck until he giggled. When the threat of tears disappeared, Jane solemnly told him, "Crayon smudges are the reason God made washing machines."

"God didn't make washing machines," Teddy pointed out with preschool wisdom.

Touché. "Well... he made people and people made washing machines."

"I thought the museum we went to with Aunt Courtney said we revolved."

"Evolved." Jane grabbed the Tide pen from a kitchen drawer.

"Well…" She uncapped the pen and scrubbed at the stain, wondering what she should say. Then Jane saw the clock. "Whoops. It's time for your piano lesson." She swept him onto his feet and smoothed her hair back into a ponytail, quickly adjusting her gym shorts.

"I haven't practiced."

"You've been busy lately…" *Recovering from an abduction at gunpoint after dangling from a Black Hawk.* That was better left unsaid. Maybe the traumatic encounter would come in handy when writing college application essays. "It'll be fine."

Teddy slipped on his sneakers, and she grabbed her bag of water and snacks, then cracked the front door and peered out. "The coast is clear."

Quickly, they kept their heads down and hustled for the main house. The piano teacher might already be waiting.

Teddy faltered when high-pitched, sing-song voices rolled from the far side of the deck. Jane couldn't see Gigi and the camera crew, but knew their trajectory was on course for a collision.

Teddy pulled her hand. "Janie, run!"

CHAPTER THIRTY-FOUR

HAND IN HAND, they vaulted over the flower beds and around lounge chairs. She pushed Teddy ahead of her as they skittered onto the paved walkway that led to the east wing of the house. Just as they hit the stone staircase, Jane heard Gigi call, "Yoo-hoo! Jane!"

Busted. Jane stopped. Teddy clutched her side. She kissed the top of his head and whispered, "Just smile. It'll be over before you know it."

"Fine." He grumbled and didn't let go.

Footsteps and voices approached behind them. Jane hoisted Teddy onto her hip and turned. *Three* cameras focused on them. One large video camera. One cell phone camera. One paparazzi camera.

The television reporter took a surprised step back. Jane cringed inwardly. Her pocked and flaking skin had made the woman recoil. That was exactly the ego boost she needed.

The video camera lens extended and zoomed in on Jane, shedding snake, and Teddy with practiced but still heart-melting smile.

Lark, Gigi's publicist, stepped around from the group and caught Teddy's attention. She pulled her finger over her upturned lips, signaling their smiles should be bigger.

Gigi held her hand out. "Jane is our wonderful nanny, and this is my dear child, Teddy."

"Hello," Jane managed.

Gigi faced the reporter. "As I mentioned." Her low voice took a somber, practiced tone of sympathy and compassion. "Jane's blisters and burned patches are an unfortunate result from our trip."

Burned *patches*? Jane would've flinched at the description but indignation had hold of her backbone. She wouldn't cower, but hell if she didn't want to offer a nicer-sounding description such as third-degree *sunburn*.

"Her injuries occurred as we raised awareness about women and children with nowhere else to go but refugee camps," Gigi continued.

Not exactly. Jane repositioned Teddy, waiting until they were no longer on display before allowing her aggravation to show.

"Her blisters may scar. Her complexion will never be the same." Gigi grimaced sympathetically, covering her hand to her heart. The sun glinted off her ring set with a diamond the size of a marble. "But when you look at Jane, you can see the vicious suffering that others face without our help."

And with that cheerful description, Jane was done. "Off to piano, or we'll be late."

That was how Gigi saw her? A wonderful nanny who was the living, breathing illustration of mass casualty suffering. Angry tears burned the back of her throat.

The group mumbled as Jane hurried away.

"*Jane.*" The click-clack of designer heels hastily followed. "Jane?"

If only Jane could teleport to piano lessons. She turned and set Teddy down. "Run to the bathroom before your lesson. Okay?"

He agreed and ran off before Gigi came within arm's reach. Jane wasn't sure what Gigi might say. Maybe she realized her word choice had been cruel. Perhaps she wanted to tell Jane that she was appreciated. Jane didn't count on it, but hope springs eternal. "Yes?"

Gigi gestured the direction they had come. "They're filming a special quick-to-air mini-documentary."

Not an apology. Jane wasn't surprised. "Sounds wonderful."

"Everyone in the world wants to know how we're doing—you know, after the *incident*."

"Got it."

"Isn't it absolutely *thrilling*? Almost as if we have our own reality television show, without any of the tacky PR-whore conventions. It's all about *us*!"

Just like everything else. "Sounds exciting."

Gigi beamed. "If the ratings are good, there's no holding us back. We'd be household names." She leaned closer to Jane. "That's something money can't buy."

Speechless, Jane rolled her lips together.

"It's so close I can almost feel it."

Jane didn't know what to say. She hooked a thumb over her shoulder. "I need to check on piano practice."

"Oh, of course!" Gigi said theatrically, stars in her eyes. "Oh, I forgot. Dax is in the piano room, being interviewed by *Entertainment Tonight*. Why don't you see if you can get the piano instructor to teach on the Steinway in my sitting room? And I have some people inside, updating the décor. Make sure Teddy doesn't get in their way." Then, with a wrist flick, Gigi dismissed Jane.

"*Household names*," Jane muttered as she quietly slipped inside the house and found Teddy's piano teacher alone.

Jane took the teacher into the west wing, depositing her in Gigi's sitting room and then searched for Teddy. He wasn't where she expected him, and Jane returned to the east wing, where his bedroom was located. There she found him. He sat on the floor of a hallway bathroom, crying.

"Teddy." Jane crouched in front of him. Had Dax yelled at him for interrupting the interview? Was he still worried about the lapse in piano practice? Teddy made no secret of the fact that he didn't enjoy piano, along with just about everything his parents made him do. "What's wrong?"

The sound of wood splintering penetrated through the wall followed by a harsh, "be careful." Jane turned toward the noise as though the wallpaper could explain what was happening.

Teddy pointed toward the wall also. The bathroom backed to his bedroom, and her stomach dropped. Jane inched into the hallway but saw nothing to account for the sounds. Teddy's bedroom was bigger than the house Jane had grown up in, and Gigi kept it fashionably decorated. In Jane's opinion, Teddy's room looked more like an adult bedroom. But even if it were painted in primary colors with fun wall posters, his room still missed little touches that made a child's bedroom unmistakably theirs. Like, toys.

But toys were in the playroom only. That strictly enforced rule from his mother kept their house picture-perfect.

Warily, Jane left Teddy and walked to his bedroom door. She held her breath and said a little prayer before opening it.

Three men were dismantling the furniture. Any sign of Teddy had been boxed up. She moved into the doorway. "Um, hello?"

"We know," the man closest to the door said. "Keep it down."

"No, I mean…" The framed prints had been removed. The curtains were gone. "What are you doing?"

"What's it look like, lady?" he said, unfastening a bolt from the bed. "Time for another round of renovations."

The home décor update that Teddy was supposed to stay away from was for his bedroom. Dang it. Teddy just got used to the new design. She shook her head as she walked back to the bathroom.

Teddy looked as if his whole world were ending.

"I'm sorry, honey. But I bet—"

Tears slid down his cheeks. "They threw away Bun Bun!"

Bun Bun was his very special stuffed animal. It was the only thing he'd been allowed to keep from the moment he was born. Every night, he clung to it as he fell asleep. Sometimes he didn't let go until after breakfast. "Isn't Bun Bun at my place?" Though she didn't remember seeing Bun Bun next to the crayons and paper.

"No."

She balked at the impossibility of purposefully throwing his toy away. "I'm sure they just moved him. I'll go check."

"Okay. Thanks, Janie." He buried his tear-stained face against his knees.

Jane rushed back into the boy's bedroom. She poked around, nothing. "Did you see a turquoise bunny? Like a stuffed animal?"

"That's all gone."

She stepped past them, looking where Bun Bun should've been and then in a trash can. "What do you mean *all gone?*"

The man closest to the door shrugged. "First thing on the list, remove personal touches."

"And do what with them?" Teddy kept his *personal touches* in the playroom or her cottage. The only thing in his room that didn't come from a designer was his Bun Bun.

The man shrugged as though Jane needed to take her argument elsewhere. She gritted her teeth. This, apparently, was where she drew the line. She would not let his parents destroy Bun Bun.

The Thanes had their trash receptacle area hidden on a wooded side of their property. Everything disposed of from the house, from kitchen scraps to donations, passed through there, and she guessed that's where Bun Bun would have gone.

Jane stormed from the bedroom, swept him into her arms, and spoke with forced cheer. "While you're at piano, I'll go and get Bun Bun back. Okay?"

His eyes filled with tears again. "B-But I want to go with you!"

She should've expected that. Jane decided he'd earned the right to save his stuffed animal. "All right. You can miss your piano lesson today." Jane would hear it from Gigi, *if* Gigi ever peeked out from her bubble and found out, which was a big *if*. At least, Jane would spare the precious Steinway. "Let me tell your teacher, and we'll go look. Okay?"

He nodded, and a small smile broke on his face amid the tears.

As she led the piano instructor downstairs, Dax was *still* pontificating about himself and his wonderfulness. They said goodbye to his teacher. A reporter Jane recognized flagged her over. She groaned that the reporter had been let inside the gated community, but the guardhouse let Lark and the Thanes call the shots.

"Jane!"

"Nothing to say." And they had a stuffed animal to save.

"What do you say about the rumors?" the reporter called from the sidewalk.

"Rumors are a dime a dozen," Jane muttered, backing them away so that the piano teacher could back out the driveway.

"You don't care about problems between Dax and Gigi?"

Jane stopped and glanced at the reporter holding his phone out to catch her comments and then pointedly to Teddy. "Do you mind?"

Thankfully oblivious, Teddy pulled on her hand.

If his parents had problems with their relationship, Gigi and Dax wouldn't be on television, constantly exposing their family, home, and habits. Unless... her stomach turned. Well, honestly, she wouldn't put a stunt like that past them if it meant a few new headlines.

Together, she and Teddy walked away. Her curiosity grew. Once they were out of the reporter's sight, she let him run ahead. Jane took out her phone and scanned the gossip pages. Sure enough, several gossip websites had various theories.

Jane scanned the articles and comments, and no one offered anything specific but mentioned rumors of upcoming television appearances.

"Janie!"

Sighing, she pocketed her phone and lifted her gaze to Teddy. "Coming."

After walking the perimeter of the expansive property, they stopped at the wrought-iron gate that protected the trash from reporters and dumpster divers who wanted to sell Dax's half-eaten apple on eBay. Trash receptacle was just a pretty name for a dumpster. She could smell it. Ugh.

"Are you sure Bun Bun's in there?" Teddy asked hesitantly.

"I think so. He's on a wild adventure." She squeezed Teddy's hand.

"You're going to get him for me?"

She laughed. "Yup, and I hope you still love me when I smell like garbage."

He giggled. "I'll always love you, Janie."

And that was why she adored him so much, why she would risk a thousand smelly dumpsters for him. No one in her life had ever loved her unconditionally. She ruffled his hair and took a deep breath, and prepared to go dumpster diving.

After searching through all sorts of grossness while Teddy looked on, Jane finally emerged victorious, holding the blue bunny above the rim of the dumpster to Teddy's wild applause.

She climbed out and presented it to him. He hugged the dirty bunny and then hugged her, even though she was, in a word, disgusting.

"Thank you, Janie."

All in a day's work.

CHAPTER THIRTY-FIVE

THE LAST WEEK had been unbearably slow. Outside of PT and one mandatory safety briefing entitled *How to change a lightbulb like you're not buffoons intentionally trying my patience*, led by Mr. Personality, Jared Westin, king of all and everything, as he called himself during the training, Chance realized he needed an assignment like he needed air to breathe.

Maybe today would be the day. He checked his wristwatch then took the stairs to the first-floor lobby. Chance nodded to a few familiar faces of the construction crew and walked behind the reception desk. He wound down the office hall and stopped outside the war room. A bright yellow, half-crumpled piece of paper lay on the floor. Chance picked it up and grinned.

WARNING
Behind These Doors Are Men
Highly Trained in Weapons That Go…
Ping, Ping
Pew, Pew
Kaboom

Unable to hide his laugh, he smoothed the warning sign against the wall and made sure the tape stuck before he opened the door. Everyone on the team already sat around the conference table. They'd stopped talking and looked at him as though he was late.

"Hey," he muttered, sneaking a glance at his watch. *Right on time.* "Did I miss something?"

Jared pushed from the head of the table and cracked his knuckles.

"You make that sign?"

Chance tried his best not to laugh. Who the hell was the sign grand master? "Roger that. It was me."

He growled. "Take a seat."

Chance pulled back an open chair. "I didn't realize we were starting early."

"We did," Jared grumbled. "You didn't."

Puzzled, he wanted to question why, but at the same time, he noticed Liam. "Hey, man." They shook over the table. "When did you get in?"

"Last night."

Westin cleared his throat. "If you two are finished gabbing."

Chance lifted his hands apologetically. He didn't want to aggravate Boss Man before his first gallon of coffee.

"We were talking about the Thanes," Jared continued.

Chance's stomach sank like a rock. "My favorite people. What about them?" He glanced around the room and couldn't get a read on anyone's expressions. "That good, huh?"

Jared grumbled.

"What?" Chance shifted uncomfortably. "Dax is suing us? The photographer didn't capture his best side when we hauled his screaming ass into the helo?"

No one laughed. His stomach bottomed out again. "Did someone—" *Jane* "—get hurt?"

"No, nothing like that." Jared pinched the bridge of his nose and shook his head with a sigh that sounded like he already had a headache. "They want to hire additional security to their personal team."

Chance didn't see why that would cause a headache. Ace's parent company, Titan Group, was based in Virginia and handled jobs like that. Still, no one made a peep. He was missing something. "All right. So, what am I missing?"

"They want you on a temporary security detail."

Chance sat back in his seat. His forehead furrowed. It'd be an opportunity to see Jane—should that make him say yes or run like hell? He couldn't stand the Thanes. That would be an immediate problem. Not to mention, Chance didn't like monotonous wait-and-see of a security position. He'd tried his hand alongside Liam before they'd joined Aces. While he would gladly do it again for a buddy, Chance wouldn't consider it for the Thanes. Except… that he'd see Jane.

"The thing is," Jared interrupted his thoughts. "Gigi Thane specifically requested you."

"Me?" Chance rubbed the back of his neck. "Why?"

"She wouldn't say." The room stayed quiet while Jared paused. "If they hadn't received new threats, then I'd be a hell of a lot more likely to ignore her request and pass the job along."

"There are new threats?" he asked.

"Apparently. Something about privacy invasions and reporters treading too close to the family." Jared's lips thinned. "I'd call them concerns. Either way, she asked for you."

With everyone watching him, Chance couldn't stop thinking about the opportunity to see Jane again. And, the more he thought about her, the more he realized he couldn't—or at least, shouldn't—see her again. Were his teammates thinking the same thing? Chance glanced around the room. "That's why you met without me?"

"I wanted to know their opinions," Jared said.

Chance swallowed hard. "About?"

"Whether or not this job would fuck you up."

"I'm not going to fuck up—"

"I asked if the job would fuck *you* up or not," Jared clarified.

His eyebrows arched, and while he trusted his teammates with his life, he didn't know what they'd say to that question. Hell, he didn't know what they saw or thought they knew. Chance rolled his lips together. "I'm not going to let a gig mess me up."

Jared's eyes narrowed. "What about a woman?"

A long, heavy silence hung over the room. Chance swallowed hard. "I wouldn't let a woman mess me up."

Forever ticked by. Finally, Jared nodded. "They agree."

Thank fuck for that. Relief rolled down his back, but still, Chance couldn't relax. "Then, you're sending me to the Thanes?"

An uncontrollable excitement pulsed through his veins. Jane was the reason, and he didn't like it. Time and time, he'd seen men ruin their lives when their dick made their choices. Was that happening now?

"Are you volunteering?" Jared asked.

The correct answer was hell no. But, of course he was. Chance couldn't walk away from an opportunity to see Jane. "Guess so."

Chance didn't say another word during the rest of the meeting. Finally, it ended, and he pushed out of his seat, stalked to the door, and almost jogged down the hallway in search of fresh air.

The main lobby was a whirl of activity. A forklift beeped as it lifted material to scaffolding. The quiet hum of repairs multiplied in the cavernous space. Chance stopped and watched a group unload the forklift, wondering what the walls might look like when they were finished.

Liam and Hagan joined him, each flanking his side.

"What do you think it's going to look like?" Hagan asked. "The only thing I can come up with is expensive."

"Is that a color?" Liam asked.

Hagan chuckled. "And a texture."

"Yeah, this place is going to look pricey," Liam finally said, then turned to Chance. "So, the Thanes?"

Hagan turned into the conversation. "You agreed easier than I would've guessed."

Chance didn't like what this was leading up to. "Is that right?"

"Hagan and I were talking," Liam said.

"Of course you were."

"And, we have questions," Hagan finished.

The two of them exchanged smirks like schoolboys in the back of the classroom. Chance acted as though he couldn't tell and didn't care. "About?"

"What the hell happened between you and Jane?" Liam asked, raising his eyebrows in unison with Hagan like they'd rehearsed it all morning.

He feigned cluelessness. "Nothing."

"Give me a break," Hagan laughed. "I talked with her on the plane—"

Chance lifted his hand. "Don't tell me."

Liam shrugged. "Chelsea thought—"

"Chelsea? Why does *your wife* have anything to say?" His skin felt too tight. Not only had his teammates made assumptions about his time with Jane, they were discussing outside the team.

Liam punched Chance's arm and chuckled. "Aw, shucks, Midas. If I didn't know better, bro, I'd say you had a little crush on your hands."

Chance wasn't willing to touch the accusation. "Screw off, guys. Liam, if you want the assignment, it's yours. No skin off my nose."

Liam grinned. "Hell no. Chelsea would skin my ass if you didn't spend time with your girl."

"She's not my—"

Hagan sighed. "Chance and Jane would have cute kids."

"Very," Liam concurred, with equal wry. "Will they invite the Thanes to the nuptials?"

"Good question." Hagan barely kept a straight face.

Chance growled.

Hagan folded over with laughter and slapped his leg. "What an image."

"Another happy couple." Liam contained his laughter. "I was getting sick of being the only family man around here." But then he broke and cracked up.

Chance shoved his hands into his pockets. "Hardy, har, har, dicks."

Hagan and Liam only howled louder. Chance searched for a reasonable excuse to hightail away from the conversation without looking like he couldn't handle their ribbing. In truth, he couldn't. Didn't that just grate his nuts.

"All right, all right." Hagan, perhaps sensing Chance's growing agitation, settled down and then slapped him on the back. "We're just giving you hell."

Maybe Chance deserved a little razzing from Liam. Chance had outed his friend's quiet relationship in the name of security. Chelsea's life had been in danger, but Liam went on to marry her. It worked out in the end. But Hagan didn't have a reason to bust Chance in the balls. He pointed at Hagan. "When your time comes…"

"Wait." Liam arched his eyebrows with renewed interest. "Are you saying *your* time has come?"

"Hell." Chance glowered and waved them away without success. It didn't work, so he turned for the stairwell.

"Midas," Hagan called.

Chance turned but kept walking backward. "What?"

Hagan lifted his chin, still jovial but far more subdued. "She's a good girl."

He stopped. "Yeah, I know that."

"Whatever happens when you see Jane…" Hagan tilted his head with a humorless grin. "Don't overthink it."

"I never overthink."

"And," Liam said. "Never underestimate a woman who walked out of hell and smiled the next day."

Chance could picture Jane's smile while she had been *in* hell. But, he'd keep that to himself. "Who knew you two were such oracles of wisdom?"

CHAPTER THIRTY-SIX

TEDDY WAS GONE and in good hands. Aunt Courtney had surprised Jane with a request for one-on-one time with her nephew. Courtney tried to do that as often as she could. It amounted to every month or so, when she spent time at her beautiful Kalorama home in Washington, DC. This time, her weekend itinerary included the National Zoo and Teddy's choice of Smithsonians.

Dax and Gigi were gone before they knew of Aunt Courtney's unscheduled visit. They had left early in the morning, under the cover of darkness, on a romantic getaway to a spa in the Shenandoah Mountains, something that wasn't *that* unusual for them. Though the secretive part was odd. No matter. The schedule changes meant Jane had free time.

She grabbed a paperback romance novel and went out on the porch of the pool house, ready to fall back into her favorite re-read, a second chance love story between a GI Joe type and a therapist.

She picked a spot under an umbrella that was close to the pool but out of the sun's baking rays. Jane put her ice water and cell phone on a side table and curled onto a lounge chair. "Where was I?" She opened the book and enjoyed the soft breezes as she paged to the chapter where GI Joe tossed the therapist over his shoulder and hauled ass from a shootout. "She's gonna give you hell for that." Talking to the characters had to be one of Jane's favorite reasons not to use a bookmark. When she flipped through pages, not knowing where she'd stop, she'd get a few extra seconds to relive what she'd already read.

Jane skipped a few more pages and found a good place to start reading again. "Here we go." She let the words surround her—until her cell phone buzzed. It was a number she didn't recognize, and she silenced it. "Not today, Satan."

Answering unfamiliar numbers meant chatting with a gossip blogger or celebrity journalist who wanted the dirt on the Thane family and weren't afraid to pay for it. The last time she answered, someone had offered her five thousand dollars for Dax's calendar. Tempting, but she would never dish.

Jane read a few pages and then checked her phone. No voicemail. Of course the caller wouldn't record their bribe.

A moment later, it rang again. Same number.

So much for having an unlisted number. It was going to be one of those days. What did they want? What would they offer? How often would they call until Jane picked up the phone and lost her temper.

She groaned, already imagining how the headline would read: "Insane Thane Nanny Loses Her Mind." Of course, every gossip-covering website would have the audio file accessible for the world to hear her rage.

The notion of acting like the *insane Thane nanny* was almost amusing, or maybe she just liked how it rhymed. Either way, Jane snickered and declined the call again, turning back to her book. If this tough-guy hero didn't fall to his knees and beg his smart, sassy lady for forgiveness, Jane wasn't sure she'd take their happily ever after seriously. Though she knew what would happen, having read this book a few dozen times. Did that make her a literary sadist? Her brow scrunched, but she returned to the familiar chapter.

Jane couldn't turn the page fast enough, sparing a momentary glance at her phone. No message. As always.

She started a new chapter when the phone rang again—unknown number. They might call all day. She decided to answer and have a little fun. Jane answered with her best game-show host voice, "Hello, caller, you're on the air!"

After a pause, a low voice that she'd heard in both her nightmares and dreams said one word. "Jane."

She couldn't breathe. The phone nearly dropped from her hand. "Chance?"

"How's your day off?" His voice was sure and steady.

This was another dream. Or a nightmare? Sometimes they seemed the same after she woke up. "What?"

"What are you doing on your day off?"

Dumbstruck, she blinked. "How do you know I have the day off?"

He chuckled. "I have my ways."

"Uh…" Her breath shook, and she tried to hide her reaction. The simple act of breathing sounded as though her gasps danced in her chest. "How did you get this number?"

His quiet laughter continued. "I have my sources."

"You have ways and sources," she managed.

"And you have a few days off."

Her sense jumped to full hyper-alert status. What was happening? Then her stomach plummeted. There was only one way to know she was alone. "Did you make friends with the paparazzi?"

"Ha. No. Come outside."

"I am outside." She sat up straighter, looking around, though she wasn't sure what she was looking for. Chance, staring at her through binoculars, from the canopy of a tree? The estate was huge and bordered by a big metal fence. Not to mention… he wasn't in the United States. He didn't work on this side of the world. He'd made that very, very clear. "I can't see you."

"Let's fix that problem." His carefree laughter sent shivers down her neck. "Show yourself, or, I'm coming in."

Jane fumbled to make sense of their phone call. "Where are you?"

"Waiting for you."

Shivers cascaded over her skin. Jane didn't have the words. She realized that her mouth hung slack and slapped it closed. Her fingers strangled her cell phone, and she pulled it from her ear and stared at the screen. The tips of her fingernails gripped the screen to the point that they were white.

She stood and sprinted to the front of the house. There he was. Chance leaned against a big, black, badass truck. His clothes were casual. Dark jeans and a light cotton T-shirt that stretched across his chest. And his smile? It made her knees weak.

"You're slow," he said, a teasing lilt to his voice. "How long does it take you to get out of that house?"

"I was in the backyard."

His long strides closed their distance. Her breath shook and, eyes locked, her head tilted back to keep his gaze. He stopped, towering over her. "Nice to see you again, MP."

"I can't believe you're here."

He lifted a shoulder. "Surprise."

Jane pushed her flyaway hair behind her ear and wanted to hug him. Instead, she crossed her arms, suddenly very aware of her appearance. She'd healed significantly since he last saw her, but as Gigi Thane had pointed out, Jane wasn't a pretty sight.

"Damn, Jane. You're so beautiful."

CHAPTER THIRTY-SEVEN

CHANCE CRINGED, KICKING himself for leading with a cheesy, expected one-liner. His words were true enough, but that wasn't what should've come out of his mouth. He could've picked from a laundry list of her non-superficial qualities. Yet, one look at Jane, and his world tilted to the side, wiping away his uncertainty and aggravation.

He no longer cared that his transatlantic journey had been the equivalent of a red-eye ride in a cargo plane. Nor did he give a flying monkey shit that the high-maintenance Thanes canceled their scheduled meeting via a text message from someone named Lark.

As a matter of fact, right then, he wanted to find Lark and say thanks. Lark had given Chance two things: the Thanes's home address and Jane's cell phone number.

The combination was enough to mask the bitter taste of exhaustion and aggravation. Too bad he couldn't think of anything better to say than the equivalent of You, Jane. Me, Tarzan.

★   ★   ★

ALL OF THE blood in Jane's body rushed to her head. "Ha, ha," she tittered, self-consciously then twisted away. "Welcome back to America."

"Thanks." Amusement danced in his beautiful eyes. "How have you been?"

She pressed her palm against the small of her neck and could feel her pulse jumping like it raced hurdles. "What are you doing here?"

He tilted his head as though weighing her reactions. "You don't know?"

Jane glanced around the yard as though any minute a television reporter and camera crew would jump out of the bushes. "I must've missed the security memo."

His brows knitted. "The Thanes do security *memos?*"

"No," she quickly amended. "Only joking. They don't do anything with security unless it creates headlines—" She stopped before saying too much. At least, according to her nondisclosure agreement.

"I was supposed to meet with them, but they cancelled on me."

"You flew across an ocean, and they cancelled?" Though she wasn't the least bit surprised.

"I should've called."

Her? Them? Jane wasn't sure what he referred to, and she fumbled for what to say next. "Do you have time to hang out for a little bit?"

Again, there was that expression she couldn't read. If she had to guess, she'd say there was humor mixed with the slightest hint of skepticism.

"I'm going to be here for a bit."

"Oh." Why? He didn't like the Thanes. Or, rather, he detested them. "I'm the only one here. Teddy's with his aunt, and Gigi gave the staff time off while they were gone."

"Just you and me." Chance pursed his lips together. "How about that timing?"

Butterflies fluttered in her stomach. She should invite him in—but where? To the main house? Her cottage? "I was reading by the pool."

Chance tossed his truck keys in the air and caught them in the same hand, then shoved them into his pocket. "Lead the way."

Okay. That was easy enough. Jane guided them to the backyard. They walked down the slate rock path and passed through the gate. Their arms brushed, and her body flamed. During their daytrip in the souks, she could semi-ignore her reaction to him. But after their elevator kiss and his surprise arrival, Jane's nerves hit a fever pitch.

He saw where she'd been reading under the poolside umbrella and took charge. He shifted their dynamic, guiding *her* to her lounge chair. She appreciated the subtle ways he took charge, especially when it was just the two of them.

Chance pulled a patio chair under the umbrella. She chose a patio chair also and reached for her sweating water glass. The ice cubes had nearly melted. Jane took a sip, watching out of the corner of her eye as he relaxed. "Are you on some kind of top-secret mission?"

He laughed. "Why do you think that?"

"Because, you've been…" She pinched her thumb and pointer finger together. "The *slightest* bit vague."

His laughter rumbled in his chest. "If I were in the neighborhood on a classified job, do you think I'd swing by here?"

Jane rolled her eyes. "Well, of course not."

"Then you'd be wrong."

Her insides turned to molten mush, and the memory of their time in Abu Dhabi flooded back. Was she supposed to ignore their kiss? Wouldn't he have called if he wanted to see her again when he was dropping by a different continent? "I hope you didn't stop by after they cancelled out of misplaced…" Remorse? Disgust? "Guilt."

His eyebrow crooked. Chance's lips parted as though he might respond, but instead, ran a hand over his chin and leaned back. "Why would I feel guilty?"

Come on! He was the Adonis-like man who'd kissed the leper woman. She didn't know why, but guilt should've covered it. A sheen of sweat dampened the back of her neck. "I don't know."

Chance reached for her book. "What are you reading?" He held up the saucy book cover with a quick bark of laughter.

Jane snatched the book. "Don't make any judgmental comments!"

He grabbed the paperback back. "Is it judgmental to assume that I'll cast judgment?"

Her eyes narrowed. "Don't be cute."

"Oh, I'm not." He flipped through a few pages. "I'm curious." Chance stopped. His eyes drifted across the page until his amusement sobered, and he turned the page. "Huh—"

Self-preservation kicked in. "Give me that." Jane stole the book away but kept her finger on the page that he'd been on. After he left, she'd check the page he'd read. Jane crossed her fingers that the chapter focused on gunfights instead of getting it on.

"I always wondered what was in those books." He gestured playfully. "Now I know."

"No." She shook her head. "You didn't."

"I did." He crossed his hand over his heart. "*Very* interesting."

Her curiosity bulldozed over her trepidation. So much for waiting until he left. Jane quickly opened the page.

> *"Give me my hands back, Colby."* *She screwed her legs tight on his thighs. Her hair splayed out on the bed, wild in every direction.*
> *"Not a chance, doll."*
> *"That's not fair."*
> *"Mia, honey, if you find yourself in a fair fight, you didn't plan your mission correctly."*

Her jaw fell open. Taken out of context, those few lines could give Chance the wrong impression. Jane buried the book in her lap. "All right. So—"

"Colby's right." The corner of Chance's lips coyly turned up. "Ya know…"

No. Jane didn't know a thing. Her brain spun, not letting her articulate an appropriate response while her womanly parts jumped to life, begging Jane to ask him to tell her more.

The corners of his eyes crinkled. He was loving this!

Jane swallowed hard, reaching for any sarcastic lifeline she could find. "I'm glad his military lesson was what had caught your attention."

"Actually." He rolled hours' worth of provocative play into that single word. "It was the way she said one thing but wanted another."

Chance didn't look away. Jane couldn't breathe. She knew Mia all too well, wanting what she couldn't have. Their reasons were different. But in that moment, they were the same. Chance was beautiful. She was not. Chance lived on the other side of the world. Yet, here he was. Their time together had been so confusing. But that kiss… She'd never forget it—or understand why—just like she still didn't understand the reason he was in front of her.

"You're not here to read my books," she whispered.

"No. I'm here for work but, really…" Eternity lingered. He didn't smile. Didn't blink. Then he simply said, "I couldn't stay away from you."

CHAPTER THIRTY-EIGHT

W ISE MEN TALK *when they have something to say.*
Fools talk because they have to say something.

Chance wondered who said that? Maybe Plato. Maybe his grandma. Either way, he wasn't sure if it were wise or foolish to be so blunt with Jane.

She jumped from her chair and tossed the book aside. "We should go inside."

Jane didn't wait for him to agree. She turned and left him in her tracks. Nothing he'd said or done had gone according to his plan. He glanced at the book one more time, still *very* interested, and followed her up a set of stairs that led onto a deck.

She left a sliding glass door ajar, and he stepped into a bright, white kitchen. The vaulted ceilings and stainless-steel appliances made the room cold. His hotel kitchenette had more character and could fit in the space occupied by the kitchen island.

"Do people eat in here?" he asked.

Jane stood on the far side of the island. Her finger clutched the beveled granite edge. "Sometimes."

He gave the room another assessment. He supposed it was well designed, but in his opinion, it came off as clinical. "Does anyone cook in here?" He opened the refrigerator, shocked to find food neatly stored.

"They have a chef and staff to do that."

"Have you ever seen Dax or Gigi cook?"

Jane shrugged.

"Never?" He always thought of a kitchen as the central hub of a home. Even in his hotel room. Every conversation started over a beer or can of dinner. "That's strange."

"This isn't a normal place. If you see everyone here, it would look different."

"Why did you stay when everyone else is gone?" he asked, thinking about his luck.

"It happens. I didn't expect Teddy to go with his aunt." She shifted around the island as though the conversation made her forget her need for distance. "I'm the house sitter, I guess. They didn't want anyone to know they snuck away."

"Weird."

She agreed. "So… You know why I'm here."

He pulled out a barstool chair with a high back and sat. "They have security concerns and contacted our office."

Jane seemed to think that over, then turned for a cabinet, took out two glasses and removed a pitcher of lemonade from a small refrigerator that he thought had been a dishwasher. She filled the first one and paused. "I thought your team doesn't work in the US."

"We usually don't." He watched her gaze slightly narrow. Did she believe him? He tacked on, "It was a special request."

She finished pouring the lemonades and placed one in front of him.

Chance sized up her reaction before he took a small sip. "You really didn't know I was coming?"

Her eyebrows arched. "Does it look like I knew?"

Sure? What the hell did he know. "You would look different?"

Jane pressed her lips together. "I didn't know."

"Gigi hired me. She asked for me by name."

Her eyes widened with surprise and her mouth opened. A long moment crawled by. "Excuse me?" Jane blinked and then her forehead furrowed. "I didn't know you two met."

"We didn't."

"Then how…?" A bright blush flamed over her cheeks. "Oh my God." The glass of lemonade trembled in her hand. She set it down. "Do you think that I have something to do with that?" She gripped the edge of the island counter. "After what happened between us?"

It'd be a lie to say he hadn't wondered. It would've been equally false to ignore his response—that is, his response that surfaced *after* his interest in seeing Jane again. Jane wasn't manipulative, and they'd been clear that they wouldn't see each other again. If she had been involved in Gigi's request, he would have been flattered—as much as it would've made him uncomfortable. Chance lifted his shoulders. "I think it was hard for Titan to deny the Thanes's request."

"Story of my life," Jane muttered. "What they say goes."

"Did you mention me to Gigi?"

Jane gasped. Her cheeks reddened. "No."

"Okay." He stood from the barstool, taking his time to approach Jane. "I believe you."

Jane rolled her eyes. "If I had told her, she would've found a way to exploit it—" Her gaze cut back to him. "Did you tell anyone…" She rolled her hand and looked away.

"That I kissed you?"

She stiffly straightened as though his words took her by surprise.

Chance eased closer. "No."

"Of course not." Her chin dropped as she stepped away. "I don't know why you would—"

Chance cut off her escape with a strong hand on her hip. Jane's breath hitched. She didn't look up even as he closed the remaining inches, clasping his hand on her other hip. Their chemistry was off the damn charts, yet she kept running away. How could she ignore the searing desire pouring between them?

"Are you upset about what happened in the elevator?" Because, if so, he would get to the bottom of that.

"You don't need to coddle me or explain yourself or why—"

"Jane, *stop*."

Her eyes shot to his. "Stop what?"

Jane didn't see what she did to him. Hell, she didn't see what he saw. Pouty lips that could make his dick twitch. Kind eyes and a sexy attitude. His arousal blinded him from everything except for her. The more he stared, the more he could feel her uncertainty—about him.

A dull ache hollowly thudded in his chest. He pressed his hips to her. Her eyes widened. There was no mistaking his swollen thickness. Chance didn't imagine her naked, he didn't need to taste her sweet mouth. Simple proximity to this woman was enough to drive him over the edge. "Stop pretending I don't want you."

Her eyelashes fluttered. The rise and fall of her chest grew more noticeable.

"Because I do." Chance touched his mouth to her pink cheek. "I want you." The softness of her skin twisted him in knots. "In more ways than I know how to explain."

"*Chance.*"

The quiver in her breathy voice ignited a wave of goosebumps down his back. With a painfully lazy slowness, he grazed his lips over her cheek, nuzzling over her skin until he could nip her earlobe. He hadn't though. Not yet. Jane would first understand that he needed her in a basic, carnal, desperate way.

Somewhere at the back of his mind, he recalled wanting to talk, to make certain they were on the same page. But now he knew a conversation wouldn't work, and he would prove to her that his words weren't meaningless. He couldn't do that without her though. His warm breath teased behind her earlobe. "Put your arms around me."

For once, Jane didn't hesitate. Her hands locked behind his neck. She lifted her chin and met his gaze. Time stilled. They pressed together, and Chance watched her until he saw her understanding shift.

"Thank you." He let the word linger, almost pressing his lips to hers. The anticipation of another kiss made him feverish. He wanted her mouth, her tongue. Chance wanted her pussy to quake on his cock. But for that split second, he would revel as Jane found her trust in him.

Impossibly, they seemed closer and yet too far apart. Their lips touched. Heat ignited, wicking over his nerves. Unlike in the elevator, he was certain they'd kiss again. Chance didn't greedily take what he needed. He savored every one of her delicious reactions.

She opened her mouth to his, and their tongues touched, danced, slowly memorizing the feel and taste of their mouths together. Needy murmurs burned from her lips. Jane had surrendered to their drawing power. When she let go, he shivered with awareness that went far beyond physical needs.

He lifted Jane onto the granite countertop. Wanton, she wrapped her thighs around his hips, giving him irresistible access. He ached for her pussy. He would die with that first thrust and when she climaxed on his cock. The satisfaction wouldn't come soon enough—yet he refused to rush. Chance opened his eyes and inched back. She was everything he hadn't known existed.

"What?" Jane asked quietly.

He grinned and rolled his lips together. Just minutes ago, she'd been ready to run. "You listened."

Jane didn't shy away or steal her gaze from his when she smiled. "Sometimes I do."

CHAPTER THIRTY-NINE

"*A HEM.*" BRIGHT LIGHTS flooded the kitchen.

They jerked apart as a slender woman in high heels and a business-professional dress crossed to the kitchen island. Without another mention of what she'd walked in on, the woman took the lemonade pitcher to the side counter and poured herself a glass.

Chance stepped back. Jane wasn't fast to jump off the kitchen island. He sensed an animosity between the women.

Jane slid down and stayed close to his side. "I didn't know you were working today."

The other woman raised her eyebrows and then assessed the way Jane stood by his side. Then she smirked. "I see you've been introduced." She took a sip of her lemonade, put it down, and stared at him like Chance was a prize to conquer. After a none-too-subtle look he was familiar with, she strode forward and extended her hand as though he might kiss her knuckles.

He shook it instead. "Chance Evans."

"Lark Dyson."

So this was Lark. He sized up Gigi's right hand. Platinum blond hair framed her flawless face. With mischievous light blue eyes and a perfect smile, she carried an air that went well beyond confident and leaned precariously close to entitled. "Thanks for the text."

"If there are any *problems.*" Lark pointedly looked at Jane. "You can let me know. I'll handle them until you can meet with Gigi."

"No problems." Chance wondered what the other Thane staff would be like. He was certain he could get on well with security. But how many were like Lark? She came off as cold as this kitchen, and more judgmental than he'd been of Dax.

Lark tapped a manicured fingernail against the counter. "If you could spare me a few minutes, we can go over logistics." After a beat, she tacked on, "*Alone.*"

Jane squeezed his forearm. "I'll be around back. Call me when you're done."

Chance mustered all of his control not to pull her back and kiss her goodbye. But, that'd be pushing his luck in several ways. He lifted his chin, quietly saying goodbye, then turned to Lark.

She eyed him coolly. "Sometimes I have lunch in here. Please don't fuck where I eat."

He crossed his arms, knowing an enemy when he saw one. What he didn't know was why. "Any other important rules?"

"Image is everything. You already look the part. Make sure you act it as well, or you'll be gone before you know it."

"Are you always so kind and welcoming?" He narrowed his eyes. "Or am I just lucky?"

"Kindness has no place in this household," Lark said. "We hired you: good looking, single, and knows how to use a gun."

He snorted. "Yeah, lady. That's exactly what it says on my resume."

"I wouldn't be surprised."

This was why he didn't do celebrity security. Lark the Enemy made his skin crawl. "Let's talk about logistics," he said, changing the subject. "What—"

"Gigi will handle everything when she returns. She'll introduce you to her current security and share the threats that they've decided to keep from the press." Lark coolly smiled. "Until then, I'll be your point of contact. Give me a few hours, and I'll text you a housing assignment."

"All right. I'll be waiting."

"I'm sure." Lark tartly crossed her arms. Her pink lips pursed, and she studied him as though she were analyzing that Kandinsky he noticed hanging in the hallway off the kitchen. Like the painting, Lark could see his value, knew what others had said of him, but for the life of her, she wasn't sure why he was considered world class. At least, that was how

Chance felt about the Kandinsky.

Lark sipped her lemonade and then added, "If the nanny becomes a problem, we can ship her and the kid off until we're through with you."

The nanny and the kid. His molars clamped—but it was that moment when Chance understood Jane's concern for Teddy. The boy's parents weren't the only problem. These people saw a child as a commodity.

JANE PACED THE length of her small living room. While she should've been worried about Lark, she didn't care. Chance preoccupied every crevice of worry and wonder in her head. He'd thrown out every assumption she'd made about him—and *them*, if that wasn't too presumptive, out the door. And that kiss…

A wicked burst of shivers slid down her neck. She could still feel him. The hard heat of his body wrapping to her soft one. His hungry, full lips, and his arousal. The rapid cadence of her heartbeat exploded, weakening her knees and resolve. Jane took a shaky breath and closed her eyes. The memory of him against her, long, thick, and hard, would forever be seared into her memory. She pressed a hand to her heart. The poor thing was trying to jump from under her sternum.

But she didn't know what to do next. She still didn't trust herself… or understand what he saw in her—she stopped cold. Even if she didn't get it, he did see something in her. He demanded that she accept that. It was scary but exhilarating. Without saying so out loud, he'd declared himself hers and demanded she admit the truth. He wanted her like she did him.

None of that helped with Lark, though. There would be ramifications if the Thanes's publicist told Gigi about their indecent on the kitchen island. Jane took a seat on her couch and pulled a large knit blanket up to her neck. Lark and Gigi were working with Chance. They'd asked for him by name and hadn't mentioned his visit. Jane couldn't wrap her head around the situation.

A solid knock rapped on her door. "Jane?"

A clap of arousal thundered in her chest. She didn't know it was possible for anticipation to show up at the knock of a door. But it had. So much for thinking with a clear head around the man with the golden touch.

She unburied from the protective cocoon on the couch, ordering herself to "keep it together." Then Jane let him in. "You found me."

"I'll always find you." Chance ambled into her place like this was just another day and he wasn't casually dropping lines that made her cling to the doorknob for support. "Lark's a real peach, huh?"

Jane snorted her agreement and moved back onto the couch and pulled the blanket onto her lap. "Is peach a special word for—" She stopped herself and pulled the blanket to her chin. "Never mind. Gossiping over Lark isn't worth the bad karma."

"I might disagree." Chance took a seat on the couch. "One might consider it sharing intel on the enemy, not gossiping." His cool, relaxed demeanor was the epitome of confidence. He leaned an elbow on the back of the couch. His long, powerful legs cavalierly spread as though he wasn't aware that his pants strained at the bulk of his thigh muscles. "After the conversation I just had with her." He shook his head, gaze unfocused like he were rehearing Lark. "I can think of a few more deserving names for that lady other than peach."

Jane could only imagine. She tossed a corner of her soft blanket to him. "It helps to cuddle something soft and forgiving when this place gets to be too much."

Chance cut her a quick look. "Is that why you're under there?"

"Maybe."

"Lark bothered you that much?" He gestured toward the door. "'Cause I'll make sure she—"

"No, don't bother with her."

"I wouldn't be able to handle your job," he admitted.

"Sometimes the reasons that I don't quit are the same reasons that I want to quit."

Chance rolled his bottom lip into his mouth and released it, but tension remained tight in his jaw. "Because you have to protect that little boy."

A lump formed in her throat. She smiled halfheartedly and gave a short nod before she trusted her voice. "Yes."

He pulled her under his arm. "You're a protector at heart."

Jane wanted to correct him. Her cold upbringing and lack of caring parents had given her textbook boundary issues. She wasn't protecting Teddy as much as she loved and cared for him, basking in the love he returned. "Not quite."

His arm tightened around her shoulder and rested his chin on the top of her head. "Agree to disagree."

She leaned into him, and whether he wanted the blanket or not, she didn't care. Jane tucked it over his legs, enveloping them in the large knit cocoon of safety. She didn't want to have a thought-provoking discussion right now. Jane would much rather kiss him like they had in the kitchen. But, if they were going to get deep, she appreciated his arm around her. The world didn't seem as scary and ugly when curled under there.

"Until Gigi is back in town, I want to get to know you better, Jane. The real you. Not the nanny. Not the woman in Syria or Abu Dhabi. Just you."

Butterflies danced in her stomach—except, she didn't have a new side of her to show off. Anxiety needled, and a small wave of self-consciousness dulled her growing bliss. "That was me." She hated to disappoint him but owed Chance the truth. She took a shallow breath and faced him. "I already showed you who I was. I'm not sure much will change."

"I meant," he tried again. "I want to spend time with you, no bullets or fancy-ass hotels, before—"

She hung on the answer, but his mouth clamped shut.

Before? Obviously, before he left again. Could she trust herself to him, knowing he would eventually leave? No. Why didn't he continue his thought! Unable to wait any longer, she prompted, "Chance, before what?"

He hesitated and frowned. "I don't know."

That wasn't true. He knew. So did she. No matter how much of her heart she opened to him, how much he claimed to want her, Chance Evans would leave when Aces needed Midas.

CHAPTER FORTY

A CELL PHONE rang between Jane and Chance, and she gave him room to remove it from his pocket. He glanced at the screen, and she could tell he had to take it.

"Give me a minute, okay?" He accepted the call and stood. "This is Evans."

A few seconds of lag time passed as she recalled that Evans was his last name, proving they needed to get to know each other still. It didn't matter that she felt like he was a long-lost boyfriend—who knew what he'd think of that description—they didn't have the basics down.

Did he leave the toilet seat up in the middle of the night? Who did he admire? How many women felt as though they had a soulmate-like connection to Chance? Those questions were leap years beyond recalling his last name. They had work to do, and she needed to pull her head from the clouds.

Chance listened to the phone call and walked an easy circle around her open floor plan. The small space benefited from the Thanes's designer's eye, and what could've felt like a cramped pool house seemed more like a cottage oasis. One of the many reasons why Gigi liked to pop in with a camera crew on occasion.

Jane tried to read his expression but Chance was a blank canvas. He didn't say much, and she liked that he was an attentive listener. She also liked the way he filled out his clothes. But that wouldn't be high on a get-to-know-you list.

Minutes ticked by. Chance mouthed an apology, silently adding, "It's work."

Would he be leaving already? His face didn't offer any insight, and

Jane promised herself that she would not be upset if he had to leave. She'd had more time with him than she'd ever expected—oh, whatever. It was going to suck when he left. Her voice of reason nodded woefully in the corner of her subconscious.

"Sorry about that."

She jumped to face Chance. "Is everything okay?"

His pursed lips already said no. "Do you know why the Thanes report some credible threats but not all?"

"Of course." Jane snorted as though the answer were as clear as the summer day was long.

He crooked an eyebrow, apparently not seeing the reasons as clearly. "*Credible* threats. Not just bullshit from…" He rolled a hand as though searching for a word. "Gossip rags or whatever."

"Yeah," she said with the same level of certainty.

Chance plopped back onto the couch, and his game face was firmly in place. Even his blue eyes didn't give a hint of the conversation they'd just been having. "Want to tell me?"

Jane shrugged. "Sure, it's not a state secret."

"Okay."

"Some problems create better press than others."

He blinked twice before his eyebrows pulled down, forehead furrowing like he tried but failed to hear her speak a language he understood. "Come again?"

"Well, stalkers get a huge amount of attention."

His mouth hinged but he gestured for her to continue.

"Think about it like… Did you hear about that time Dax's phone was hacked?"

He made a face. "No."

"Pictures were leaked." Jane tilted her head, indicating the nakedness with a simple look. "Gigi filed a police report, but she also went on an intense media blitz."

He folded his arms over his chest. Disgust pulled at his frown. "What type of problem would be reported to the *police* but not the press?"

Jane hummed. "Anything financial, or anything that could show

Thane Insurance in a bad light."

"I see." His jaw flexed.

"Last week, I read something about trouble between Dax and Gigi. Nothing abnormal happened at home," she said. "But when I checked some celeb and gossip sites, they had pictures—though out of context— and details that sounded bad for them. Lark was all over it, but I think she only fanned the fires. They love the attention."

"Doesn't make sense," he muttered.

"That's what I always think." She shrugged. "But people eat it up, and crazy enough, it makes them even more money."

Chance rubbed a hand over his chin and then refolded it against his chest. "The money part is where it gets tricky."

"How so?"

He pursed his lips. "I work with a guy you might've met. Parker Black."

Jane wasn't sure. So many faces and names blurred together. "Maybe."

"Anyway, the office is keeping tabs on things too, but he had some questions about a few recent pictures."

"Why?"

Chance shrugged. "I think they're trying to give me as much infor-mation as possible. This isn't our usual gig. Especially since plans changed before I landed." He sucked in his cheeks, then shook his head. "Don't worry about it. If they need to talk again, I might need to jump on the phone for a while. Headquarters wants to make heads and tails of what's going on."

Remembering why he was there, her shoulders dropped, but she of-fered a fake smile. "I know you're here for work. You don't have to explain yourself."

He stepped closer as though he could clearly see through her veiled reply. Chance brushed her hair back and cupped her chin. "Yeah, I go places when I'm told. That's my job."

"Really, you don't have to explain. I know." And she did, though her throat clogged with disappointment. Jane swallowed hard.

"If I'm gone, you know where I'd rather be." His thumb caressed over her skin.

She blushed. "Sure."

Chance wrapped her in his arms. His mouth covered her. She melted, opening for him. The delicious velvet slide of his tongue against hers now had the unbelievable hint of familiarity, even as he erased the room around them.

Then his lips softened. Their hunger hadn't disappeared. The tangle of their kisses slowed until they were barely lip locked. He pressed his forehead to hers, holding her close. Jane drank his scent, his feel, without opening her eyes. His lips moved to where his forehead had just been, sweetly kissing the same spot.

Then his phone rang. Her heart clenched.

"Let me jump back on the phone with Parker for a bit, and then I'm all yours."

She knew he had to pull away, and she almost trusted he'd come back to her. He wouldn't stay. That would be an impossible dream. But right then, Jane didn't care. She wanted to pretend it was possible for someone like Chance to be with someone like her.

CHAPTER FORTY-ONE

A N HOUR LATER, Jane experienced déjà vu when she answered the phone call from Chance. He had disappeared into his truck for his phone call with Parker. Once again, she'd been reading, but this time when he called, she'd raced to meet him in the front yard.

His smile made her giddy, and as they ambled into the backyard and toward her poolside cottage, Chance unceremoniously took her hand like he'd done a hundred times before. Her neurotic mind tried to make sense of their handholding. Chance chatted about a work and a colleague's baby.

He didn't show any nerves as they stepped into her little home. Meanwhile, Jane stumbled through the conversation and tried not to trip over her feet. Basically, she determined, Chance was unflappable. He jumped out of helicopters, camped in war-torn deserts, and didn't shy away from PDA—or whatever might happen between them behind closed doors.

Jane shut the front door, eyeing him as he walked around the quaint living room. Chance paused, pointedly glancing at her paperback romance novel on the coffee table and then giving her a wicked grin before inspecting a row of framed pictures on a side table.

While he poked around, she tried to see what he might—her stomach turned. Semi-folded laundry waited for her on the floor. In her rush to greet him, Jane hadn't thought about hiding her plain cotton underwear. She scooted in front of the clothes and heaped them into her arms. "Be back in a minute."

Thankfully, he continued to check the pictures.

She returned. Chance held a framed picture of her and Teddy at a water park. "Nice bathing suit."

She flushed. Her suit wasn't skimpy, but until then, she hadn't noticed the angle of the shot. It made her nonexistent chest look like major curves. Jane tried to snatch the frame away.

He held it out of reach. "What are you doing?"

"What are *you* doing?"

"Admiring your tits."

"Chance!"

He laughed but squinted. "Too vulgar?"

"No." Heat crawled up her neck. "It's just..." She jumped for it again. "Don't be silly."

He moved his arm out of the way but stepped closer. Her hands landed on his chest as she tried to catch her balance.

"Not silly, babe. Sexy."

Her mouth fell open. Jane couldn't think of a retort.

He lifted an eyebrow as though challenging her. "You haven't been told that enough, have you?"

"Ha." She choked. "You're the sexy beautiful one."

The corners of his lips curled but she didn't think her haphazardly thrown comment was the reason. Purposefully, he placed the picture frame down.

Her stomach jumped. "What are you doing?"

Chance took her hand and led her to the couch. After they sat down, he hauled her closer. Her fingers rubbed her knee, and her pulse jumped. Playfully, he walked his fingers up her leg, teasing along her inner thigh.

"What are you doing?" she asked again.

"Making a list."

"Of?"

"Places I want to kiss you."

She blushed and fidgeted. "Guess you can cross a kitchen off your list."

"I meant *where* I want to kiss you." His fingertips slid closer her shorts. "Like here."

Her breath hitched.

He turned his hand over and trailed his knuckles to her hip. "And here." He skimmed the pads of his fingers under the hem of her shirt. "Everywhere."

Jane swallowed hard. She couldn't tear her gaze from his wandering hand as he caressed down her hip and back to her leg. Her hard nipples pressed against her t-shirt. She wasn't even wearing a bra. Most times, she didn't need to. They were too damn uncomfortable. Yet, the way her breasts perked against her shirt made Jane feel incredibly feminine and… sexy.

"What do you want to do today?" he asked.

Jane wanted to say something about his kiss list. But she couldn't.

"Lie down with me." He pulled her to his chest then down. Their heads shared a throw pillow, and he snaked his foot between hers. Their bare legs tangled. "Better."

"Better," she repeated.

"All right. You don't know what we should do." He hummed. The corners of his lips quirked. "Finish your laundry?"

He did see her piles of boring cotton undies! "No!"

"You're right. Besides, I have a better idea."

"What?"

He laughed. "We'll go on an adventure where no one will try to kill us—or show up unexpectedly when I'm kissing you."

"If I lock the door, Lark can't come in," Jane pointed out, then slapped her hands over her face. "I didn't mean we should stay on the couch and—"

He kissed her. "In due time."

Her stomach backflipped even as she wanted to die from embarrassment. Chance pulled her off the couch and guided her out the front door. An excited, mischievous smile curled on his lips. "We need to go for a drive."

Chance didn't give her an opportunity to ask more questions. They retraced their steps to his truck. He pulled the door open and lifted her in. "There's something I want to show you."

Jane stared back, wary. "Maybe I should change first." Her flip-flops weren't good for anything but hanging around the house, and *again*, she wasn't wearing a bra! She was ninety-nine percent sure her employment agreement with the Thanes required her to be presentable in public—she was no lawyer, but even loosely defined, presentability probably meant wearing a bra.

"Do you want to change?"

She gestured to her super casual outfit. "I should."

"No one will see you but me."

That didn't make her ratty outfit any better. "I *am* comfortable."

"Comfort for the win." He closed her door as if that had determined the final answer.

Jane buckled her seatbelt. Nerves and anticipation mixed with compounding lust that freely flowed through her veins. She had absolutely no idea what the hell she was in for and couldn't wait.

He climbed in the driver's side with a million-dollar smile and muscles that flexed without meaning to. Chance seemed better suited for a rugged truck commercial than taking her for a surprise jaunt. Even the sun cast a brightly glowing halo around him before he shut his door. Jane wasn't entirely sure this was actually happening. If it wasn't, it was one hell of a good dream.

CHAPTER FORTY-TWO

THE ENGINE RUMBLED when he turned it over. As soon as they slipped through the gates that surrounded the Thanes community, Chance rolled down the windows. Her hair flew in the wind, and he cranked the music loud enough for them to sing.

Maybe Chance didn't have a specific place he was taking her to. That'd be okay. Music and the open road worked for her.

An hour might've passed. She could only guess. The drive had been like a road trip of winding hills and two-lane straightaways. He never looked at a map, and she didn't question where they were going.

They slowed, and his truck rumbled onto a well-worn driveway draped on both sides by thick trees. Chance slowed in front of a rustic sign. Jane read it aloud, "The Mud Palace."

"The Mud Palace," he repeated affirmatively.

"What does that mean?"

He grinned, lifting a shoulder, then urged his truck off the gravel road. She pushed up in her seat as they bumped along. The makeshift path was hard to see. After a few seconds, the ride smoothed out. He'd found a groove in the dirt tracks and followed them even as they disappeared into the tree line.

The road wound up a hill and opened into a cleared area. A handful of mud-caked sport-utility vehicles were parked in the field—then the name clicked. It was some kind of off-roading extravaganza. Chance rolled to a stop and she took it all in.

Dense woods surrounded the field. Several marked and blazed openings were wide enough for monster trucks to pass.

"Where do you want to go?"

She didn't have a clue. The trail markings might have well been written in Greek. Jane pointed toward a trail on his side.

"Good choice." He angled to the far left and drove back into the tree cover. The incline sharply grew until they summitted the hill. It opened into another clearing—except it had small hills and valleys like a golf course on steroids.

Instead of sand traps, Jane saw... her eyes rounded. "Is that *mud*?"

They rolled to a stop. Chance dangled his wrist over the steering wheel, laid back even as the truck engine revved. "It's not called the Mud Palace for nothing."

"I've never heard of anything like this." She tried to take the sprawling space in, then turned.

He grinned. "You want to drive?"

Jane balked as though Chance asked her to land a shuttle on the moon. "I think I'll let you start."

"All right. Let me know when you change your mind." He rolled up their windows. The engine roared. "Hang on, Mary Poppins. It's gonna be a bumpy ride."

Jane was certain this place wasn't on a map. "Did you grow up around here?"

They rumbled forward. "A little farther south, more in the mountains."

Midas the mountain man... He'd wanted to see the real her, but she loved seeing the real *him*.

Across the mud pits, Jane watched other off-roaders—a Wrangler, a dune buggy, and one monster truck—splash and spin over the landscape. Her heart raced as their truck approached, ready to do the same. He cut her a quick, mischievous glance and pressed his foot to the gas.

They headed straight for the nearest mid pit. Anticipation built in her chest. Her fingers clenched, and Jane held her breath as the truck dove into a pit. Mud splashed. She squealed in delight. They rocked side to side. The engine rumbled as they streaked through the mud and up the embankment.

"Fun?" he asked.

"Yes," she laughed and hollered at once. "Wait—we can't see!"

The wipers swiped some of the mud away. "Sure we can."

Not nearly enough. Nothing would be in their way, but the low visibility heightened her excitement. Chance jerked the steering wheel. They fish-tailed over the slick field. His laughter boomed, mixing with her eager shrieks.

"Eeek!" She pointed then gripped the door. "Watch out—*whee!*"

Mud rained in clumps. The truck slid and spun, and the poor windshield wipers raced to remove the never-ending coat of mud. They squished into swamps and carved out tracks as their wheels spun. She jostled back and forth in her seat, shouting where he should go next.

Finally, Chance pulled to the side. She pressed her hands to her chest, surprised to find her heart racing. "I need a break to catch my breath."

He laughed, and she tipped her head back. After a moment, she faced him. "Wow."

He agreed. "Adrenaline packs a hell of a punch."

She smiled. Her eyes sank shut. Adrenaline still buzzed through her. The hairs on her arms had stood, electrified. Her eyes opened, and she looked at him. His casual posture belied the fierce hunger on his face. Jane could blame her adrenaline rush all she wanted, but that didn't change the fact that Chance was the reason for her visceral reactions.

The space between them was too small, too warm. Heat crawled up the back of her neck. Everything about Chance—physically—made him mind-numbingly gorgeous. But his kindness and laughter, his sense of humor and easygoing yet fiercely protective nature—that made him hotter than the sun on an August day. But even that wasn't the reason Jane's heart jumped and her panties dampened. She was vividly aware of his feelings toward her. The man had made a list of *places* to kiss her, and he liked to hold her hand. That combination was one hell of an aphrodisiac.

He pulled in a deep breath and shook his head as though holding himself back. Then he quickly grinned.

"*What?*"

His blue eyes danced. "Your turn."

"Oh no! No, no, *no.*" Jane inched back, trapped against the door. "I didn't survive Syria to die at a place called the Mud Palace."

"Babe." His finger motioned her closer. "Get behind the wheel. No more running from what you want."

CHAPTER FORTY-THREE

*I*F THE MAN *only knew.* Jane *wanted* his mouth on hers. But three important things surfaced in her mind. The first was simple. *Babe* would never be her preferred term of endearment, but it was infinitely better than Mary Poppins. Second, despite that, the way that Chance said babe made her shiver. His voice dropped and the corners of his eyes tightened. She couldn't explain the arousal-inducing formula, but she couldn't ignore it either. Finally, third, no matter the situation, Chance knew what she wanted—sometimes before she realized it herself. Kissing him would be awesome. Driving his truck through the mud? That'd be pretty amazing, too.

Jane didn't need more convincing. They switched places, and she repositioned the driver's seat to reach the pedals. Her heart galloped, but she wrapped her hands around the steering wheel.

"Ready?"

She couldn't explain her nerves. "I'm a little scared."

"I won't let you get hurt." He lounged in the passenger seat as though they weren't tempting death with her at the wheel.

Still, her stomach tied in knots. "What if I destroy your truck?"

Impish humor curled on his lips. "Don't do that."

Jane pressed her head to the steering wheel. She *really* wanted to drive into the mud. The consequences were terrifying. They could wreck. They could… *die.* Along with any number of possibilities that existed in between. She rolled her head until she could see him. Chance terrified her. He was beautiful, she was plain. He was amazing. She was normal. Yet he didn't see the same thing she did. In his eyes, she was beautifully amazing, and in his words, he wouldn't let her get hurt. Jane met his eyes, trusting what he believed, and sat up. "I'm not going to wreck your truck."

He nodded. "I know."

"You're pretty amazing, Chance."

"Eye of the beholder, babe. But I'm glad you think so."

Her heart squeezed, and Jane shifted into gear. "Here we go."

She licked her lips and pressed the gas pedal. She clenched the steering wheel tighter as they approached the mud pit, and the split second before they dove down, her breath locked in her lungs. She closed her eyes as it felt like the truck was free-falling. A split second felt like a century. The truck straightened. Her eyes flew open. Jane hollered and fed the truck more gas. They rocked side to side. Mud splashed. The wheels burned and churned. Her fingers ached and her heart slammed against her ribs until they summited the far side of the pit.

She took her foot off the pedal and threw her arms into the air. "I did it!"

His grin matched hers—but without her ecstatic screaming. "Now do it again."

So she did. Jane flew through the field. They raced and spun through mud. She traversed hills and valleys, searching for their next run. The wipers barely kept the mud off the windshield. She trusted herself, and he trusted her. Jane crisscrossed the field until she didn't think her body could fly any higher.

Jane eased up. They slowed, and she shook her hands out and took a long breath. This had been cathartic. Her nervous tension had ramped up but disappeared somewhere in the mud, leaving her relaxed and alive.

"Go that way." Chance pointed toward the darkening tree line.

Jane eased them from the field and headed onto a new trail. They rolled along a rocky road. The steering wheel easily slipped back and forth in her hands. She let the truck rumble as it found its path, knowing she was still in control as they headed deeper into the woods. Shadows wrapped around them. The sinking sun only reached them in patches between the branches, seeming to promise that they were the alone with nature. It felt like there was nothing near them for miles and miles.

Jane slowed at a fork in the road. "Which way?"

"Your choice," he said.

"Mine? I don't have a clue."

Chance gestured. "That way leads out."

She studied it, not sure she wanted to leave the quiet oasis where they'd taken respite but not sure that she wanted to rumble in the mud again. After all the excitement, she liked sitting next to him in the quiet. "What about the other way?"

His blue eyes met hers. The connection sparked over her as though lightning cracked. Chance bit his bottom lip as if he wasn't sure where the other path led. Then his jaw ticked. He cocked his head toward the mysterious trail, and no matter what he said, she was certain she wanted to go that way. "Eventually, it'll lead to a dead end."

Lightning cracked between them again. Her fingers tightened on the steering wheel, and she shivered. Alone with Chance. No one to interrupt. He didn't say another word. He didn't have to, and she realized what he had done. Jane had to choose what she wanted—which, of course, was him. Saying that she wanted him, doing things that signified what she wanted... that made her vulnerable. She had to trust herself and him. She had to believe that he wanted what she did, no matter what barriers she'd once constructed in her mind.

Looks didn't matter. Assumptions were pointless. She wasn't as bold as him, honestly answering and reacting to whatever came before him. But that was what he needed from her.

Baring herself in this way was impossible. Her heart tripped over itself, racing with desire and... *certainty.*

Jane closed her eyes, certain what she wanted... what *they* wanted. Serenity filled her chest, and Jane opened her eyes. The corners of her lips curled as she angled his truck along the path that would give them time alone.

They didn't say a word as she drove. Arousal warmed in her blood, and while she anticipated what might come, she was embarrassed of her desire. The trail disappeared. Jane shifted into park when she didn't see anywhere else to go.

"We're here." Her heart slammed as she turned. "The middle of nowhere."

His mouth quirked. "You handled the mud like a pro."

"Thanks." She chewed on her bottom lip. Jane didn't know how to act next now that she'd made clear what she wanted. Her short breaths couldn't keep pace with her sporadic pulse. She'd half-expected Chance to jump across their seats, but she knew better. He liked to be deliberate. That careful, intentional way he went about kissing her made her ravenously weak.

His seatbelt unclicked. Her heart jumped. Slowly, as if he were savoring her tense, shaking breaths and multiplying desire, he reached across the truck. Deftly, Chance released her seatbelt. The metal latch unclicked. The chest restraint rolled back. Neither were a sound she ever noticed before, but now, they caressed her senses like a promise of what was to come.

CHAPTER FORTY-FOUR

STRONG HANDS LIFTED Jane from the driver's seat. Chance pulled her onto his chest as though she were light and graceful. His next fluid movement dropped the back of his chair. She became acutely aware of their proximity, and had this compromising position happened any time before today, she might not have enjoyed it as much. But she did, reveling in the way he stared up at her.

"You approve of the trail I picked?"

His hands rested on her hips. "I would've been good with whatever you wanted." His fingers squeezed. "But this one had my vote."

Jane angled closer and breathed him in. His scent had mixed with the outdoors, and a memory flashed of her first night with him in Syria. His lips brushed hers, and she melted against his mouth, falling prey to its infinite sweetness.

She let herself go. Heat built into their kisses. Her body hummed. His hands and tongue explored her. Unguarded, she basked in his touch and sought to bring him a fraction of the pleasure washing through her.

Chance nuzzled to her ear. "Damn, Jane."

She appreciated the tremor of hunger in his voice, understanding she'd caused his reaction. "I like the way you sound."

He kissed her as though he had never done so before today and might never have the opportunity again. Chance tasted like heaven and felt like a haven. Her palms explored the slope and angles of his muscles sculpted through blood, sweat, and tears when lives had been on the line, and gratitude filled her.

Chance reached into her haphazard ponytail and tugged the band free. Her hair swooped down, covering their faces like a curtain closing over stage. He moderated their frantic kisses with lazy, maddeningly sensual circles of his tongue. Desperation flooded her veins. Their clothes hindered skin-on-skin contact. She craved the sensation of their bodies becoming tighter; her soft, sensitive thighs sliding over his powerful masculine ones.

Needy rumbles purred between them. Jane rocked her hips, savoring the friction of his engorged cock against her sex. With more deliberate motion, she rubbed against him. He sucked in a sharp breath. His palms gripped her ass and held her in place. Chance flexed against her, grinding his erection with identical speed and pressure—except he was in charge. Jane gasped. Her eyes opened and met his as he held her in place. She didn't know it was possible to feel so in control of what she wanted, yet simultaneously so completely and so *gratefully* controlled.

"How do you do that?" she gasped.

Chance wrapped his arms around her back, cocooning her in his hug. He whispered, "Do what?"

Explosive tears caught in her throat. She had wanted to rip their clothes off, but when he stopped stroking his cock against her, she simply wanted to crawl inside his strength and burst. "Take me from zero to a hundred."

"Neither one of us have ever been at zero together."

That was the truth. Her hand touched his cheek. He let her explore, tracing the outline of his mouth and jaw.

He kissed the back of her knuckles. "I could watch you all day. Every day."

In her mind, a faraway warning reminded Jane he would leave soon. This job was temporary. His home was a world away. Both promised he could never stay. But, instead of listening to the little voice at the back of her head, Jane pressed her lips to his.

Who cared if he left tomorrow? Today, they were on the same page. They wanted, needed, and tasted each other. She'd never been so safe and fulfilled. Maybe the here and now was all that mattered.

Jane deepened her kiss and pushed her worries away. Chance would take care of her, and it felt so damn good to give up her role as the responsible one, the person who took care of everything and made sure she was protected, to just live and feel and be.

As though Chance could read her mind, his hands slid under her tank top. His rough, calloused palms skimmed up her spine and held her in place against him. She flexed onto him, rocking for the needed friction. His fingers kneaded her back, melting her neck muscles and fueling the desperation in her core. His hands curved around her ribs until the weight of her small breasts filled his rasping hands.

She writhed. Need spiraled deep inside her body. Arousal soaked her underwear. "Chance—"

A horn blared. Jane jolted upright. Not a car horn. A freaking *air* horn. Then her world spun topsy-turvy. Her head spun, and she blinked until she could find her bearings.

They weren't on the passenger side of the truck. The steering wheel wasn't far from her face. Chance's mountainous weight had her pinned beneath him. She struggled against his hand clasped over her mouth. Then she froze.

She didn't have his attention. Laying prone, he searched the mud-splattered window. His hand held a *gun*.

Where the freaking hell had that come from? And, more importantly, what the fuck was happening?

Chance repositioned, fruitlessly searching out the windows. "Stay down."

A metallic thump echoed from the back of the truck. Before she could freak out, Chance rolled out the passenger door in one fluid motion. His fierce face and drawn handgun pointed toward the woods, leaving Jane to watch whatever might happen.

CHAPTER FORTY-FIVE

"EASY THERE, SON." The raspy words from a pack-a-day smoker chuckled as though it weren't the first time he'd had an armed man barrel roll out of a truck. "Lower your weapon."

Jane twisted to her knees to watch but couldn't see out the back window. Her head swiveled to watch Chance. He relaxed and lowered his gun. "Didn't expect company."

His tone was decidedly more apologetic than when he'd ordered her to stay down. Jane peeked out. Chance strode closer to the older Marlboro Man who caught sight of her leaning out the door. Jane jerked back into the truck.

"I can see that," the Marlboro Man chuckled. "But everyone's supposed to get gone at sunset. Ya'll need to head out."

"We lost track of time." Chance and the Marlboro Man both sounded as if they were coming from a place of understanding.

Jane wasn't sure what she thought about that. Did he bring girls here? To this… wooded lovers' lane? She scowled as their conversation wrapped. Just like that, the horn-blaring emergency ended.

Chance shut Jane's door and then ambled to the driver's side. He gave her a wink when he climbed in and fired up the engine. Her cheeks heated as though they'd been caught necking at a high school dance—except, they'd been caught in the throes of foreplay by the Marlboro Man. Embarrassment curled down her spine.

The air-conditioning immediately blasted. She realized that their make-out session wasn't the only thing that had made her hot. Despite the tree coverage, the summer heat did her no favors. She tied her hair into a ponytail again and grumbled. "What's with the air horn?"

Chance laughed.

"I thought we were under attack."

He quickly glanced her way as he threaded them through the grounds. "Sometimes it's best to announce yourself."

Probably good advice. They picked up speed over an empty field. The setting sun had dropped behind the forest, making the sky an orangish purple. It reminded Jane of dinner in Abu Dhabi. She and Chance had danced with each other that night and crash-landed in an elevator lip-lock. How did that advice pertain to them now? They'd made their intentions and desires clear. The only thing that wasn't clear was what the future would hold.

Chance mumbled to himself then turned on the radio.

"What?"

He eyed her with a quiet head-shaking laugh. "Definitely didn't realize it was so late."

True and funny, but there was an uneven cadence in his laughter that didn't sound as amused as he let on to be.

Jane bit her lip. "Time flies when you're having fun."

THE TRUCK RUMBLED along the trail. Gravel spun in his wheels. Branches and bushes slapped the side of truck bed. Chance fiddled with the radio, aggravated with himself. It was a good thing that old man had come along when he did. A few minutes later, he would've had Jane in a far more precarious situation. From the sounds she made and the way her body moved with his, she would've been on board to strip their clothes away.

A fresh wave of arousal needled down his spine. They'd been so close. So fucking close. It killed him that Jane wasn't on his cock that very second. His chest heaved, and he slapped the radio off as he turned the truck onto a paved road.

She repositioned her legs. "Back to civilization."

"Yup." A heavy silence blanketed them. Now that they'd left the densely packed woods, they seemed to be in another country.

"Do you always have a gun with you?"

"Yeah." Chance glanced at Jane. It was easy to forget that most people didn't assume an enemy lurked behind every corner. "It's part of the job."

She nodded. "Our real worlds are so far apart."

Chance didn't know what a weapon had to do with their jobs. After all, it was her job that brought them together in the first place.

A gas station sign glowed ahead, and he pulled over. Not only was he hungry, but in his hasty rush from the Mud Palace, he hadn't cleaned up his mirrors and windows like he should have. After a few minutes of scraping mud from the mirrors and loading up on junk food, he returned behind the wheel. Jane sorted through the options, splitting snacks between them as he pulled onto the road again.

They ate in silence. The miles became a blur. After a few mile markers, he noticed the uneasy tension was gone. Chance polished off the last cookies from a snack-pack, realizing that sanity had crept back to mind. Getting busy in the woods hadn't been his intention. Even when he told Jane he wanted to kiss her without interruption, that hadn't meant fucking in his truck. At least not the first time they got together.

What he needed was another list to accentuate his first one, appropriately titled 'places to kiss *Jane*'. That second one would be called '*places* to kiss Jane.' He grinned, eager to show her the differences between his lists.

They pulled up at the gate that surrounded the Thanes' exclusive neighborhood. Chance stretched in the driver's seat. He hadn't realized how tight his muscles were and couldn't think of any reason why—unless the vicious blue balls that always seemed prevalent around Jane had metastasized into knotting aches in his back, shoulders, and chest.

"Oh no." Jane wrinkled her nose. "They're not going to let you in."

He scowled, long limbs aching to get out of the truck. "Yeah? Why not?"

She eyed him as though green antennas sprouted from his head. "They have rules."

"Who?"

"The people who live here. Think of it like a homeowner's or condo association with the world's most particular board."

"Yeah… that doesn't mean much."

"There are rules," Jane explained. "But even if there weren't, Gigi Thane has many rules that can be generalized in one tenet. Only *perfect* things may enter the Thane bubble."

God, these people. Chance pinched the bridge of his nose. "We'll go find a car wash."

"There isn't one close by. Folks over here have help for that."

"Right." He shook his head, not believing—yet totally believing—that his truck wouldn't pass neighborhood muster. "Well…" Chance decided to test their luck and inched toward the gate house anyway. "The truck *is* a *perfect* mess."

She snort-laughed. "Nothing fazes you, does it?"

He gave her a quick look. "You do, sometimes." He winked then rolled down his window, greeting a guard. "Evening."

The man stepped out, gesturing for the truck to back out. "This is a closed community—"

Jane leaned over and waved. "Hi, Sal."

A vaguely horrified expression crossed the guard's face when he peered into the cabin of truck. He squinted, still ready to wave them away like muddy river lunatics, when he caught sight of her. "Jane?"

She tilted her head and cheerily greeted, "It's me, Sal. Can you let us in?"

Sal didn't look convinced. His expression darkened with concern, and casting Chance a wary look, he carefully asked, "Is everything all right?"

"It is." She unbuckled and scooted closer to his window. "This is Chance Evans, Gigi's newest addition."

"I see," Sal said, not moving to let them in. "And the truck? Is that some kind of stunt?"

"No—"

"Because we're all supposed to be on the same page when Mr. or Mrs. Th—"

"No, Sal. I promise. It's not. Everyone's out of town, and Chance took me to play in the mud."

"I see." Sal crossed his arms, still unconvinced. "What's the phrase I'm looking for?"

"Enjoy your night?" Chance offered.

The man smirked. "Let's try… Not a snowflake's chance in hell."

Jane grumbled. "Sal, I have to pee. Let us in."

He shook his head. "Careful, Jane. The paparazzi lounging across the street will start sniffing to see who the hell you are."

"So let us in," Chance suggested.

Sal scoffed. "If your truck dirtied the Thanes' street…" He clucked. "That's a risk I'm not willing to take."

Chance found an enormous amount of humor in the guard's reasoning. "I thought the Thanes have a 'Risk it all' motto?"

Jane and Sal groaned simultaneously.

He looked incredulous. "Syria's okay, but mud isn't?"

Sal pinched the bridge of his nose. "You have a lot to learn." But then he pointed toward a small enclave of staff parking. It was cordoned off by a protective layer of hedges. "Park in our lot and don't tell a soul."

"Thanks, Sal." Jane grinned. "Appreciate it."

Chance threw the truck in reverse and pulled into the hidden lot. The manicured landscaping barely hid his truck in the farthest spot. He stretched and unbuckled his seatbelt. "Ready?"

Jane gave him a shy but sly smile. "I think so."

His eyebrow arched, watching as she fidgeted with the hem of her shorts. "What?"

Her chin dipped. "I'm ready so long as…"

"What?"

Jane met his eye, tugging her lip between her teeth. It took a moment, but she finished, "So long as we pick up where the Marlboro Man interrupted us."

CHAPTER FORTY-SIX

CHANCE FALTERED, DOUBLE-CHECKING that his mind hadn't dubbed over her actual words. "The Marlboro Man?"

The look in her eyes—a mix of uncertainty and lust—assured him that he hadn't. "I didn't catch the man's name."

His throat tightened. The visceral memory of her on his lap rocketed across his skin. For a moment, he wasn't sure if he could trust his voice. Tension filled the truck as Chance slowly lifted his chin. "We'll pick up where we left off."

"Great." Jane jerked away and jumped from his truck, her nerves leading her retreat as she slammed her door shut.

"But we'll wait until you're ready." He found himself smiling and shaking his head.

She rounded the corner of the hedges, not glancing back, and he hustled to catch up. He'd never *run* after a woman before—until today—but waved at Sal as he loped toward Jane.

Jane slowed when he reached her side. Chance took her hand. As his fingers knit with hers, he could feel the anxious tension melt away. "The neighborhood's kinda nice. If you like this kind of thing."

She snort-laughed, ambling as they rounded a corner. "Who likes award-winning architecture anyways?"

Hand in hand, they followed a winding road of perfect lawns and well-appointed homes. Chance wondered how many *normal* houses could fit between the neighborhood's mansions. Finally, they turned down the Thanes' street. The neighborhood was eerily perfect. Not a single blade of grass or manicured flowers was out of place. The homes rarely showed signs of life. It was summer, but the sound of kids playing and laughing didn't fill the air. The warm night didn't hold the scent of backyard grills. What was the point of their rigorous standards when Chance didn't see a soul enjoying it?

He didn't know but knew he wanted to spend his time with people who appreciated life more than furnishings. "Even if I were a billionaire, I wouldn't live here."

"Same." Her phone dinged from the back pocket of her shorts. It quickly dinged again and served as a reminder: this neighborhood was simply their job.

Jane retrieved the phone. Her warm expression shifted. The corners of her lips pinched as she read the screen, and Chance didn't need three guesses to know who it was.

★   ★   ★

"OH, BOY." JANE frowned at her phone. Gigi's text messages popped onto the screen, one right after the other. The first ones were silly ones, asking that Jane double check the sprinklers went off at the right time and reminding Jane that Gigi's man-candy pool guy would be there on Tuesday.

The last one, though, threatened to ruin her night with Chance. Jane re-read Gigi's text message: *Lark can't stay in the main house tonight. We REALLY need to give the appearance that we're at home. Please spend the weekend in the main house.*

She understood Gigi's concern. For whatever reasons, the Thanes were trying to keep their super-secret trip as on the down low. Jane hated to stay in their massive house when she was all alone, though... she glanced at Chance. She *wasn't* alone.

"What's going on?" he asked.

Before she could reply to Chance, another text came through from Gigi: *Hello? Are you there? I'm not sure why you're ignoring me.*

"Oh, good grief." Jane rolled her eyes and held up her phone for Chance to see. "Ignoring her? It's been less than a minute."

Another text pinged through. Jane glanced at the screen. Gigi sent a row of praying hands and heart emoticons followed by: *Please. We're sorry if you already had plans elsewhere. Just turn some lights on and off. Pretend you're playing house. Just keep the paparazzi off our tails.*

Another text pinged.

Jane, stop ignoring me!!!

Jane snorted, and Chance read over her shoulder.

He let out a slow whistle. "She can be a little manic?"

"Yeah." But that wasn't what bugged her. She still didn't understand why the attention-hungry Thanes wanted to lay low. That could be a mystery for another day. Before Gigi could send another text, Jane responded: *That's not a problem. Enjoy your vacation.*

They started toward the Thanes' again. Jane's thoughts raced. Would they care if Chance stayed with her in the main house? They wouldn't know if he spent the night in her pool house—her stomach flipped. Spending the night was insanely presumptuous. Except, between the interruptions in the kitchen and his truck, Jane had made assumptions. Tonight, they could be together and alone. It didn't matter when he would leave, or if they spent the night together in her cottage or the main house. Once they were behind closed doors, Chance would touch her again.

Her heart skipped a beat. She would touch him too. They'd kiss. They'd undress. His body would press against hers. *Into hers.* Despite the warm summer night, a chill rolled down her spine, and heat spiraled up Jane's neck. They'd be intimate. That's what she wanted, wasn't it? It better be. That's what she told Chance she wanted in his truck.

Jane fidgeted but then turned. Where was Chance supposed to be staying anyway?

Their trek finished, and they stood at the bottom of the Thanes' large cobblestone driveway. She bit her bottom lip and twisted to face Chance. "Did they tell you where you were staying? Security doesn't usually stay on the grounds."

Security rarely ran twenty-four-hour shifts, per Gigi's requests for privacy, and they rarely stayed on the grounds. But their property could house guests and staff. Two guest houses faced the opposite side from Jane's poolside cottage. There was an apartment over the garage, or maybe they planned for Chance to use one of the guest rooms.

He shrugged. "Lark said she'd get back to me, but I haven't heard from her."

"Hmm. Lark was supposed to stay in the main house, but now she can't."

"Did I mention how Lark seems like such a nice person," Chance muttered.

Jane laughed though her nerves still jittered. She felt like a schoolgirl asking her crush on a date. Where had her bravery gone? Jane shuffled her foot. "Since I have to stay in the main house, later, if you want, you could stay there with me."

Chance offered a closed-lip grin.

She couldn't read his silent answer. Was that hesitation? "*Or don't.* There are guest rooms and guest houses like mine." She grimaced. "Actually, forget I even mentioned it. We'll hang out and then—"

"Jane." He took her hand and led the way toward the front door. They stopped on the porch, and before she could let them in, he spun her to face him. "Do you always think the worst?"

When it came to someone spending time with her... "Maybe?"

"Why?"

Her parents was the easiest answer. They'd taught her to distrust before she knew how to walk. "You gave me a weird look a minute ago."

Chance grinned. "I forgot my bag in the truck." He chuckled. "You left, I followed. We walked all the way up here, and I didn't bring a thing."

"Oh..." She laughed, covering her warm cheeks with her hands. "So, you want to stay with me?"

"Tell me one reason why I wouldn't stay with you."

In that calm demand, Chance seemed so intent and true, set on re-minding Jane of every kind and sentimental word he'd shared. "I don't know."

He wrapped her to him and rested his chin on the top of her head. Silent laughter rumbled in his chest. "I won't even complain if you force me to sleep on nice sheets."

A calm grin curled on her lips. "Oh, I will."

With renewed conviction, she pressed the security code on the keypad next to the front door. The locks clicked, and she threw open the doors. "Welcome back to crazy town."

CHAPTER FORTY-SEVEN

THE SECOND TIME in the Thanes's home was no less impressive than the first. But Chance didn't care. Finally, they were alone.

Then Jane's phone blew up with another round of messages from Gigi. Between the quick responses, Chance decided to jump in the shower and let Jane deal with her—*their*—boss.

He walked around a bathroom that was the size of his house in the Shenandoah Mountains. The bathtub was like a swimming pool and the shower had a number of heads, all pointing in strategic locations. As he programmed the hot water to turn on, Chance decided he would avoid the main house whenever he had the opportunity. But not tonight.

He'd said he'd spend the night with Jane and he'd meant it, however uncomfortable his surroundings made him. Opulence was a reason he didn't like Abu Dhabi and Dubai. Yet here he was, in a guest bathroom with technology to rival NASA.

Chance splashed some water on his face but didn't dare touch the fluffy white towels. He didn't know a shade of white this bright and clean existed. Jared Westin had been right. The Thane mansion was his worst nightmare.

"Chance?" Jane knocked.

He dried his hands on his shirt then opened the door.

Jane held a stack of clothes. "I found these and thought they might fit."

"Thanks." He took the pile. Their hands touched. If Jane had been any other woman, he wouldn't have noticed. She didn't flirt or do anything special, yet desire twisted in his chest.

"Let me know if you need anything." Jane stepped from the door threshold.

Chance tossed the clothes onto the counter and reached for her hand. "Wait a sec." He pulled her close and shut the door. The steamy air surrounded them when her body drew flush against his. "Where're you going?"

She looked up at him with her big eyes, her lips parted. "I thought you wanted to shower."

His eyes searched her face, her hair, and all of her pretty features—each one he desperately wanted to explore at length. "I do." He cupped her cheeks in his hands, letting his thumb slide over the soft skin. "With you."

Chance held her against him, savoring Jane's hold as realization dawned. He hadn't just said the words. His desire had electrified the air. His heart thumped with a mind-numbing yearning, and he was positive another word wasn't needed to clarify the depth of his hunger. *I want you. I need you.* Every conceivable variation he could imagine felt trite.

His hands slid down her jaw. At the base of her neck, Chance relished Jane's strong, racing pulse. She licked her bottom lip. The tiny pink flick of her tongue drove him to the edge. He hooked his fingers under the straps of her tank top. Jane's eyelashes fluttered. The pink hue of her cheeks deepened.

Slowly, he slid the straps from her shoulders. His mouth dipped to the corner of her neck, eliciting her shiver. His lips curled, and Chance parted them. His tongue swept over her skin, and encouraged by her sharp breath, he nuzzled and kissed his way to the soft spot below her jaw.

Jane leaned her weight into one of his arms. The more pliant she became, the deeper his need burned. His cock throbbed. Jane swayed against him until his mouth took hers. She opened for his kiss, letting him nibble, suck, and explore. Steamy air swirled around them, and with his eyes closed, Chance mapped her mouth and memorized her reactions as though nothing in the world could interrupt them.

His hands reached her waist, and his eyes opened to meet hers. Their lips parted, and she didn't look away as he lifted her shirt, slowly exposing her stomach and then her bare breasts. Her tight, dark nipples reached for him, and Chance dropped to his knees.

Surprised, Jane leaned back. His hands remained her waist, and he stilled her, watched her, promised without a single word that he would make her feel like heaven. A second passed. Then another, and when she relaxed, he buried his face in the valley of her breasts.

Chance released her waist. His hands skimmed up her back then along her side until he cupped her tits in the palms of his hands. She trembled, breath shaking.

He took his time, licking and kissing each mound, rolling his hot tongue over the perked tips. He let the stubble on his cheeks graze her creamy skin.

Jane's fingers gripped his shoulders. Her nails dug into the muscle, urging him on, and when her hips swayed, he took that as a sign to finish undressing her.

Her shorts fell away. His fingers traced up her calves and up her legs. Still dressed and on his knees, he'd never felt more in control of and responsible for a woman than he did at that moment. "Fuck me," Chance whispered reverently. His hands drifted from her thighs, and he stared in appreciation. "You're beautiful."

"*I'm naked.*"

He grinned and took his time standing. "Naked and beautiful."

"You're dressed," she murmured, her voice rich and lusty.

"Not for long." Without any fanfare, Chance pulled his shirt over his head and unfastened his jeans. Her eyes widened. Desire made their hue richer than he could recall seeing. "Beautiful and strong and smart, and…" He didn't fucking know enough words to explain why she made him harder than steel. "You're everything."

That was a hell of a thing to say. Undefinable. Unexplainable. It just… was.

He pulled a condom from his wallet then kicked away the last of his clothes. Steam swirled around them, and Chance breathed it in as he reached for her. Their naked bodies meddled tighter, and with an absurdly chaste kiss, he backed Jane into the shower and placed the condom next to the shampoo.

Hot water wrapped around them. Her face nuzzled against his chest, and she hugged their slick bodies together like they were slow dancing in a warm rain. He wanted to slide back onto his knees and bury his face in her cunt. He wanted to taste Jane, feel his tongue inside her, to know he was between her legs when her orgasms hit.

Jane shifted, reviving him from his trance. Her hand wrapped around his shaft, and he sucked in a deep breath.

Her chin tilted up. "Is that okay…" The pad of her thumb slid along the thick head of his cock.

His molars clamped, and he trembled under her touch. "Carte blanche permission, babe."

She laughed, grinned, and sank to her knees. She covered the crown of his member with her white-hot mouth. His eyes shut. A ravenous thrill coiled in his back muscles and ripped through his frenzied limbs. Hot water beat on his back and his chest, and her tongue teased and tormented him until she made his toes curl.

How did his plan go haywire? His orgasm loomed, but hell if he would come anywhere but inside Jane. "I need to—"

She drew away. "So *do.*"

Chance teetered dangerously on the vicious edge of climax. He broke away, breathless. "I can't."

Uncertainty listed in her dark eyes.

"Jane." He commanded her gaze and dared her demons to ruin their moment. "I want more than your mouth. I need to be inside you." His words and racing breaths mixed. "Tell me you understand me."

She nodded, and Chance lifted Jane onto her feet.

"Promise me. When it comes to you, you will not doubt me." His lungs hammered, and to hear him, he sounded angry. But he wasn't. Not at her. Maybe the rest of her world. Maybe because a powerful climax begged for release. But never Jane.

Her lips parted. "You're amazing—"

"*Jane.*"

"I'm naked. Let's have sex." She pushed onto her toes for a kiss.

He didn't know what boiled deeper: the need to come or her wavering trust. Tension ticked in his jaw. Sanity and pleasure battled.

Painfully, he side-stepped her kiss and vowed to set her straight. "You were worth finding, and you're worth waiting for. I don't want your body. I want all of you. That includes every scar and layer that came before we met." He inhaled and held it until he had the strength to back away.

"You want to have sex with me…"

He didn't know if that were a question or an understanding left unfinished.

Jane pressed her palms to his chest. His heartbeat slammed under her touch. "I want that part of you that you hide. That you refuse to show anyone." He took her chin and inched it up until her eyes settled on his. "And, I gotta tell you. That scares me to death. But I'm good with it."

Her watery laughter was nearly drowned away by the shower, but her faint smile stayed. "You're a warmonger with years of training."

"A cocky one at that." A smile tugged on his cheeks, but he suddenly sobered. Maybe he was asking too much of her. Chance had never thought about romance or relationships. But at that moment, he realized that so much of what he *knew* was all wrong. Like the way people thought beautiful homes would make happy lives. They were in one of the most beautiful homes in the world. It wasn't a happy one.

Shower sex made a relationship as much as roses and candy defined romance. They were child's play. Romance meant… he didn't know. It meant giving himself and building trust. Right now, he was ready to give and give and give until they couldn't move. But that wasn't the kind of giving she needed. Jane needed the opportunity to believe in them.

He pushed her wet hair off of her face and cupped her cheeks. Their lips connected. The world fell away until a building need made him hum for more. "Let me touch you."

She nodded. "Carte blanche."

His lips stayed on hers, and his hands slid over her back, letting the water sluice between them. The lull of the water washed away the strain. Chance guided her to a wood bench that lined the large shower. "I never knew what these things were for."

Jane held onto his hand as he sat down. "A comfy place to shave legs?"

He pulled her into his lap, legs on one side, her back propped in the crook of his arm. "A comfy place for something." His hand glided up the inside of her thigh. Jane kissed him. Their tongues languidly tangled as he stroked up her thigh and down again. Each time, he inched higher until Chance reached her sex. Jane parted her legs and squirmed.

For now, this would be better than shower sex. The subtle way she writhed made him want to master her body. Water didn't fall over them, but a warm swirling mist mixed with the steam and kept them warm.

Chance grazed his fingers along her sensitive skin. The buds of her nipples tightened. "That feels good?"

Her eyes slipped shut, and Jane nodded. He grazed her clitoris and delicately teased. Her hips swayed, and her back arched as her chest drew quicker breaths.

"I like the way you move."

Her eyelashes fluttered, and Jane shifted to give him more access.

He liked that move too. Chance took advantage of the way her legs spread, stroking her silkiness that was slick with arousal. He circled her entrance, mesmerized by the quiet mews that fell from her lips. He'd wanted trust, and with her eyes closed and body bared, she'd given him what he'd asked for.

Chance slid his fingers into her pussy. Jane's chest hitched. Her head tipped back. Her body clenched him as he withdrew, and her hips lifted for more. He pressed into her again. He crooked the angle of his fingers while keeping pressure against her clit, experimenting and studying the woman in his lap.

"Oh," she breathed harshly. Her hips swayed in rhythm with his hand. "That's…"

"Good," he finished.

She nodded. He plunged in and out of her, living for the burn in his muscles as his forearm flexed, finger-fucking Jane as she begged for more. Her hand clamped to his bicep. Her fingernails dug into his arm. Her other arm wrapped around his arm, he struggled to maintain what she desperately needed.

"Come for me, Jane. Give it to me."

She thrashed her head against his chest. Her body thrashed. Jane rode his hand as much as he drove into her. Her muscles clenched.

"Please," Jane hoarsely whispered, grinding for release. "Chance, please."

He couldn't take this anymore. His cock throbbed, threatening to come from just her wet, slippery ass grinding against his erection. He growled and gave her everything he had.

"God." Her moaning cry echoed in the shower as her body quaked in orgasm. Her canal rippled like a hurricane of pleasure.

She twisted toward his stomach, legs and hands still wrapped around his arm until she shuddered. Trembles still pulsed around his fingers, and Chance withdrew his fingers. She gasped then pliantly nuzzled against his chest.

He dropped his head against the wall. One arm held Jane. The other hung limp, wishing to God he had the strength to grip his cock and—her fingers wrapped around the heavy, throbbing length between them. "Jane—" Her fist slid the base of his shaft with a long, fluid motion. His eyes closed. His teeth clenched. Painfully erect and dangerously close to orgasm, he hissed at the flick of her wrist and strong grip. Jane spared no time with preambles, jerking his cock like they'd been lovers for years.

Had this been any other woman, he would've forced the pleasure back as though he had to wait an imaginary time threshold for manly reactions to hand jobs. But he didn't care. She made him feel too damn good.

His body tightened, and his climax coiled deep in his nuts. The arm around her back squeezed. His exhausted hand threaded into her hair, and he flexed his hips. Chance groaned and came until his cum spurted, marking her stomach and thigh.

Her slippery hands slowed. A full-body shiver overtook him. Even as they collapsed together, more satisfied than he knew possible, he wanted more.

"Wow." She pressed a kiss to his chest. "That was amazing."

No. He didn't want more of Jane Singleton.

He *needed* more.

CHAPTER FORTY-EIGHT

FOUR DAYS PASSED, and the Thanes still hadn't come home. Jane stayed in contact with Aunt Courtney, who decided to extend her weekend getaway with Teddy into a weeklong visit to her second home in upstate New York. All of this meant that Jane and Chance continued to play house in their parallel universe where responsibilities and jobs didn't exist.

That meant *a lot* of time spent getting to know each other. In bed. Out of bed. In the shower again. And, they talked about everything and nothing. She liked how the quiet times didn't feel awkward. She didn't feel pressure to fill the day with witty banter or come-hither flirtations. In truth, their time together felt real.

Except, it wasn't. They were playing pretend. Any time his cell phone buzzed, her stomach dropped to the floor like a boulder thrown into a canyon, certain that Chance would be called to the other side of the planet.

But ignoring the ticking time bomb of real life, Jane could almost pretend that this make-believe fairytale would live on indefinitely.

A warm breeze rolled over the pool, sweeping flyaway strands into her face. Jane set down her newest reread and pushed the hairs away. The large umbrella next to the pool had shielded her from the bright afternoon sunlight, but now the sky held an orange hue. It was later than she realized, and she was feeling snackish. Jane checked the time on her phone. Not quite dinner time.

Gigi had encouraged Jane to use a food delivery service while they were gone. Uber Eats and Postmates were part of her grand plan of evasion as though gossip reporters would never question that she and Dax were home if they needed meals brought to their door.

But, delivery was getting old after a few days in a row. Such a first world problem, but be that as it may, Jane placed a bookmark in her paperback and went in search of her man.

She walked into the massive kitchen to find Chance standing in front of the fancy-pants double oven, a mitt on his hand and a dishtowel over his broad shoulder.

After days of delivery and no mention of cooking, the scene in front of her stopped Jane short. "Are you *cooking*?"

He winked. "One of my many talents."

"Really?" She arched an eyebrow and sauntered to the set of super-complicated double ovens. "Do you know what you're doing?" Word on the street was that using them was akin to programming the space shuttle. Only those with culinary degrees or experience with mass spectrometers could get the thing to turn on—that never struck Jane as a benefit, but to each their own. The thing likely cost more than the house she grew up in.

"It's a roast. Not rocket science." He flicked the hand towel against her shoulder as she peered inside.

"You'd be surprised." Though, she was the one astounded to see a very lovely-looking roast surrounded by root vegetables. "I'm impressed," she added, her mouth watering at the delicious aromas emanating from the oven. Turning around, she noticed the kitchen island had been set for two. How was Chance Evans a single man? He was too good to be true.

She slipped onto the stool and watched as he moved around the kitchen like a professional chef. He poured her a glass of wine, and she took it. "You think of everything, don't you?"

He grinned, poured himself a glass, and raised it. "We're only here for a short time, let's make it a good time." He laughed. "I read that in a fortune cookie once."

She grinned and sipped to hide her melancholy. He drank, seemingly oblivious to the depressing idea that their time together would end abruptly. The oven timer sounded, and he hopped back to his chef duties, pulling the roast out and working the kitchen like he'd lived in this house his whole life.

He sipped his wine. "How are you supposed to know if this stuff is any good?"

"Do you like it?" she asked.

He shrugged. "Guess so."

"Then it's good." Her heart squeezed when he grinned. Amusing him might just be her superpower. There was no other reason a guy like Chance, the Midas-like man with the golden touch—and looks *and* whoa, those bedroom moves—liked her romantically.

With expert finesse, he moved the roast onto a cutting board.

"Did you ever work in a kitchen?" she asked.

"Nope."

"You didn't do time at some prestigious culinary academy?"

He snorted. "Not unless you count KP duty in the army."

Her brow furrowed. "I don't know what that means."

"Kitchen patrol," he explained. "A lot of peeling potatoes and washing dishes."

"Ohhh." She wrinkled her nose. "Fun—but you have to tell me how this became *one of your many talents.*"

His lightheartedness sobered, and Chance concentrated on slicing and then plating the roast beef. "When I was a kid, it was just my mom and me, and my mom was sick. She had issues with food." He moved the plates from the prep area to the kitchen island. "I got it in my head that if I made the right food, and she really liked it, she'd get better. So, I was constantly in the kitchen, making all sorts of stuff from a pretty young age." Pain flickered in his eyes. "Turns out, you can't show your love through cooking and fix someone's struggles."

Jane pursed her lips together. "Chance... I'm so sorry."

With a flat shit-happens grin, he tilted his head toward her and met her gaze. That eye-locking connection turned a switch in her chest and maybe did something for him as well because he didn't put up the false bravado to hide his pain. "You'd think I'd hate cooking," he added quietly. "But, I don't. I think she knew, and damn did my mom love me." He glanced away for a long moment before he continued, "I cook for people I care about."

A knot tied in her throat, and hell, she felt like one wrong word, and she'd cry.

Chance dropped a kiss onto the top of her head, pulled the hand towel from his shoulder, and tossed it to the counter. He cleared his throat and settled onto the chair next to her. "Ready to eat?"

With a story like that and half a glass of wine polished off, she couldn't do anything more than nod.

He placed the linen napkin on his lap and began eating, a clear signal that he was done with the emotional chitchat and waited for her to do the same. The lights were low, the kitchen smelled buttery delicious, and despite her near tears, the surprisingly romantic ambiance of their dinner for two made her fall a little bit harder for him.

He speared a piece of roast beef. "Hope you like it."

So tender she could cut the meet with a fork, Jane tasted it as he watched. Her eyes sank shut. Rich and flavorful and *homemade*. That made it even better than a Michelin-star chef-prepared meal. "Oh, my god, Chance…" She savored that first bite like she had their first kiss. For as much as she wanted both, she'd been unprepared for her intense response. "It just *melts*."

He laughed modestly and took his own bite, then nodded his approval. "Not bad."

"Ha," she managed between mouthfuls.

The conversation lingered over their dinner and refills of wine. He told her a few KP stories that made her grateful to have always had a dishwasher, and more than a few Army stories that made her wonder how he was still alive.

As they finished their dinner and the last of the wine disappeared, Jane thanked him again for the delicious meal.

Again, he demurred. "The kitchen isn't what I'm used to, but I made do with what I had."

She laughed, and then added solemnly. "I understand. It must be hard to work with a brand-spanking new appliance."

His eyes scanned the kitchen. "Yeah?"

"Oh. Yeah. The Thanes constantly remodel. New appliances right before our trip, and they're redoing Teddy's room for the hundredth time."

"Why?"

She rolled her eyes. "I think it must be like clothes to them. Some people don't like to be photographed in the same outfit over and over. They like to keep everything fresh for the public."

Lines etched across his forehead. "They let people tour their house?"

"Oh, sorry. No." She waved her hand in the general direction of the main sitting rooms where most of their interviews took place. "Gigi is obsessed with the production of their new miniseries documentary—you must've heard about that one." How couldn't he? Even if he didn't follow pop culture closely, someone should've mentioned it to him to be aware of from a security point of view.

"There were a lot of media appearances listed in my intel package. Past, current, and future. I was more interested in which security threats were bogus hype and which ones were real."

"Oh, you're missing out on a lot of great stuff then," Jane added with biting sarcasm. "How else will you know what shade of gray is the right shade of gray? Which five-figure double oven is best for roast beef?"

He groaned. "I don't think I want to know any of that." He slid from his chair, placed their plates in the sink, and took her hand.

Jane placed their napkins in the small laundry basket under the counter and put the silverware on top of the plates as Chance poured them more wine, handing hers back and slipping his arm around her shoulder. "I have an idea."

She didn't drink much but knew the warm tingle that rolled down her spine couldn't completely be blamed by the vino. He smelled sexy and delicious, a combination of his cooking and that familiar scent of red-blooded, hard-bodied man that she'd come to associate with him. Jane leaned into him and let Chance lead them from the kitchen into the main living room.

The ceiling reached high above, over two stories tall, and the central focal point of the well-designed room was a massive stone fireplace in the center.

"If I really lived here." He faced them toward a wall, and with the lift of his glass, he pointed. "That'd have to go. I'd knock it down." His wine glass gestured toward the hall that they'd just come from. "That one too. Maybe all of the walls over here."

"Why?"

"So that the family room was a part of the kitchen."

Her stomach clenched, and she didn't know what to say. "They call this the living room." Gigi has been very specific that they didn't have a *family* room." There was the great room, the living room, several sitting rooms, a dining room, a media room, and on and on and on.

Chance snorted his thought about that classification. "I don't think much *living* has happened in this room. I'd bet my ass, not as a family."

How right he was…

Chance turned them and walked across the grand open space. "And instead of that spindly little sofa thing?"

"Something more comfortable," she suggested.

"Yeah, something that doesn't look like it'd give a guy hemorrhoids if he wanted to kick back and watch a ball game."

Jane snickered. "No one wants those."

"I'd put in a big leather sectional instead."

She agreed. "One that's big and comfy."

"Where the whole family could lie on and watch Sunday football games."

A blistering wave of awareness streaked straight to her womb. Her unsteady breath hitched, and Jane gulped from her wineglass.

He ambled to the spindly little sofa—she'd never look at that thing again without hearing his description—and sat in the middle. With his long torso and muscular legs, he dwarfed the designer sofa as though he were a giant—a playful one. Chance wriggled on the cushion, giving it a little bounce. "Definitely a high risk for hemorrhoids over here."

She laughed. "Good to know."

He jumped up and walked over to a delicate statue precariously sitting on a narrow pedestal. Jane bit the inside of her cheek to refrain from warning him to be careful. It was ingrained in her as she constantly had to warn Teddy to "Watch out" and to "Be careful."

"This is probably a masterpiece, huh?" he asked.

Her nerves settled the tiniest bit that he was aware the abstract design had major significance. "Yup."

He cocked his head, eyes narrowed. "How do you fill your house with breakable shit when you have kids?"

"You don't." She shrugged. "Unless you're the Thanes. Then you hire a nanny and staff to make sure things won't break."

"How do you do that?" He kept his head at an angle as he studied the statue as though he were a rare art collector.

"We stay away as much as possible."

With a small shake of his head, Chance drank from his glass, then asked, "Do you want kids?"

What? Jane blinked hard as though her eyes had anything to do with her ears. She'd heard him correctly. But... *what?*

He grinned and swept his wine glass in front of him. "A house this big needs a couple dozen kids."

"A couple *dozen?*"

He shrugged. "No one needs this much square footage unless they have a score of kids."

"If not realistic, your reasoning makes sense." She didn't know what else to say and imagined the buttoned-up room filled with a giant big-screen television, lumpy sectional, and dozens of kids running around with all their toys. His idea was a definite improvement.

"So, do you?" he asked, his attention steady and keen.

Jane tried not to read into that little life-compatibility question that every dating website on earth weighed heavily in its equation for happily ever after.

"I do," she admitted, thrilled that she didn't sound like she'd been huffing helium from balloons.

"I do, too." His expression didn't change, and as though this were everyday banter, he asked, "A lot or a little?" A playful smile broke. "Or, if we lived here, one dozen or two? Given the square footage."

This had to be the wine talking. If they lived here? With their future offspring? "You're awfully casual about our future brethren of kids."

He laughed and took her hand. "We're knocking down walls to remodel, why not fill it up too?"

Yeah, sure. Why not hold his hand and dream about a future that would never happen. A pang of jealousy strummed in her chest. One day, when he retired, or life changed, he'd still want a warm, open home and a handful of kids. She wouldn't be the one who shared that with him. "It's always nice to imagine."

"What else would we remodel?" He led them out of the elegant room into one of the attached sitting rooms. The wall directly across from them had been covered with photographs of either Gigi or Dax and some celebrity, famous politician, or renowned philanthropist. Several showed them at award shows. Another wall in this room had been dedicated to framed magazine covers with one of their faces emblazoned on the front.

"This room..." Chance guffawed. "Says a lot."

"No kidding." She and Teddy never came in there. It felt as though the hundreds of Thane eyes were watching them. Definitely creepy. She couldn't imagine how Teddy must feel, his parents looking at him from every direction.

"Where are their family pictures?" His brow furrowed as he quickly reviewed the walls.

"Here's one." Jane pointed to a red-carpet picture. Gigi and Dax flanked a two-year-old Teddy in a white tuxedo—an ensemble determined by a comment-poll from Gigi's Instagram.

"That doesn't count." Chance rolled his eyes. "I'd knock down these walls too."

She laughed. "Maybe you just need a smaller house."

His eyebrow arched. "For our two dozen kids?" He shook his head. "Be practical, babe."

She laughed. None of this was real. He didn't want dozens of kids. The wine had clouded his jokes with romantic daydreams. "You're nuts."

He didn't deny the accusation. "All of this shit would go."

"Gone." She flicked her wrist. "Replaced by a tasteful selection of family pictures. Birthday parties, football games—"

His expression brightened. "Hey, we'd have more than enough kids to fill our own teams."

"*Bonus.*"

He chuckled.

Jane tried to envision their imaginary, ridiculous future as freely as he did. It only made her wistful. "I'd be one of those moms who sent out holiday cards every year. Ya know, the cute ones with the annual family photo. I always wished my parents had done that."

He gave her shoulder a small squeeze but then humor curled on his lips. "We could do holiday calendars. A couple kids for each month. We could group them by birthday."

"Two dozen kids would take a while." The idea made her laugh, and then she couldn't stop laughing. They were acting as certifiable as Dax and Gigi. Yet, she was surprised how easy it was to talk about something so important and intimate. Kids. Family. *Marriage?* Sure, why not. It was her imaginary future.

CHAPTER FORTY-NINE

"WOULD YOU TELL me more about your family?" Jane asked.

Chance choked on a joke about his willingness to practice making kids. He hadn't expected the change in topic, but could see how they got there. Jane didn't want to drudge up pain. But she had the right to know events that formed him as a man. More somber, he rocked back on his heels. "Well…"

She faltered. "Actually, never mind. You said enough before."

He offered too quick of a smile and his body language shifted. Chance took a deep breath, not willing to hide from Jane's question. "There was more to the situation with my mom."

"You don't have to tell me anything if you don't want to." She took both his hands and stroked them as though she knew he needed something. "I didn't mean to press."

"Damn, Jane." His mouth went dry, but he pulled his hands free and wrapped her to his chest. "You're smart, beautiful, and can read my mind. Quite the trifecta."

She tilted her head back, resting her chin on his sternum. "Sensing unsaid family problems is my secret talent."

"That sucks." He wasn't eloquent but that was the truth.

She leaned back into his arms. "When I was a kid, I spent a lot of time watching what went wrong in other families."

"Why?"

She shrugged and rolled her eyes, stepping out of his arms. "I was a sadistic juvenile. Actually… I watched other families. I wanted to see their problems. To know that I wasn't alone. But then I realized theirs were always different than mine." She paced, never stepping out of his reach, but Chance could tell she needed space. "Normally, something happened. There was always an action and then a consequence."

He crossed his arms over his chest to keep from holding her. She'd come to him when she needed him. "That made your family different?"

Jane stopped and stared into the distance for several seconds before facing him. "I couldn't see the actions that caused consequences with my parents. Their behavior, the way they treated me..." She sighed sadly. "I was too young to understand."

He wasn't sure he understood her meaning now. "What didn't you get?"

"Do you know what narcissism means?"

"Your parents were narcissistic?"

She nodded. "Clinically."

Her clarification didn't shed any light. "They thought they were very attractive?"

Tensely, Jane wet her lips. "They believed the world revolved around them, individually, and they'd manipulated or abandoned anything that didn't react accordingly."

"Ouch," he said.

"It is what it is. Lots of people have it better and worse."

He didn't know which his childhood qualified as. "My dad was our problem," Chance admitted. "My mom was really sick. She needed him. I did, too. But my dad left us to be with a younger woman." He let out a strangled laugh. "You know how it is. I don't fucking know why it still bothers me. I guess because I couldn't do more for my mom. She wasted away until... she was gone."

Jane stepped close again. "She died?"

"Yeah." Chance cleared his throat. "The doctors called it an eating disorder. She was so beautiful—as much on the inside, if not more, than on the outside." Again, his throat clogged. He swallowed hard. "When I was Teddy's age, I didn't get why she just wouldn't eat. I knew she was hungry. That's why I learned to cook."

Jane rubbed his arm, and he couldn't stop talking, inching closer. He'd thought she'd come to him when she needed him, but oh the irony, he needed to hold onto her. "As I got older, I could see how she tried to control everything by controlling herself. Everything meaning his philandering ways, I suppose." *The jackass.* Chance ground his molars. "He once told me that men get better with age. Then he just looked at my mom and let his unsaid words hang." That was the first time Chance hated how others perceived him. The good-looking kid. The golden boy. It had fucked him up for years. Maybe it still had. "I was eighteen when she passed. Angry and with something to prove. So, I enlisted. Tried to leave it behind and prove to the world that real men weren't superficial pieces of shit."

He dropped his head back and stared blankly at the ceiling. Jane curled her arms around his torso. With his eyes shut, he let go of all the anger and tension. He rested his chin on top of her head and waited until his resentment regulated. "Did a shitty job of leaving it all behind, obviously."

Jane eased back and met his gaze. "You don't leave behind the things that make you who you are. You use them to make yourself a better person."

He worked that over in his head. "Spoken like the strong woman you are."

Her cheeks heated. "Speaking from experience. That's all."

"I never told anyone about what happened. Or, rather, why things happened."

"Maybe you're still figuring it all out," she suggested.

He didn't know about that, but of other things, he was certain. Beauty came from within, and *that* fueled attraction.

Jane pressed her mouth to his. The kiss lingered. He relished in the way she soothed the dark shadows in his soul.

She whispered against his lips, "Thought you needed that."

"You have no idea." Chance took her hand and led them from the overdone living room until he found an unadorned anteroom. An oversized couch faced a large picture window. The dark sky melted into the backyard, partially lit by the aqua blue glow from the pool.

He tugged Jane onto the couch and waited until he had her complete attention. He was ready to battle her uncertainties and dismantle her defenses or doubts, and he'd keep doing it until she understood the truth, and that was simple. He was in love with Jane.

CHAPTER FIFTY

C HANCE TUCKED HAIR behind Jane's ear. "You have no idea how much you mean to me."

A content, almost peaceful, warmth grew in her chest. She couldn't describe the sensation in any other way other than *safe*. She trusted him—and she trusted herself too. "I know I do."

His gaze sharpened. "You do?"

Unhurried, she basked in the calm confidence that he cared about her—and that he wanted her. Mentally and physically. She grasped what he'd been struggling for her to comprehend. Nothing could make this man more attractive than his authentic... availability. Chance had patiently given himself completely to her. Her heart squeezed. "You mean so much to me, too."

His dark blue eyes burned. Jane pressed her hands to his cheeks, and tension in his jaw ticked under her palms. "That sounds inadequate. But it's true," she promised. "I trust you."

She reveled in the quickening pace of his breath. Her fingers slid down his face and feathered down his neck. The steady beat of his pulse teased her fingertips until her fingers hooked over his t-shirt collar. "I'm ready."

His nostrils tightened. Chance tensed as though holding himself back. He didn't move a muscle. Then his tongue wet his bottom lip. Jane's heart raced. She wanted to crawl inside his mind and know what he thought. She wanted to show him what was in her head.

Jane smoothed her hands down his hard chest. She took her time and savored the rapid-fire beat of his heart. Hers thundered in time. Heat bloomed in her cheeks. Arousal flooded her senses, and merely watching him *fiercely* watch her was enough to make her wet. She saw the moment for what it was—Chance wasn't hesitating. He was appreciating. *Her.*

Her fingers knotted in his shirt and lifted the fabric up. With one hand, he ripped it over his head and pulled Jane to straddle his lap. The thick length of his erection bulged in his jeans. Shivers rushed across her back. He would soon be inside of her.

Jane pressed her forehead to his. Their eyes locked, and she repeated herself, whispering, "I'm ready."

His pupils dilated. "Thank fuck."

She laughed. Chance tore off her shirt and bra. Jane wrapped her arms around his neck. Their bare chests met. The tight, sensitive tips of her nipples brushed against the rough smattering of his chest hair. Her mind spun, not sure she'd ever experienced this desperate level of desire.

Chance kissed as though he'd been unleashed. His mouth devoured hers. His tongue whipped her into a fever pitch. With the tight grip of his hands on her hips, he ground her against his erection. The fruitless friction packed a punch. Jane writhed for more.

She kissed his neck, sucking and teasing with playful nibbles. He groaned with satisfaction. The intoxicating taste of his skin mixed with his masculine scent. She inhaled deeply, swooning with another wave of arousal, then fumbled to release him from his jeans.

"Hang on." He lifted her to his chest, removed his wallet from a back pocket, and tossed it to the side. Chance settled back, hands firmly holding his hips. Without a word, he questioned her again. Jane nodded.

The corners of his lips quirked. He lifted her onto her feet, standing between his knees. "Gorgeous." Then he stripped her shorts and underwear away. "Goddamn fucking gorgeous."

She shivered under the thrill of his stare and watched as he unfastened his jeans. The deep thud of her heartbeat marked every second until Chance was gloriously naked. She wasn't sure how many times she'd seen his body. Since that first night in the shower, they had found a million ways to play. But now, she simply needed to be closer than ever before.

As though another unsaid conversation had passed, they agreed that everything before tonight had been foreplay. He reached for his wallet, withdrew a foil wrapper, and sheathed his thickness with the condom.

Then, dangerous as a wolf but sweet as sugar, he looked to her and took her hand. Her breath hitched as he pulled her over his lap again. Her bare, soft thighs straddled his powerful ones. Jane appreciated his brawn, and she rubbed and played, exploring her ability to excite a man this virile.

"Tease." Chance wrapped his arms around her back, grinding her slick sex to his shaft. He groaned, and his mouth found hers. Their tongues played. He was everything at once. Confident and potent. Careful and powerful. Jane liked the way he smiled against her lips, how he could transition from a thousand miles an hour to slow drawling kisses that made her pray for more. "I can't wait another second."

His half-cocked grin was like an empowering challenge. "You can do whatever you want."

And she would. Her stomach fluttered. Jane lifted herself from Chance. Cool air kissed their fevered skin. The blunt head of his cock pressed to her entrance. He inhaled sharply, and Jane gave herself over to his thickness.

Jane's jaw dropped. He stretched her, filled, made Jane frantic for more. Restraint showed in his tight jaw. Pronounced tendons tensed in his neck. "Sweet Jesus, Jane."

She couldn't speak. The need was too great. Chance gripped her hips. His stormy blue eyes held her still when every part of her screamed to move. Then Chance let loose. He owned her, fucking her, driving in and out, making her cry with empty sensation and beg for mercy as he thrust himself into her again.

Again and again, he took her to the edge. He drove until orgasm after orgasm melted into one mind-numbing cry of ecstasy. The pull of another climax had her begging for release. Chance pounded into her, demanding, *growling*, that she come. Jane had no choice. The climax hit her, more intense than she'd ever dreamed. Chance strained, holding her impossibly tight, grunting into her shoulder. His orgasm rolled through her until he had nothing more to give.

They didn't move. Didn't talk. Their hearts seesawed against each other. Jane didn't have the strength to move from Chance. His arms hung heavy over her back, holding her close.

He angled his head and kissed her cheek. Jane was glad she waited until she could give herself completely, glad she believed in him enough to know he'd given the same.

Chance drew a deep breath then lifted her away. "Give me a minute."

He headed toward the nearest bathroom. Jane wrapped a large chenille blanket over her naked skin, laid back on the couch, and closed her eyes. She heard his returning footsteps. Chance lifted the blanket and slipped next to her, possessively pulling her to his naked chest. This was everything she ever wanted. She loved him.

Warm and fuzzies made her heart clench. Jane nuzzled closer. "Can we sleep here?"

"Anything you want. The world's your oyster, babe."

"Everything I want is right here—"

The piercing cry of the alarm system blared. A mechanical alert barked, "*Intruder alert. Intruder alert.*"

CHAPTER FIFTY-ONE

"SOMEONE'S IN THE house." Jane couldn't move—but Chance could. "Clothes on, babe."

An unknown person had entered the huge house. She didn't know where or how or why. But the answers weren't good.

"*Jane.*"

She jerked from her panic. "What?"

Somehow magically dressed, he tossed her clothes and paced for the eternity it took for her to redress.

"Come with me." He pulled her to his side. "Stay close."

Thank God that Chance, the resident white knight and protector, would know what to do. Though, truthfully, she should know too. They'd had drills before, and she could make it to a safe room with her eyes closed. Yet, she felt like they were moving in slow motion.

Chance led them to the first-floor office that the security team kept. He reviewed the security system panel with a quick gaze and flipped a switch. A wall of video footage came to life.

She didn't see anything but empty rooms. There's wasn't even a stray cat roaming the grounds—not that there would be in a place like this.

His fingers flew over a keyboard, silencing the alarms, and explained, "Back of the house. Looks like a sensor activated on one of the sliding glass doors."

She scanned the monitors. "There's no one there."

"Right now," he pointed out. "They could have left. That loud-ass alarm is a hell of a deterrent." He tinkered until he found a video prompt and rewound the footage. There was nothing to see. "What the hell."

"Yeah," she muttered. "Should I call the gatehouse? They might've heard it, and—"

A phone rang from a desk beside them. Chance picked the receiver up without hesitation while she stared at it as though they were in a horror movie and the call was coming from inside the house.

The conversation consisted of one-syllable agreements that could've doubled as grumbles or grunts.

The distant wail of police sirens stole her attention.

"Yeah, we hear them. Thanks." He hung up, took her hand, and after a quick review of the monitors again, he led them toward the back of the house.

"It's shut."

"And still locked." He tugged on the locked door to be sure and then flipped the latch and slid the door open.

Jane followed behind him as he stepped onto a patio. The evening summer sky was filled with purples and oranges. If the alarm hadn't just blared, she would've thought the setting ideal.

Chance walked the edge of the patio and then glanced over his shoulder. "Are there many false alarms?"

She shrugged, only having heard drills. Those were apparently conducted at half the volume as real alarms. "I don't think so. I don't know."

They walked back inside. Chance continued to check the rest of the house while Jane headed toward the front door, where the police were banging and announcing their presence. She rushed, certain that the paparazzi had come in with their cruisers.

Sure enough, an arc of cameras pointed toward the home, filming and snapping the police cars with their lights spinning as she opened the door.

Several police officers filed in, and Jane pointed them toward Chance. After a brief discussion, most of the uniformed officers did a thorough check of the house, finding the same thing Chance had found—nothing—while two others followed Chance toward the security office.

Gigi was going to freak out. Jane found her cell phone and sat in the kitchen, wondering if this news would come better as a text or phone call. Really, she'd only know the correct answer if she knew Gigi's current mood. Jane checked her social media and found nothing.

Another knock came from the door, and a man announced himself as "from the alarm company" and then bustled by her. He knew where the office was, so she assumed letting him in was okay.

Jane decided to call Lark before Gigi, but Jane only got Lark's voicemail. Well, hell. She needed to let the Thanes know. Jane called Gigi and then Dax. Neither answered. Of all the days for everyone to go quiet.

Chance, the alarm company man, and the two officers returned to the living room, announcing that a faulty sensor had expired. The alarm company said they would send someone out to repair it in the morning, and the officers said they'd tell the photogs it'd been a false alarm. They all knew it was wishful thinking to hope that would send them away. If Gigi and Dax were home, they'd be on the front driveway preening for the cameras. Even the most newbie gossip hound would believe there was a problem if the Thanes didn't make an appearance.

Jane assumed everyone would clear out as fast as they'd arrived. But she'd been wrong. An inordinate amount of care was taken to make sure the precious mammoth house was safe and that the reports were as detailed and well-written as could be mustered on electronic tablets.

Several hours later, around midnight, Chance and Jane walked the remaining police to the front door, thanking them as they left. Cameras flashed. Videographers rolled next to their day-glow lights perched on tripods. Jane hadn't peeked at the gossip blog websites, but she knew tonight's excitement had made top-of-line news.

Before the last of the police cruisers rolled away, a gray Tesla pulled up the driveway.

"What timing," Chance muttered.

A roar of questions from the celebrity press pool ignited as Dax and Gigi parked in the center of their driveway—a first—and proceeded to pose for pictures while saying, "No comment."

Jane and Chance slipped back inside the front door, spying from a side mirror. The Thanes relished the onslaught of the cameras and questions, and Jane noticed they both had perfect hair and makeup. Weird look for a late-night while on vacation...

The front door opened, and Gigi called for her without coming in.

Jane groaned and trudged toward the commotion. She absolutely hated when Gigi used her as a pawn in her act.

Chance stayed close behind her, and when they entered the foyer, the snapping camera lights behind Gigi sparkled like tiny explosions.

"Oh, Jane!" Gigi grasped Jane's shoulders, smoothly angling them for the perfect picture. "We came as soon as we got notice! Is everything okay?"

Jane tried to tell her that everything was fine, but Gigi didn't appear to be listening. Instead, she turned toward the reports, pressed a hand to her neck, and expounded on the *terrifying* events of the evening. "Just had a small break-in. Of course, very frightening, but we're all okay. Everything's insured, of course, with Thane Insurance, and at least our son wasn't here. Something like that would really scar him for life…"

Right, a broken sensor would scar him for life, but a Syrian refugee camp was all fun and games? Jane glanced at Chance. He remained off-camera and rolled his eyes.

Gigi didn't let Jane go as she continued to speak until Dax stepped forward. Gigi swiftly moved to him as the cameras swung his way. Jane inched back, unable to turn away. Their entertainment value was sickly addictive. She listened to Dax add his commentary and a rather lengthy tutorial on the importance of having a great insurance policy to cover one's home. Ridiculously, the camera crews ate it up.

Finally, after the reporters had gotten their fill of the Thanes, they thanked them and waltzed in the front door, waving like they were walking a red carpet.

"Well, hello." Gigi abruptly stopped in front of Chance, giving him a head-to-toe inspection. "You're my new security man?"

Out of the corner of her eye, Jane saw Chance shift uncomfortably. She didn't know if it was the way she spoke about him or the appreciative way she studied his body.

"Yeah." He extended his hand. "Chance Evans."

"I see. You're very photogenic. You'll do just perfect." Gigi held her hand out as though she wanted him to kiss her knuckles. Instead, Chance gripped her awkwardly extended hand and gave it a quick shake. The corner of Gigi's mouth tightened downward. "I see we have some work to do."

Before Jane could break up the uncomfortable exchange, Dax approached and shook Chance's hand, speaking in his gruff-man voice, but still talking a mile a minute. "Yeah, man. Good to have you here. Thanks for all that help with the situation overseas. You're a good man to have around."

Chance couldn't get a word in edgewise, but from the look on his face, he didn't want to. There was no doubt that he was ruing the day he'd accepted the Thane assignment. If he thought they were bad now, all he had to do was wait. Jane didn't put it past Gigi to insist Chance wear face powder or prance around shirtless or whatever she thought might get the miniseries better ratings.

Whatever was going to happen, it definitely would get a lot worse before—she stopped herself before thinking that it would get better. Because it wouldn't. The job would end. Chance would leave.

Their time playing house and imagining their football teams of children was officially over.

CHAPTER FIFTY-TWO

CHANCE SAT AT the poolside cabana, directly across from Jane's house, massaging the migraine from his temples. It had been four days since the Thanes returned. And precisely four days since he started wondering why the fuck he'd decided to accept this assignment.

Jane, he reminded himself as he took his hundredth glimpse of her house, right across the pool. She was likely in there, with Teddy, doing her best to keep him occupied while Gigi Thane busied herself getting ready for another day of shooting the Thane family documentary.

In Chance's opinion, documentary wasn't the best description for the tabloid-esque reality show that Gigi had orchestrated. Jane had said she would do as much as possible to keep Teddy's time at home out of the public eye, so whenever the cameras were around, he never saw them.

But when he and Jane were off the clock, and the camera crews were gone for the day, and Teddy was tucked into bed, Chance kept Jane in his bed.

The Thanes hadn't picked up on their relationship, and he'd guessed that Lark kept what she saw to herself. He hadn't seen Lark since his first day. Neither Gigi nor Dax asked where Chance had been sleeping. They'd passed his housing assignment along as though he'd just arrived—as though the world stopped and started with their arrival.

His place was perfect; an apartment over their six-car garage. The space was meant for the chauffeur. However, Dax considered himself a car enthusiast and didn't employ a chauffeur. From what Chance could gather, Dax's enthusiast title was merely a loose description for driving like a maniac with blatant disregard for speed limits and stop signs.

The best part of Chance's apartment was the location. It was only a two-minute walk across the vast grounds to Jane's cottage. They got their "together" time, and no one was the wiser.

One of the sliding glass doors that fed onto the deck opened, and the now-familiar sound of a camera crew spilled out. From his vantage point, he could see the group without turning, but it was another bodyguard who went by Pennebaker that held Chance's attention.

Pennebaker's bald head shined in the reflection off the pool as he lumbered down the deck stairs and lifted his chin to Chance. "Midas." He hooked a thumb over his shoulder. "You're up."

Chance managed not to groan. He'd been artfully positioned poolside by one of the camera crew people, and he wasn't in the mood to move from location to location all day as though he were furniture. Who the hell would've thought he'd miss the routine of Abu Dhabi with its opulence and a makeshift war room?

"Good luck," Pennebaker muttered as he pulled out a chair next to Chance and took up his poolside assignment.

Before Chance had the opportunity to stand, Gigi leaned over the deck railing and snapped her fingers at him. "Chance, please come here."

Pennebaker readjusted his chair and gave a subtle but knowing glance. "Good thing she pays well."

The pay was nice, but the perks—or, rather, one beautiful perk who made his fucking dick twitch—were what kept Chance on the clock for a woman like Gigi, who snapped at him like a dog.

Still, he readjusted his sunglasses and hoofed it up the stairs and onto the deck. The production crew focused on Gigi drinking a tall glass of iced tea as though she hadn't just snapped for his attention.

"Mrs. Thane." He greeted her as professionally as he could muster. She wore a bikini and a sarong suitable for an island vacation and posed with a hand on her hip. He wasn't trying to eyeball her, but it was hard to ignore the skimpy bathing suit. Chance shifted uncomfortably, very aware that any reaction would be caught on film.

After a deliberate assessment, Gigi placed the iced tea glass on the rail and peered over her dark sunglasses. "Chance, honey, where is your gun?"

Honey and gun. Two words he hadn't expected to come from her mouth. He gave her a look. *Is this a trick question? Another opportunity to showboat for the cameras?* He pulled off his own sunglasses. "Why?"

"Well, you *do have* a shoulder holster, don't you?" She stared at him expectantly, as if she really wanted him to have a conversation about his gear. "I'm sure you know that women go crazy for a man in a shoulder holster." Gigi winked for the camera. "Especially this one."

He had a shoulder holster, but since it was balls hot and he liked to carry on his hip or small of his back, he never thought to wear it. But it didn't matter. He was Aces, not a movie star or prop. Chance cleared his throat. "Ma'am," he said, aware that calling her the M-word would have a chilling effect. "Can we have a minute, please?"

Her lips pinched at the corners and then flicked her hand to the side.

"Cut," a man called, and the crew morphed into a flurry of chatting and repositioning.

"What?" she asked tersely.

"My superiors didn't know there'd be a camera crew here."

"Yet they are." She took a sip of her iced tea and then waved her hand. A woman scurried over and powdered Gigi's face.

"I'm positive that your contract with my company won't allow you to air video footage of me."

"*That's* why we stopped the shot. For an explanation of contracts?" She scowled.

The urge to walk away needled under his skin. "I don't want to waste your time."

She tilted her head and ogled him. "How could you possibly do that?"

"They'll need to edit me out of whatever media thing you're doing."

She drew a heavily-pink-painted lower lip under her top teeth and sighed. "*Chance.* Don't be like that."

"Like what?"

She sauntered closer. "We could be having so much fun."

His jaw tensed, acutely aware of her tone and positioning. "I didn't take the job to have fun." He willed her to back off. "Actually, the security briefings I've been privy to have been few and far between. I'm not sure that you need me here." Though he'd do it all again for more time with

Jane. "Definitely not on camera."

She took off her sunglasses and pouted. "Think of the opportunities this could open for you. I mean, Dax is cute and funny and handsome. But you? You're sex on a cracker, Chance. Women would go crazy for you. It's a shame they'll have to miss out."

Chance sucked in a breath, understanding why she'd requested him by name. His superficial good looks were as much home décor accents as her designer candles. "Yeah, a real shame."

Gigi dismissed him with a cold roll of her eyes, demanding he return to the background and for Pennebaker to return.

He didn't wait for her to finish pouting. Chance high-tailed it off the deck, broke the bad news to Pennebaker, and settled under the poolside cabana, counting down the minutes until he could see Jane again.

CHAPTER FIFTY-THREE

JANE WAITED UNTIL she was positive Teddy had gone to sleep for the night. When his quiet breaths found an even cadence, she kissed his forehead and slipped out of his bedroom. The main house was quiet as she crept down the hallway. Both Gigi and Dax were home but retired to their quarters. Part of her wondered why they didn't tuck their little boy in, and part of Jane knew the sad answer. Tucking him into bed never crossed their minds.

This time of day should've been her favorite part of the day. It usually was. Within minutes, she would be at her place, and Chance would knock on the door. They would fall into bed. The rest of the world would disappear. But right now, she wanted him to *hug* the world away.

"Why so glum, Mary Poppins?"

She jerked toward his voice and found Chance sitting in a chair, illuminated by the pool and moonlight. "I didn't see you there."

He pushed from the chair as though he were a century old. "Is everything okay?"

She walked to him, feeling like she could breathe better near him. "Nothing I haven't mentioned before."

He didn't respond, instead taking her hand in his and leading her to her cottage. Warmth radiated from his hand, and while his touch could soothe her soul, she still needed to be wrapped in his arms.

They walked through her door. If it had been any night before, they would have jumped each other, tearing clothes off, and trying for a how-was-your-day conversation in fits and bursts until he slid into her body, killing off the remnants of a conversation that would be picked up against later.

Instead, she shut the door and curled into his chest. He didn't reach for the lights or the hem of her shirt but rested his chin on top of her head and held her close.

"That's exactly what I need right now," she whispered.

"Rough day?"

Jane nodded. "Yeah."

Chance pulled her toward the couch, and they tangled together in the dark.

"They don't tell him good night." Her voice broke, and her eyes threatened to water. "I don't know why it's bothering me so much tonight. But it is."

He stroked the back of her head.

"He's such a sweet kid."

Chance nodded. "Seems like it."

"And, it's crazy to say he deserves better. He'll never want for anything. He's set for life. But it just seems so, so…"

"Heartbreaking."

"*Yes,*" she cried. "And I don't know how he can have both everything and nothing."

"That's easy." Chance inched her from his chest and caught her eye. "The best things in life aren't *things.*"

"I really wish I was Mary Poppins." She snapped. "I could fix Teddy's problems. Get rid of the camera crews and move his aunt into the mansion next-door."

"That would be one hell of a good start."

Face to face, they laid together, legs entangled, holding each other in a weighty silence. She snuggled against him and drew patterns on his chest. The smallest amount of moonlight mixed with the blue light from the pool, filtering through her windows. It cast a silvery glow over them. "Why were you sitting by yourself in the dark?"

Chance inhaled a long breath and let it out slowly. "Long day."

She recalled his interaction with Gigi and grimaced. "What she said is still bothering you?"

He tensed. "You heard that?"

Jane nodded. "Sorry. She shouldn't objectify you like that."

"She shouldn't objectify anyone like that."

"Yeah."

"Sex on a cracker," he finally muttered. "Who says that?"

Jane snickered. "If you think about it, it's kind of a weird thing to say."

Chance snort-laughed. "Cheese on a cracker works. Sex on a cracker, not so much."

"And…" She leaned closer as though she had a secret to tell. "I think she has a crush on my man."

He tensed for a minute then laughed and tweaked her side. "You heard a lot, huh?"

Jane giggled. "I don't think it's possible to ignore Gigi. She's kind of loud and relentless."

After he stole a kiss, he stopped tickling her side. "I don't know if I'd call Gigi's proposition a crush."

"True. What do you call that rabid look that glints when a wolf circles a piece of fresh meat?"

He groaned. "I don't know if anyone's ever called me fresh meat before. Do you think she's pretty?"

That caught Jane off-guard. Gigi certainly had all the attributes that could make a person pretty. But she wasn't. "I don't know. Do you?"

"Nah. She could be, but the looks dissolve the moment you meet her." He shook his head. "You know what?"

"Hm?"

"Gigi and Dax were made for each other. I've never met a more drama-filled couple in all my life."

"Yup."

"Ironic, considering they're in insurance. They should be risk-averse, yet they seek out craziness and live for risks."

"They *are* the crazies," Jane pointed out. "There have been times that I wonder if they've lost touch with reality. Not like, they aren't in touch with us common folk. But as if they aren't mentally stable. As though the fame and adrenaline have permanently altered what they understand as right and wrong."

After a long minute, Chance shrugged. "Upside: If they weren't batshit crazy, I wouldn't have met you—"

A noise came from the front door. Jane turned as it swung open. Bright lights blinded her. Her surprised scream died in the second it took her to comprehend the arrival of a camera crew.

"Get out," Chance barked. He flew off the couch and blocked their shots. "Turn it off. Get the hell out!"

"Where's Jane?"

She recognized Lark's voice and squinted toward the bright lights. "What?"

"Can you come over here," Lark called, unapologetically.

"Turn the fucking cameras off!" Chance growled.

"Never mind. We got what we needed," Lark called. "Forget you ever saw us."

What did they need? Dread hardened in the pit of her stomach. They couldn't use that footage in the documentary! Could they? It wasn't as though they'd filmed anything intimate but it had been private. This was their time, and they didn't have to share it with the Thanes, Lark, or a camera crew.

Chance slammed the door closed, re-locking it. He turned and leaned against it, then scoffed. "Good thing we weren't naked."

Jane pressed a hand to her chest. "Naked or not, they can't just walk in and film us."

"I'm not sure what your contract says, but mine won't allow it."

She dragged her knees up to her chest, still wondering what shot they wanted. "I think Lark just set us up."

A long, thoughtful minute crept by until Chance sat down next to her. "You're right. But hell if I know why." He grumbled and scrubbed his hands over his face. "I hate security work. And the mind games?" He shook his head. "No, thanks. I'll leave those to the spooks."

"Me too."

He laughed. "Don't worry about the Thanes. They're crazy, but they're not dangerous."

She wished she could believe him.

"At least, as long as you don't get on a plane to Syria again."

Jane had to laugh. "It's a plan."

He said good night and locked the door behind him. Jane tried to sleep, but the adrenaline rush remained in her system. When she closed her eyes, she could still see the camera's bright lights. Sleep didn't come, and as she lay alone in bed, worried and awake, staring at the ceiling, she fretted over what the next morning would bring.

CHAPTER FIFTY-FOUR

CHANCE TOOK A deep breath and strode into the living room of the main house the following morning, ready to kick ass and take names. Or, at the very least, lay down the law with the Thanes. Lark had known damn well what she was doing with the camera crew the night before, and Chance was certain that meant Gigi had been involved. Perhaps no one ever told them *no* before. Today, they'd learn what his limits were.

He'd also explain the reality of his relationship with Jane. They were an item. If there was a contractual issue with that, he'd wait for them to work it out. It was in the Thanes' best interest that he and Jane remained on their staff. Chance would make that a simple ultimatum. Boss Man would back him up. The drama would blow over, and he could continue on his merry way, providing security for this shit show.

But a little voice in the back of his head whispered that nothing ever went according to plan in the Thane household. Common sense didn't rule the roost, and ratings dictated most decisions.

After several minutes searching for Dax, Chance gave up. He'd have to speak with Gigi first. It would be fine, he told himself. He'd had much bigger problems on far more dangerous jobs.

Gigi sat with her back toward him as he entered one of the sitting rooms with a knock.

The second she looked up, he knew there was trouble. He swallowed hard, fearing nothing good would come up with a conversation with her now. Circles darkened under her eyes, and recent tears were evident.

"Just the person I needed to see," she said as she rifled through a drawer, her movements clipped, full of determination.

He took a step back, knowing he needed to escape as a camera crew bustled in, appearing out of nowhere. They boxed him in place and focused on Gigi. She didn't react to their arrival but pulled out a familiar dark blue booklet. "Ah. Here it is."

"What is?"

"My passport." Gigi swept her hair from her face. "Of course, with all of your travel, you have yours, too."

He rocked back onto his heels, uncomfortable with the conversation and the camera crew. "Of course, but—"

"Good. Get packed. We're leaving shortly."

"*What?*" He ground his molars.

"I need alone time, Chance," she snapped and muttered under her breath.

Did she say something about betrayal?

Gigi abruptly rose from her desk and strode to him, stopping far too close for comfort. He awkwardly stepped back, but she knotted her fists into his shirt.

He froze, pinned between the camera crew and Gigi. "Ma'am—"

"Go pack. *Now.*" She spun away and slammed the door.

Alone and trapped with the camera crew, he turned toward them. "What the hell just happened?"

They ignored him as though he were talking to himself. Chance scowled, shook his head, and turned.

"Cut—that was beautiful."

The sudden whirl of conversation made him spin toward the camera crew again. "Would any of you tell me what the fuck this is all about?"

One of them smirked. Someone else rolled their eyes. A few people filtered out the door.

Chance blocked the last two men from leaving. "What happened?"

They glanced at each other and then him again.

Why did *they* look confused?

"You haven't been read in for the day?"

What did that mean? These people didn't have security protocol. They didn't operate with any sense of order. He'd *never* been to a regularly scheduled meeting to be *read into* anything. "I guess not."

"Oh," the other man said. Both of their confusion disappeared. "Dax is dropping Gigi for a younger piece of ass, half his age. Juicy shit that the network can't get enough of."

Dax was no different than Chance's father. For everything he hated about Gigi, he couldn't help but understand her pain. After all, he'd lived through it once before.

Except for the wealthy and callous parts, Gigi might be his mother. Absolutely beautiful but abandoned and replaced.

Exhausted, Chance backed against the wall. He covered his hands over his face and pulled them down. He hated drama.

"And, hey, if you hadn't realized which way this will play out," the other man warned. "You're the odds-on favorite to serve as her consolation prize."

Chance ignored them and frowned as he headed back to his house to pack. Even if Gigi was a high-maintenance pain in the ass, she was Dax's woman. Chance had no respect for men who did that to women. Visions of his mother's broken heart made his chest tight, and no matter how much he hated drama, he felt an ever-increasing pity for Gigi.

He texted Jane but didn't receive a response as he walked to his garage apartment. By the time he'd closed the door and pulled out his go-bag, he'd forgiven Gigi for her blundering flirtations. Dax hadn't just left her; he'd planned to tell the whole world that a younger woman was better than his wife. It made Chance seethe.

He quickly packed, then headed to Jane's cottage. There was no answer when he knocked.

His text message buzzed with her reply to his earlier text.

How'd everything go? Teddy and I are at a playdate. Be back late afternoon. xoxo

Unsure how to summarize what had happened, he asked her to call when she had a private minute, and then Chance trudged back to the main house, go-bag slung over his shoulder.

Gigi stood in the kitchen, surrounded by her ever-present camera crew. She had changed into a tiny sundress and was giving a monologue to the camera. "I didn't see this coming. I'm not sure what life without Dax looks like." She sniffled and wiped at her eyes. "He's my rock. My one true love."

A production person gestured and said, "Great, and, cut."

Gigi wiped at the area under her eyes and caught sight of Chance, standing in the doorway. "Hi," she said, sounding fragile and a little embarrassed.

The crew scattered at the orders of the cut-man, following orders to tape b-roll. Gigi swept over to him, much calmer than he last saw her.

"Hey. Look," he offered. "You'll be okay. Just take some time away. Things'll work themselves out. Do you need anything? A snack?"

"Thank you, Chance. You're right." She went to him and draped herself onto his arm, patting his chest. "I just need to be away from everyone else."

His spine straightened, uneasy in her emotional embrace, and awkwardly waited for her to release him. She didn't budge, and no matter how he shifted, she didn't let go.

Chance tried a new tactic. Conversation. "Where are we headed?"

"The Caribbean." She squeezed harder.

He wanted to escape but couldn't. Shit. "I bet Teddy likes the beach."

"I suppose."

Maybe she didn't know. "You could show him—"

Gigi arched from his chest. "No. He'll stay with Jane."

"He will?" Chance swallowed hard.

She fluffed her hair and waved her hand as though his suggestion was a silly thought. "He'd be bored to tears in the Caribbean."

Not likely. Then it dawned on him—*they* were the only ones going to the Caribbean. When she said she wanted to get away from everyone, she hadn't meant the camera crew. She meant *everyone.*

"Just a quiet beach house. Nothing to do except watch the waves lap onto the sand."

The situation was getting more and more serious by the moment. He'd thought maybe they were going to stay with her family or with close friends. *Isn't that where people usually go to mend a broken heart? To the arms of people who love them?* "Who will join us?"

"No one. Just us."

"Just us?" Suddenly the consolation prize comment started to make a lot of sense, and he *really* didn't know what to say to Jane. "Pennebaker wouldn't mind time in the sun."

Gigi sashayed toward the counter and picked up a large-brimmed hat as though she hadn't heard him. She went to a decorative mirror and adjusted the dramatically slanted brim angled over her head. "I really love the beach."

"Right, yeah." He cleared his throat, worried that she skipped over his question. "So, what do you mean by just us?"

"Oh. No. Not *just* the two of us."

Thank god. "I see."

"I'm contractually obligated to continue filming, so a cameraman is coming, too. The Thanes can't handle more than one legal problem at a time." She smiled as if she faced the paparazzi. "Shall we be off?"

Then she disappeared. Chance stared after her, stunned.

A cameraman stepped in from where Gigi had swept away.

For a moment, it almost seemed as if she'd known a camera would be waiting around the corner. But, of course, she would. They were every-where.

The man set his equipment on the ground but gave Chance another look. "You okay, buddy?"

"No."

He snickered. "I remember my first couple of weeks. You're not in Kansas anymore."

CHAPTER FIFTY-FIVE

WHEN JANE PULLED up at the front of the house, she knew something was wrong. Everything seemed very quiet and still. Even the camera crews' trucks were gone.

Unbuckling Teddy from his car seat, she wiped some hot fudge from his chin and helped him out of the car. The second they reached the front door, it swung open, and Dax stood there, looking wild-eyed and unfocused.

Oh no, Jane thought. *Here we go again.*

"Big problems," Dax said, fidgeting from side to side.

Jane tightened her grip on Teddy's hand. "What? Is everything okay?"

Rather than answer her, he spun and stalked through the foyer and into the living room.

"Hi, daddy." Teddy held up the stuffed animal he won from an arcade machine.

Dax didn't seem to notice Teddy. Jane tickled the boy to distract him as she watched Dax pace back and forth, running his hands through the dark shock of hair at the top of his head and muttering to himself.

One of the housekeepers hurried by, and Jane called for the woman to help. They had a quick discussion, and the housekeeper took Teddy to the kitchen. Their chef could prepare a snack—not that he would be hungry. They'd just had a big helping of ice cream. But Jane had seen this side of Dax enough to know that when he got like this, everything was far from okay.

Jane waited for him to say something, but he only paced. "Okay, well, I'm going to make sure that Teddy is—"

He wheeled on her, eyes wide as if noticing her for the first time. "No.

Don't go anywhere. I want to… I don't know. It's got to be big. Something really wild and out there. But what?"

Out there? The last time Dax had talked about *out there*, they'd ended up on a plane to Syria. "I… don't know," she said softly.

But if his unfocused eyes were any indication, he wasn't asking her. It was more like he was asking himself, asking the universe. And she was caught in the crossfire. "Dax—"

He grabbed fistfuls of his hair and faced the window then suddenly spun on them. "I got it. Free insurance for life for the person who pulls the craziest stunt and posts it on our Facebook page. Yes!" He reached for his cell phone and came up short, patting his pockets. "I've got to get that to our marketing team."

Why wasn't there another voice of reason available? Jane gnawed on her bottom lip. "But, what if someone gets hurt?"

He waved the idea away. "That's what my legal team's for."

The front door opened, and Aunt Courtney stepped in, arms crossed, looking like she was out for blood. She strode across the room, heels clicking on the marble floor, and sighed at her brother as Teddy's voice called from the kitchen. Jane heard him racing to his aunt, and she only stopped when the little boy threw himself into her arms for a hug.

Aunt Courtney whispered into Teddy's ear. He giggled and nodded, then kissed her on the cheek and raced back toward the kitchen.

Soon as he was out of earshot, she rekindled her wrath and focused it on her brother. "Stand down, you crazy son of a bitch."

Dax moved his mouth and his hands, mimicking a puppet's mouth flapping. "*Womp, womp, womp.* There goes the fun."

She pinched the bridge of her nose. "Really, I don't know why anything you two do surprises me."

"*Womp, womp, womp.*"

"Dax! You need to take a Xanax. Or whatever meds you decided to skip." She scowled. "Did your psychiatrist refill your prescription? That one you restarted?"

He matched her scowl, and then his face lit up. He rushed across the room and snagged his cell phone off an ornate hall table. The camera crew appeared with the lights on and the film rolling.

"Dax," Aunt Courtney yelled. "You can't—"

"Stay away, Court. I'm in the middle of something important." He scrolled through his phone. "Something *epic*."

Courtney whirled on the camera crew and stuck her hand over the lens. "Turn this shit off."

"Don't touch the equipment."

"I will own your network if you don't get those cameras out of here in the next thirty seconds."

"Always the buzzkill," Dax complained.

Apparently, Aunt Courtney had threatened the crew with magic words. They cut the shot and killed the lights.

Courtney opened her mouth and paused, turning to Jane. "Would you mind taking Teddy upstairs or outside?" She pursed her lips together. "Somewhere else for the time being?"

Dax didn't argue, and Jane nodded. "Of course."

Jane found Teddy with the chef, licking peanut butter off of celery. The two adults exchanged a knowing glance before Jane picked Teddy up and took him to her cottage.

"You're so sticky." She pushed out the door and quickly moved down the deck. The sun warmed her shoulders and made his little hands that much stickier. "How about a bath before we do anything else?"

"Yes!" Her bathtub had jets, and he loved to play in it.

It only took a few minutes to strip off the ice cream and peanut butter covered clothes and set him in warm water. She got out toys, and he played with them in the tub.

Suddenly, Teddy stopped. "Is everything okay with Daddy?"

His big chocolate eyes made Jane's heart ache. She nodded. "He'll be okay. He's just a little wound up tonight."

Bath time wasn't much fun after that. She cleaned him up, redressed him in fresh clothes, and curled around him on her bed, turning a movie on. They hadn't had a nap, and he didn't always need one, but after a day like today, they could both doze off without complaining.

As the movie started, Teddy pulled the covers up over his chest. "Do you think there could've been a mix-up at the hospital?"

She laughed quietly. "What do you mean? When?"

Teddy turned, and his little face studied her. Whatever he was about to say had required him to wonder and think.

Uncertainty prickled in her chest. "Teddy?"

"Maybe Aunt Courtney is my mom." His sober expression gave way to a small slip of hopefulness. "And someone else is my dad."

Jane tried to hide the moment her heart broke into pieces. A golf-ball-sized knot lodged in her throat, and she vividly remembered her own childhood, when she wondered and prayed that her own parents were not her real ones, too. "Oh, baby. Teddy." Tears spilled from both their eyes as she wrapped him to her arms. "I'm so sorry."

He sniffed. "But what if the doctors just gave me to the wrong person? What if it was an accident that they gave me to them?"

She couldn't stop her tears and kissed his forehead. The movie came on, and she quietly promised, "I know grownup problems don't make sense. But, you and me? We'll keep going. We'll stick together. We'll love each other very much."

"And Aunt Courtney," he said.

"*And Aunt Courtney*," she agreed, then let the opening scenes distract him from her silent tears. Jane's heart aching. Poor Teddy was asking the same question she'd asked herself when she was only a little older than his age: Why couldn't his parents find it in them to love him?

CHAPTER FIFTY-SIX

A LONG, LONELY week followed. Jane missed Chance in ways she didn't expect. She'd become used to the way he brought her coffee every morning, and she missed his good night kisses every night. She missed talking to him too, and couldn't believe, given modern technology, they couldn't keep a simple phone call connected.

The morning sun brightened her apartment. Still, Jane lay in bed, staring at the ceiling. She didn't want to get up and face another tense day of tiptoeing Teddy around his father's erratic mood swings. It had been, in a word, exhausting. Not to mention demoralizing, draining, and soul-killing. Still, she'd do it all over again if it protected the kid.

Taking a deep breath, she got out of bed and slipped into her "uniform" for around the camera crews—a nice, wholesome flowered sundress. As she was braiding her hair behind her back, someone rapped on the door.

She opened it, thinking it was one of the housekeepers who continually serviced the main house, saying Teddy was already awake and asking for her before breakfast.

She nearly broke down when she saw Chance there, holding out a cup of coffee. "Oh, my God! You're home!" She took the coffee, placed it on a nearby table, and jumped into his arms.

He laughed, kissing her as he walked her inside, closing the door behind him with his foot. "One would get to thinking you missed me."

"I did!" She kissed until he laid her gently on her bed.

"One second." Chance disappeared and returned with her coffee.

God, she loved him. "I missed this too."

He placed the coffee on her nightstand. "Probably more than me."

She grinned, shaking her head. "Did you miss me?"

"More than you know." He traced a finger over her lips.

"What did you do the whole time? Hang out with Gigi?" she asked.

He shrugged. "Not much. Just a few crying spells early on that I had to talk her through. For the most part, she was fine. How was everything here?"

She cringed at the thought. "Dax was worse than ever. All I've been doing is protecting Teddy from his weird flights of—" She stopped in a cold panic and pushed off the bed. "If you're back, Gigi's home. She and Dax are probably fighting."

Chance grabbed her wrist. "You can't jump between them."

"I know." Jane pushed her hair back. "I meant I need to be a buffer between them and Teddy."

As she tried to slip away, he grabbed her again. "Jane, that isn't your job."

She pulled her hand free. "Yeah, it is."

"Where's the line?" He stood from the bed. "When it comes to this job, where does your life start and end? They do whatever they want, and you do exactly what they expect you to do."

Tears filled her eyes. "Yeah. I take care of their son."

His shoulders slumped. "When you put it like that…" He grabbed her coffee. "Let's go."

Jane was right. When they got into the main house, the tension hung thick in the air. Feet were stomping, and doors slammed. Chance took the sound of a glass breaking to head toward the security office in search of a comrade to discuss the situation.

She wasn't so lucky. A text message alerted Jane that she and Teddy would have to stay on the property, per Dax's request. Another day of tiptoeing, but this time, Jane had two adults behaving like children to avoid.

Jane dressed Teddy in a bathing suit with plans to spend the day swimming. They walked out of his newly styled bedroom, running into Dax.

He put a hand on her shoulder. "Jane. Good thing you're here."

She was always there. But her annoyance gave way to dread. His tone didn't bode well. "What's going on?"

"Bring Teddy to the living room. We're having a family meeting."

As fast as he appeared, Dax left.

"What's a family meeting?" Teddy held up his arms.

She lifted him to her hip. Her trepidation tripled. They stepped down the massive curved staircase. "It's when family members sit together and talk."

Teddy perked up. "Aunt Courtney's here?"

Wishful thinking. Jane wriggled him as a distraction. "Even if she's not, we can report all the details to her."

"Good plan."

She forced a lighthearted grin but faltered as she stepped into the living room. Chance and Gigi sat on a couch. His stiff posture made Jane uncomfortable, though he lifted his chin in a quiet hello. Gigi angled her legs toward Chance, half-covering her mouth with her hand as she spoke to him in hushed whispers.

Dax paced through the center of the large room. A camera crew followed his movements from their position in the corner.

Jane kept her focus on her only ally in the room, Chance, but he seemed busy ignoring Gigi. Time ticked by. Teddy wriggled in her lap. What were they waiting on? A producer to tell them how to host a family meeting? Maybe Dax's younger woman would sashay into the house. That would make outstanding reality television.

Every so often, Chance readjusted his place on the couch, clearly perturbed that Gigi inched closer. Jane studied him and decided that wasn't the only thing wrong. His hard-set jaw ticked as he tightly folded his arms over his chest. He wasn't uncomfortable—he was suspicious.

She bit the inside of her lip and scanned over to Dax. Jane had thought Dax had been throwing eye daggers at Gigi, but no. Clearly, his rage was aimed toward Chance.

Dax stopped pacing in front of Gigi and Chance. "So glad you brought your bodyguard to our meeting."

"Is there a reason you're looking at me like that?" Chance asked. His rough, cool tone left no question about his distaste for Dax. If this had been high school, Jane would've been sure the two men were about to fight. "Whatever your issue is, maybe you should think twice before bringing it into your home."

Jane swallowed hard, suddenly seeing how Chance's opinion of Dax and Gigi might have shifted in light of Dax leaving Gigi for a younger woman.

Teddy pulled for her attention. "This is a family meeting?"

Jane stroked his head and tried to change the subject. "We'll go swimming soon."

"Soon," he agreed.

Jane noticed one of the cameras focused their way. She ducked Teddy close to her chest, still stroking his hair like her arm was wide enough to block him from view.

"Good," one of the producers said.

Jane didn't know who he was speaking to or what was good. This was the world's most uncomfortable and *boring* family meeting.

Dax turned and held out his hands as if greeting the room. He glanced at them one by one with a nod as though he were ready to announce a hostile takeover in his corporate headquarters. "Now that we're all here, I can say what I need to say."

Jane situated Teddy on her lap, trying to gauge everyone's expressions. Dax took a dramatic deep breath. Did he have cancer? Had he sold Thane Insurance? Were they telling Teddy about the impending divorce in such a heartless manner? She had absolutely no clue.

She hugged Teddy closer. Dax stood in front of Gigi again. She gripped Chance's thigh. Chance jerked from her touch. "I don't think I'm needed at your family meeting."

Dax smirked. "Gigi and I have made it through one of the toughest tests of our relationship. *No thanks to you.*"

Chance froze. His legs were wide apart as though he might tackle Dax. Jane could see him analyzing the situation, and she didn't have a clue what he'd figured out. She was completely lost.

Then, Gigi dramatically swept off the couch and threw herself into her husband's arms. Their theatrical embrace lingered. Jane wanted to cover Teddy's eyes. She waited for them to wrap it up when she realized they were posing for the cameras.

She turned to Chance. Furrowed lines creased over his forehead. His eyes were tight and narrow.

Dax and Gigi changed positions and kissed like horny teenagers. Jane cleared her throat and shielded Teddy from the over-the-top PDA, only vaguely aware that the cameras filmed her range of reactions, from disgust to distrust.

The messy kiss ended then Dax motioned to Teddy. "Come on here, buddy. Get in on this family hug."

Dumfounded, Jane blinked and clutched her arms around Teddy like a seatbelt. The little boy didn't move.

"Teddy, my love, come here," Gigi cooed.

A cold chill ran down Jane's spine. She hated Dax and Gigi more now than she had hated her own parents.

"I don't wanna," Teddy whispered.

Dax and Gigi held their arms out and, as if choreographed, surged toward Teddy. They pulled him off Jane's lap and into a three-way embrace.

Teddy disappeared between his hugging parents, and Jane searched Chance's face for answers. He scowled, his expression radiating with contempt, then mouthed what she already knew, "Acting for the cameras."

Sickened, she turned toward the camera crew and glared. Everything had been for the television crew; the cheating accusations, the Caribbean vacation, and Dax's maniacal behavior. Neither even spoke to their son all week! Though that wasn't terribly out of character. But still, Teddy heard the slamming doors, shouting, and had to live in this virtual minefield of a home? For what? A publicity stunt? A great episode of daytime television?

The cameras cut, and the Thanes immediately abandoned Teddy with a slap on the back, all but confirming everything she just guessed.

Teddy, confused and bewildered, looked as though he'd been holding his breath during their family hug. He raced to Jane and took her hand. They had to get out of there.

She waved to Chance, certain this would be a hell of a topic to scrutinize later when they were off the clock and alone, and hurried the fastest way outside. Playing in the pool might be the only thing that turned this morning around. That, and *breakfast.*

She groaned. The day had just barely started. What craziness would come next?

CHAPTER FIFTY-SEVEN

JANE SPLASHED HER feet in the pool. Teddy splashed on the top step, making waves for his toy boats. The sun reached high overhead. They'd needed the free time to compress after the insanity of the Thane family meeting.

Teddy raced a speed boat toward her legs and then back to his plastic fleet floating along the top step. "Hey, Janie?"

She smiled, putting far too much effort into the acknowledgment. Yes, she was overcompensating, but the kid needed an overdose of love. "Yes, honey?"

"You finished malting."

Her eyebrow arched. "What does that mean?"

"Snakes malt," he explained then jumped into the water. His little body made a big splash. Then he kicked and paddled to her spot on the ledge. "You stopped malting."

"Ah." She couldn't help but laugh. "Molting. With an O." Jane held out her legs then examined her arms. She had already noticed the changes, trying not to obsess over them with topical lotions, aloe vera, and vitamin E oil. But while her flakiness was gone, sections of her skin were still discolored. A dermatologist explained that in some sections, the change in pigmentation or due to scarring would be permanent. "I've finished molting."

"Do you feel good in your new skin?"

Man, that was a deep question. Teddy didn't mean to probe, but she found herself reflecting on his question.

"It looks nice," he continued. "Same as your last layer of skin."

Out of the mouth of babes. "Yes, baby. I feel good in my skin." She smiled, somewhat surprised at herself. "I feel *comfortable* in my skin." Her smile deepened. Had Chance been the reason she'd been more accepting? Jane rolled her lips together and realized he wasn't the root cause. It certainly didn't hurt that the sexiest man on earth couldn't keep his hands off of her. But, this body of hers had been through a lot. Physically. Mentally. And, here she was, smiling. Happy.

Jane wasn't a fool. Finding comfort in her body wasn't easy. She'd had recent shaky moments, but more often, she'd had ones of lenity. Almost as though she'd given herself permission to be human. *Fragile* acceptance. But she had to start somewhere.

"I *don't* feel comfortable in my skin when I get out of the pool." Teddy held up his pruning fingers. "My fingers are swiggly. Then I dry off, and I feel like I've been stretched."

Jane tipped her head back and laughed. He pulled himself out of the water, kicking water over her legs until he sat on the ledge, side by side. Dripping, he leaned against her side. They kicked the water together.

Her stomach rumbled. They couldn't stay outside forever. "Are you hungry?"

"Yeah."

"Me too. Besides, if we spend any more time in the pool right now, you might really turn into a prune." She stood and retrieved their towels. He giggled and squirmed as she toweled him off, then he raced toward the deck stairs.

Jane gathered her bag and followed, knowing they were about to run into trouble the moment Teddy faltered at the top step. She climbed the remaining stairs and saw Gigi was lounging in the sun, engrossed in a magazine.

She and Teddy could creep down the stairs and enter the house a different way, but then their avoidance would be obvious. Plus, Jane didn't want to reinforce Teddy's avoidance of his mother.

"Go on," Jane whispered. "It's okay."

The little boy kept his eyes down and ignored the woman lounging on the patio in a tiny red bikini, reading behind massive dark sunglasses. They quietly walked toward the sliding glass door. If Gigi noticed them, she chose to ignore the interruption.

Jane pulled the door open. It squeaked. She was sure it'd never made a sound before, and she cringed.

As if on cue, Gigi called, "Jane?"

Her skin crawled as her name drawled out. Teddy froze like a deer in headlights. Jane twisted, not moving away from the boy or the door. "Yes?"

Gigi nonchalantly flipped a page and then another as though testing how long they would wait for her to speak. "Lark mentioned that you have a little infatuation over Chance Evans."

Irritation prickled under Jane's skin. She tried to hide it and kissed Teddy on top of his head, ushering him through the open door. "Go to the kitchen, and I'll meet you in a few."

He scurried off, grateful for a reason to leave and certain that meant he'd get to eat whatever he asked for. Jane slid the door shut, took a calming breath, and approached her boss. "Actually." She cleared her throat. "I wanted to talk to you about him."

"I bet," Gigi cracked, never raising her eye from the magazine. "He's very attractive. Men with physical traits like his are few and far between."

And do much more. "He's—"

"Quite the specimen," Gigi finished for her then folded her magazine into her lap, finally glancing toward Jane. "A man like Chance can't be caged."

Already uncomfortable with Gigi's description of Chance, Jane faltered, having never thought of relationships like cages before.

"They're primal beasts," Gigi continued. "They have needs and desires that cannot be met under normal circumstances." She paused pointedly. "Not from ordinary, *Plain Jane* women."

Jane clamped molars together, not willing to jump at the bait.

"However." Gigi pulled her sunglasses to the tip of her nose and eyed Jane coldly. "Men like Chance Evans will alleviate their urges with substandard stand-ins until someone more appropriate comes along." She left off the predictable *like me* and pushed her sunglasses up again. "I *do* like spending time with him. He has an ass you just want to bite."

Her lips flattened. From territorial to down-right bitchy, a million responses flooded her mind. But that was what Gigi wanted. Jane wouldn't stoop to her level. Her teeth ground, but she managed, "If that's all. I'll go find Teddy."

Gigi held up a hand. "Not before I'm sure you understand my point."

Her point? She was gorgeous. He was gorgeous. They should have gorgeous people sex. A few weeks ago, Jane might have crumbled under self-doubt. But now she didn't disguise her revulsion. The only thing she had to be concerned with was keeping her job for Teddy's sake. She twisted her fingers into the wet towel. "You want to bite someone who works for you?"

Conceited contempt curled across Gigi's bright pink smile. "My, my, Jane. You do have a little crush." She picked up a magazine, snickering. "How very perfect."

Anger pound in her ears. The longer her boss tittered, the tighter Jane's chest became. "Gigi."

Rolling her head, she sighed heavily in response.

"Just because I work for you—" Her ears rang. Words jumbled together, and her dry throat ached. "I care for your son. I give him everything I have. Don't take advantage of that to be cruel." Tears burned her eyes. "I don't deserve it." She swallowed hard. "And, Chance—"

Gigi smirked, callously amused. "Chance, what?"

"Beauty is only skin deep." Jane seethed. "Whatever you think you see, you're missing out on everything that makes him amazing."

Gigi pressed her hand to her chest and giggled. Her laughter swelled, and she covered her mouth, hysterical. "The ugly duckling has a *big* crush!" She tossed her magazine and doubled in laughter. "How fantastically cliché."

Tears spilled over Jane's cheeks. "You have no idea what you're talking about. He's my..." She swatted the tears away, furious but suddenly aware she and Chance hadn't had a relationship-defining conversation.

Gigi stopped laughing but didn't hide her caustic delight. "Your what?"

Her hands trembled. "Boyfriend."

Gigi pressed her hands to her chest again and folded, cruelly laughing.

Furious and humiliated, Jane rushed inside. White-hot tears burned down her cheeks. She hid her face and ran to the closest bathroom. Behind the safety of the locked door, she dropped to the floor, wrapped her arms around her knees, and wept.

She cried until depleted. Her swollen eyes hurt, and her head pounded. Exhaustion made her weak. Jane dropped her head back against the wall and concentrated on her breathing.

Someone knocked on the door.

"Jane?"

She cringed at Lark's voice.

"Jane, honey? Gigi's worried about you."

She snorted. "I'm fine." The growing absurdity made it hard for Jane to do anything more than shake her head. "And, I'll be out in a minute."

Jane waited until she was certain Lark had grown bored and left, then she stood to face herself in the mirror. The hours spent poolside didn't help her tear-stained appearance. Jane leaned closer and studied the reflection. With pin-prick accuracy, she knew every spot that had changed as she'd grown older and after her time in Syria. She saw the tiny indentation just off center of the middle her forehead. That spot had been with her since her freshman year in high school. The hellacious pimple that wouldn't go away. Mostly because she picked at it. The remaining mark was near impossible to see. Yet, she always saw it—and, for most of her life, she'd considered it one flaw of many.

Chance didn't care about that stupid spot.

Truthfully… *She* didn't care either. Not anymore. But not because of him.

Jane leaned back from the mirror, knowing she'd still always see that spot. Though maybe not as a shortcoming.

"Jane, are you still in there?" Lark called.

She had to laugh. "Yeah, Lark. Bad breakfast burrito."

"Ew, gross. Go to your cottage if that's the case."

Her grin reached her eyes. Jane liked the way they smiled with her mouth. "I'll keep that in mind next time. Thanks."

This time, Jane heard Lark leave, with disgusted stomps and a trail of muttering comments.

She sighed, unexpectedly at peace with herself. "I see you." She meant to point at the tiny scar on her forehead, but it felt like more. Her hand fell away. "And I like what I see." A little voice in her head cheered. "I have to get out of this place."

Her chin dropped. Jane didn't know what to do. She couldn't leave Teddy alone in a toxic home. Somberly, she slung the pool towels over a hook and stepped out of the bathroom. There had to be a way to protect the little boy and get out of this job. Maybe Aunt Courtney was the answer? Chance could help her brainstorm.

With her head held up, Jane headed toward the kitchen, vowing not to react if she saw Gigi or Lark. Or, hell, Dax, too.

She found Teddy seated on a barstool chair at the kitchen island, watching videos on an iPad under the watchful eye of one of the housekeepers that Jane considered an ally.

The woman opened her mouth to greet Jane but stopped short, forehead furrowing. "Are you okay?"

Unable to trust her voice, she lifted a shoulder.

"Your friend," The housekeeper dropped her voice. "The bodyguard. He and another were in the security office." She flicked her hand to shoo Jane. "I have the boy. Go. Take a moment."

Jane nodded on her gratitude and took off to find Chance.

CHAPTER FIFTY-EIGHT

CHANCE LEANED FORWARD on the office chair. He and Pennebaker had been huddled in an intense discussion for the past thirty minutes. If he'd thought it would shed light on the chaotic household, Chance had been wrong. They shared passing conversations with Lark and the camera crew conversations, and both men wondered what was for real and for show. Were Dax and Gigi a danger to themselves? Or, more likely, unable to satiate their desire for attention?

A quick knock on the security office door preceded it swung open. Jumpy, they turned quickly. "Jane?"

Her puffy eyes and faltering hello were enough to turn his stomach. Pennebaker muttered a greeting and appraised the situation. After a confirming look to Chance, he stepped toward the door. "Just on my way out."

Jane crossed straight into Chance's arms. She curled her arms between them, knotting her hands between their chests. Whatever had happened, she needed to be held. He pulled her close and backed onto his chair again.

Her face buried into his neck, and she curled tightly on his lap, silently begging him to keep her safe. Chance stroked the back of her head. Her quiet sniffles made his blood boil. One of the Thanes were responsible. He wanted to kill them. Which meant he needed to get the hell out of dodge before he actually did. Neither one of them should be in this job. He didn't know what to do about Teddy, but he had to act fast. "Want to talk about it?"

She shook her head.

"When you're ready." And then, after he knew what had happened, Chance would make a phone call to Boss Man. If he wasn't available,

Chance would call his teammates until he had someone with a clear perspective. Both he and Jane were in too deep to see the situation with any clarity.

"I said you were my boyfriend." Her lips tickled on his neck.

Chance chuckled and inched her from his chest, with a lopsided grin, he hoped he could make her laugh. "And that made you cry?"

She smiled. Not laughter, but he'd take what he could get. He kissed her forehead. "Guess that means you're my girlfriend?"

She sniffled and *almost* laughed.

"My woman?" he tried again, dropping his voice low, again hoping for a laugh.

Jane smiled, gave a short laugh, and wrapped her arms around his neck. He'd take that triplicate for a win.

She met his eyes. "We need to get out of here."

His neck muscles stiffened. For Jane to say that... "What happened?"

Her eyes closed, and with a slight head shake, she said, "The details don't matter. You were right. This place is toxic." Her voice broke. "But we need a plan."

"For Teddy?"

She nodded.

Knowing she was right but not having the slightest idea what to do, his stomach turned. He reached for the bottle of antacids that Pennebaker had left behind. Jane shifted from his lap and pulled a chair closer. Once they were settled again, face to face, she admitted, "I still don't know how. But I won't abandon him."

A rough knock pounded on the door, and Pennebaker announced, "Coming in."

The door swung open, and just as his stomach had lurched when Chance saw Jane, it did when he saw the dread on Pennebaker's face.

"What?" Chance hand over the bottle of antacids.

Pennebaker popped a few and capped the bottle. "They've called *another* family meeting."

"JANIE!" TEDDY'S VOICE echoed down the hall, and it was the only thing that could have propelled Jane out of the security office.

She found Teddy still on the barstool. Several members of the staff lined the wall behind a large kitchen table. To Jane, it almost looked as though they were hiding with the hopes of blending into the wallpaper.

Teddy leaned away from Dax, legs kicking and reaching for her arms. "We're having another family meeting."

The omnipresent camera crew positioned in a corner. Unlike usual, they had lights strategically stationed as though the room was set up for an interview.

Gigi swept in for Teddy. Jane could've ripped the boy from her arms but stepped back. Teddy seemed ready to cry.

The heavy footsteps of Chance and Pennebaker approached. Jane didn't look toward them, but knowing Chance was close somehow made her feel better.

"Now that we're all here," Dax said and hung an arm over Gigi's shoulder. "We have an announcement to share."

Gigi leaned against Dax. "We're renewing our vows!"

Jane's jaw dropped. No one made a sound. Bile churned in her stomach, and she could use the security office's bottle of antacids.

Gigi placed Teddy on his feet, just short of dropping him, and turned to Dax. With all the talent of a soap opera wannabe reject, her eyelashes fluttered, and she tossed her hair dramatically off her shoulder. "I love you."

Dax clinched her waist. "And, I love you."

Teddy ran toward Jane, jumping into her arms.

The happy-again couple turned toward the group, angling for the video camera. Dax said, "I bought Gigi a campy little resort."

Bought her a resort? Though… why not? An everyday guy might grovel and makeup *at* a mountain hotel. Dax Thane would buy the whole damn mountain and give his wife a resort.

"Campiness is vogue at the moment," Gigi explained. "And I can't wait to post the pictures."

Clearly, this conversation wasn't for anyone in the room. The Thane minidocumentary was turning into a weird mishmash of the Real Housewives, Survivor, and Punk'd.

Teddy leaned close to Jane's ear. "They're going to camp?"

His hopefulness in his voice sliced to her heart. "I'll explain later, honey."

Dax clapped his hands and rubbed them together as though he were about to dive into a meat lover's buffet. "Champagne glass hot tubs and heart-shaped beds."

"We're leaving tonight!" Gigi beamed. "Off to the wild, rugged Poconos."

Jane recalled the time she and Teddy visited an indoor water park in the Poconos. They'd had the absolute best time. Dax and Gigi refused to join them. Looking back on the rural area, Jane wondered how the locals would take to the Thanes.

"Say that one more time," a producer called.

Gigi and Dax restarted their banter, repeating themselves word for word. Jane rolled her eyes. But a realization hit Jane like a semi-truck. They were essentially filming a commercial. Nothing was ever what it seemed.

CHAPTER FIFTY-NINE

JANE MOVED TO another window of an alcove in the east wing where she'd had a stash of crayons and coloring books. Teddy happily colored, while she watched as the paparazzi grazed on the front lawn. They'd been allowed inside the gates at Lark's direction.

"What a shit-show," Chance muttered and left the window he'd been spying out of. Instead of joining her at the better vantage point, he walked toward Teddy and dropped on the carpet as the little boy happily killed his blue crayon.

"That's a good description," she agreed. Gigi and Dax had given the photogs a few pictures and extolled the excitement of their campy vacation. Jane nearly gagged as they saw off a caravan of their staff, all now on paid vacation, with gleefully charitable waves.

Jane, however, was not on vacation. She and Chance would watch Teddy—though they didn't notice Chance had stuck around. They'd decided to use the quiet time to concoct a viable escape plan. She watched Dax help Gigi into their favorite Range Rover. He waved to the paparazzi and pulled out the driveway.

"They're gone." She turned for her guys. Both were now coloring. Though Chance wasn't as hard on the crayons as Teddy. "What are you drawing?"

"Ghost blocks in a field. The cows fall through them." Teddy held up his paper.

Jane could make out a cow. Maybe two. "Very nice."

"And you?"

Chance grinned and mimicked Teddy.

Her eyebrow arched. "A stick figure holding an umbrella?"

"Oh, come on." Chance inspected his work of art. "It's *Mary Poppins*."

Teddy leaned over to look and nodded. "It's Mary Poppins."

Jane plopped next to them. Chance signed his name on the bottom corner and handed it to her. "For you, MP."

She took the drawing but then kissed her man. Just a little peck.

"Are you going to get married?" Teddy squealed.

Heat rose to her face. "Kisses mean you care—"

"One day," Chance said, giving Teddy a wink.

Her heart flipped, and her jaw fell.

Chance grinned, teasing her with the lift of his eyebrows. "And we're gonna have enough kids to play football."

"Cool!" Teddy picked up another crayon. "Can I play too?"

"Absolutely."

Jane was absolutely one hundred percent in love with Chance. If they were alone, she'd tell him. But it would have to wait until bedtime. "I'm going to make dinner."

"We'll be up here," Teddy explained. "Coloring."

They were cute and content. Jane left them to their creations and headed for the kitchen. The doorbell rang, and lyrical tone took Jane a minute to place. No one ever used the doorbell. The guardhouse would call up for guests who showed up without notice.

Then again, Lark had given the guardhouse the okay to let everyone in. Jane groaned and ignored the door, but the bell chimed again. She walked into the foyer, curious who would drop in when Dax and Gigi had left. The beveled, glazed front door glass didn't show who was on the other side. It was the first time she had needed to use a peephole and realized the designer front door didn't have one. The doorbell rang again.

The shadow on the other side knocked on the glass pane. "Jane Single-ton?"

Her eyebrow crooked. Who knew her name? Weird, but not insane. Most gossip hounds would call with a bribe, not brazenly knock on the door.

"Jane? A little birdie told us you were home."

She sighed. One day, she'd figure out how to get Lark back for every little headache. If the reporters knew she was home, they'd keep at it until she opened the door. Reluctantly, Jane cracked the door and saw a woman she recognized. Then, she saw all of them. Most of the paparazzi hadn't left, and several gossip reporters hurried toward the empty door.

"No one's here," Jane announced, stepping outside for all to hear. "You know that. You saw them leave." That didn't make a difference. She shielded her face. Hours had gone by, but her eyes were still puffy and her nose still red from her meltdown in the bathroom. She didn't want that recorded for prosperity's sake, no matter how happy she was in how own skin.

Jane backed inside the door, but a reporter caught it. The hairs on Jane's arms stood up. "Let go." She readied to throw her weight against it, knowing if she cried out, Chance would fly down the stairs. "Let go. Or I'll break your fingers when I close the door."

"*Jane*," a reporter called. "We don't want them. We want to talk to *you!*"

She should have ignored the bait. After all, she had a thousand times before. But something in the woman's voice gave Jane pause. She inched the door open. "Why?"

"I want to hear your side."

The reporter's faux sympathy prickled down Jane's back. "On?"

"The Thanes' vow renewal?"

She wasn't sure if loathing or annoyance crossed her face, but Jane knew she hadn't been able to completely mask her reaction. "People renew their vows all the time. I don't care—"

"But not after your boyfriend sleeps with your boss."

Jane froze, looking out into a sea of blinding flashbulbs. *Boyfriend?* "Excuse me?"

The reporter's face twisted. Her expression was a strange mix of pity, sadistic enjoyment, and triumph—after all, Jane didn't deny her claims, mostly because Jane couldn't wrap her head around whatever Gigi and Lark had done now.

The reporter gave her phone to Jane. Her fingers trembled as she took it. The headline of a familiar entertainment news website exclaimed *NEW*

BODYGUARD TURNED LOVER CAUSED THANE RIFT.

Horrorstruck, Jane scrolled down. Not bothering to read the fictitious article, she stopped on the photographs. They were grainy, but they were still clear enough to see Chance and Gigi at the beach. Jane scrolled down the page and froze, unable to look away from a picture of Gigi, topless and lounging, as Chance approached with a drink in hand.

The logical part of Jane's brain screamed that she knew better. Chance wouldn't touch Gigi. But the gossip-blog-reading part of her mind balked at the evidence on the screen.

"There's more." The reporter reached for the phone and opened another app, scrolling for Jane. "In bed."

The images weren't just grainy but dark and shadowed. Still, that was Chance in the dark. Behind him, there was a shadowed woman, identifiable only by her long hair. There was no question, though. That was Chance. Jane knew the angles of his face, the broad reach of his shoulders. Jane swallowed hard. Her hands trembled, and she forced the phone back into the reporter's hand.

There had to be an explanation. But she couldn't figure that out standing with a mob of reporters. Jane knew better! She did. She trusted Chance. Still, tears brimmed in her eyes. "No comment."

This time, the reporter let her shut the door.

Jane staggered toward the living room.

"Hey, Jane," Chance called from upstairs. "My boss is on the phone. Teddy's coming your way."

"Okay." All of the air left her lungs. She wanted to scream. Or throw up. She dropped onto a couch, and her tears spilled, unable to shake the dark images from her head. How could that have been the same man? Chance held her hand, he made love to her, whispered secrets at night, and made her feel like a queen. *His* queen.

"Janie?"

Shit. Jane fought against the cold lethargy that paralyzed her muscles and wiped her tears away. "Hi, honey. Sorry."

Teddy dropped next to her on the couch. "Do they make you cry too?"

"I'm not crying," she lied. "It's nothing. Everything's fine."

Teddy wrapped his arms around her. "That's what I say sometimes, too. Even when it's not."

Hell. Her tears swelled again. "Oh, Teddy." She returned his hug and stroked the back of his head, sniffling. "It's different, but I'm so sorry."

"How's it different when mom and dad make you cry?"

Jane bit her lip to keep from falling apart. "It just is. Give me a second." She swiped her cheeks dry. "And I'll have dinner ready. Okay?"

"How about we have ice cream before dinner?" Teddy asked.

She laughed. "Boy, do you know the best time to ask."

Teddy took her hand and pulled toward the kitchen. "For Chance too."

Weakly, she agreed. Jane followed Teddy, thinking of the first night in this house with Chance. With painfully vivid recollection, she recounted which walls they would redecorate. The ones they wanted to tear down. Her thoughts spiraled. She couldn't believe they'd been upstairs, Chance drawing her pictures, minutes away from the moment when everything would be called into question.

"I want mine on a cone." Teddy tugged her shirt. "Janie?"

"What? A cone? Sure." She walked to the walk-in pantry and found two types. "Cake or cookie cone?"

"Both!"

"Ha, try again." She decided on a cake cone for him and a cookie one for her.

"Cake—you already knew!"

"Wait a minute. How do you know this one is yours?" She hid the hurt in her voice and held up her cookie cone. "Maybe I want the cake cone."

"No way. I know you. You'd never eat a cake cone. Never ever."

She laughed. "True. You know me well."

"What about Chance? Which cone does he want?"

Her stomach turned. "He's on a work phone call."

"You know him so well," Teddy said. "What would he choose?"

Me. He would choose me. "I don't know, honey." Jane turned for the freezer and stopped cold. She knew Chance. She loved him, and while they hadn't said the words, he loved her. He'd shared that with her in a hundred ways.

Her mind flashed through the pictures. She tried to set aside her disgust and recall the dark bedroom photographs.

Oh, God.

That hadn't been Chance with Gigi. That was Chance and *her*. The night the camera crew barged into her cottage. But why?

Teddy nudged her hip. "Are we still having ice cream?"

"Yeah, baby." Jane hurried to make Teddy's cone. "And afterward, we'll have a real dinner. Okay?"

She set him on the barstool with a scavenger hunt book and his ice cream cone. As he announced the items he found, Jane paced, waiting for Chance to wrap up his phone call.

His footsteps approached the hall. Jane pivoted to face him. She knew the headlines were bogus, that he wouldn't lie or hurt her. The only thing she had to deal with now was her guilt—for faltering in her conviction of them.

Chance walked into the kitchen. The fury in his storming blue eyes confirmed everything Jane already knew. "Chance." Her heart pounded. "I love you."

CHAPTER SIXTY

CHANCE STOPPED SHORT. His eyes shut, and damn if Dax and Gigi didn't want to ruin everything. He sure as hell wasn't going to let them color when, what, and how he and Jane spent their time together.

He opened his eyes and closed the distance between them, placing his hands on her shoulders. "I would do anything to make sure you just said that because—"

"I saw the pictures."

Fury knotted in his jaw. "They're not—"

"I know." The corners of her mouth tightened. "But it took me a minute, and I'm so sorry that it even took me that long. I trust you." Tears slid down her cheeks. "*I love you.*"

"Babe." He pulled her close. "I'm in love with you. It's been that way since the moment we hit go." He cupped her cheeks. "I hate this place. And I don't want any part of it to stay with us. Do you get that?"

She nodded, and he held her close, clasping a hand around the back of her head and holding her to his heart. "Jane. I love you. I'm going to marry you." Euphoria flooded his system when she squeezed his sides in response. "Maybe we won't have dozens of kids. But I'll give you everything you ever want. Okay?" He kissed the top of her head. "Let's just get the hell out of here first."

Again, Jane nodded. She wrapped her arms around his neck. "They set us up."

"Yup." His earlier conversation about an exit strategy with Jared had quickly derailed into his boss reading him the riot act for fucking the client. As soon as Chance recovered and caught Boss Man up to speed, Chance could see everything clear as day. The Thanes had set them up.

Lark was very much involved, from arranging the unwelcome visit from a camera crew in Jane's cottage to the photoshopped Caribbean vacation. "We're the collateral damage in another Thane publicity stunt."

The outside world wouldn't be able to see events as they really happened or even in real-time. Every incident had been scripted, choreographed, and surely edited to suit a production schedule that they weren't privy to. Chance could see their entire playbook. Their depravity made him shake. "Good news, though."

She hooked her arm in his. "You already heard ice cream's for dinner?"

He cast a glance at her, appreciating for the umpteenth time how well Jane could dust herself off and keep trucking. "We have the start of a plan."

"Oh, really?" Jane deposited him on a barstool next to Teddy.

As she made them ice cream cones and prepared a real dinner as well, Chance shared what Jared had said—as much as Chance could in front of Teddy—ending with their first action item. "Later tonight, I'll track down Courtney Thane and have a long conversation on Teddy's behalf."

CHAPTER SIXTY-ONE

AFTER DINNER, JANE kissed Chance goodbye and turned for Teddy. He had his scavenger hunt book sucked under his arm.

"Can we have dessert?" He smiled, making a point to show as many teeth as possible in hopes of another ice cream cone.

Jane ruffled his hair and shook her head. "No, but we can go outside with your book."

"And look for fireflies!" He skipped toward the sliding glass door, impatiently waiting for Jane to disarm the security system.

She approached the closest panel, housed in the pantry. The screen normally emitted a low green light, allowing her to swiftly swipe the code, but the dark screen made her pause. She searched for the light switch and illuminated the pantry. The alarm panel was definitely not working. "Hang on a sec," she called to Teddy then ambled to the foyer. That security panel was dark also. "Teddy?"

"Yeah?"

"Try the door now."

"Is it unlocked?" He knew to wait for the mechanical voice to announce *disarmed*.

"It's glitching, I think." Jane pressed the dark screen futilely. "See what happens when you open the door." What was the worst thing that could happen? They'd trigger the alarm, the police and security company would rush to the house, and she'd explain the panels were dead, unable to cancel the alarm. Easy-peasy.

Jane walked toward the kitchen and heard the sliding glass door before Teddy called, "Opened."

"Weird," she muttered and followed him outside.

The summer night made for an orange and purple sky. Shadows hung over the backyard. But they didn't create enough shade for the backyard lights to turn on.

Teddy plopped onto a lounge chair. She pulled a patio chair close and rested her feet on the edge of his, watching as the little boy flipped through his book.

"Look," he said, barely looking from the pages. "I found the pirate and the treasure."

Jane grinned. "Good job."

"They were over here." He tapped a page. "I always forget he's not where he's supposed to be."

Teddy had completed every hunt in the book several times. So had she, and still, she forgot that the pirate wasn't on his ship and the buried treasure wasn't near the X on the map. "They're never where they're supposed to be," she repeated as goosebumps chilled down her back. She didn't know why.

"Jane?"

They both jumped and turned as Gigi emerged from a side patio.

Gigi's long hair was chicly tied back, and she wore a black jumpsuit that Jane realized she hadn't seen in a week or two. Apparently, the time for mourning their Syrian disaster had passed. Uncharacteristically though, she wore flats. Surely designer but not sandals nor heels that made a statement. It was the most blasé outfit Jane had ever seen the woman wear. "Gigi—what are you doing here?"

She sashayed across over then pet her son's hair as though he were her pet. "It's my house." Her too soft smile didn't reach her eyes. The hairs on the back of Jane's neck stood. "And I realized something important."

Jane glanced at Teddy, frozen like a statue. "What's that?"

"You never get time off." With one last pet, Gigi finished the awkward show of affection and sat next to Teddy on the lounger. "You're always alone in this big house."

"I'm with Teddy."

Gigi glanced at the boy. "True. But that can still be very lonely."

Teddy perked up. "But we weren't—"

"Lonely," Jane quickly finished. She wanted to keep Chance's name out of the conversation. There was no point in creating drama. "We're fine. But thank you for worrying about me."

"Aunt Courtney offered to take Teddy for a few days."

"I'm going to Aunt Courtney's?" His little legs bounced with excitement.

"Isn't that great?" Gigi's voice held an unfamiliar velvet softness that almost covered its razor edge. "You have such a great auntie."

"When?" Teddy scooted to the edge of the lounger. "Tomorrow?"

Jane's belly knotted. Chance was on his way to Courtney's. Had the conversation gone that quickly? She wished he could've filled her in before Gigi returned.

Gigi stood. "Now, if you like."

"Yes! Please, can I go now? Please?"

"Of course, honey." Gigi's smile was beautiful in the way that broken glass could shimmer in the sunlight. "Jane, would you run inside and prepare his bag for a few days?"

Teddy slapped the book shut. "I want to help pack!"

Gigi clapped a hand on his shoulder. "He can stay with me."

Jane fought against an overwhelming urge to grab Teddy and run. "All right." She bent on her knees, meeting him at eye level. "Any special requests?"

Teddy's bottom lip pushed out, but his desire to see his aunt kept his pouting at bay. "Bun Bun."

"Of course." Jane squeezed his shoulders. "Anything else?"

"No, that's it."

She nodded. "Okay—"

"That's it," Gigi repeated tersely.

Dismissed, Jane straightened. Her heartbeat thumped faster than it should. She could taste adrenaline but didn't know why. "Everything's okay?"

With a quick pinch of her lips, Gigi's icy demeanor surfaced into its usual place. "It will be so long as you can listen and do as instructed."

The woman's recognizable bitchiness was almost welcome. Jane kissed

Teddy on the head and forced herself to walk away.

Each step made her anxiety grow. She climbed the deck stairs and re-entered the kitchen through the sliding glass door, pausing as she recalled the security system problem. Jane could tell Gigi, but what would that do? Gigi would tell her to do what she already planned to do after Teddy's bedtime: Notify the security company that their system was acting up again.

Actually, she had planned to call Chance and then the security company. More so than before, Jane needed to hear his voice. She reached for the back pocket. Her stomach fell. She'd left her phone on the table by the pool. Normally, it wouldn't have mattered. She wasn't tied to her device. But now, it did, and she couldn't articulate why.

Shivering, Jane turned to retrieve her lifeline of communication.

"Hello, Jane."

Jane spun. Her arms flew up, ready to defend herself like her uncle had trained her years before. "Dax?" Surprised recognition trumped her fight instinct. Her hands pressed to her heart. "You scared me to death."

"I'm sorry." He stepped from a dark hall. "Didn't mean to startle you."

Hands still clutched over her racing heart, she tried to shake paranoia. "I didn't know you were here."

"You didn't see Gigi outside?" He glided by her and leaned against the kitchen island, eyeing her thoughtfully.

"I did." Jane forced her hands to her side. "She didn't mention you were lurking in the shadows."

He laughed. "I don't know about lurking. But are we ever apart?"

Jane shook her head.

"You're on vacation now. I'll fix you a drink. What'll it be?"

She shook her head again. "I'm fine."

"Oh, come on now. You're off the clock."

"I have to pack a bag for Teddy."

"Ah, right." Dax tossed his hand. "Better get to it."

"Thanks." She rushed deeper into the large house. Even though Dax wandered the first floor, Jane jerked at every little sound. The quiet hum of the air conditioning. The way her bare feet padded over the thick carpet.

It didn't take long to pack Teddy's bag. Jane hid Bun-Bun at the bottom in case Gigi peeked in his suitcase and decided to toss the stuffed animal. She returned downstairs, glancing out a large picture window at the deep purple sky. The backyard and pool lights were off. Gigi and Teddy were nowhere to be seen.

Dax met Jane on the last step. He took the suitcase, and in place, he handed her a glass. "Cranberry vodka. My gift to you."

"Oh, really. I don't—" She faltered with the glass, and the cocktail sloshed. "Shoot. Sorry."

"Jane." He loomed over her. Too close. Too tall. "Relax."

Every passing second ensured that she wouldn't. The hall lights were off, and the expansive passageway was only lit from the hallway connecting to kitchen. Dax blocked her way, forcing Jane to angle her head back. "Excuse me."

A lazy, almost seductive grin curled on his face. She'd always understood that Dax was an attractive man. His good looks were magnified by his large build and broad shoulders. Right now, those same qualities pinned her in place. She could back onto the stairs or dive around his side. What was he doing so close? If he touched her, she'd throw the unwanted drink in his face.

"Can we talk?"

The glass trembled in her hand. "With Gigi?"

Dax shrugged and set the suitcase down. "Would that matter?"

"*Yes.*" Or, no? "What's going on?"

Gigi and Lark stepped into the hallway. Jane pushed by Dax. "Where's Teddy?"

"In my car," Lark volunteered and took the suitcase. "We'll be back in an hour."

Jane watched the two women head toward the kitchen. She placed her glass on a decorative table that cost a small fortune, not caring, and hurried for the front door.

"Where are you going?" Dax asked.

"To say goodbye to Teddy." Jane reached the security panel out of habit then simply unlocked the front door. No cars. She turned. "Where are they?"

"This would be easiest if you sat down and talked with me." He approached cautiously. "Shut the door. Sit down. If cranberry vodka isn't your drink, tell me what is."

"Where are they?"

"Lark parked on the backside of the lot. We thought it would be best to avoid attention."

"Why?"

Dax sighed. His stance loosened. "She mentioned you spoke with a reporter a few hours ago."

"Lark sent the reporter to talk to me!"

"Come with me, Jane."

At a loss, she slammed the door shut and followed Dax up the stairs. They followed the pathway toward the west wing. She rarely came to this side of the house. It housed the master quarters, which were expressly off-limits to Teddy unless directed otherwise. "Where are we going?"

He paused, giving her an odd look. "The sitting room."

There were a half-dozen sitting rooms in this damn house. Still, she followed deeper into the west wing. Was Dax about to fire her? She hadn't said a word to the reporter! And, if they did that and didn't let her say goodbye to Teddy? God, she'd kill him.

They entered the sitting room attached the master bedroom. Gigi's clothes covered a fainting couch and matching chairs. A row of high heels lined over the keys of their Steinway piano. Dax stood in the middle, amused. "Guess she packed in a rush."

In what world did Gigi pack her own bag? "Dax?"

His eyebrows arched.

"Are you going to fire me?"

He laughed. "Would you have that drink if I said yes?"

The world spun. Her knees went weak.

"No." Dax grimaced. "Bad joke. Sorry. No." He flicked his hand toward the clothes. "Throw those onto the bed or something. Then we can talk."

Funny, how they were so adamant she was on vacation. Yet, here she was, lugging slinky dresses and piles of lingerie around. Jane grabbed handfuls of hangers, cleared them out. Dax took a seat after and pulled out his phone. Within seconds, a video of what sounded like teenagers jumping on top of cars had his full attention.

Awkwardly, Jane moved Gigi's underwear to her bed. It wasn't organized, but for now, that wasn't her problem. She took a seat and waited for Dax to look up. He didn't until she cleared her throat.

Reluctantly, he put his phone away. "You sure you don't want a drink?"

Jeez. "*No.*"

He stood and paced. Each tight revolution seemed to amp him up, reminding Jane of football players psyching themselves up before a big game. This is what Dax did. It was as though he craved adrenaline so much that he called upon it constantly—most recently, in family meetings. He curled his hands into fists, clenching and unclenching with exaggerated movements. Tendons strained in his neck as his cheeks grew darker.

"Dax, are you okay?"

He pivoted like a sumo wrestler. His jaw flexed, his nostrils flared. Jane pushed against the back of her chair. She'd never been the sole focus of his adrenaline-driven mania before.

"Dax?" Fear broke in her voice. "You're scaring me."

He bounced on his toes, and his lips pulled back, revealing teeth sealed tightly together. Through clenched teeth, he managed, "Should've drunk your drink."

He lunged. Two hundred pounds pinned Jane to the couch. She thrashed and kicked. His hand covered her face, forcing a cloth over her nose and mouth.

She gasped and choked. Her muscles weakened. Jane prayed for strength. She needed to kick and claw. The room spun. She closed her eyes, fighting the room's awful tilt as the ceiling and the floor played hopscotch.

"Breath," Dax cooed.

She battled the snowfall of psychedelic trails until her arms and legs were too heavy to lift. Dax floated back, kneeling next to her and staring as though she were important but worthless. Jane couldn't move. He pushed her chin up and closed her gaping mouth. Jane tried but couldn't part her lips again.

"You've done your job," he whispered reverently. "I promise. This won't hurt."

Slowly, the edges of the world bled black and fuzzy and quiet.

CHAPTER SIXTY-TWO

THE LIGHTS WERE on, but no one was home. Chance returned to his truck. He'd parked in front of Courtney's Kalorama home and, no doubt, any moment now, someone would call the cops on him if he continued to lurk. Maybe they already had and Titan Group had rerouted the calls.

Once again, he double-checked the address that Parker had given him. It matched the address number on the bronze mailbox at the foot of the double stairs. Chance called back to Parker's IT lair.

"Status update?" Jared barked instead of Parker's affable hello.

He pinched the bridge of his nose. "Not much to share."

"Damn these Thanes. Always causing problems."

"To be fair—"

"I don't give a donkey's crap about fair."

Chance shifted. Perspiration dampened the back of his neck. The stuffy air in his truck did him no favors as the night seemed to warm. Between that and Boss Man barking at him, he'd have preferred to get out of his truck. But if he hadn't scared the neighbors yet, he didn't want Jared's booming growl to do the trick. "She didn't know I was coming."

"She would've if she'd answered the phone."

Courtney Thane had to be the polar opposite of her brother. She shied away from the pomp her family's wealth could bring, she stayed offline, and, apparently, didn't answer her phone after eight at night. "We're sure she's in DC?"

"Yeah, we're sure." Then, not to Chance, Jared demanded, "We're sure she's in DC?"

"Affirmative," Parker supplied in the background.

Headlights turned onto the street. It didn't see a lot of traffic. None of which had slowed like this Mercedes was now. Chance squinted to see the driver. Definitely a woman, but despite the glowing streetlights, her shadowed profile wouldn't allow him to identify Courtney Thane. "What do you have on a dark silver Mercedes. Tags—" He checked his sideview mirror. The orange turn signal blinked. "It's her. Gotta go."

The Mercedes disappeared into the alley. He hung up and jumped out of the truck, giving her thirty seconds to drive down the alley, wait for the gate, then pull into her garage.

He bounded up the stairs again and waited for a thirty count. Through the decorative, clear glass panes along the door, Chance didn't see movement.

Forty seconds passed. Then fifty. After a full minute, he wondered if she'd spotted him lurking. He pulled out his phone and tried her cell phone number again. No answer. Just like his and Titan's calls before. Damn it.

Seemingly far from the front foyer, a light turned out. Then another. Courtney had finally made it inside and was apparently on her way to bed. He knocked. No answer. The last of the first-floor lights turned out. Then she moved slowly into the hall.

Chance knocked again, wishing he'd thought to bring night-vision goggles. What was she waiting for? Hesitantly, she stepped closer until he was certain she was at the peephole.

"I work for your brother," Chance called loud enough to penetrate the heavy wood door. But, that revelation didn't gain him entry. Though, why would it? Her brother was batshit crazy and, according to Jane, Courtney Thane knew it. "My name is Chance Evans. I work for the security company employed by your brother," he tried again, "Titan Group."

"If you don't leave," her whisper floated from an unseen intercom speaker. "I'll summon the police."

"For all the waiting I've done, they're probably on their way."

"What do you want?"

He ran a hand over his face, not sure what would convince her to open the door. "A conversation about Dax and Gigi."

"No."

"It's important. If you would check your phone. My boss has been reaching out to you."

She didn't respond.

Maybe Chance should've watched Teddy, and Jane could have come for Courtney instead. "You have to trust me."

Waiting for her felt like years. Finally, she added, "I don't."

Chance had hoped the delays meant she'd been checking her phone. "It's about Teddy."

She didn't answer. He continued to wait, mentally willing her to open the door. No dice. She must've gone to bed. He dropped his head back— the door cracked open.

His chin snapped down then his stomach dropped. Courtney clutched her phone while holding a sleeping little boy to her chest.

"*Teddy...*" Chance couldn't breathe. "What's going on?"

"I listened to the voicemails," she replied, not lessening his growing panic. "Your name again?"

"Chance Evans."

Courtney narrowed her eyes but stepped back. "Come in and close the door. I'm going to put him to bed."

Chance wanted to steamroll her with questions but bit his tongue and agreed with a lift of his chin. He locked the door, then walked into a formal living room. Leather-bound books lined the walls—and toys lined the floor. In the corner, an art easel waited to be used again, while a row of Teddy's artwork lined the windowsill, haphazardly taped in place like the little boy had been allowed to do it himself.

His heart raced as he walked farther in. Wood furniture gleamed, no less beautiful under a pile of coloring books. The sofa and couches matched, upholstered in dark blue silk, but they looked comfortable and, dare he think it, well-used.

Carefully, Chance lowered himself onto the couch. It *was* comfortable, and though he was still alarmed, he felt a sense of unpretentious comfort.

Courtney returned, folding her arms over her chest. She stayed at the edge of the living room, wary. Chance wasn't certain of everything that made her cautious, but he didn't want to be on that list. "I apologize for barging in on you."

"It's been one of those nights."

He swallowed hard and pressed his hands to his knees—but stopped himself from rising. He wanted her to trust him, and without more than a few voicemails and messages, he was on shaky ground. "How much did my boss say?"

"Enough to allow you in the door."

His heart raced. "Is Teddy okay?"

"I need a glass of water." She nudged her head and left. "Would you like one, too?"

"All right," he said, on her heels.

Courtney filled two glasses with tap water and gestured for him to sit at the table. "You're the one who bedded Gigi?"

He cringed. Jane had warned him that Courtney didn't pull punches. But the thought of touching Gigi made his stomach roil. "I'm the guy they'd like you to think bedded Gigi."

Courtney regarded him carefully, then handed him the glass of water. She sat in the chair across the table and set hers down, untouched.

"Before I jump into everything. I need to know." His pulsed raced. "Why do you have Teddy?"

"My brother and his wife are off on another trip and their nanny called in sick."

Fuck. He needed to speak with Jane immediately. "Excuse me a second. I need to make a call—"

With the razor-tipped edge of an ice-cold stare, Courtney denied him. "Sit down."

His jaw clenched until white spots danced in his vision. Alarm and terror seesawed in his chest. If Chance didn't speak with Jane soon, he'd explode. But if he didn't listen to Courtney, he'd lose valuable intel and a possible ally. Agitated, he took a seat.

"What urgent conversation demanded phone calls from the Titan Group and a visit from Gigi's—" She stopped herself. "A visit from their security personnel."

Chance didn't know where to start. "We're concerned—"

"*Concerned?*" Courtney massaged her temples. "What are you going to tell me that I don't already know? My brother's a manic asshole? His wife's a self-centered bitch? They're hopelessly addicted to attention the way some junkies crave a needle? *I know.*" Her hands dropped to the table, and she couldn't hide her exhaustion. "Trust me, I know."

"I left their house after dinner with Jane and Teddy. She wasn't ill. If she got sick, she would've called me." He leaned forward. "Jane's the reason I came to find you. She's scared for Teddy. But, since Teddy's here? I'm scared for her."

Courtney's eyebrows drew together. She tapped the pad of her index finger along the table as her wheels turned.

"Dax and Charlotte had left," Chance emphasized. "They didn't know I was home with Jane and Teddy."

Courtney's finger tapped faster. "Call Jane."

Chance laid the phone in the center of the table and called, pressing the speakerphone button. A flash of her contact picture—a selfie of them—flashed before the first ring. Courtney lifted her gaze to him, but she didn't question the way Chance had held Jane.

Voicemail picked up. He gripped the edge of the table as he listened to her recorded message. "Hey, MP. It's important you call me back." He ended the call and shot off a text message with the same request.

"You didn't say where you were," Courtney pointed out.

"I don't know why she's not answering the phone." He rubbed his hands over his face. "They took Teddy from her—"

"Their nanny."

"Who's not sick." His mind had a hundred nightmare scenarios in queue. "We both know they're crazy."

Courtney rubbed her temples again. "But how crazy…"

CHAPTER SIXTY-THREE

SLOWLY JANE CAME to. Her head ached. Voices swirled around her; she could almost see them tumbling across her vision and she couldn't decipher which word meant what. A meaningless rush of familiar sounds.

Her tongue felt as though it didn't fit in her mouth, her cheeks like they'd been air dried in a dentist's chair. She couldn't swallow. Her dry throat wouldn't allow it. Just like her eyes wouldn't stay open.

Jane tried to roll over but couldn't. She had no feeling in her limbs nor strength in her neck to lift her head. Had she died? Jane didn't think death would give her such a painful headache.

So, not dead. Not awake. She was too tired to care.

Unable to sleep, bits of memory teased the edges of her mind. Chance made her happy. Teddy made her...worry. A cold prickle of panic tingled at the back of her neck. Why did she worry for Teddy?

"This is killing me," Gigi's theatrical cry rang clearly and broke through Jane's fog.

Yet Jane still couldn't move. But she could hear—and remember. Memory upon memory came into focus and zoomed away as though she were watching a slide show. The reporter and the damning pictures. Chance explaining the truth. She whimpered, recalling how Dax pressed a caustic cloth over her face.

Though her eyes were closed, she sensed someone approach. Jane lay perfectly still, scared to take a breath.

"Did she make a noise?" Lark leaned close on Jane's right.

"I thought I heard something also." Gigi lifted Jane's wrist and dropped it.

Helpless to control her body, her arm bounced to her side. Jane couldn't have moved it on her own if she wanted to.

"There's nothing to hear. She's not waking up," Dax said.

"I know," Gigi muttered. "But this is a lot of work—"

"Think of all the shopping you can do." Lark moved away. "Think of the media bookers that will want your story on their shows."

Jane's ears burned. She still couldn't move and didn't understand. Where was she? And what were those sounds?

"What about this?" Lark asked.

"Yes!" Dax cheered. "Throw it against the wall."

"Do *not* throw that against the wall," Gigi cried. "At least not until we're ready to leave. A little Chanel is fine. A bottle soaking in the carpet?" She gagged. "I won't stick around."

"How much more should we do?" Dax asked. "Everything?"

Both women hummed in contemplation. Jane moved her pinky finger. Her ability to orient herself came back to her in spurts. She could feel fabric under her palms and, minutes after Lark had been by Jane's side, the tilting sensation of her crawling close—on a bed—came back. It was as if her senses were on a delay.

Jane opened an eye. Her headache throbbed. She could see, but that didn't matter. Nothing registered yet. Her other eye opened. If she could've winced she would have. The lights weren't bright but they stabbed into her eyes—she almost knew where she was. The familiar location was on the tip of her tongue—the Thanes's bedroom. She was in their bed.

The sound of rips and tears mixed with the clicks of wooden hangers tangling. Jane could stretch her fingers. Her fingernails dug into the comforter.

"Remember this one?" Gigi called. "I wore it to the Met."

Dax laughed. "It looks like a trash bag with sequins."

"It *is* a trash bag with sequins," she agreed.

Jane tilted her chin and squinted toward the voices. With a knife in one hand and the dress in the other, Gigi stabbed and sliced her bag dress until it looked like it had been used to capture clawed animals.

Jane opened her eyes wider. Dax, Gigi, and Lark worked diligently through Gigi's clothing. They cut, tore, and shredded. *Why?*

More confused, panic pressed on Jane's chest. Her fear and lucidness came in bursts. She clenched her fingers, wriggled her toes. Jane fought the stranglehold that had paralyzed her. The pounding headache worsened. Jane wanted to vomit. Instead, she opened and closed her fists.

One by one, her muscles returned to her control, but she wouldn't make a move until she could run. Jane managed movement in her right leg, but not her left. She couldn't do anything with her arms beyond her wrist. Carefully, she tested her neck's range of motion. She froze, staring at the nightstand. A vodka bottle and container of cranberry juice were lined up next to a row of Gigi's Xanax bottles.

"Where's that pencil skirt I hate?" Gigi asked.

"On the bed?" Lark suggested.

Jane closed her eyes and returned to her original position as best she could.

"No, never mind. I already did that one."

"I think we're almost finished," Lark said.

Dax's heavy footsteps crossed the room. He opened a closet and returned, dropping something next to Jane's head. He cackled. "I haven't used this thing since that IPO went buck wild."

Gigi groaned, muttering, "Don't forget, you got sick for days."

Jane cracked her eyes when Dax walked away. A red funnel connected to a long plastic tube laid on the pillow next to her. *A beer funnel.*

Jane's clarity came in one astonishingly calm second. The slashed clothes. The liquor, pills, and funnel. If it would have done any good, she would have screamed. They were going to kill her and the story would tell itself. The brokenhearted nanny who lost her handsome boyfriend to the billionaire beauty drowned herself in booze, ending it all in a jealous, *newsworthy* rage.

CHAPTER SIXTY-FOUR

H OW CRAZY ARE *Dax and Gigi…?* The question might haunt Chance for the rest of his life. It was certainly on repeat as he pressed the gas pedal and sped out of DC. When he and Courtney couldn't answer that question, they'd known the answer. Their next call had been to Jared.

Boss Man had answered on the first ring. He didn't question their combined situational assessment and conclusion: Jane was in danger. No one had seen that coming, but that would be another thing that would haunt Chance.

Outside of National Airport, they could land a helicopter in DC without the risk of scrambling military fighter jets. Between Jared and Courtney and their fleet of helicopters, they promised Chance they'd get him in the air faster than he could drive to the Thanes's. All he had to do was cross into Virginia. By the time he got there, they would know who had the closer chopper with the shorter preflight checklist.

Chance rounded the corner of the highway, passing under the Virginia is for Lovers welcome sign. His phone rang; the Bluetooth speakers picked the call up as he sped by the Pentagon. "Yeah?"

"Pull onto the left shoulder and stop," Jared ordered.

"Stop?"

"Yeah, pull the fuck over."

"Hell," he muttered. "Roger that." He tore onto the shoulder. Debris and rocked rolled in the wheels and under the truck as he slammed the breaks. "Stopped."

"Then get out," Jared said.

Chance didn't have time to question. He tucked his Glock in a holster and grabbed the keys and his phone and squeezed out his door. He wouldn't have parked so close to the cement barrier wall if he knew he'd have to hoof it. Then he looked up, feeling the stealth helicopter before he heard it as the beast lowered into the closed HOV Express lanes.

"Holy shit." He jumped the cement barrier and ducked for his next ride.

The hatch door opened. Two men greeted him by way of handing him gear and weapons. They had a way about them. Chance could tell they knew his world well. Each seemed to know that this was one of those jobs where names weren't mentioned because this job never officially existed.

He grabbed a headset and listened as the pilot called in their liftoff.

"Midas?" Parker's voice reverberated.

Chance took a deep breath, reassured to have someone he knew on standby, even if it was only by radio transmission. "Midas checking in."

Parker gave a quick update and run-down. They opted out of an emergency call to the police until they knew the situation. Jared had reached out to Pennebaker, who reached out to Sal. They'd be their eyes on the ground until they touched down again. If they saw anything suspicious from the outside, the men had the wherewithal to pull in the cops. Otherwise, they wouldn't enter and would wait for Chance to call the shots.

His instructions were simple: assess for immediate danger and collect intel. Use Sal and Pennebaker as backup. Lean heavy on the man who went by "Winters." The other man, call sign "Cash," would "disappear and do his job." Judging by the sniper rifle at his side, Chance gathered Cash would be their eyes and cover.

What could've been a forty-five minute or longer drive was whittled down to eighteen. The pilot had shaved an additional two minutes when he announced they'd arrived.

The hatch opened. Cash slipped out like liquid spilling into the night. One second he was there, another second, gone.

"Midas, Winters," Parker called. "Don't wrack up a body count."

Winters glanced at Chance. "Formality. Mostly."

He snorted. They bumped fists, pulled their night-vision goggles on, and hustled toward the house that Chance couldn't stand.

★   ★   ★

EXCEPT FOR HER legs, Jane was ready to run. She kept up her unconscious performance as wooden hangers were tossed aside and dully clicked together, though she'd been able to covertly take in the room. Gigi's clothes were in tatters, torn and shredded. Her makeup had been thrown. Strips of a red-carpet dress hung on a lamp, and one of Gigi's dangerously high Louboutins had been used to murder a keepsake pillow.

Then the ripping and hanger-tossing stopped. Dax, Gigi, and Lark milled about, inspecting their work. How long had they planned this? How much longer until Jane needed to run? She tried in vain to move her thighs. It was as though her brain couldn't connect correctly with those limbs. Her toes would wiggle and ankles roll, but that wouldn't help if she couldn't get off the bed.

Jane's brain wasn't a hundred percent either. Two of them approached her again, but she couldn't tell which two. Dax had to be one. He was close enough to block the light on the nightstand.

"So." Gigi sat on the edge of the bed. "What's next?"

"The pills," Lark instructed.

"Yeah. The pills." Dax knocked one of the bottles over and cursed. "My hands are shaking. I've never felt a rush like this."

"Think of the one to come," Gigi cooed.

"Think of my bonus," Lark added, just as sing-song as Gigi.

They laughed. *At her.* At the situation and how brazen they were. Jane couldn't understand but also knew they'd get away with it. She had thought them fools, but they'd constructed the perfect crime. The reporter who saw her reaction to the pictures. The cocktail left by the door. Even her fingerprints on the hangers—but, Jane almost gasped. They didn't know about Chance. He had to know something was wrong by now.

The lamp jumbled on the nightstand and Dax muttered, pushing it out of the way. The mattress dipped as he sat by her head.

"Can someone move her over?"

Gigi and Lark rolled Jane. She tried to act limp, but even if she hadn't, they were too keyed up to notice.

Pills rattled from their container. Dax expertly crushed them. Why wouldn't her legs work?

"Think that's enough?" Dax asked.

Lark leaned over Jane. "Hmm, think so. Maybe do one more. Just to be safe."

"I think that's enough, really," Gigi countered. "It'd be enough to kill me."

They laughed again. She wanted to scream. But instead, she focused on the impossible task of moving her legs.

"Don't be greedy," Dax snickered. "You have more than enough."

They laughed *again*. Jane's leg jerked out, surprising the hell out of her. But not nearly as much as them. They jumped and screamed. Jane didn't move. Her face pressed into the mattress and she tried not to move again.

"What the fuck," Gigi gasped.

"I think that happens sometimes," Dax added.

"How would you know? Go around knocking out women often?"

Dax nervously laughed. "Take it easy, Gigi."

"Poke her," Gigi demanded. "With a pen. Or a pin."

"*No*," Lark cut in. "We cannot leave a mark on her. Not a single bruise. *Nothing.*"

Gigi sighed. "I don't think they'll even check."

God, fuck you, Gigi! Jane's other leg twitched.

Well, hell. The jig was up. They'd poke her or she'd keep twitching. Either way, Jane was done laying on her face. She screamed and threw herself off the bed.

CHAPTER SIXTY-FIVE

CHANCE AND WINTERS skirted the grounds, both pulling on their night-vision goggles as they approached the pool. Sal and Pennebaker were on a side portico and Chance directed his new partner toward their backup. He lifted his chin in greeting, taking in their clothes.

With slicked-back hair and cologne, Sal wore a tightly-fitted shirt and expensive slacks. "What? I was out."

"In the club," Pennebaker nodded, exceedingly more comfortable in his Hawaiian shirt, pool shorts, and flip-flops.

"Every time I think I've seen it all, Boss Man throws me for a loop," Winters muttered.

The nightclub getup didn't change Sal's rosy demeanor. "Who's the kid?"

Winters ignored the jab.

"Lights are on," Pennebaker offered instead. "As always. No sign that anyone's home. The GPS indicator on their Range Rover don't have them within two hundred miles of here."

Chance studied the large home. "Did you go inside?"

"Hell no," Sal quipped. "I'd like to keep my job."

"We eyeballed Jane's cottage and swept the perimeter." Pennebaker gestured. "No one's home. All's quiet on the home front—except for the womp, womp of your stealth copter. What's this all about? Your office wouldn't say shit."

"Jane." Chance reached for his cell phone and called her again. Dread curled in his stomach.

A cell phone chimed. The foursome pivoted. The bright light of Jane's phone glowed from a poolside table. He killed the call and rushed over.

She hadn't seen his calls or messages. Chance turned—and stopped. His eyes locked on Teddy's scavenger hunt book, haphazardly laid open on a pool lounger. He picked up the phone and book and returned to the men, holding them up like evidence.

"The boy's missing too?" Pennebaker's jaw tightened. "You want to tell us exactly what's happening?"

"Teddy is with his aunt." Chance tucked their phones into his back pocket. "Jane's gone."

"Eyes up," Cash said in their earpieces. "Movement in the west wing."

He and Winters shifted. They weren't at the best angle but nothing caught his eye.

"Heavy drapes," their sniper continued. "I've got nothing more than shadows."

Chance recounted the update to Sal and Pennebaker. They moved to the garage. Pennebaker unlocked the door.

"The system's not armed," Chance pointed out.

"The systems not *on*," Pennebaker corrected.

They filed through a hall. "We're out a job if you're wrong and they're upstairs fucking," Sal added.

They stopped in the large kitchen long enough for Chance to eye the dirty dishes abandoned on the counter. Sal and Winters, opposites in nightclub clothes and tactical gear, hustled through the hall. Pennebaker peeled off, heading toward the back stairs. Chance took the lead and charged up the stairs. The place was a maze of dark corridors and halls, but gut instinct directed him toward the master bedroom. The walls were lined with priceless works of art, but for a split second, he recalled the moment in Syria when a wall fell and separated them from Teddy. Jane questioned him. He'd heard the fear in her words. At the time, he didn't understand how a job could possibly be so important. Now, he was certain the fallout from this job would dictate the rest of his life.

They approached the end of a hall. The master bedroom had multiple points of entry, including through a sitting room. He put his hand up. Winters and Sal paused. Chance listened. Nothing. His heartbeat drummed. He pointed at Winters and the far bedroom door. Silently, he moved as ordered, positioning himself to the side of the grand French doors.

Chance met Sal's eye. "If you want out, you can roll."

"Sometimes you gotta risk it all." Sal smiled weakly. "I don't have any training. Not like you guys. I'm just a guy who sits in a guard house."

"Maybe that'll change today—or we'll all get fired."

Sal chuckled then froze. Muffled voices came from the bedroom. They certainly weren't fucking, but Chance couldn't decipher their words or tone. He posted Sal behind him, against the wall. "Wait for my word. Then pull the drapes."

"Why?"

"For another set of eyes. In case we need help."

Unconvinced, Sal rolled his bottom lip but gave a curt nod. "Got it."

Pennebaker stepped from the back stairwell. Chance directed him opposite Winters. Once in position, Chance crept for the sitting room door. He tested for the doorknob—unlocked—and eyed the men at the end of the hall. Winters and Pennebaker nodded, ready to go. Winters and Chance had their weapons drawn. He held up his hand and gave a three count and signaled go-time.

They pushed through the doors. Glock in hand, Chance found himself in the middle of a clothing explosion. Lark screamed, throwing her hands into the air. Gigi's surprised cry rang out as well.

"What the..." Sal edged into the sitting room and skirted along the wall.

"It's not what you think," Lark tried, easing her arms down.

Chance shook his head. Her arms jerked higher. "Where's Jane?"

Sal ripped the drapes back.

"You don't understand," Lark fumbled.

Sal stepped into the bedroom, continuing to rip open the windows.

"Go." Chance ordered Lark into the connecting master bedroom.

She tripped over a pile of hangers, further scattering them in her rush. Gigi sat on top of a clothes-covered bench at the foot of her bed. Lark took a seat, too.

Winters cleared a walk-in closet and searched the half-open wardrobe before he moved to the next walk-in closet.

"Clear?" Gigi demanded. "You're in my bedroom!"

Pennebaker stepped over strewn shoes. "What happened in here?"

Chance searched for an answer. The bedroom was worse than the sitting room. Glass shards from a broken mirror covered the vanity. Makeup had been thrown across the room. Red lipstick had been used to write slut across the wall. Shredded clothing hung everywhere.

He directed Sal and Pennebaker. "Help Winters clear the room." The master bedroom had more alcoves and walk-in closets than necessary for two people, no matter their wealth. "Where's Dax?"

Blotchy red patches grew on Gigi's face and neck. "Not here."

Winters stepped from the second walk-in and caught Chance's eye. "Clear—destroyed, but clear."

He towered over the women. "Where's Jane?"

"We don't know," Lark said coolly. "We just walked in—"

Hangers clattered. Curses tangled with the familiar sound of flesh hitting flesh. A struggle thundered in the walk-in that Sal and Pennebaker had stepped into. Winters rushed across the room. Chance ordered the women to stay put.

"Gun," their sniper announced in their earpieces. "Third tango is armed with a hostage."

Chance repositioned as Dax stepped into the bedroom, eyes wild, nostrils flaring, with Pennebaker's weapon pressed against his throat. Winters dropped for cover behind the bed.

"Do you have a clean shot?" HQ requested of the sniper.

"Negative."

Gigi stood. Chance refocused on her. "Sit down."

"He's confused," Gigi explained. "We just came home, and this is what we see. You're here. Of course Dax would protect—"

"Sit. Down."

Dax yanked Pennebaker into the room. His finger haphazardly curled over the trigger. The security guard didn't struggle. Winters stood from his defensive position, searching for cover and a better shot. Their options weren't great.

"Dax, put your weapon down," Chance said calmly. "Then explain."

He scooted closer to them. Winters repositioned, following Dax.

Gigi slapped her thighs. "You know what? You're going to jail. All of you. Breaking and entering into my house." Her breaths shook. "Just leave!"

Dax sidestepped. His sloppy grip on the weapon made sweat form on the back of Chance's neck. Winters angled inside the bathroom door and faltered, cursing under his breath. Their comm system amplified it in Chance's ear.

Winters backed into the bathroom. "HQ, we need immediate medical transport."

The floor felt as though it had fallen from under Chance. A cold wave of nausea rocked hit. He struggled to keep his weapon up as his earpiece transmitted the sound of sloshing water.

"We just walked in," Gigi screeched. "Dax, damn it, put the gun down. We *all* just walked in."

"Midas," Winters called. "Now."

His stomach churned. Chance kept his weapon up but moved to the bathroom. "What?" He glanced in and saw *I loved you* scrawled over the mirror in lipstick. Coldness burned in his limbs. "What'd they do?" Chance forced himself into the bathroom. Only the bottom of Winters's boots were visible from around the corner. The steady thud of chest compressions thundered in the stark white bathroom.

Chance gave Gigi, Lark, and Dax one last look. "If you—*when you* run, I will find you. Whatever you've done. You will pay." Then he stepped into hell.

CHAPTER SIXTY-SIX

C HANCE HOLSTERED HIS weapon and prayed. He hadn't done that much in his life. Maybe he needed to do it more often—or maybe not. But as he knelt next to a tub filled with blood-red water and Jane laying lifelessly on the bathroom floor, his prayers were vicious, savage requests for retribution.

"Her wrists." Water dripped off of Winters as he spoke between chest compressions. "Hold the towels." Another chest compression, then he positioned her airway and gave two breaths.

Winters had wrapped towels tightly around Jane's wrists, but they still needed pressure. Chance held them as best he could.

Pennebaker rounded the corner. Sweat dampened his Hawaiian shirt and he stumbled back as he caught sight of them on the floor, but got to work, taking one of Jane's wrists from Chance. "Sal's still out. Dax got me with something—" he gagged "—over my mouth. Just for a minute. Long enough."

Jane choked. Water gurgled from between her lips. Winters turned her head. Her stomach convulsed. Her breaths returned, faint and choppy.

The back of Chance's throat ached. "There you go, Mary Poppins." He watched her eyelashes. They fluttered, not opening. "You're going to be fine." Sirens wailed in the distance. "Everything will be fine."

"I'll get the door." Pennebaker nodded for Chance to take Jane's wrist again—but he stumbled to find his balance.

"You stay here." Chance switched with Pennebaker. The front door seemed miles away. He promised Jane that everything would be okay, then hustled from the bathroom. Of course Dax, Gigi, and Lark would be gone. Chance would ruin the rest of his life if it meant he could ruin theirs.

Until then, he needed for help to arrive. Chance bounded down the front stairs and across the foyer. Something moved in his peripheral vision, and he spun toward the living room. Their sniper had pulled a wingback chair in front of a couch. The man they called Cash cradled his rifle and wore a look that said *try me*. Inches away, Dax, Gigi, and Lark sat on the couch, thigh to thigh, bound by plastic zip-ties.

The sniper smiled darkly. "They've requested a lawyer."

Chance's eyebrows arched.

"To which I explained in no uncertain terms, I didn't give a shit."

If he weren't waiting for Jane's ambulance, Chance might have laughed.

"I don't know who you are," the sniper added. "I'll never see you again. But I know Boss Man would give his stamp of approval to whatever you want to do with these three before we hand them over to the cops."

What did Chance want to do? He stared at them. Though Dax was coming off of an adrenaline high, he seemed unfazed, Gigi was put out and indignant, and Lark was clearly calculating how best to spin the situation to the press. They weren't worried that Chance would tear them limb from limb—nor were they worried about Jane.

"What do you want to do?" Cash prompted.

The only thing Chance wanted was to be by Jane's side. "Let them rot in a prison cell. I don't care."

Gigi scoffed.

Loathe curled over his lips. "You'll be surprised to learn that karma is a bigger bitch than you." Chance turned to meet the emergency technicians, adding with a cold laugh, "Finally, something that will hold my interest about the Thanes."

CHAPTER SIXTY-SEVEN

WHEN JANE AWOKE in the hospital with machines whirring and beeping around her, she needed a minute to figure out where she was—and why. Vaguely, she grasped at pieces until she recalled enough to understand. Her last memory was Dax holding a cloth to her face a second time. They'd tried to kill her—they'd do it again.

Panic gripped Jane. She struggled upright and opened her eyes. "Chance." He gripped her hand in his. His lips moved. She could hear him—but couldn't, as though he were far away. What had they done to her? "I can't hear you."

He squeezed her hand as he spoke to her again. Fear climbed in her chest. She clung to him and then saw the gauze bandages around her wrists. Her head pounded and her ears ranged loudly.

"Chance." Jane shook his hand. "My ears. My arms."

He climbed onto the bed and tucked her under his arm, petting her, soothing her like he believed it would be fine. Tears flooded her eyes and Jane buried her face into his neck.

"You're okay," he said.

She jerked back. She'd heard that. Or, had she only felt the vibrations in his throat? Either way, she *could* hear a never-ending ringing.

He reached for a small pencil and notepad laying on the table by his chair, then Chance jotted a note and gave it to her. It read: *Are your ears ringing?*

She nodded.

It took him another second to write out a response. *Doc said that would happen. It will stop.*

"Can you hear me?" she asked, unable to regulate how loud her voice should be.

He grinned and nodded.

"They tried to kill me." Jane glanced to her wrists. "I don't know what happened. I don't—"

Chance cupped her cheeks. "I know."

She understood and, relieved, Jane didn't have the energy to care about how or why; just that she would be safe.

"Jane." He pushed her hair back and then, slowly made sure she understood. "I love you."

Her heart flooded. "I love you, too. With my whole heart."

He reached for the notebook and pencil again, turned the page, and wrote her a longer message. After a quick re-read, he handed it to her.

In her head, she read his words as though she could hear his voice.

I was wrong before. There wasn't a right or wrong time to tell you that I love you. I love you—at work, in a hospital bed, anywhere, good or bad. I will always love you.

She nodded. Tears slipped free. "Always."

He pressed his forehead to hers. "Good." He took the book back and penciled another message. She laughed, swiping away her exhausted-but-happy tears.

With a sweet, goofy grin on his face, Chance stood after he handed the note back.

Jane glanced down. He'd drawn... a ring. She looked up, but he dropped down onto one knee.

"Chance!" Then she read his words through a sheen of blurry joy.

I'll do this again—out loud and with your pick of rings. But I can't wait to ask you to spend the rest of your life with me. I'll be your family. I'll be your whole damn world. Marry me.

EPILOGUE

Two Months Later
Abu Dhabi, United Arab Emirates

J ANE WALKED INTO the newly-finished hotel suite that would serve as their new home in Abu Dhabi. She'd taken a look at the hotel room that Chance had been living in and, with Angela's help, decided that they could do better. Better wasn't on the thirteenth floor, next door neighbors with his teammates. Their new apartment on the fourteenth floor was close enough that Chance didn't mind and Jane wouldn't feel like she lived in a fraternity house.

They'd also been able to convince Liam and Chelsea to set up an apartment on their floor. Jane guessed that Chelsea and the baby would be part-time residents of the under-construction hotel soon enough.

She tossed her keys onto the hallway table. "Hello?"

"In here."

Jane eyed a box that must have come from his old apartment. Angela had had her things boxed, shipped, and unpacked before they returned from their honeymoon. "What's in there?"

"Cans of stew," Chance explained as he and Hagan lounged at the kitchen table, T-shirts appropriately damp with sweat, drinking beer and basking in their recent victory—moving his couch that he couldn't live without to their new place. It had looked like a perfectly ordinary couch to Jane, but he'd insisted that it had conformed to his body. He didn't want to start all over again. Such was married life.

Jane sat in his lap and took a sip of his beer. "I can't believe you got that thing up here."

"The bastard's heavier than it looks," Hagan added.

Chance flexed his muscles and grinned. "But, ya know, piece of cake."

She rolled her eyes.

"So?" he asked. "How'd the call go?"

Jane beamed and handed the beer back. "That's what I wanted to tell you about. It went way, *way* better than expected."

"Don't kill us with suspense."

"They each took a deal," she said.

"Wait—what? Really?" Chance popped his knees up and made her squeak. "Seriously?"

"Yup, really!"

"Gigi vowed to go down fighting." He snickered. "At least, that's what I thought she said when I swung by federal lockup for a quick hello."

Hagan snort-laughed. "That's not passive aggressive at all."

Chance shrugged, then faced Jane. "I don't get it. Just like that?"

"Well, as it turns out, staging my death for ratings wasn't their only problem." She bit her lip. "Remember that time I asked you if the bullets were real?"

"No—" Chance sobered and cocked his head. "You mean in Syria?"

Jane nodded. "The federal prosecutor shared a hell of a story."

"I knew it," Chance whispered.

"They planned the whole thing?" Hagan searched their faces for clarity. She nodded again.

Chance added on, "Until the locals realized they had the upper hand."

"True," Jane said. "But they didn't fess up *until* the photographer from the trip found himself in hot water."

"With the Feds?" Chance crooked his eyebrow. "Like the production company?"

The Thanes and Lark hadn't been alone in their greed. The more Jane learned, the angrier she became. But then it clicked. They went to extremes, desperate for happiness. Money and fame were like drugs. As soon as she accepted that, Jane pitied them. They'd destroyed their lives, willing to do the same to others, to find what was available and free. Love and acceptance. "Yeah. The photographer cut a similar deal, but only after they got him with blackmail."

"What?" Both men hooted.

"I know, right? She shook her head. "Dax told him what to expect. Joe played his part, believing the whole thing was a farce for most of the trip. Until he didn't. Then he blackmailed Dax and Gigi."

"Bet they gladly paid up," Chance muttered.

"And," Jane continued. "Because they planned the trip, the Feds got all of them on several new charges, from child endangerment to manipulating consumers and shareholders."

Hagan whistled.

Sad, but her story had a happy ending. "All of which means… drum roll, please."

The guys obliged, laughing and drilling the table.

"I don't have to testify in person," Jane announced.

They cheered. She took a bow as though the show were finally over. Chance gave her a big kiss. Hagan popped up to retrieve another round of beers. He cracked the top off of a fresh one and gave it to Jane. "Congratulations."

They clinked bottles and took a drink.

"There's more good news." She rolled her bottle between her palms. "You are looking at the newest martial arts instructor for one of the hotels across the street. They have a beautiful dojo and will be ramping up a children's program. I start next week."

"Awesome." Chance lifted his bottle. "Let's hope your new employers aren't as crazy as your last ones."

"Let's hope so."

Hagan held up his bottle hesitantly. "Any other good news?"

Jane smiled. "Courtney emailed an update. Teddy loves his new school and joined a Lego club. He's so happy now." Her eyes grew watery. "But I'm going to miss seeing him every day."

A loud knock shook the front door, killing her misty moment. Chance and Hagan groaned.

Jane arched her eyebrows. "Who is that?"

"Boss Man," Chance explained, finishing off his beer. "And he sounds so cheery."

She tsked them. Hagan chuckled. Chance cracked open his second beer. Jane went to answer the door. The second she opened it, Jared blustered in.

Maybe the guys were right… She hurried to catch up and sidestepped the angry storm of a man. Jared had a basket in one hand and a crumbled piece of paper in the other.

"Hi—"

He thrust the basket into her arms. "Angela says you need this."

"Okay." Jane eyed him suspiciously then read the card with a grin. "It's a housewarming gift."

He grumbled. "I gave you a house. Isn't that enough of a gift?"

"Thank you." She gave him an awkward but well-meaning squeeze. The gesture shut down his grumpy tirade, though it left her husband and his teammate speechless. "That was very thoughtful."

Jared cleared his throat. "Enough of that. Let's talk about this." He flung the half-crushed paper onto the table. It softly landed between the beer bottles. "Is this your way of owning up to the signs?"

Jane stepped closer. Chance and Hagan sealed their lips. They didn't say a word, turning a dark shade of red as they tried to hold back their laughter.

"What is it?" She flattened the paper on the table.

WARNING

Love is in the air

Take all precautions

Face Masks. HazMat Suits.

Do Not Drink the Water

Jane set the housewarming gift basket down and flipped the paper over and back. Blank. She glanced at Jared questioningly. "Where did you get this?"

"Taped to your door," he groused.

She squinted, trying unsuccessfully to decode what was going on. Jane turned to Chance. "I just walked in. Nothing was on our door."

Hagan stood like a lawyer making a closing argument. "Proof that it was not us."

Jared didn't speak so much as he growled—without opening his mouth. Apparently Boss Man didn't need words to say *shut your mouth*.

"Well, guys." Hagan grabbed his beer and retreated. "This is where I leave you. Enjoy the couch and the company. I'm out."

He quickly disappeared. Still grumbling, Jared snatched the paper and stormed out behind Hagan, leaving Jane confused. "Um, what am I missing?"

Chance bellowed with laughter before he clarified. "Someone's hanging signs around the building. They're driving Boss Man to the edge."

Her lips quirked. Maybe their apartment wasn't on the frat house floor, but she could tell the antics couldn't be avoided. The more she thought about it, the more Jane liked having the Aces team so close. They could be like her big, rowdy, paper-sign-making family.

Their laughter subsided and she pulled Chance to the new-old couch. Their place was very nice. She noticed a few more boxes that had arrived with the couch. They could unpack and figure out what else needed to be done. She already had a list brimming with ideas on how to make their hotel room suite look like a home. She leaned into her husband. "What should we do now?"

He pulled her close. "Since love is in the air… I think we're supposed to do each other."

Laughing, she pressed a kiss onto his lips.

"What?" Chance gave her a not-so-innocent look that made her toes curl. "That's not an option?"

"It's the best option." She kissed him again but stopped short. "I just thinking about something and realized I had it all wrong."

His eyebrows knitted. "HazMat suits aren't needed for birth control. We're fine."

She slapped his chest playfully. "I was thinking about how to make this place look even more like our home."

"Jane, babe. Right now, I don't care about anything other than the mattress."

"Hear me out." She grinned and wrapped her arms around his neck. "So long as I'm with you, it will always *feel* like home. See what I did there?"

He shook his head and jumped up with her in his arms, muttering about making her feel at home as he raced to their bedroom. Jane giggled until they fell into bed again.

"See what I did there?" he asked then stripped away their clothes and wrapped her close.

With nothing between them, she nodded. "You gave me everything."

THE SURVIVOR

Ten years ago, against the advice of the most influential people in the world—her family—Amanda Hearst walked away from her security detail. She wouldn't allow another person to risk their lives to save hers.

Hagan Carter wants the truth about the mystery woman who works with Titan Group. Her lethal moves and skilled evasion fuel a volatile attraction.

Their past should stay buried, and their future is impossible unless the couple risks their lives to understand why they can't be together.

THE SURVIVOR is the next book in the Aces series. Get it everywhere books are sold!

ABOUT THE AUTHOR

Cristin Harber is a New York Times and USA Today bestselling romance author. She writes sexy romantic suspense, military romance, new adult, and contemporary romance. Readers voted her onto Amazon's Top Picks for Debut Romance Authors in 2013, and her debut Titan series was both a #1 romantic suspense and #1 military romance bestseller.

Connect with Cristin! Text TITAN to 66866 to sign up for exclusive emails.

The ACES Series:
Book 1: The Savior
Book 2: The Protector
Book 3: The Survivor

The Titan Series:
Book 1: Winters Heat
Book 1.5: Sweet Girl
Book 2: Garrison's Creed
Book 3: Westin's Chase
Book 4: Gambled and Chased
Book 5: Savage Secrets
Book 6: Hart Attack
Book 7: Sweet One
Book 8: Black Dawn
Book 9: Live Wire
Book 10: Bishop's Queen
Book 11: Locke and Key
Book 12: Jax
Book 13: Deja Vu

The Delta Series:
Book 1: Delta: Retribution
Book 2: Delta: Rescue*
Book 3: Delta: Revenge
Book 4: Delta: Redemption
Book 5: Delta: Ricochet
*The Delta Novella in Liliana Hart's MacKenzie Family Collection

The Only Series:
Book 1: Only for Him
Book 2: Only for Her
Book 3: Only for Us
Book 4: Only Forever

7 Brides for 7 Soldiers:
Ryder (#1) – Barbara Freethy
Adam (#2) – Roxanne St. Claire
Zane (#3) – Christie Ridgway
Wyatt (#4) – Lynn Raye Harris
Jack (#5) – Julia London
Noah (#6) – Cristin Harber
Ford (#7) – Samantha Chase

7 Brides for 7 Blackthornes:
Devlin (#1) – Barbara Freethy
Jason (#2) – Julia London
Ross (#3) – Lynn Raye Harris
Phillip (#4) – Cristin Harber
Brock (#5) – Roxanne St. Claire
Logan (#6) – Samantha Chase
Trey (#7) – Christie Ridgway

Each Titan, Delta, and 7 Brides book can be read as a standalone (except for Sweet Girl), but readers will likely best enjoy the series in order. The Only series must be read in order.

ACKNOWLEDGMENTS

As with all of my books, this one would not be possible without the love and support of my family. Courtney, I knew what to name Teddy's aunt the moment I re-read her description—blunt and practical. Two of your many awesome qualities. Whether it's wrestling away chemistry sets or teaching the kids how to fly, you are the coolest sister and aunt in the world.

I want to thank my readers for sticking with me as I took much needed time to spend with my little ones. Over the years, so many of you reminded me that they are only young once, and that time flies. I took your comments, emails, and messages to heart. Thank you for your patience, encouragement, and incredible stories that you've shared with me.

Thanks to the great team behind this book, including cover designer Kim Killion. Cindy, I would never have attempted an outline if we hadn't talked—even if that outline was twenty thousand words. This book didn't follow my usual pants-it-to-the-end approach, and because of that, I was able to work with many wonderful editors. It was a pleasure! Finally, Amber. *fist bump* Titan strong all the way. Do what you do. You're amazing.

Made in the USA
Monee, IL
23 December 2019